ESKAONUS
BATTLE FOR THE HEART

THE DAY AFTER ALWAYS

BOOK THREE

BY

CHARLES EARL HARREL

ISBN: 978-1-965352-54-0

To all those who helped with this novel,
believed in it, and prayed for it to make a difference:

Thank you!

Contents

Till the sea runs dry, till the moon don't shine.
Till the rainclouds are all left behind.
Till the wind don't blow, till the stars don't show.
I'll praise His name till the day after always.

—Song lyrics by Paul Dee Allen (1988)

CHAPTER 1

Eddnok Flees Briacap

Sixty cycles ago, Lord Eddnok awoke two spans before firstlight. He couldn't sleep. Thoughts plagued his mind. Senior Commander Bolgog and others were stalling on his orders to raise an army to attack the Lower Realm. Lady Saephira and Narleen recently escaped from capture, and a group of southern rebels destroyed the catapult he'd hidden in the Kunakk Vineyards.

The words from the mysterious scroll promised he would become a ruler of fate, but why wasn't it happening? To make matters worse, the mystical knowledge tree had disappeared from the hidden cave, and the ten fruits he kept locked inside his office were stolen. Someone or something thwarted his efforts at every turn, including his plan to rule all of Eskaonus. Distraught and frustrated, he fumed with anger.

He toppled out of bed, not caring if he disturbed Flissae, and dressed quickly. He took a swig of kunakk, tossed the half-empty skin on the floor, clutched his dagger from the top dresser, and tucked it into his belt. As soon as Eddnok unbolted the door, the sentry bowed. "Good nightrise, my Lord. How may I be of service?"

"You can't." Eddnok raced down the hallway and exited his Briacap residence. Darkout still covered the horizon. He grabbed a torch, struck it aflame, and continued on to the watchtower. By the time he reached the tower, firstlight had dawned. Sub-Commander Brappt and two sentinels stood guard at the entrance. He ignored their hails. "Where's Bolgog?"

"The commander is atop the battlement," answered one of the watchmen.

Eddnok tossed his fiery torch at the sentinels' feet, forcing the men backwards to avoid burning their boots. "Take care of this torch." He climbed the circular stairwell and found Bolgog standing behind the parapet on the wallwalk, staring through his magnifier.

"Perhaps you should take a look, Lord. Although it's hard to see the details in the morning twilight, I think a warband approaches from the south."

Lord Eddnok peered through the looking glass and handed it back to Bolgog. "You better alert the compound. I think Lady Saephira has gathered a contingent and plans to attack our citadel."

"They'll never be able to breach Briacap. It's impregnable, and besides, by the time they surround us, we'll have hundreds of soldiers on the ramparts and more in reserve. They'll be slaughtered before they get close."

"So you say! I assume you've forgotten about the raid where a small band of militia freed Lady Narleen nine cycles ago. Not only did they get close, they scaled the wall, entered our stockade, overwhelmed our warders, and escaped—making a fool of your invincible forces."

"I was at the hidden cave with you when—"

"That excuse did me little good. I should have relieved you of command then." Eddnok turned to leave.

"Where are you going, sir?"

"To my quarters."

"Lord, if a southern battlegroup intends harm, don't you think you should stay and oversee the defense?"

"No, I have other matters to attend." And Eddnok rushed away.

Once he reached his room, rage filled his heart. The sentry could see the anger on Eddnok's reddened face. The guard said nothing, only bowed. Eddnok pushed on the entry and stomped inside. The door hit the sidewall with a crash and awakened

Flissae. "Lord, come back to bed. It's too early to be up."

"Get out!"

"But Lord, you have my comfort until dayrise."

"It is dayrise! Leave!" Flissae slid from the bed and began to dress.

"Just take your garments and go. You can dress elsewhere for all I care. You know, Flissae, you're no better than my two worthless concubines, Bovi and Seirlai, and you cost more to maintain."

"Lord, that's cruel and unfair. I have been a faithful servant for yarns."

"No longer." Eddnok withdrew the dagger and thrust it at her. "Depart before I . . ."

Flissae bundled her clothing to her bosom and stumbled into the hallway, weeping and mumbling curses. The door sentry noticed her flushed face and tears as she passed, but again, he said nothing. Seeing a prostitute exit Eddnok's chamber was a common occurrence in Briacap.

After she departed, Eddnok grabbed a spare satchel from his trunk, packed it with several sets of clothing, and then called for his doorman. The man cautiously peeked around the corner. "Yes, my Lord, how may I—"

"Shut up and listen." Eddnok fiddled with his dagger's handle. "I want you to rouse Menarbat and Preaverca. Have them meet me at the main gate in one span. And tell them to have three kacks ready, mounted with side carriers containing rations and supplies." Fearing for his life, the guard simply nodded and scurried off. Eddnok scanned his quarters for additional items, spotted the half-empty skin of kunakk and added it to his carrier, then departed for his office.

From an early rampage, his office remained in shambles: potted plants knocked over, furniture broken, and litter strewn everywhere. The whole place lay in disarray. The chest that contained the knowledge fruit sat empty on the floor with a broken lid. He kicked it twice, tipping it on its side. "If I discover who stole my ten fruits, I'll have their hands cut off."

He circled his desk, righted an overturned chair and plopped down. Eddnok opened the bottom drawer, withdrew the notes on constructing catapults and formulating liquid fire, rolled up the sheets, and placed them into his carrier bag. Next, he unlocked a hidden compartment and withdrew the black token he had taken from the Archives yarns ago. None of the archivists knew the talisman's significance or the meaning of the *TREOW* symbols engraved on the front. When a recordkeeper reported it missing, Eddnok lied concerning its whereabouts. He liked the rectangular shape and texture of the strange, smooth stone. After rubbing it several times between his fingers for luck, he tucked it into his satchel.

From his second drawer, he removed Lundy's translation of the ancient scroll and read it:

If treasure is what you seek
Then don't be meek
Nor forgo the rift
Near the highest cliff

Buried deep within lies a secret twin
Of the richest gift
Known to gods or men

Take an uphill pace to seek a taste
Of wisdom sublime
And power divine

So follow the trail to the mountains red
Through the forest dead
Past waters shed
And peaks that grow during daylight glow
Past ancient grave lays hidden cave
Where treasure awaits
For a ruler of fate

Eddnok tore off the last three stanzas that mentioned wisdom, divine power, and ruler of fate. He folded the paper in quarters and stuffed it into his pants pocket. The remainder of the document he angrily crumpled into a ball and tossed on the floor. He stood, threw his chair against the wall, snapping off three of the legs, then walked over to the empty chest and kicked it again, screaming, "If I'm this destined ruler, why am I not succeeding?" Eddnok stomped out of the room and returned to his quarters where he spent the next half span. With a final search of his chamber completed, he headed for the city gate.

By the time Eddnok approached the exit, forecycle had begun. Observing a flurry of activity, he asked Commander Rennard to explain the commotion.

"Lord, two battlegroups are forming. We counted more than 160 militia, some mounted, others on foot. They carry spears, harpoons, and axes. There are two squads on each side of the main contingent—armed with devices that launch those strange floating rocks and magical flying sticks. All available troops have been called to man the ramparts." As Eddnok listened to the report, dread gripped his heart. He started to make a comment when Menarbat arrived, leading a spare ride. Preaverca followed close behind him.

"Well, Tracker, are you and Preaverca ready to go?"

"Everything is packed as you ordered, my Lord. We have three haversacks of rations, spare torches, and two full waterskins. So, where are we bound?"

"Through the main gate and to safety."

"I'm sorry, Lord. Senior Commander Bolgog ordered the gates barred," advised Rennard. "No one is allowed to exit our fortress. We're under siege."

"You're to disregard those orders. I'm in charge here. Unbar the exit. Now!" Eddnok pulled his dagger and leveled it at Commander Rennard. Menarbat moved his mount to within striking distance of the officer's neck, unsheathed his curved saber, and drew back for a swing.

The commander paused for a moment, then pointed to the five men on the gate and yelled, "Do it!"

Eddnok mounted his kack while Menarbat sheathed his sword. As soon as the entry cracked open, the three of them bolted away at a full gallop, traveling east. Rennard shook his head as they departed, adding, "If those fools choose to die, then let them. Close and secure the gates. I'm joining the sentinels on the battlement."

Lady Saephira noticed three shapes racing away from the

citadel and sent a company of mounted militia to subdue them. As the riders closed in, Preaverca glanced toward the rear. "They are gaining on us, Lord."

"Do we have time to go north and enter the Nae through Narnj pass?" asked the Tracker."

"No!" shouted Eddnok, not bothering to look at the two companions riding by his side.

"Let's go south," Preaverca suggested.

"Too risky. It would put us in Lower Realm territory."

"Lord, they are almost in spear range." Menarbat withdrew his sword, fearing the worst.

"Entering the Lost Forest is our only option." Preaverca and the Tracker hesitated, not wanting to disagree with Eddnok. "What are you two scared of?"

"Aren't those woods haunted?" asked Preaverca.

"If you believe those foolish tales, you two can stay behind. I'm leaving."

"They're only paces behind us now and have aimed their spears." The raspy sound of Menarbat's voice revealed his distress.

"Die, be captured, or escape with me," declared Eddnok, his tone belligerent. "Make your choice."

The Tracker and Preaverca briefly discussed the matter. "Okay, she and I will go with you."

Lord Eddnok, Preaverca, and Menarbat galloped into the forest. None of their pursuers cared to enter this mysterious grove of timber. They knew the rumors all too well. The Lost Forest kept even the bravest persons at bay. Saephira's militia watched as the riders disappeared into the thickets and then turned around to rejoin the assault forces surrounding Briacap.

MAP OF ESKAONUS

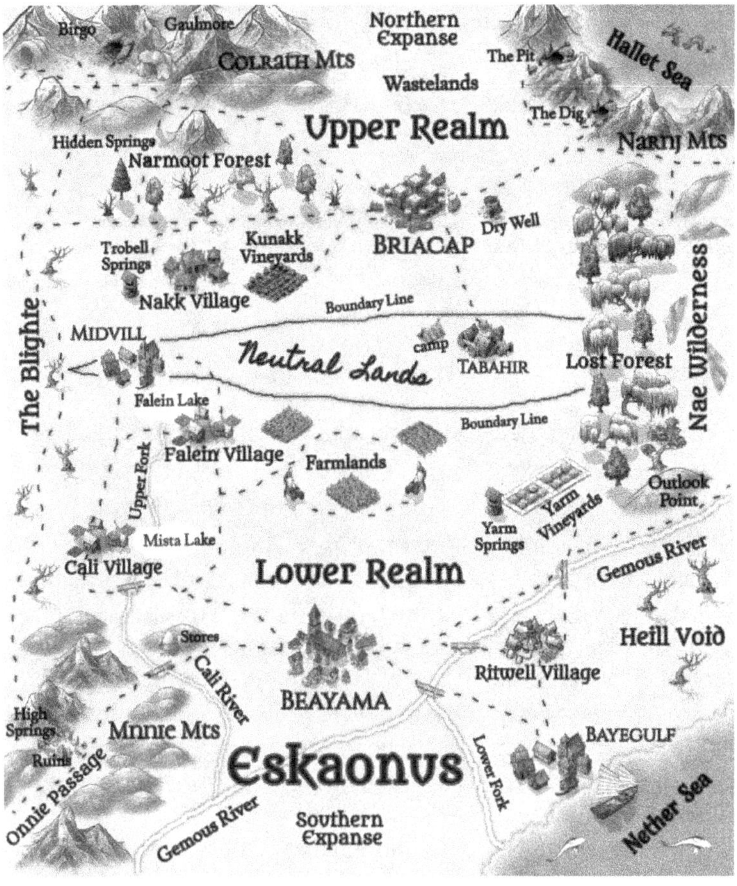

Eskaonus has two main provinces called the Upper and Lower Realm. The landmass contains two oceans, one landlocked. Wilderness areas in the east and west are largely unexplored. There are no suns or moons. During the days, called cycles, a glowing light similar to an aurora borealis shines forth until fading into a gloomy twilight.

CHAPTER 2

RIDE TO BAYEGULF

A few cycles ago, Maximus was in Camayah with Jesse and his team, trying to restore order to a dystopian society. Now he's back in Eskaonus, his spouse is pregnant, half the fleet has disappeared, and he's racing toward the Postal Tower. Questions rattled his mind. He wondered how things were going on Camayah. Had the Council of Twelve implemented the suggested changes and edicts? Were the believers growing and sharing their faith? How many minds had been freed from the restrictive programming? Did they resolve the quawner issues? His thoughts continued to churn as he ran.

Learning of Narleen's pregnancy after everyone else bothered him. Okay, it wasn't everybody. Still, Nar should have told him first. Her being exhausted and nauseated all the time made more sense. Maybe that's why she acted moody, too. Max felt happy about finally having a baby. On earth as a Roman centurion, the opportunity to birth a child ended when barbarians killed his betrothed. Now he had a second chance to raise a family. A boy would be nice: a son he could train in soldiering ways. On the other hand, a girl might be best: a daughter who took an interest in learning music like Miss Anna or doctoring like Mender Ottaar. Either way, he'd cherish the child and protect him or her with his life. Perhaps Nar was right; thinking about the upcoming birth drew his attention elsewhere. He'd better focus on the situation at hand.

The missing ships from Bayegulf were his priority now. The delay could be nothing more than bad weather. Maybe the fleet tarried at sea to catch a larger bounty of tarkks. As he rushed to the mail tower, he pushed all other thoughts out of his mind and decided on a course of action. He climbed the stairs to the top of the tower and found a person holding two homing flyers. She looked confused.

"Good dayrise . . . um . . . I don't believe I know your name, ma'am."

Startled, a young woman with wavy blond hair, turned around. As soon as she saw Maximus, she curtsied. "My name is Lurah, sir." She placed both flyers into the same cage and dropped the lid.

"Where is the Postal Overseer?"

"We don't have one." Her lavender-blue eyes sparkled as she talked. "Lady Narleen hasn't appointed a replacement for Preaverca who abandoned her post. The mailroom is only being staffed part time, a few spans a cycle. This dayrise is my shift."

"I see. Can you show me the original dispatch from Bayegulf?"

"I'm sorry, Captain Maximus, I didn't realize we were supposed to keep the originals, so I tossed it in the burner. This mail system is confusing to me. In fact, I'm having a hard time determining which homing flyers go in which cages."

"Shouldn't the flyers and cages be numbered by location?"

"I think they were before Preaverca destroyed the labels. In fact, where is she?"

"Unknown. Preaverca was last seen entering the Lost Forest with Lord Eddnok and the Tracker. We consider them traitors. Later, you can ask Nar, I mean, Lady Narleen to provide additional details on their offences. Excuse me for being abrupt, but I need to ask if the dispatch from Bayegulf said anything more referring to the lost ships."

"Nothing, other than they've been missing for several cycles, and the city magistrate is concerned. He's awaiting a reply."

"Alright, send a message to inform Hyneil I will arrive by

midcycle. Ask him to meet me on the docks for an update."

"I'll write one and fly it off immediately."

"Thank you, Lurah. From now on, keep a copy of each dispatch in a filing cabinet, whether it's sent or received. I believe there are several filers in the overseer's quarters."

"No one has been in there since Preaverca departed. I think she ransacked the place prior to leaving town."

"No doubt. Please clean up the mess and try to get this place organized again."

"Yes, Captain Maximus."

"Just call me Max. And one more thing."

"Yes, sir, I mean Max."

"You are the new Postal Overseer for Beayama, if you'll accept the position. We require a fulltime person here."

"It would be an honor to serve. Raydoo will be so proud of me."

"Is Raydoo an acquaintance?"

"He's my younger brother."

"Apparently, dedication runs in the family. Good, I will ask my spouse to confirm your appointment when I get back from Beayama. As the overseer of messages, those living quarters are yours. And you'll be part of the leadership council. Accordingly, you're invited to the banquet tonight. You will have a place at the main table with the other city officials."

"Are you sure Lady Narleen will want me? It would be a dream come true."

"I've never been surer." Max smiled, bowed, and then bolted down the steps, exiting the tower. He found Militia Chief Phauch waiting outside, sitting on a kack. Another mount stood nearby.

"I figured you'd be going to Bayegulf to check on the missing ships, so I readied your ride for travel."

"Thank you, Chief." Max walked over to the kack and stroked its forehead. The animal neighed, enjoying the attention. "Did you see Lady Narleen safely to Residential Hall?"

"Indeed. She's doing well. Ottaar and Holley already checked on her. Since the Lady had sufficiently recovered, she dismissed them."

"My spouse is not one to complain . . . much." Max said

with a grin.

"I assume you're not opposed to having an escort to Bayegulf. I packed two torches in case we don't return before darkout, a haversack with a loaf of kin, several chaws of antaloop jerky, and your longbow."

Max unstrapped his bow from the side carrier, slung it across his back, and attached the quiver of arrows to his belt. "No, I'd appreciate the company. And you can give me a report on the happenings while I've been away. It seems like I've been gone for half a period."

"Not really, sir. Only one cycle."

"Hmm . . . just one?" *Guess I forgot about the time variance between outer realms.* "No matter, let's ride. I need to meet the magistrate on the docks by midcycle."

They rode their mounts at a gallop, hanging on to their long fluffy manes for stability, steering the kacks by using gentle leg movements and touching their necks to make turns. The men stopped at the Gemous River ford to rest and water their animals, where a conversation ensued.

"Captain, I've heard rumors from some of our militiamen that you were not born in Eskaonus; is this true, sir?"

Max scratched his chiseled jaw as he considered his answer. "The rumor's correct, Chief. I was birthed in a different place."

"And you recently hailed from a high realm?"

"Also correct. However, my past is not as important as the present. Since you are interested, I can confirm that I served as a military commander, called a centurion, in charge of ninety soldiers. Lady Saephira recognized my former experience and asked me to help resolve conflicts with the Upper Realm, including rescuing prisoners. Later, she promoted me to Militia Chief and then to Captain of the Militia. Although I've only been here for a short time, I fell in love with Lady Narleen, and we betrothed sixty cycles ago. These facts are common knowledge."

"But, sir, I was wondering—"

"Let's sit down sometime, hoist a cup, and talk in more detail. Right now, though, we have pressing matters in Bayegulf. It's time to ride." The duo mounted up and continued on to the coastal port, covering the league between Beayama and Bayegulf in one span, arriving at midcycle. They waited at the docks, watching sailors load and unload cargo.

Finally, Hyneil, Bayegulf's magistrate, arrived with a delegation of three skippers from the fleet. Two skippers bowed and one curtsied to show their respect. "Good dayrise, Captain Maximus and Chief Phauch. How can we assist the Militia this fine dayrise?" asked Hyneil.

"Good dayrise. Tell us what you know regarding the missing vessels," replied Max.

"Three crafts left port seven cycles ago for their normal fishing tour. They should have returned two cycles ago. There has been no word by homing flyer or otherwise. The sailors' families are worried, as am I."

"Do you think weather has been an issue?"

"Perhaps. The seas can be dangerous, especially farther out, or the crews might be following a school of tarkks in hopes of a bountiful catch. Either way, they should have notified us of any delays."

"Are delays normal in the fishing business?"

"Yeah, quite often," confirmed Hyneil, "but failure to receive homing flyer updates is not."

Max stomped around in a circle as he pondered the circumstances. "How many ships are docked in port?"

"We have four, sir," answered Master Haleema, the skipper with the most seniority.

"Then I recommend you send three to search for our lost ships and keep the fourth in reserve."

"That was my intention, sir."

"I'm sorry, ma'am, I didn't mean to insinuate . . . well, never mind. How long until your vessels can get underway?"

"I can gather crews and sail by postcycle on the outgoing currents. We should have word in a couple cycles. We'll send flyers once they're sighted."

"Alright, Master Haleema, please keep me posted." Max nodded to the skippers and thanked the magistrate. After a few more pleasantries, Phauch and Max mounted their kacks and rode off. They stopped by Ritwell Village to talk with the village elders before heading back to Beayama, reaching the stables at twilight.

"I'm gonna check on Nar. I'll see you at the banquet later.

Thanks for riding with me; I enjoyed the company." And Max hurried off to Residential Hall.

CHAPTER 3

THE BANQUET

After Max checked on his spouse's welfare, they both walked to the Great Hall to join the banquet. In addition to dinners, Beayama's citizens used the hall for public events, exhibitions, and business meetings. The building contained a large dining section, side conference rooms, and two kitchens. Although community banquets were occasionally hosted in the hall, most of the time, residents shared nightrise meals in their own homes.

As the guests filed in, Narleen noticed Lurah standing in a corner, alone, looking like a lost kack foal, so she rushed over to speak with her. "Good nightrise, Lurah. My spouse tells me you've been volunteering in the mail tower."

"Yes, my lady." Lurah curtsied. "Only trying to be helpful. I'm still learning the system and which cages to house the returning flyers in. Sadly, I have misplaced several of the dispatches."

"Not to worry, the former overseer, Preaverca, did worse than that. Fortunately, she decided to quit." Narleen touched Lurah on the shoulder, offering reassurance. "Captain Maximus said you're doing a wonderful job, and based on his recommendation, I've officially appointed you to Postal Overseer of Beayama. The position comes with a stipend of credits and private quarters in the tower. Please come join my spouse and me at the leadership table. I want people to meet you."

Lurah curtsied again. "Thank you, my lady. You have no

idea how—"

"I believe I do." She took Lurah by the hand and led her to a place setting next to hers. "And since you're on the council, please call me Narleen." Jesse and Lady Saephira arose from their seats and hailed the newcomer with nightrise greetings and smiles.

Before Jesse returned to his chair, he glanced around the hall and noted the seating arrangements for his team members and other invited guests. Holley and Lundy had gathered with Mender Ottaar; Anna sat next to Gelr, surrounded by several safeguards; and Seth hung out with Raydoo and Calrin in the rear. Phauch and Chepho occupied the circular board with a handful of militia, and Membarb, the woodsmith, lounged at a counter with four people Jesse didn't recognize.

Lady Saephira offered a brief welcome, introduced Lurah as the new Postal Overseer, and signaled the servers to begin delivering the dinner fare for tonight's banquet. The feast included entrees of baked tarkk, dishes with filleted river eel, and several trays containing antaloop roast. The kitchen staff delivered baked kin, platters of colorful squashes, plates filled with maize, saucers of candied dallups, bowls with various types of yarm berry desserts, kettles holding steaming-hot Azollie tea, and pitchers of slightly fermented yarm.

Hoping she had built up her immunity by drinking yarm when she first arrived in Beayama three cycles ago, Holley tried a small serving of yarm berry pudding, saying to herself, "Moderation is best until I understand these side effects."

At the central table, Saephira, Narleen, Lurah, and Jesse listened to Max's report concerning their missing ships and the proposed search. Maximus told them the delay was likely weather related, or that the crews had tarried for a bountiful catch. Bayegulf's magistrate felt they should know more in a few cycles and promised to keep them posted.

Once Max finished with his update, Narleen shared her pregnancy news. Everybody congratulated the couple; Jesse already knew about the situation, and Saephira had somehow discerned it. After the group satisfied their appetites, Max and Narleen excused themselves. Max wandered over to visit with Chepho, and Narleen headed for the mender's table to talk with

Holley. Narleen motioned for Lurah to come join her, assuming Saephira and Jesse desired privacy to discuss Camayah. She knew about the mission; Lurah didn't, and it gave Narleen an opportunity to confer with Lurah regarding mail tower protocols.

When Saephira and Jesse were alone, she asked, "How did things turn out?"

"It's a long story."

"We have time now, and I have many questions. Can you explain to me how you, Captain Maximus, my vice-leader, and your colleagues traveled to a different world?"

"It's called portal jumping. I'm not exactly sure how it all works. We just think where we desire to be and we're there."

"Do such journeys always succeed?"

Jesse frowned. "No, and I'm not sure why."

"Hmm . . . I guess we can discuss it later." Saephira slid her chair a little closer to Jesse. "What did you encounter on Camayah?"

"An advanced world with unimaginable contraptions."

"Like what?"

"Fanciful machines, stun weapons that shoot light beams, flying ships, portal transporters, and electronic communications. Messages on Camayah use dataflows, not homing flyers."

"Electronic communications?"

"Talking devices more advanced than this." Jesse removed the radio from his satchel and showed it to Saephira. "This is called a transceiver. We brought several of them from the high realm." She examined the strange item and handed it back to Jesse. "I think Narleen holds the one I gave Max. She can show you how it works, or I can, but later." He quickly placed the device into his carrier, not wanting to draw attention.

"This information is most intriguing. What else did you do there?"

"We located a handful of missing individuals and rescued them from exile on a moon."

"A moon?"

"It's a large rock circling a planet."

"What's a planet?"

"A world orbiting a sun."

"Sorry for being so inquisitive; I don't understand these

terms.”

Remembering that Eskaonus didn't have a sun, only a yellowish, aurora borealis glow, he decided to forgo the astronomy lessons and summarized their accomplishments. Feeling a bit apprehensive and somewhat hesitant, Jesse chewed on his lower lip before describing the problems still faced by the Camayahnites. He left out the details about the Burning, artificial intelligence, pleasure pills, and other deceptions they encountered. He ended by saying most things turned out favorably and promised to elaborate on specific matters when time permits.

“Perhaps we can talk more candidly next cycle. I'm planning an excursion to inspect the storage huts burned down last season by northern raiders. Volunteers are rebuilding them. I want to transport a load of stores and could use the help. Would you care to accompany me? If you have no other commitments, meet me at the stables at firstlight, and we can ride together. It's a short trip.”

“Don't you require a militia escort?”

“No, things are peaceful at present. We should be safe.”

“Alright, it's a date. I mean, I'd be happy to accompany you. Besides, my sole agenda for the morrow was to catch up on my journal entries, but it's not a priority.”

“Good, I'll see you at dayrise.”

Jesse rose, bowed, and excused himself. He hoped to talk with the mender before retiring for the night. Saephira remained for a while at her seat, pondering the things Jesse had related, then arose to make the rounds and visit with her invited guests.

At the rear board, Raydoo, Calrin, and Seth scarfed down several helpings from each platter, enjoying the meal and friendly banter between friends. Finally, the teasing abated and Calrin asked, “So, Seth, where did you guys go? We inquired with Mender Ottaar; she merely said your group traveled out of town for a few cycles.”

“Oh, man, it sure seemed longer. Sorry, dudes, I'm not sure JW wants me to spill the beans.”

“Gonna get all secret on us, are ya?” teased Calrin. “Well, fine. How much trouble can a person stir up in a couple cycles?”

“More than you realize.”

"What does that mean?"

"Nothing, forget it." *If they only understood the troubles we faced in Camayah.* "Let's rap on something else. Last time we banqueted together, you guys mentioned harpooning for tarkkies at one of the local lakes."

"Yeah, catching juvenile tarkks might be fun, but we have a better idea."

"Cool, what is it?"

"River angling," Raydoo replied. "I hear the eels are swarming on the Cali River, a quarter league below the village by the ford. We could camp on the eastern side of the river and have an eel roast. If you've never caught a slimy eel, you'll love it. They are real fighters. And we don't need a boat or a net. We can fish from the shore with a whirling hook and line."

"Dudes, I'm not afraid of the water anymore."

"We remember. Rule Number Two, right?"

Seth nodded. "Good rule."

"At any rate," continued Raydoo, "we've already been harpoon fishing at Mista Lake. That was two cycles ago before you left town for wherever you disappeared to."

"The place was called Camayah, but I don't wish to discuss it now."

"Fine, we aren't really interested." Raydoo flashed a taunting smirk at Seth. "Knowing your stories, it's probably some sort of wild tale, anyway."

"Yeah, if you say so." *Maybe I should give them the whole skinny.* "What time are we leaving?"

"Let's meet before firstlight at the stables. Calrin and I will bring the gear."

"If you two are done yapping," uttered Calrin, "pass me the yarm pudding. I'm getting hungry again."

Captain Maximus noticed his militia lead exiting the hall and hurried to catch him. "Chepho, wait a moment."

"Sir?"

"I've decided it would be prudent to conduct military drills with the Militia. Gather the men on the practice field at dayrise. Have everyone bring their longbows."

"What span?"

"Forecycle. We'll run drills for three cycles, starting with bows, and later I'll demonstrate advanced quarterstaff tactics. The following cycle will involve swordplay. On the third, we'll finish with slings, spears, and knife throwing. I realize it's short notice; nevertheless, I believe it to be expedient."

"We'll be there, sir." Chepho bowed, and together they walked out the entry. Max stopped suddenly, realizing he had forgotten his spouse. He turned around and raced over to the mender's table, hoping Narleen didn't see him leaving without her.

"Pull up a chair, Captain Maximus," said Ottaar. "Lundy and I are discussing a trip to Onnie Passage."

"Aye, the mender and me are gonna check on the life tree, gather more healing leaves, and see if any fruit has sprouted from the pip she planted."

Gelr overheard the conversation and inquired, "If the trip involves an escort, I'll volunteer to lead it." He slid his chair across the floor to sit next to Lundy. "A couple of my safeguards have been itching to see this mysterious tree."

"Sounds like an interesting outing." Anna rose from her spot and joined Captain Gelr.

"More than viewing some mystical tree," Gelr added, "I need to pay my respects to the fallen militiamen. I started the landside on the passage that slaughtered them, not to mention injuring you, Anna, and almost killing Phauch. Everything was my fault because—"

"No, it wasn't!" exclaimed Annabelle. "Evil Lord Eddnok forced you. He's the one to blame, not you. You were simply following orders."

"True, except I still feel responsible. Lady Saephira told me an honor guard buried Captain Melmandus and his comrade along the passage. I must make my peace and ask for forgiveness."

"Yahweh always absolves those with repentant hearts like yours. I'd be happy to accompany you and offer spiritual support. Besides, I want to see this life tree. Hey, Jess, care to tag along?"

"I better pass, Annie. I'm staying in town. Lady Saephira asked me to ride with her to inspect the repairs at their storage area. Crews are replacing huts and restocking supplies that raiders pilfered last season."

"How about you, Max?" wondered Anna.

"I'm also remaining here. I'll be conducting drills all cycle with the Militia. And if Captain Gelr is providing escort, my time's better spent on the practice field."

"Wanna go, Holley? It's an interesting place. We think the ruins were an ancient temple compound."

"Thanks, Anna, but I intend to spend the day alone, relax, and read my doctor's manual. Because of our recent circumstances, I haven't had time to study it."

"I have a better idea, Holley," interjected Narleen. "Why don't you join me at forecycle to break our fast? I know a popular eatery near the town center. They make the best yarm berry tarts. Afterwards, we can do a little shopping. You best have proper Eskaonite clothing if you plan to be seen with a vice-leader." Narleen smiled, hoping Holley realized she was jesting. "And if there's time, I'll show you a few of our sights. It'll be fun; you can always study your mender scrolls during nightrise. Please say yes . . ."

"Sure, I'd love to. It does sound enjoyable."

"Wonderful, I'll stop by Ottaar's place and pick you up."

"I hate to interrupt this conversation." Jesse moved closer. "I came over to ask the mender a medical question."

Ottaar looked at him. "Go ahead, Sir Jesse. What's the concern?"

"I've been having pain and stiffness in my right knee. It's an old injury. For a while, I was better, except the condition has returned. And my eyesight is getting blurry again. I used to wear spectacles."

"If you mean wearable magnifiers, I don't make those. You can talk with our glassmith and see what he recommends. His shop is by the Archives. Regarding the knee injury, Helixzon salve should alleviate your pain, temporarily. Netherute might help too. Sorry, I don't have remedies for poor vision. It happens to all us older folks at some point."

"What about healing leaves? Would they cure my sight problem?"

"They might. Unfortunately, my leaf supply is gone. That's another reason I need to visit the ruins at Onnie Passage. I plan on collecting more leaves for my mending potions." She glanced at

Holley. "Do you still have the ones I gave you?"

"No, I left them on Camayah with Layshura for treating Triverphol Disease."

"Guess my Helixzon will have to suffice."

"I could use a wee bit of your ointment as well," added Lundy. "Me joints have been aching."

"Okay, I'll give you gentlemen one or two bottles apiece, depending on my supply. It should provide relief until I can brew a batch of healing tea. The drink may resolve all your ailments, permanently. Those healing leaves have amazing properties."

With the span being late, the banquet festivities wound down and everyone departed the hall, heading for their homes. Outside, nightrise had faded into darkout, so each person struck a torch to see in the pitch darkness. Max and Narleen strolled arm-in-arm, following Lady Saephira to Residential Hall. Jesse's group shadowed Ottaar to her house. The other attendees, who included the leadership council, militia officers, and invited guests, likewise retired to their respective residences.

Once Jesse's party arrived at the mender's home, Ottaar opened her mender chest and withdrew three bottles of Helixzon salve. She gave one to Jesse and two to Lundy. "Apply a small amount of salve at bedtime and rub it into the affected areas. Do the same thing again at dayrise and every nightrise until the pain and stiffness subside." She closed the chest. "Remember these are only temporary treatments. I'm hopeful the healing leaves we harvest at High Springs will provide lasting cures for everyone. Good nightrise, my friends." Then she climbed the stairs to her bedroom and shut the door.

Jesse and Lundy no longer had immortal bodies like they did in heaven. The youthful endurance Lundy felt in eternity had gradually slipped away, and Jesse's eyesight had reverted to the time on earth when he wore glasses to see clearly. Moreover, Jesse's knee injury had begun to bother him again. The younger members, Anna, Seth, and Holley, seemed unaffected by the change to mortal bodies.

After Ottaar left for her room, the partners sat around the large kitchen table and shared their plans for next cycle. Based on their itineraries, Jesse redistributed the radios, giving one to Seth and the second to Anna. He kept the third for himself. He assumed Narleen retained the fourth unit because Max shied away from using walkie-talkies, unless absolutely necessary. Jesse instructed his team to set the dials to their originally assigned channels and suggested discretion in case they operated them. Although Narleen and Saephira were aware of their existence, he thought it unwise to reveal advanced messaging devices to a world unfamiliar with technology.

"Jess, is it alright to play my nyeflute?"

"Sure, Annie, just be careful which tune you choose." Jesse grinned. "We don't want any adverse effects this evening."

"Thanks, I'll play it quietly."

"Does this mean no midnight rides on my hoverboard?" Before Jesse could answer, Seth added, "I'm joking, JW."

The gang enjoyed a good laugh, then climbed the stairs and entered their guestrooms. As soon as everyone settled in for the night, Jesse flipped on his candle lamp and pulled out his journal, intending to make a log entry. However, feeling exhausted and in pain, he returned the diary to his satchel. He rubbed some salve on his sore knee, extinguished the lamp, slipped under the covers, and fell asleep.

CHAPTER 4

THE LOST FOREST

Lord Eddnok, Preaverca, and Menarbat entered the Lost Forest. The group paused for a moment to see if the company of militia would follow them. They didn't. Feeling they had escaped, the three rode deeper into the interior. Green branches and oak-shaped leaves from cottlepines spread across the canopy blocking out the light of dayrise. The air smelled as if a rotted corpse lay nearby.

The farther they traveled into the grove, the darker it became, and soon torches were necessary to see. Since Menarbat had packed two, he struck both aflame and gave one to Eddnok, keeping the other for himself. The party pressed on with Eddnok in the lead, followed by the Tracker, and then Preaverca.

They slowly urged their mounts forward, threading their way around cottlepines until the trees and foliage became too dense to continue, forcing everyone to dismount and proceed on foot. By instinct, their animals followed them hunched together in herd formation.

Unnatural hissing penetrated the silence, which seemed to be coming from all directions at once. The kacks whinnied, bothered by the noise.

"Hey, Tracker, go check on our rides and see what's spooking them," demanded Eddnok.

"Probably nothing, Lord, but I'll investigate." Waving his

torch from side to side, Menarbat jogged to the rear and bumped into Preaverca, leaning against a cottlepine in the shadowy darkness. "See anything?"

"How can I? You two have the only torches for light. Those strange sounds frighten me. I'm heading to the front with Lord Eddnok."

"No! Stay here and don't move. I'll return in a few moments as soon as I check on our mounts. You'll be fine."

It didn't take long for the Tracker to determine one ride was missing. He shined his torch in a circle, yet didn't see the animal anywhere. He petted the remaining kacks. "Take it easy you two; it's merely forest sounds, nothing more." The kacks continued to stomp their hoofs, snort loudly, and shake their heads, uncomfortable with the foul scent in the air. Menarbat scanned the area for hoofprints. Seeing no trail, he turned and rushed back to pick up Preaverca.

As he approached her location, Preaverca screamed. Gazing into the canopy, Menarbat saw a plant at least six paces long and four paces wide, holding a wiggling body between two jaw-shaped pods. Preaverca's cries were unrelenting. "Help me, help me!"

The thing's mouth contained sharp thorny stems similar to fangs. They were dripping blood. After one more muffled shriek from Preaverca, the plant rose into the boughs and disappeared. Lying on the ground, he found her waterskin and remnants of clothing covered in green slime. He picked up the waterskin in his right hand. The substance burned his fingers. Ignoring the pain, he raced to the front where Eddnok waited, holding the torch in his left.

"What's happening in the rear? I heard shouting."

"A huge plant appeared out of nowhere and devoured Preaverca. And one of our kacks is gone."

"We'll assume it was hers. Fortunately, two rides are left. You better backtrack and lead the remaining mounts forward."

"How?"

"Use your sword. Beat them if you have to; just drive them this way. We'll need transportation once we exit these woods, including the supplies inside those side carriers if we plan to survive in the Nae Wilderness."

"Lord, I think you should go with me. If these things attack again, I'll—"

"No, no, I'm staying here. In fact, you had better give me Preaverca's waterskin. We don't want to lose that as well." Menarbat wiped the slime off the container onto his pants. The acidic substance soaked through his clothes and burned his thigh. Instead of handing the skin to Eddnok, he sprayed water on his leg, trying to wash it off. "Stop! We need to conserve our water supply. Now, get going, brave Tracker." Angry at the slight, Menarbat threw the waterskin at Eddnok's feet, turned, unsheathed his saber, and took off running.

The hissing continued. A kack moaned in torment. When Menarbat reached the area where he left the mounts, he couldn't find their second ride. The third one was bucking and shaking its long mane as if trying to fight off an invisible predator. "Take it easy, gal." After the animal settled down, he noticed pieces of a side carrier lying nearby on the ground. The Tracker rifled through it, searching for salvageable supplies, and found a haversack of rations. While examining the contents, a deafening hiss arose, sounding like a viper preparing to strike. He stood, turned around, and watched as a long vine dropped from the heights. The carnivorous plant grabbed the remaining kack in its mouth. The animal released a long screeching whinny as it vanished into the canopy. Then silence. Menarbat dropped the haversack of rations, tossed his torch on the ground, and ran, holding his sword extended in front of him. Without light to see the path, he bumped into trees, tripped over rocks, but kept running.

Dins of *sissssss, sissssss* echoed round about him, growing more intense and louder. In the darkness, he spotted the faint glow of a torch. He stumbled toward it and approached Eddnok. Before he could report his findings, a vine dropped from its hiding place and clamped onto his legs. "It's got me!" The Tracker tossed his saber to Eddnok. "Quick, cut the thing above . . . Aaaaah! . . ."

Eddnok leaned over and clutched the sword, then stepped back two paces and watched as the greenish monstrosity lifted Menarbat into the darken dome. Menarbat's screams lingered for a moment before growing silent. Eddnok raised his torch, scanned the heights for more plant creatures, and noticed movement in a limb above him. Gripped with fear and hardly breathing, he bolted away, holding Menarbat's saber in one hand and his torch in the other. The satchel containing all his belongings dangled at his side.

The shrieking noises were unrelenting. Eddnok raced ahead, yelling, "Stay away, stay away!" With only a curved blade to defend himself, he scrambled past the shadows and swung at anything slithering above him in the canopy.

As Eddnok neared the grove's edge, light began to filter through the tree branches. No longer needing the torch, he extinguished it and slowed his pace to a fast walk. Faint hissing resonated behind him.

He exited the woodlands to behold a vast wilderness lying eastward as far as the eye could see. The air felt dry, the temperature, hot. Other than a few hills, the landscape looked barren with no water in sight, anywhere. Lord Eddnok didn't care about losing his friends; they were simply pawns. The fact that none of their rides survived is what disturbed him the most.

CHAPTER 5

INSPECTING THE STORES

During the banquet, Saephira and Jesse had decided to spend the day together, visit the stores, check on the rebuilding progress, and finish their conversation from the previous night. The mender's Helixzon salve helped with Jesse's knee pain, so he applied a little more in the morning. He placed the bottle into his satchel, which contained his radio, candle lamp, journal, and a handful of nourishment tablets. Remembering he wanted to write an entry, Jesse withdrew the journal and flipped to an open page. Using the special pen that never seemed to run low of ink, he began:

Entry Eighteen

Here we are again, back on Eskaonus. As I noted in my last entry, I felt my team needed a break for a couple days, I mean cycles, before we returned to heaven. Our group looks forward to the moderate climate and lush greenery of the Lower Realm instead of the barren sectors of Camayah. Even the cold is preferable to its arid conditions. Hopefully with time, the Camayahnites can terraform their landscape and improve their living conditions.

I had anticipated that Maximus would depart with us, but since he married a local gal named Narleen, I'm not sure how that affects things. I recently discovered he's gonna be a father. I'm still trying to wrap my head around the baby news.

They say heaven is a place of second chances. Perhaps this is his. On earth, Max was deprived of marriage and raising a family when barbarians attacked his village and murdered his betrothed. He seems happy here, and the residents depend on the military experience he gained as a centurion in the Roman Empire. I get it. I think he would rather be here than floating on some celestial cloud in heaven for all eternity. And if eternity is supposed to be a place where our hopes and dreams are realized, then his choice to stay in Eskaonus is the right one for him. As for me, I continue to ponder my purpose.

The only adverse issue is the missing fleet from Bayegulf. It may be nothing more than a weather delay. Max sent three ships to investigate. Other than this concern, all is well. Our party is involved in various activities: Lundy and Annie are traveling up Onnie Pass to see the life tree; Seth is hanging with his friends; Holley wants to visit the local establishments; and I'm joining Lady Saephira to inspect the storage facility near Beayama.

In other news, we ate to our hearts content at yestercycle's banquet. It was nice to have actual food and drink instead of nutrition and hydration pills. We plan on portaling to heaven soon. Of course, time is relative. Just a little humor in case Chesedel reads this log. Better end this entry now; I have to meet Saephira at the stables. She's probably waiting since it's already past firstlight.

Jesse tucked the journal and pen back into his satchel, slung it over his shoulder, and hurried down the stairs. He found Holley, Annabelle, and Lundy sitting at the table with Ottaar, sipping cups of tea. "Where's Seth this morning? I thought he'd be here."

"We think he rose early, removed an old loaf of kin from the pantry, and departed," replied Holley. "Last night Seth mentioned a fishing trip with Calrin and Raydoo." She took one last sip and pushed her cup aside. "As for me, I'm waiting for Lady Narleen. We're breaking our fast at an eatery near the town square, and because I'm unfamiliar with Eskaonus, she wanted to show me the sights. She also mentioned shopping."

"Yeah, I heard part of your conversation at the banquet. And you three?" Jesse glanced at the reverend. "Still going out of town?"

"Aye. Me, Annabel, and Ottaar are waiting for Captain Gelr

to arrive with his escort. Then we'll travel up Onnie Passage to see the ruins. Be gone two cycles. I wanna check on the life tree and explore the spot for more clues. I'm pretty sure it was a temple at one time."

"And I plan to pick several totes of healing leaves," added Ottaar. "I'm confident a healing-leaf tea mixture will improve your degenerative knee condition. It did wonders for my stiff joints. It might even mend your failing eyesight."

"Last time the mender visited there, she said the life tree had blossoms." Annabelle's brown eyes widened as she talked. "If purple fruit has developed, it might work the same way it does in heav . . . I mean, the high realm. Wouldn't this be wonderful, Jess?" He simply nodded; his mind seemed focused elsewhere.

"Care to break your fast here? I have Azollie tea simmering on the stove and several loaves of kin in my oven, baking. It should be ready in a quarter span or less."

"Thanks, Mender, except I better scoot. Lady Saephira is waiting for me." Jesse bowed, then rushed through the doorway, heading for the stables.

Saephira stood in front of the stall, dressed in a shapely-fitted riding outfit. Her braided brunette hair hung down across her left shoulder. When Jesse drew near, Saephira's face brightened, causing her bluish eyes to glisten in the morning twilight.

She already had Salie, her white-striped kack, saddled with side carriers and stacked with totes. Her animal had gone missing during the conflict with the Upper Realm, but Commander Bolgog returned it during the peace negotiations in Midvill. Salie was strong, a good runner, even though she measured two hands shorter than Jesse's mount, whose height marked eighteen hands at the withers.

"Sorry, we can't ride double. I must deliver four totes of dried maize to the storage area, and your kack is already loaded with cottlepine slats required for the rebuilding project. We need to take two animals. Do you still remember how to steer them?"

"Yep, hang on to their long fluffy manes for stability, guide them by using gentle leg movements, and touch their necks to make turns. Most importantly, don't pull back suddenly on their manes. It's a good way to land on your fanny."

"I assume you learned these lessons the hard way. Have you broken your fast yet?"

"No, I left before I had a chance."

"Fortunately, I packed a haversack. We can stop on the way."

The riders took their time, walking their mounts at a leisurely pace. They approached a series of hills at forecycle and stopped near an outcropping of cottlepine saplings to eat their meal.

"Hope you're hungry."

"I am. What did you bring to munch on?"

"Just a few things to hold us over until banquet time." Saephira removed a small sack from her side carrier and unpacked kin rolls, a container of yarm berry jam, and a half skin of cold Azollie tea. She spread out a blanket, and they sat down. As they shared breakfast, the kacks wandered around, nibbling on the nearby bushes and grasses.

Their conversation jumped from topic to topic. They discussed Eddnok's entrance into the Lost Forest, Camayah, the Unseen One, Jesse's comrades, her dreams for the Eskaonites, and their concerns for the absent ships, until the exchange landed on technology.

"Tell me more about this tekknowledgie. Is it magic?"

"Actually, it's pronounced *tek·naa-luh·jee*. And no, it's not magic; it's . . . hmm . . . a type of advanced knowledge or science."

"Is it good or evil?"

"Depends on how it's used. Here, let me show you." Jesse pulled the walkie-talkie from his satchel. "Lady Narleen is probably carrying the device I gave Max. He shies away from using these transceivers." Jesse flipped to Narleen's channel. "Let's give your vice-leader a call."

"How do you do that?"

"Like this." He held the radio near his mouth. "Jesse to Lady Narleen, do you copy?"

The unit remained silent. "It doesn't seem to be working," noted Saephira.

"Narleen might be somewhere she feels uncomfortable

using it. Here, you try it this time." Jesse handed the communicator to Saephira. "Speak into the screened hole at the top."

"Vice-leader, do you hear me?"

"Is that you, my Lady?"

"Yes, Jesse is demonstrating what he says is advanced knowledge."

"I know; I had to get used to it on Camayah. These talkies are wonderful devices and much faster than sending messages by homing flyers. And the Camayahnites have even more amazing things."

"You mean tekknowledgie?"

"Indeed, I . . ." Narleen's voice faded. "Wait a moment, my Lady. I am drawing stares from people who are probably wondering why I am talking into a little gray box. I better cut this call short. Besides, Holley and I are about to break our fast at Ellee's Place. If everything's okay, I mean no emergencies, then I'll say goodbye. You and Jesse have a fun time."

"Interesting . . . this knowledgie science." She gave the radio back to Jesse. "I'd like to learn more, but right now, we better inspect the repairs and drop off the supplies we brought with us."

Jesse gathered the food while Saephira rolled up the blanket. Afterwards, they mounted their kacks and rode uphill to the storage location, passing a large mushroom patch on the left.

"Max mentioned picking mushrooms. Are those—"

"They are. Most locals use this patch. These dallups are the best tasting ones in the Lower Realm, or so I'm told. They seem to flourish by this grove of cottlepines. If time allows, we can gather some before we return to town."

When they approached the site, the forelady scurried forward and curtsied. "Lady Saephira, what a surprise. We never expected the leader of the Lower Realm. If I had known, we would have—"

"This is not an official inspection, merely a drop-by visit to view your progress in getting the structures fixed. Please give me a tour." Saephira and Jesse dismounted and followed the forelady. She showed them a series of huts: five were completed; the others were in the process of renovation. After a lengthy walkthrough of the storage area, Jesse and Saephira dropped off the building supplies and four bags of maize kernels. Prior to leaving, Saephira thanked the forelady and her crew of laborers for all their hard work in restoring the burnt huts. On the way down the hill, they stopped at the dallup patch.

The patch contained various sizes of mushrooms. Their caps were shaped like little Christmas trees with green gills underneath. "Be careful not to disturb the large dallups. Those are the seed spreaders; they keep the patch full. We only pick the middle-sized ones."

"You mean these things grow by seeds, not spores?"

"Correct. The bigger ones keep the patch full by spreading their seeds during darkout."

Because the harvestable fungi were the size of an open palm, it didn't take long to fill two small totes. As soon as they finished loading the bags onto the side carriers, Saephira asked, "Do you mind if we sit for a span and continue our conversation? It's still early. Latecycle is spans away."

"Sure, there's no hurry. I'm mostly vegging today."

"Vegging?"

"It means taking it easy."

"Interesting word." Saephira motioned to Jesse to join her. "May I ask you a question?"

"Sure, if it's not too personal."

"Regarding the places you hail from, do they have . . . betrothals?"

Jesse thought for a moment, wondering where the question was leading. He didn't want to give a dubious reply. "On earth where I was born, the inhabitants have similar arrangements called marriages. On Camayah, those relationships are known as bondings."

"What about the high realm?"

"Hmm . . ." Jesse figured this question would arise at some point, so he paused to consider his answer. "Things are different there. People neither marry, nor are they given in marriage."

"That's sad."

"Not sad, per se, just different. It's more of a spiritual domain, an eternal realm beyond time."

"I really don't understand your reply. Since Max also came

from this high realm before he decided to live here, perhaps I should talk with him."

Feeling he had dodged the bullet, Jesse agreed. "Yes, Maximus might be the better individual to query. I only resided there for a brief time prior to my arrival in Eskaonus."

"How brief?"

"One day, I mean cycle."

"Obviously then, Maximus would be more knowledgeable on high province matters. I'll inquire with him later."

Hoping to change the focus from his circumstances to hers, Jesse said, "My turn to pose a question."

"That's fair, assuming it's not too personal." She smiled, remembering Jesse's reply.

"Are you planning to get betrothed again?"

"You mean after Eddnok tricked me into accepting his proposal, thinking it was sincere when all he sought was a concubine. No, I'll not be deceived again. Besides, I've only met one man I'd be interested in betrothing."

"And who's the lucky guy?"

"Now you're getting personal." She smiled again. "Perhaps it's a good time to end these queries. Before we depart this place, I can show you the biggest cottlepine in Eskaonus." Saephira pointed to a small grove of trees adjacent to the dallup patch. "Let's walk closer. We think the middle one is more than a hundred paces tall and ten paces wide."

Jesse studied the tree, estimating the height at over 350 feet tall with a base thirty feet around. "Wow, this evergreen is huge. It's the largest tree I've ever seen, even bigger than the Sequoias from my homeworld. What are those markings on the trunk?"

"Residents come from far and wide to carve their initials into it, believing their actions will bring good fortune. Here, look at this one." She touched two faded letters. "W + K were placed by my mother and father when they were younger. And these." She indicated a fresher set of letters. "N + M are marks Narleen and Maximus whittled into the bark. If you search around the base, you'll find hundreds more."

"Interesting tradition."

"Let's add ours."

"I didn't bring a knife."

"Don't worry; I did. I've begun carrying a dagger ever since the day we were attacked by assassins on our way to the Archives." Saephira withdrew a small knife, hidden in her sash, and ran her finger across the blade to test its sharpness. "The lady's initial always goes first, followed by the man's." Saephira carved an S and passed the blade to Jesse. He hesitated. "You don't have to if you feel uncomfortable. I merely thought it would be a nice reminder of your visit to our land."

Jesse didn't have the heart to tell her he planned to leave for heaven in a few days. "No, I don't mind." He carved a J next to the S and handed the dagger back to Saephira. She added a + between their initials and tucked the blade away.

"We better leave for Beayama. It will be nightrise soon, and we'll need torches to see if we tarry much longer." As they climbed upon their rides, Saephira asked, "If you're not busy on the morrow, would you care to spend the cycle together? I promise no more inquiries, just a nice time."

"Sure, I've got no real plans, other than to rest and recuperate before I gather my colleagues together to discuss our next options."

Although Saephira's eyes revealed sadness at his comment, her voice gave no hint of disappointment. "Where would you prefer to go? My schedule is open. The Vice-leader can handle things. Narleen wants to stay close to town and give Holley a tour. She and Holley have become close friends."

"It appears so." Knowing the party's next options involved leaving Eskaonus, Jesse worried their medic had gotten overly involved. "Actually, I have a hankering to travel to Tabahir, visit with Nanlon and his son, get the latest news from Briacap, and see the scenery."

"Not much scenery in the barren lands surrounding Tabahir. However, we could have dinner at the Copper Rail, spend the night, separate rooms of course, and return the next cycle. I'd also enjoy seeing Nanlon and his son. He's a precious little boy, and I don't even know his name. I have a gift for him, an official militia belt, which is awarded to all soldiers once they finish training."

"No doubt, he'll love it. Sounds like a needful visit, and it's what the mender recommended for me. In fact, Ottaar felt our whole group should take a few cycles to recover our health, not to mention, consume real food instead of nutrition tabs."

"Nutrition tabs?"

"Let's leave that explanation for another time. Concerning a trip to Tabahir, I agree. Fits my timeframe." They mounted up and trotted back to the city, continuing their conversation about less-serious matters, arriving during twilight.

CHAPTER 6

TOURING THE TOWN

Max slipped out of bed, trying not to disturb his spouse, and dressed quickly. "Where are you going so early?" Narleen glanced out the window. "It's dark outside."

"Sorry, Nar, I have militia training this cycle." Max strapped on his Gladius and slung the longbow over his shoulder. "I need to arrange the practice field before firstlight when the militiamen arrive."

"How long will you be gone?"

"All cycle, probably. I plan to conduct another session on the morrow, and if necessary, the following one. I hafta make sure the Militia is prepared."

"For what? Is there an issue?"

"No, not really. I'm just concerned about the missing ships. However, it may be nothing more than a weather delay. We'll discern more in a few cycles. What are your plans?"

"I'm meeting with Holley to break our fast at Ellee's Place. Afterwards, I'll take her shopping for clothes. She's still wearing Ottaar's hand-me-downs. Since the eatery is near the practice field, why don't you join us?"

"I can't, Nar; training comes first. I'll stop by the kitchen and grab a bite to eat on my way out. I gotta run."

"Aren't you forgetting something?"

"Oh, yeah." Max walked back to the bed, bent down, and

kissed Narleen on the cheek.

She pulled him closer and returned the kiss on his mouth. "Are you sure you don't care to stay a little longer?"

"I wish I could, except I better leave now or . . ." Max headed for the door.

"Or what?" She smiled, assuming he got her hint.

"I'll see you at nightrise when we have more time to continue this conversation." He grinned.

"Fine, I'll be waiting, but aren't you forgetting something else?"

"Like what?"

"Your quiver of arrows."

"Thanks, Nar, you're right. I must have other things on my mind."

"I hope I'm one of them, Captain," she said with a teasing sigh.

"You are, my lady." He winked his left eye and bowed deeply. "You're the most important thing." He surveyed the room to see if he had missed anything and noticed his *persuader* leaning against the wall. He grabbed the quarterstaff, seized his quiver in the corner, and rushed out.

Once he left, Narleen snuggled under the covers and slept for another span. As soon as firstlight appeared in the window, she arose, shuffled over to her dresser, and gazed into the mirror. She rubbed her hazel eyes, trying to wake up, knowing she had to meet Holley in a couple spans. If she went out among the people, she wanted to look the part as their vice-leader. Narleen brushed her auburn hair—*it'll be long enough to braid soon*—and donned a long cream-colored dress, which seemed a little tight at her waistline. *Ottaar was correct; I have put on extra weight.* She laughed, realizing it was because of the child in her womb. She smoothed the dress across her slightly rounded stomach. *Better shop for roomier outfits for myself.*

Narleen met up with Holley at Ottaar's home, and they strolled down the road toward the town square. As the duo approached Ellee's Place, the radio inside Narleen's satchel sounded twice in rapid succession. She didn't have time to respond to the first call from Jesse. The second one came from

Saephira. She quickly withdrew the device and replied the way Max had taught her. After a brief conversation, Narleen signed off and tucked the radio away, mindful of the stares from passersby and diners.

The owner, a plump, short-statured woman with graying hair, curtsied and led them to a streetside table. As she arranged their plate settings, she asked, "What would you ladies like this fine dayrise?"

"Your famous yarm berry tarts."

"And to drink? We have yarm, berry juice, flavored teas, and kunakk."

"A pot of Azollie tea would be nice."

"Yes, my lady." She curtsied again and smiled at Holley. "I'll have our waiter bring them right out."

As Holley and Narleen broke fast, their conversation revolved around local events, Holley's medical experience, Narleen's marriage to Max, and birthing children. Once they finished their meal, Narleen requested a bag for the leftover tarts. "If you don't mind, I'll take the rest for Maxie; he loves these pastries."

"Fine with me. I've eaten enough for a week. Although the nutrition pills from Camayah worked well enough to satisfy hunger, they're no comparison to real food. Their supplements had no taste. In fact, that whole place was a—"

"Talk about places, there are a few here in Beayama worth seeing. The Archives is one. It's close by, down the alley. The merchant carts are fun to browse. We can also stop by the practice field and watch the Militia. Maxie has training this cycle, so it's best not to intrude while the guys learn soldiering. Besides, I don't care to embarrass the captain in front of his men." She paused as a grin formed on her face. "You know, Holley, I'm a better slinger than any of his soldiers." She giggled at her truthful jest.

"And if you're not too busy, on the morrow, we can visit the former vice-leader, Yhmim, who's serving time in our stockade for treason. The guards say she's unrepentant. Even so, I feel sorry for her. She's really been depressed, not eating. Perhaps your medical advice can help her. However, before we engage in additional activities, we must get you proper clothing." Narleen paid the bill, leaving a tip of five credits for the server, and the two women departed.

As they wandered across the street, Narleen explained that Beayama had three weaver shops: One made utility products, curtains, blankets, and general clothing; the second produced ropes, cloth lines, tents, and banners; the third specialized in decorative wear and mender clothing. "In Bayegulf, the port seamsters construct sails for ships, sea tarps, harpoon lines, and outfits for sailors. Our tailors are experts with their craft. Each village maintains at least one workshop."

"What do they use for knitting material?"

"Cotta, a yellowish-tan plant with spiny branches. The soft fibrous balls bloom all yarn long, which gatherers harvest for weaving. Knitters dye the fibers to obtain various colors. Cotta grows along the riverbanks and tributaries in abundant supply. Kacks love nibbling on the fuzzy tips and would probably eat the entire bunch if we allowed." She slowly shook her head and chuckled. "Fortunately, the kacks consume other flora, so when we stop at riverbanks to hydrate them, we move our rides away from the cotta plants and hobble them next to our leafy field grasses."

After stopping at two merchant carts in the square, they approached a weaver shop and entered. "This facility specializes in mender garments."

A tall, lanky clerk with scraggly black hair greeted the women. "Good dayrise, ladies, how may I serve you?"

"We're in need of clothing for me and menderware for Holley."

"Wonderful. We have a wide selection in stock, and our stitchers in the rear cubicle can design whatever style you prefer."

"Lady Narleen, I'm not sure I require—"

"Yes, Holley, you do." Narleen moved forward and leaned on the counter. "What colors do menders request?"

"Well, most either wear green or blue matching outfits, pants and tops, no dresses, unless it's an official gathering. We have those, too. And of course, purple sashes with marking tassels. Each tassel indicates the number of yarns of mendership. How many for the young healer?"

"One would be fine." Holley joined Narleen at the counter. "I'm fairly new—"

"Make it five yarns," interrupted Narleen. "She has much experience elsewhere."

"Oh, which province?"

"A distant realm that we would like to keep private at this time."

"I understand. Menders prefer confidentiality in such matters. Does the young lady seek a mender bag?" The man grabbed several from a hanger and placed them on the counter. "These styles are popular. All very roomy inside."

"No, I will stay with my silver satchel." Holley showed it to the salesman.

"Nice, unique design. I've never seen this style before. If you ever choose to make a trade or sell it, I will accommodate. Would fifteen credits suffice?"

"Although I appreciate your generous offer, I'm keeping mine." The clerk removed the bags and hung them back on his display rack.

"Fine. Regarding outfit colors, Ottaar prefers blue. What's your preference?"

"Blue works for me," replied Holley.

"Perfect. Come back for a fitting on the morrow. We'll have the outfits completed by the following cycle. You can take the purple sash now." He handed it to Holley. "Wear it as a belt, a shawl across the shoulder, or a head scarf, but please don it. People should know you're an experienced healer."

"I'll make sure she does." Narleen tied it to Holley's waist. "We'll return next forecycle for her fitting. We also want to purchase general clothing and banquet outfits. And I'll require some roomier clothing. I have a child on the way."

"Congratulations, my lady. Would you like to select birthing outfits at this time?"

"No, I'll do it on the morrow. What do I owe?"

"We can settle your account later. The Vice-leader's credit is always good." The man bowed. "Oh, by the way, I hear that Ritwell Village is seeking a mender. Perhaps the young lady would be interested. Tabahir and Nakk Village are likewise in need."

"Thank you, I'm sure Lady Saephira and Ottaar are already aware. Nevertheless, we'll take your suggestions under advisement."

Narleen and Holley stopped by the Militia practice field, staying until twilight to watch Max give quarterstaff demonstrations. For the next cycle, they made plans to see the Archives, visit the former vice-leader in the stockade, and stop by the weaver's place to complete Holley's fitting. If time allowed, they'd travel to Ritwell Village to check on the mender situation. Since the span was getting late, the two friends headed home: Narleen to Residential Hall and Holley to Ottaar's place. On the way, a woman noticed Holley's purple sash with five tassels and stopped to ask questions about her son's injured arm. The mother seemed pleased with the advice and promised to follow it until her child recovered.

CHAPTER 7

TRAINING THE MILITIA

Max rose early, said his goodbyes to Nar, and rushed out, heading down the street. He stopped by the kitchen in the Great Hall and snatched a couple kin rolls to eat on the way. He arrived at the practice field at firstlight and found Militia Lead Chepho arranging the targets for archery. "I assumed we're starting with longbows."

"Yes, Chepho, then we'll switch to advanced battlestaff tactics during midcycle."

"What about swords, slings, spears, and throwing knives?"

"As I mentioned at the banquet, we'll practice with those on the morrow and the following cycle. Where's our militia chief?"

"Phauch is on the way. He's rousing the troops now. In fact, I hear the shuffling of footsteps." Max glanced over his shoulder and spotted a band of twenty militiamen approaching at a run; most carried longbows; others held a set of spears. All had sheathed swords strapped to their sides.

Before the men arrived, Max whispered in Chepho's ear, "I have a plan. Follow my lead." After roll call, Phauch gathered the men in a circle around Max and Chepho. As soon as the outfit was settled, the taunting began. "They say you are better than me at archery."

"I am, old captain, sir. While you've been off gallivanting and wedding the Lady Narleen, I've been practicing the bow," replied Chepho, provoking Max for a response.

"Perhaps you should try betrothal yourself. It might do you good or at least tame your tongue." Max's face appeared stern, almost angry.

At first, the men appeared shocked at the conversation, including Phauch, yet no one said a word, fearing a reprimand. More insults flowed forth between the captain and his militia lead. The men wondered if their two senior officers were serious or playacting. More teasing followed. Judging by their actions, the militiamen delighted in the unexpected diversion. Some stomped their feet, others clapped, a few banged their spears together. High spirits prevailed.

"I suggest an archery contest to settle this." Max removed the longbow from his shoulder and checked the bowstring for tautness.

"Fine with me, sir. Best of three wins the cycle."

"Wager, wager, wager!" shouted the men.

"Alright, if I lose," offered Max, "I'll wager to rake the kack stalls for seven cycles."

Those who wanted the lead to win hollered encouragement while pounding their fists against their leather armor. Those who favored the captain booed and hissed at Chepho, egging him on.

"And if I lose," replied the lead, "I'll stake feeding and brushing the animals for the same period."

"Done! It's a wager." Max glared at Chepho, biting his lips to keep from grinning.

More shouts and jeers arose as the squad enjoyed their officer's banter and rivalry. Max and Chepho noticed the moral of their men rise after each taunt, which of course was their purpose.

Four comrades raced off to set up two targets at twenty-five paces. When finished, they returned to the group. Chepho strung his longbow, picked out three arrows from his quiver, and stuck them into the ground in front of him. "Do you want to go first, Captain? Rank has its privileges."

"No, let's both shoot at the same time." Max withdrew three arrows and likewise spaced them at his feet. He knew Chepho was a good bowman, perhaps even better than him. The lead had been practicing for the last sixty cycles. He, on the other hand, had been preoccupied with leadership duties and his betrothal to Narleen.

Max felt as rusty as a Roman sword left out in the rain too long.

"I agree, feeble one." The contestants notched their shafts, drew back, and let their projectiles fly: *whish, whish.*

The spotter ran over and checked. "Dead center for both. It's a tie." Cheers rose from the ranks.

"Move the targets to forty paces," Max yelled.

Both men took aim and released their second volley: *whish, whish.* The spotter checked the results. "The captain's arrow is two fingers left of center. The lead's shot is one finger right of center. Chepho's ahead." Several applauded, others booed, but everyone laughed, relishing the moment.

"Set the targets at seventy paces." Chepho smiled and notched his final arrow. "I'll give the old captain another try."

Max thanked him while he withdrew his third arrow. As soon as he did, the bronzed point fell off. He realized if he didn't shoot, he'd forfeit the contest. "My shaft is broken. Can I replace it?"

"Contest rules say you must use the three you chose," confirmed one of the men.

"Let's give our captain one more shot," replied Chepho. "Pick another and let's finish this challenge." The militiamen whispered bets to one another, hoping to make a few credits if their champion won.

Max reached into his quiver. He had one projectile left, an early prototype. It was more of a keepsake, one of the arrows he and Seth had made at Mender Ottaar's place prior to the rescue attempt at Briacap. Instead of fletchings, it had two yarn stringers to stabilize its flight. The shaft featured a whittled point, not a bronze-sharpened tip. The arrow would hit the target; the accuracy, however, remained in question. The design was inferior to the newer ones produced by the woodsmith and metalsmith for the alliance.

"Well, Captain, are ya gonna forfeit or shoot." Before he could answer, a west wind arose, stirring up a cloud of dust that obscured the target. Max rubbed his jaw; worry showed on his face. He realized the breeze would likely affect flight trajectory.

"I'll continue." Max waited for the gusts to subside, except they didn't, so he notched his arrow, adjusted his aim, squinted an eye to focus, and released. *Whish.* The Militia Lead quickly followed suit. *Whish.* Their missiles sped toward the target, landing with penetrating thunks.

The spotter bolted across the field to measure the marks. "The lead's shaft is three fingers right of center. The captain's is one finger, bottom of center. The final score is three to four. Captain Maximus wins by a finger." Gleeful hails erupted. Those who won wagers slapped the losers on their backs, offering snide comments and reminding them how many credits they owed.

"I guess Chepho will be tending the kacks from now on." Once the hooting and laughter subsided, Max added, "Okay, guys, fun's over. Let's take a half-span break, and then we'll continue."

Most sat in small clusters and shared their waterskins. Others stood face to face, arguing, trying to collect their winnings. Two cohorts crossed the street to visit with the young women who had gathered to watch. When the break ended, Max whistled to rally the unit and motioned for them to form a circle around him.

"I know we are not at war with the Upper Realm anymore. In fact, with the recent truce, we are more akin to allies. Without enemies, weapon preparedness has become a secondary concern. Most of our training thus far has been for defending the realm and defeating our enemies. Swords, bows, slings, spears, and throwing knives are killing weapons. And we need to stay proficient with them. On the morrow and the following cycle, we will drill with those. However, because warfare isn't on the horizon, I want to encourage everybody to learn the defensive tactics of the quarterstaff. We will devote the rest of the cycle to those approaches."

"Seth and Miss Anna were both given fighting staffs and were skilled with their usage; even Reverend Lundy learned how to wield one. On numerous occasions, it allowed them to escape danger or subdue their attackers. I noticed that Anna and Seth's battlestaffs, which I call *persuaders* for obvious reasons, are still in the armory. First come, first served, if anybody desires a battle-tested one." Two men raised their hands before the others responded. "They're yours. Retrieve them after practice. I'll hire the woodsmith to make more. Since we are in peacetime, I want this detachment to carry staves instead of spears."

Maximus paced back and forth as he considered his opening remarks. He stopped suddenly, tossed his staff high into the air, caught it one-handed, twirled it twice, and then swiped at Phauch's feet, dropping the Militia Chief to the ground on his behind. Embarrassed at being caught off guard, Phauch stood and quietly rejoined the circle. Having garnered his men's attention, Max began. "I've taught these techniques previously, so for some of you this instruction may be repetitive, but I feel our military would benefit from these lessons. There are four basic moves: Lunge, Strike, Block, and the last one you just witnessed, Sweep."

He raised his leadership staff high in the air. "This belonged to Melmandus, Captain of the Militia. Prior to his untimely death on Onnie Passage, Melmandus bequeathed it to Sir Jesse. When Lady Saephira promoted me to captain, Jesse passed it on to me. One yarn, I will leave it for someone else." Most of the men remembered Captain Melmandus, having attended his memory table ceremony.

Max allowed the men a moment of quiet reflection before outlining the four techniques and expounding on their effectiveness. He followed up by going through the appropriate stances and deliveries for each. "Lunge is a thrust forward, hitting a vital area like the chest, arm, or thigh. There are vulnerable targets on the face as well. Poking an eye or smashing a nose will stun your opponent, at least temporarily. Also consider lunging below the ribcage." He used his fist to indicate the best spot. "It will knock the air out of a person's lungs, allowing an opportunity to escape or respond with a different move."

"Strikes come in various forms: reverse, counter, and spin. The spin adds momentum to your strike. A hit to the neck will daze opponents. With more force, it can damage their spinal cords, permanently disabling them. Striking at an arm or leg will injure a limb, and if delivered hard enough, can break bones. I hope you'll never need to employ these more lethal methods, but you should be aware of them."

"Blocks, also called deflects, can counter whatever action an assailant tries, whether they're using a spear, sword, or other weapon in their attack. Similarly, fakes and dodges are helpful in confusing the attacker, giving you a slight advantage. All these are great defensive strategies. Use them."

"For a Sweep or reverse sweep, hit behind the knees or ankles to drop your enemy to the ground. This will facilitate the next three options: escape, immobilize, or apply a lethal blow. One of the most effective sweeps is an upward swing between the legs to the groin area. It works well, especially if the adversary is a man. Remember, a quarterstaff is primarily a defensive weapon and if used as such, can save a life. You only need to disable an opponent in order to get away."

Once Max finished his session, the band split into smaller clusters to practice archery and hone their skills. They continued drilling until twilight forced Max to call for a halt. "Remember, we have another cycle of training on the morrow, and depending on our progress, the following cycle, too. Get some rest." He wished his company a good nightrise and dismissed them. The tired troops grabbed their weapons and departed for their dwellings.

Maximus waited for the last soldier to leave, gathered his gear, and likewise headed home. Although he missed Nar and wanted to spend more time with her, his duties as captain made that harder each cycle. Maybe things would slow down after the baby was born. As Max walked to Residential Hall, he wondered if his spouse remembered to bring him a couple yarm berry tarts from Ellee's Place. They were his favorite.

CHAPTER 8

FISHING

Before firstlight, Seth scurried downstairs, half-expecting to find Ottaar at her stove baking kin to break the nightrise fast. She was nowhere in sight. He spied a loaf from yestercycle on her pantry. *Maybe the mender left it for me.* He grabbed the bread, stuffed it into his silver satchel, and looped the carrier across his left shoulder, allowing it to hang by his right side. His bag contained his folded hovercraft, radio, sling, Criunite crystals, a handful of nourishment tabs from Camayah, and several personal items. He poured a cup of cold tea, downed it in a couple gulps, and raced out the door toward the stables, excited about the fishing trip with his two friends. The mission to Camayah had taken its toll on him. He felt weary and looked forward to a fun diversion. A fish fry, even if they were slimy eels, and sitting around a campfire sounded chill.

Calrin and Raydoo were already waiting. Their three kacks had side carriers packed with supplies, a four-person tent, and all the angling gear. "Did you break your fast yet?" Raydoo asked.

"No, I didn't wanna be late, so I snatched a loaf of kin from last cycle and hoofed it over here. I can eat it on the way."

"If you get hungry, sure, but we packed enough food for a militia. Save the kin for later. Besides, we should have a limit of eels by midcycle."

"How many in a limit?"

"As many as you can catch and eat." Raydoo chuckled at his quip. "And if we hook extras, we can probably sell them in Cali on the morrow for five credits each, more if we cure them." Raydoo led their kacks out of the stables. "Let's mount up and ride. We should reach the Cali River in less than a span, and then the fun begins."

"Cool! I assume you dudes will give me the lowdown on the proper technique."

"It's a snap. If they're biting, they almost jump into your lap."

"Really?" Seth tied his satchel on top of the side carrier.

"No, I'm kidding, Seth. These slimies are real fighters, especially the bigger ones. Your arms will be sore by the time this cycle ends, but I guarantee ya the best time of your life."

"Enough bantering you two," Calrin said in a snarky tone. "Let's move out. I want to be organized and fishing by forecycle." The teens mounted their rides, galloped through the city gate, turned left on the trail, and headed for the Cali River below Mista Lake.

They stopped at a small cottlepine grove near the ford. Seth hopped off his ride and began unloading the side carriers. "Are we gonna erect the tent first?"

"No, not now, just unpack the fishing gear. We can set up the shelter and our campsite later," replied Raydoo. "We best hobble our animals, though, so they don't wander off. Then we can head to the river and get our lines in the water. When it comes to catching greenies, the earlier, the better. While I sort our tackle, you take care of the mounts. The hobbles are in my side carrier."

"Where do I tie them?"

"Away from the riverbank. Over there should work." Raydoo indicated a grassy area by two cottlepine trees. "And it keeps our kacks away from the cotta. They'll mow it to the roots while you're looking the other way."

"Cotta?"

"Yeah, those yellowish-tan plants with fibrous balls growing along the riverbank. Weavers use the soft, fibrous cotta tips to make ropes for harpoons and the fishlines we're using today. We buy them in Bayegulf; their local weavers make the best ones. They also design clothing and various cloth products.

Don't you have cotta where you hail from?"

"No, we have something called cotton; it's similar yet larger in size. Your cotta plants are no taller than a tree sapling."

"Quit yapping you two." Calrin looked perturbed. "Let's start fishing before the shoal moves to the middle of the river where they're harder to catch by casting. Our only option then will be trolling."

"Trolling?"

"If elvers aren't biting near the surface, we go deeper with trolling cords and weights. To know when they're nibbling, we usually tie the looped end on our wrists. That way, we can set the barb before the eel escapes. Greenbacks are good fighters, howbeit, soft biters; therefore, you have to hold on to the line to feel their strikes in time to set the hook. If we don't catch any by midcycle, we'll probably switch to trolling." Calrin glared at Seth with narrowed eyes. "Are your questions over?"

"Almost. How do you troll without a boat?"

Sensing Calrin's irritation, Raydoo answered, "Don't need them. People only use boats to net lake eels. For shore trolling, we toss a cord into the river and leave it. The cord has a half-sized stone connected to a secondary line that holds it to the river bottom. Your main line attaches to a leader with the whirling lure. If you hook an eel, the secondary line with the weight breaks off, freeing your main line."

"Okay, I get it. Casting first, then trolling. Do you ever use bait?"

"Sometimes. Greenbacks aren't carnivorous, unlike tarkks that attack anything moving in the water, even their own kind. Although, eels are non-predator creatures, they still love nibbling on tarkkie guts. Novice anglers use bait, but we have better luck with whirlers."

"Are there giant tarkks in the river?" wondered Seth.

"Yeah, some. However, they normally don't surface until nightrise when they migrate upstream to the lakes."

"Enough with the questions," bellowed Calrin, "or I'm gonna leave you two behind." Seth made a zipped-lip motion with his fingers, smiled, and finished hobbling their mounts. Raydoo double-checked the hobbles, and then the three of them walked to the river, carrying their fishing gear.

"This is our favorite spot," informed Raydoo, as he surveyed a nearby rocky shelf. "There's a deep channel where the shoals hide. Shiny objects attract their attention and draw them to the surface. Once they strike at it, we snag 'em."

Calrin took Seth aside and explained the procedures. "We tie the leader to the line, attach a twister to the end, and add one quarter-sized stone to make the whirler castable from shore."

"What is your leader made from? Looks like it might snap under pressure."

"Hardly, it's produced with maize sillk, which is woven together to make durable twine and threads." Calrin handed him a piece. "Maize isn't only ground up to make kin; it's used for other products as well. In fact, the husks are dried and rolled into sheets to create paper. Concerning the sillk leaders, they are nearly invisible in the water, flexible, and very strong. Try to break it if you can."

When Seth attempted to snap it in half, the leader creased his index fingers, drawing a few drops of blood. He wiped it off on his pants and gripped the leader tighter, planning to try again. "Stop or you'll slice the rest of your fingers!" shouted Calrin. "Here, use my knife." With a little sawing, Seth cut right through it. "Good. Next, we tie an eighteen-hand section onto the main line using a double-loop knot." After demonstrating how to make the knot, Calrin untied it and let Seth practice. "Experienced anglers use the same knot to attach the whirlers, weights, and twisters. This outfit is yours." Seth coiled the line the way Calrin showed him and set it aside.

He watched as Raydoo and Calrin tied their fishlines. With their tackle ready to go, the three dispersed along the rocky shore and began casting into the river. Slowly, hand-over-hand, they pulled the line back in, hoping to attract a lunker. Seth was the first to get a strike, then Raydoo.

After a quarter span, Seth hollered, "This thing is a fighting fool! I can't pull it any closer to shore."

"Keep at it. Maybe you'll land him by the morrow." Raydoo laughed as he struggled with his own lunker. "Told ya they were fighters."

The snaky creature put up a gallant struggle but finally relented, and Seth hauled it to shore. Raydoo had already landed his greenback and set it aside. Seth rushed down to the bank, clutched a rock, knocked his eel on the head, and laid it on the bank next to Raydoo's catch. He removed the lure and coiled the line. "Wanna try again, Seth?" asked Raydoo.

"Not now. My arms need a breather."

"I figured you might say that." Raydoo glanced at Calrin who remained focused on trying to snag a slimie. "Apparently, the great fisherman over there didn't have much luck; all the elvers he hooked fell off." Calrin ignored the slight and kept casting.

"By the way these things fought, I figured they'd be bigger. Mine's barely two paces long."

"The larger greenies are double that size. Be glad you didn't snare one of those, otherwise you'd be here during darkout trying to land it." Raydoo grinned. The boys quickly gutted and cleaned their catches and laid them across a rock to dry. "Besides being slimy, these water wigglers smell like rotted dallups."

"More like dead skunks."

"What are those?"

"Never mind, just a dumb expression." Seth shrugged his shoulders. "You know, dude, I can't believe these things actually taste good. Are you sure they are the same stuffed eels the kitchen serves at banquet?"

"Yep, same entree. After we season the fillets and roast them over the coals, they'll be delicious. Heat burns away the sticky slime and smoke removes the foul stench. As soon as the meat turns white, it's ready. If you eat slimies uncooked, you'll be puking your guts out all nightrise long."

A couple spans later, the angling slowed, so Seth and Raydoo decided to carry their catches back to camp and hang them on a cottlepine branch to continue airing out. Because Calrin hadn't caught anything, he chose to stay longer and try trolling.

Raydoo and Seth wished him luck, and they returned to set up their shelter, gather cottlepine limbs for kindling, and build a rock firepit. Raydoo unloaded the rest of the gear from the side carriers and stacked it by the tent, while Seth draped the eels over a nearby limb. Since neither teen had eaten for spans, Seth withdrew the cycle-old loaf of kin from his satchel, broke it in two, and handed half to his friend. Raydoo added dallups and dried yarm berries from his carrier. The two scarfed down the food while they rehashed their earlier fishing experiences. They were about to unhobble the kacks and lead them to the ford to hydrate when they heard Calrin screaming.

CHAPTER 9

TROUBLE AT THE RIVER

A span passed without even a nibble, so Calrin decided to try one more trolling attempt. He attached a heavier weight, tossed his cord as far as he could into the river, and waited for it to sink to the bottom of the channel. Calrin gripped the end for a while, waiting for a strike, but grew tired, so he lay down and slipped the looped end around his left hand, holding on to it between his fingers.

If he felt a bump, the hook would need to be set immediately, or he'd miss the bite. Calrin had already lost five eels this cycle. Three had fallen off before he could land them; the other two were slow responses on his part. Without at least one catch, he knew Raydoo would tease him for yarns.

He closed his eyes and started to daydream. Soon, Calrin felt a nibble. A slimie was mouthing his whirler. He gave a hard yank to set the hook, and the fight began. When the eel surfaced, the teen could tell it was a big one, perhaps four-paces long. With much effort, he hauled the monster halfway to shore. Suddenly, a tarkk breached and grabbed the greenback in its jaws. The predator continued swimming, dragging the attached fishline upstream. Calrin tried to untie the looped end prior to slipping into the river, except the knot had tightened on his wrist and the cord yanked him off the rocks into the current. "Help! Help! I'm being pulled . . ." The rest of his words were garbled as the giant fish drug him underwater.

Hearing his cries, Seth and Raydoo raced to the rocky ledge where Calrin had been angling. He was gone. A moment later, a huge fin breached the surface, and behind it, a body. "Shark!" shouted Seth. "I mean tarkk. The monster has Calrin. It's dragging him away."

Seth opened his satchel, removed his folded hoverboard, and assembled it in mere seconds.

"What's that?"

"I'll explain later, Raydoo. Hop on, and let's go save Calrin." Seth balanced his shuttle for the additional passenger, gunned the foot pedals, and the two rose from the ledge. He leaned forward and the craft dropped to the river, skimming above the waves. He veered right and navigated upriver. By the time they arrived at Calrin's last position, he had disappeared, so they followed the wake from the tarkk's dorsal fin.

Seth circled the area, scanning for movement in the water. "What do you think happened?"

"He probably thought he'd hooked a large elver, not a tarkk. With the cord tied to his wrist, he couldn't free himself until it was too late. It pulled him in."

Finally, a body floated to the surface. "There he is. I see him extending his left hand." Seth pulled alongside. "Try to grab it." Raydoo seized Calrin's wrist, but before he could get a firm grip, the beast submerged, pulling Calrin under the surface again. "Dude, got your knife on you?"

"Yeah, it's sheathed to my belt."

Seth continued to follow the fin's wake, hoping for another sighting. "If you see the cord, try to cut it."

The tarkk briefly reappeared. No sign of a body, just the cord. Raydoo bent over, sawed it in half, and pulled the line toward him. Slowly, Calrin came into view, his wrist still attached to the end. He appeared listless, floating face down in the water. "Slide him onto the floorboard and let's book it," urged Seth. As Raydoo struggled to pull Calrin aboard, the predator heard splashing, circled around, and swam toward them.

Raydoo untangled the knot binding Calrin's wrist and tossed the line into the water. "He's not breathing."

"We need to get him to shore where I can use CPR to revive

him." Suddenly, Seth's eyes grew wide as a long, dark, underwater shape approached. "Hey, Raydoo. We got another emergency."

"What?"

"Look behind you. *Sharkie* plans to make us his evening meal. Hang on!" Seth performed a quick 180 on his board and steered for the ford.

As soon as they landed on the closest bank, Seth flipped Calrin over, pinched his nose, and blew two deep breaths into his mouth, followed by fifteen chest compressions. He repeated the resuscitation sequence and compressions, pushing even harder on his chest. As a former surfer on earth, Seth knew exactly how to resuscitate a drowning victim. He was about to try a third sequence, when Calrin gasped several times. Seth turned him on his side to the recovery position as he coughed and spit up fluids. After a couple moments, the boys helped Calrin sit up, then stand.

Calrin's body shivered, his face looked confused, his eyes glassy. "Thought I was fish bait for sure."

"You probably would have been if not for Seth."

"How did you save me? My recollection is—"

"We can rap later; right now, let's get you back to camp and warmed up. Your body is ice cold, and your clothes are sopping wet." Seth folded his shuttlecraft, stuffed it into his silver satchel, and the teens walked to the campsite, assisting Calrin who stepped awkwardly, still feeling unsteady on his feet.

"Hey, Seth, I have a few questions concerning your flying board. Where did you—"

"Let's get Calrin settled first, and then I'll explain everything."

"You better."

Although Calrin listened to their conversation, his blank stare indicated the circumstances surrounding his near drowning and rescue remained fuzzy in his mind.

The light faded and twilight emerged by the time they reached their encampment. Realizing they had just two spans till nightrise, Seth loaded the firepit with kindling. Raydoo used a striking stone to set the wood ablaze. Calrin stood for a while to warm his hands over the flames, then sat on a nearby rock. The heat thawed his chilly body while his clothing dried out. As Calrin relaxed by the fire, Seth removed the eels from the branches and cut them into fillets. Raydoo whittled skewers and staked the meat across the firepit to start cooking. They sat by Calrin and watched the glowing embers, occasionally rising to add more wood and rotate the fillets for even cooking. Because his satchel felt a little damp, Seth placed it at his feet to catch some heat from the fire.

"Okay, friend, let's hear it," insisted Raydoo. "I expect the truth. Where did you get that flying device?"

"It's called a hoverboard, and I brought it from—" In the middle of his answer, crackling noises came from inside Seth's carrying bag, followed by a muffled voice.

Seeming more alert to his surroundings, Calrin pointed at Seth's carrier. "Hey, Seth, your pack is squawking."

"Yeah," added Raydoo, "and it's calling your name. I can hardly wait to hear your explanation."

Seth pulled out his radio and answered the call. "Who is this? Is that you, Anna?"

"No, silly, it's Rauteira."

"What? No Way! How did . . . where are you calling from?"

"Sector One."

"Not possible. Your world's a long ways away. I'm not even sure it's in the same dimension."

"Papa Lun told me your talkies had extremely long range. With his transmitter part installed in my datatop as a datacomm, I simply adapted the dataflow to your receiving band and matched the wavelength to initiate contact."

"All the way from Camayah?" Seth peered at his unit. "Apparently, these signals can travel farther than any of us imagined. Weird! How did you know which channel to use?"

"I dialed channel one, hoping it was yours. So, do you miss me? It's been over thirty dawns since I heard from you."

"You mean a month has passed, I mean period, or is it a phase? My brain must be tripping. It's only been two cycles here, I mean dawns." Seth huffed and shook his head. "Arrgh, these different time designations are confusing."

"Yes, one phase. I'm getting closer to bonding age."

Seth left her comment alone and changed the subject. "What's been happening on Camayah?"

"Lots of things: Wells have been dug and hydrew pumped to the surface. Vegetation and trees grow around the hollows. Soreseed crops flourish near the RIFTs. Ahboen is still missing and assumed dead. The Council of Twelve leads in unity, trying to implement the things Jesse suggested. And most important of all, no more Triverphol Sickness. Everyone who had the Disease has been cured by using the healing-leaf formula Holley left us."

"Does anybody know you've called me?"

"I told Cndrek and Runess that I'd been working on a way to contact you. My mom and dad are aware because they're listening to our call. Too bad your talkie doesn't have a data imager, or you would see my parents greeting you with open palms."

"Thank them for me. Please don't tell anyone else."

"Okay, if you insist. Where are you guys anyway, in the high realm?"

"No, we didn't go there yet. We made a pit stop in a world called Eskaonus."

"Pit stop?"

"Sorry, Rauteira, I gotta dip. I'll try calling you in a few cycles."

"I'll be waiting. Use channel four; it's Papa Lun's old databand connection. Fair dawn to you."

"Good nightrise. Seth out." He placed the radio back into his satchel and waited for the questions to erupt. Only silence followed.

Calrin and Raydoo gawked at Seth for the longest time, saying nothing. Finally, Seth asked, "What are you two grinning about?"

"Who is this Rauteira?" Raydoo asked. "Is she your girlfriend?"

"No, we're merely good friends."

"Yeah, like we believe that." Seth's face flushed red. "Remember, we listened to the entire exchange. Time to come clean regarding this supposed friend, your hoverboard, that talking device, Camayah, and the other places you hail from."

Too late now. I guess the cat's out of the bag. "No doubt, you dudes deserve the skinny." The two boys nodded in agreement, but the look on their faces indicated they had no idea what being thin had to do with it. Not wanting to sidetrack Seth once he decided to confide in them, they just listened. "No more woofin' it; I'll give ya the square biz. You would probably find out soon enough anyway. Except ya gotta keep what I reveal a secret, like blood brothers." Calrin started to ask about bloody brothers when Seth put up his hand. "I mean buddies. Just between us dudes. It's better if my party doesn't know I spilled my guts. Jesse might get upset since he said to be careful with what we say and do, especially with the things we brought from the high province."

"Start with this high province," insisted Raydoo.

"Alright, here's the lowdown . . ." For the next two spans, Raydoo and Calrin sat quietly as Seth came clean with the facts, well, most of them. Seth described his experiences on Camayah and summarized his life on earth. He mentioned a realm called heaven, managed by a high king who used angels and faithful servants to aid people in need. Seth avoided certain topics he felt might be harder to answer and concluded by explaining how his communicator worked. He showed them how to assemble his hovercraft and promised to give them rides on the morrow, assuming none of the locals took notice. Other than a lingering question or two, the boys were satisfied with his responses.

Once the slimies were cooked, they feasted on their dinner fare. The hungry boys scarfed down dozens of fillets, two loaves of kin, three edible gourds, and handfuls of fresh yarm berries for dessert. They packed the remaining smoked eel into totes and hung them on cottlepine branches. Not that they expected ground predators, but with homing flyers hunting for bush varmints or whatever small prey they could find during nightrise, they wanted to protect their catch.

After discussing their options, the boys decided to ride into Cali Village to break their fast on something other than greenbacks and sell their wares. Prior to darkout, the teens headed for the tent. However, with all the excitement of the cycle, revelations, and several additional questions, no one got much sleep.

MAP OF CENTRAL HEAVEN

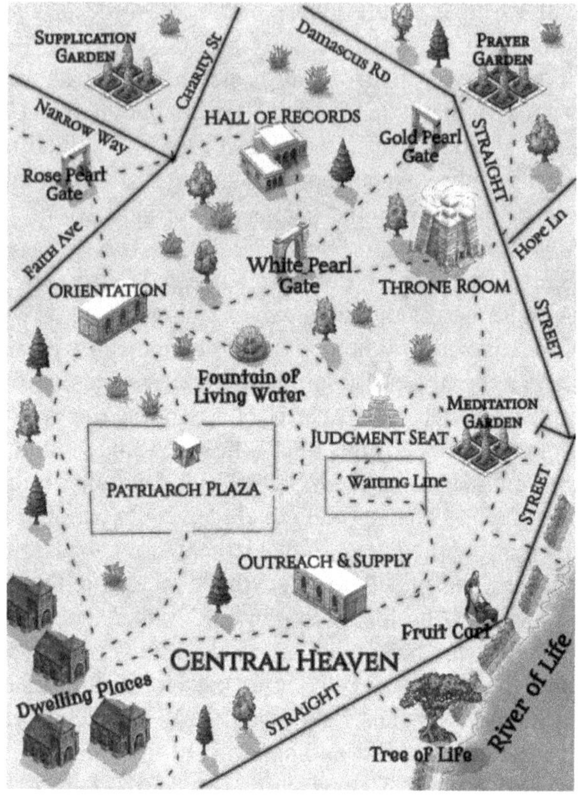

The locations and landmarks in Central Heaven are speculative. Notwithstanding, several are based on Scripture, others inspired by tradition.

"But as it is written, Eye hath not seen, nor ear heard, neither have entered into the heart of man, the things which God hath prepared for them that love him" (1 Corinthians 2:9).

CHAPTER 10

ONE WOE IS PAST

Chesedel, whose given name was elChesed, exited the Hall of Records with a copy of Jesse's latest journal entry. Because the guardian angel had constructed his journal with heavenly scroll paper, anything written thereon was simultaneously recorded in the scroll room inside the hall. These diary logs were the only source of information while Jesse remained off-heaven. Whenever he traveled to a different time and space, the guardian could no longer hear Jesse's thoughts or prayers, so he relied on the entries for information.

Because Jesse's last log, **Entry Eighteen**, mostly contained a summary of events, and since Uzziel remained on the earth, Chesedel tucked the copy he made into his blue sash. He'd show it to *the Cherubim* later. There was no reason to contact Uzziel now. No doubt, he and the other cherubim were busy watching over those who had the seal of God on their foreheads.

According to the entry, Jesse and his colleagues had completed their previous outreach on Camayah and decided to stop in Eskaonus to rest and recuperate before returning to heaven. Maybe this was for the best, reasoned Chesedel. Heaven and earth were in the middle of a great tribulation period. At least on Eskaonus, things were quiet.

Chesedel had no sooner walked down the steps of the Hall

of Records when a cherub, flying through the midst of heaven, shouted, "Woe, woe, woe, to the inhabiters of the earth by reason of the other voices of the trumpet of the three angels, which are yet to sound!" (Revelation 8:13).

After the Lamb of God opened the seventh seal, heaven experienced silence for about a half an hour according to earth time. The final seal initiated seven shofar blasts. The first four had already released terrible judgments, each one more devastating than the last. The winged cherub warned that a fifth angel would soon blow the next trumpet. The aftermath would be so dreadful that heaven called it a woe. Sadly, the final three trumpets were aptly named woes.

Following the proclamation, the fifth shofar sounded a long solitary note, and saints from Central Heaven raced to the prayer gardens. Their locale featured three gardens: meditation, supplication, and prayer. Notwithstanding, there were numerous places for prayer throughout the endless domain of heaven. Chesedel flew to the Garden of Supplication, finding it crowded with interceding saints. He knelt at a nearby bench and joined them. They all realized what the prophecies said concerning the three woes. Smoke from the bottomless pit and a darkened sun were just the beginning, more judgments would come.

Chesedel uttered a quick prayer for the collective, then rose and moved away, giving his spot to a waiting saint. The guardian fell prostrate on the ground, covered his face with his hands, and wept. The fifth shofar continued to sound, the blast loud, the echoes great and terrible, piercing heart and soul. He knew once it ended, the sixth trumpet would follow.

The Fifth Trumpet (First Woe)

"And the fifth angel sounded, and I saw a star fall from heaven unto the earth: and to him was given the key of the bottomless pit. And he opened the bottomless pit; and there arose a smoke out of the pit, as the smoke of a great furnace; and the sun and the air were darkened by reason of the smoke of the pit. And there came out of the smoke locusts upon the earth: and unto them was given power, as the scorpions of the earth have power. And it was commanded them that they should not hurt the grass of the earth, neither any green thing, neither any tree; but only those men which have not the seal of God in their foreheads. And to them it was given that they should not kill them, but that they should be tormented five months: and their torment was as the torment of a scorpion, when he striketh a man. And in those days shall men seek death, and shall not find it; and shall desire to die, and death shall flee from them. And the shapes of the locusts *were* like unto horses prepared unto battle; and on their heads *were* as it were crowns like gold, and their faces *were* as the faces of men. And they had hair as the hair of women, and their teeth were as *the teeth* of lions. And they had breastplates, as it were breastplates of iron; and the sound of their wings *was* as the sound of chariots of many horses running to battle. And they had tails like unto scorpions, and there were stings in their tails: and their power *was* to hurt men five months. And they had a king over them, *which is* the angel of the bottomless pit, whose name in the Hebrew tongue *is* Abaddon, but in the Greek tongue hath *his* name Apollyon. One woe is past; *and*, behold, there come two woes more hereafter" (Revelation 9:1–12).

The Sixth Trumpet (Second Woe)

"And the sixth angel sounded, and I heard a voice from the four horns of the golden altar which is before God, Saying to the sixth angel which had the trumpet, Loose the four angels which are bound in the great river Euphrates. And the four angels were loosed, which were prepared for an hour, and a day, and a month, and a year, for to slay the third part of men. And the number of the army of the horsemen *were* two hundred thousand thousand: and I heard the number of them. And thus I saw the horses in the vision, and them that sat on them, having breastplates of fire, and of jacinth, and brimstone: and the heads of the horses *were* as the heads of lions; and out of their mouths issued fire and smoke and brimstone. By these three was the third part of men killed, by the fire, and by the smoke, and by the brimstone, which issued out of their mouths. For their power is in their mouth, and in their tails: for their tails *were* like unto serpents, and had heads, and with them they do hurt. And the rest of the men which were not killed by these plagues yet repented not of the works of their hands, that they should not worship devils, and idols of gold, and silver, and brass, and stone, and of wood: which neither can see, nor hear, nor walk: Neither repented they of their murders, nor of their sorceries, nor of their fornication, nor of their thefts" (Revelation 9:13–21).

CHAPTER 11

HIGH SPRINGS

Ottaar, Lundy, and Annabelle sat at the mender's table breaking their fast, waiting for Captain Gelr to arrive. Holley and Lady Narleen decided to stay in town and had already left for Ellee's Place. Max arose early and departed for the practice field to train with the Militia. Seth and his two teenage friends were on their way to the Cali River to camp and fish for slimy eels. Jesse and Lady Saephira chose to spend the cycle together and inspect the new storage area east of Beayama.

Suddenly, Gelr bounded through the open door. "Are you three ready to depart? I have your kacks outside on the street. We had better leave soon, or we'll arrive at High Springs during darkout. It's a grueling two-cycle trip—nightrise there and return on the morrow."

"Do we need to pack anything?" Ottaar asked.

"No, I've got all the rides equipped with side carriers. Our gear is loaded: shelters, food, supplies, including a few tools for excavating the ruins. Just bring a change of clothes, satchels, and for the mender, your healing kit. Grab your things and let's mount up."

Captain Gelr led the six-person expedition out the western gate. The party turned left at the Cali River ford and continued up the trail to Onnie Passage. Gelr rode lead, followed by Anna and Ottaar. The senior safeguard came next, then Lundy, with the second safeguard bringing up the rear. Riding their sure-footed animals, the team made good time.

Onnie Passage was a mountain pass with high rugged cliffs, loose shale, and steep canyons. The exposed ridges contained veins of tin and copper ore, which the Lower Realm processed to make bronze tools and weapons. The route led to some ancient ruins, an artesian water spring, and a recently planted life tree.

By aftercycle, they reached the halfway point where the rockslide had claimed the lives of Captain Melmandus and one of his militiamen. Gelr ordered a halt.

"Why are we stopping?" asked the senior guard.

"I need to make peace and pay my respects since I caused their deaths." Gelr dismounted and approached a pile of stones. "This is Melmandus' memorial. I assume the one on the next rise belongs to his militiaman."

"How do you know this site is the captain's?"

"It displays an officer's sword, wrapped in a blue ribbon. The blade has been broken at the handle and the two pieces crossed over the grave to indicate a valiant life was cut short." Gelr exhaled a sigh. "Give me a couple moments to mourn the loss." He had tears in his eyes.

Annabelle slid off her ride and rushed to join Gelr. The others followed and circled the memorial behind her and Gelr. "You were not responsible for the avalanche."

"Perhaps not in one sense, yet I initiated it by releasing the first stone. The slide almost killed you, not to mention Lady Saephira, Jesse, and your entire outfit. The memories from that painful cycle never—"

"You were only following orders from an evil Lord Eddnok."

"Little comfort. I should have never agreed to—"

"Lady Saephira has forgiven and pardoned you. Now it's time to finally heal."

"Maybe you're right, Anna. I can't carry this guilt any longer." His tears continued to flow.

"You don't have to; give your hurt to Yahweh."

"How?"

Anna knelt and motioned for Gelr to join her. She held Gelr's hand and prayed. "Dear Merciful One, release my friend from the guilt he has carried for periods. He already admitted his mistakes and said he's sorry for past deeds, so please forgive him and redeem his soul for a higher purpose. Amen!" The moment she finished, Gelr stood, hugged Anna, and wiped the moisture from his cheeks.

Lundy moved closer and placed a hand on Gelr's shoulder. The reverend's eyes grew watery. "Aye, good prayer, Annabel. You know, laddies, I haven't been able to lament properly since Camayah. Without liquids in my system, I only had moistureless tears. It feels good to cry the normal way and be off those dang hydration tablets." Lundy used his shirtsleeve to dry his tears as he continued to sniffle and rub his nose.

Teardrops streaked down Anna's face as well. "Well, Reverend, I guess you have your first convert in Eskaonus."

"Ahh, me thinks so."

Slowly, Gelr arose, removed two spears from his side carrier, snapped one in half across his knee, and placed the two pieces next to the broken sword. Then he walked ahead to the next grave marker. The party followed him. He did the same thing at the militiaman's memorial. After a moment of reflection, he said, "If we keep moving, I think we can reach the ruins in another span."

By postcycle, the caravan arrived at the ruins. To Anna, they appeared the same as her last visit, except for a colorful tree growing by the springs. "Alright crew, let's dismount and establish our campsite for nightrise." Gelr scanned the area, then called to his safeguards. "You two erect our shelters: one for the women and the other for us men."

"Yes, Captain. Where do you suggest?"

"This spot seems good to me." Gelr indicated a flat area by the springs, away from any overhangs. "It'll be safer, and we won't have to worry about rockslides." He approached Lundy who was wandering here and there, turning over rocks. "Before you explore the ruins, can you gather firewood? Twenty paces down the trail I spotted a pile of fallen branches. We'll require a firepit. It gets chilly past twilight."

"I've dug a few campfires in me day. I'll get everything handled."

"Great, you'll find a shovel in one of the side carriers."

"What about us?" Anna asked.

"You and the mender can refill our waterskins at the springs. I'm looking forward to drinking water that doesn't taste like mud. I'll unpack the side carriers and hobble our rides so they don't wander off. Once we have the camp set, let's examine this life tree of yours."

With the chores completed, the group joined Ottaar and Lundy at the life tree. According to the mender who planted the seed a period ago, the tree had grown another pace. It stood six paces tall with sturdy branches. Dense multicolored leaves covered the limbs, and the purple blossoms that appeared after the tree sprouted, had now developed into tiny fruit sets. Lundy helped Ottaar pick a haversack of leaves from the lower branches. Sadly, the fruit was too small to harvest. Disappointed, Ottaar asked, "What does the fruit look like full grown?"

"A large purple mango," replied Anna. "It's the most delicious fruit you've ever tasted, sweet and juicy."

Ottaar started to inquire regarding mangos when Lundy shouted, "There's a mature one on the upper branch!"

"Where?"

"On the left, hiding between two limbs at the top."

Anna surveyed the topmost branches. "It's too high."

"I can get it," offered the senior safeguard. "I've climbed cottlepines before that are much taller. This thing will be a cinch." The man bounded up the tree like a lumberjack in a scaling competition, until he neared the top. He carefully pulled the nearest limb toward him and snatched the fruit.

"Don't drop it, lad."

"I won't." He tucked the fruit into his pants pocket, stepped from branch to branch until he could slide down the trunk. The guard handed the fruit to the mender who showed it to Lundy.

"Aye, a fully developed life fruit. I wonder why just one matured."

"Not sure," Anna responded, "although I think the tree knows what it's doing. I believe it wanted us to have this one."

"Perhaps so, Annabel. Let's save it for dessert. There's enough for everyone to have a slice, and afterwards we'll have another pit to plant."

"Any suggestions for a locale?" probed Gelr.

"No idea. Me thinks the northern province would benefit. And if so, Briacap is the perfect location."

"We can discuss this matter during dinner." Gelr gazed at the horizon. "It's nearing twilight, and we best fix our nightrise meal prior to darkout."

"Can't we explore the ruins a wee bit longer?"

"Sorry, Lundy, it will have to wait. We are losing the light."

"Arrgh! Ottaar and me had hoped to gather more healing leaves."

"We will. My safeguards will help you pick some at firstlight. However, it's banquet time, and I'm hungry." Following Gelr's lead, the crew returned to their campsite. He put torches in front of the shelters to prepare for darkout, and then hurried over to strike the wood aflame in the firepit. Ottaar and Annabelle reclined on nearby rocks while the rest of the party sat on the ground next to the glowing fire. The warmth kept most of the cold at bay.

Gelr passed out their evening rations, which consisted of smoked river eel, kin, antaloop jerky, and fresh dallups. Earlier, Anna had picked several handfuls of clover lettuce growing close to the springs. Gelr added dried herbs to make it a tasty salad. Ottaar used a kettle to brew a batch of Azollie tea. For dessert, instead of eating the yarm berries they brought with them, Lundy sliced the fruit from the life tree and passed a piece to each person. The pit he placed in his pocket.

After dinner, they set aside their bowls and cups, and gathered by the firepit to reminisce. Lundy told stories about his days as a minister. Gelr and Anna discussed the last time they were on Onnie Passage. Ottaar visited with the two safeguards as she sorted through the healing leaves she'd collected. She arranged them by color, filled seven small bags, and added them to her mender's kit. When darkout loomed, the partners headed for their shelters.

The next cycle, the group broke fast on yarm berries and leftover kin. Gelr repacked their side carriers while Ottaar and the safeguards harvested leaves from the life tree. The mender sorted and placed them inside two small totes. She decided to wait on brewing a batch of healing-leaf tea until they returned to Beayama, where she would have more time to experiment with the color varieties and proper mixtures.

Meanwhile, Lundy and Anna explored the ruins. "This way, Reverend. On our first trip here, Jesse located an altar." She pointed to a pile of square-cut stones. "It's mostly rubble, but this is where I found those Hebrew-related symbols." She withdrew a rock fragment and handed it Lundy. "What do you think?"

"I see what you mean. Closer to Paleo-Hebrew or early Aramaic. Interesting." He stuffed it into his satchel.

"And here's the crypt and capstone Max discovered. It contained the ancient scroll you translated."

"You mean the word map to Eddnok's hidden treasure cave with the knowledge tree?"

"No, the prophecy concerning our arrival on Eskaonus, two thousand years before it occurred."

"Aye, I wish I could have been present for Max's discovery. Lord Eddnok kept me imprisoned in Briacap at the time. Howbeit, I digress."

Using the digging tools Gelr brought, they excavated the adjacent fallen wall. "You know, Annabel, I think this place could be rebuilt. I'm pretty sure these ruins were a temple or monastery. I wouldn't mind overseeing the project and founding a mission here someday, I mean cycle."

"Jess says we're only in Eskaonus for a short break until we return to heaven."

"Och, me realize that. Merely daydreaming. Establishing churches was what God called me to do back on earth. Me still has the unction in me bones."

"And I have a similar desire to write music, but—"

"Hold on, lassie." Lundy's shoveling unearthed an unexpected object. "What do you think this is?" Lundy bent over, picked up a black stone, and handed it to Anna.

"It's smooth, rectangular-shaped, and has odd symbols on the front." She rubbed her fingers across it. "Feels like plastic. What do you think these symbols mean? Is *TREOW* a word?"

"Could be. *Treow* in Old English meant tree."

"Tree?"

"Not sure what it represents on Eskaonus. I might need to . . . wait a moment . . . come to think on it, *treow* could also indicate something true."

"You mean truthful?"

"Naw, more akin to loyalty, faithfulness, or a promise of favor."

"Wow! If you're right, it might confirm this place was a sacred site prior to being destroyed."

"Destroyed?"

"Yeah, Jess believed it was intentional, not a natural disaster."

"Sounds as if somebody didn't want religion on Eskaonus. Hmm . . . whether the wording on the object means a tree or truth, me thinks it's an important religious artifact. I should show it to Lady Saephira as soon as we return."

"I agree. They're puzzling symbols or letters for sure. Still, this thing was made for a reason." Anna returned the black stone to the reverend, who tucked it into the side of his boot for safekeeping. Lundy often carried things that way, especially items he chose to conceal.

"Let's not mention this find to the others until we discern more. Perhaps the archivists in Beayama will have a record." Annabelle winked her eye and pressed an index finger against her lips.

Gelr noticed Lundy and Anna standing idle and assumed they had finished with their explorations. "Come on you two. We had better head back now. We're packed and ready to go. I don't care to hang around on these ridges in case a windblower develops."

Lundy and Anna had previously experienced the local twisters, and they gladly concurred. Windblowers were dangerous storms, similar to tornados on earth. She grabbed the rake and Lundy took the shovel. "Aye, we're on our way."

With their gear loaded into side carriers, the party mounted up and started down the passage. Their return trip was uneventful, and they arrived in Beayama at latecycle.

THE BLIGHTE

The Blighte has been a mystery for ages. People considered it a vast, barren, inhospitable wasteland with no plants or animals. Besides the searing temperatures and toxic vapors, some people believed the area to be haunted. They had little desire to perish while exploring it.

CHAPTER 12

HOVERBOARD RIDE

During yestercycle, Calrin, Raydoo, and Seth decided to break their fast at Cali Village. They had their fill of roasted river eels and planned to sell their entire catch at market. After staying awake half the nightrise to talk, the teens banked their firepit, retired to the shelter, and slipped under their blankets. They slept in until forecycle, rose quickly, packed their side carriers, and departed for Cali, leaving their fishing gear and other supplies at camp. If all went well at the market, they intended to spend one more night of camping before returning to Beayama.

The three stopped at the river to hydrate their kacks, then crossed the ford, turned right, and took the trail leading to Cali. Local villagers filled the streets. A few residents waved at the boys as they entered the hamlet. They trotted up to the noticeboard and read it: *The Militia seeks recruits. Elders have a planning meeting for the morrow. A new fish cart is open on the north side of town.* "Before we break our fast, let's visit this stand to see if they're interested in purchasing our cured greenbacks," Calrin suggested.

"If they're not buying," added Raydoo, "I think the food hut will take our seasoned slimies. I've sold there several times and always received a fair price."

The man at the fish stand peeked into one of the totes holding their smoked eels. "You know, boys, you've done a fine job preparing them, but since I'm a new vendor, I'm only selling tarkk steaks. Not everyone prefers slimy eels, even when they're cooked properly." The vendor bent over and drew in a whiff of the aroma. "Mmm . . . your fillets sure smell tasty, though." Seth figured he was angling for a sample, so he passed him a piece. "Thanks, young man." The vendor popped it into his mouth. "Delicious!"

"Gnarly haul from yestercycle," replied Seth. "We slow toasted them over a cottlepine fire."

"Sorry, boys, I'll have to pass; try me next season. I plan on expanding my business, maybe even moving into a hut."

"Thank you, sir, we will," replied Calrin with a smile.

"Okay, guys, on to the food hut. And let me do the bargaining," insisted Raydoo. "The owner knows my family."

They rode back to the center of town, unloaded their catch, and carried it into the food hut. The owner stood at the counter, haggling with another customer regarding the sale price of maize. The bargainers finally agreed on two credits for twelve ears, and the man loaded his haversack and departed.

"Good dayrise, Raydoo. How are you and the family doing?"

"We're fine. Did you hear my older sister, Lurah, assumed the vacant Postal Overseer position in Beayama?"

"No, but I think she'll do a fine job. So, what do you boys have in those two totes?"

"River eel. Fresh caught and kippered last cycle."

Seth and Calrin unloaded the bags and stacked the eel fillets on the nearby cart. "Mind if I have a taste?"

"Sure, go ahead." Raydoo picked a juicy fillet and passed it to the owner.

He bit off a piece and chewed it, savoring the flavor. "Nice. Alright, I'll take a half rack. No, on second thought, I'll buy the whole bunch." He swallowed another bite. "What's your asking price?"

"Thirty credits."

"You've got to be kidding, Raydoo. I thought we were pals. Are you trying to gouge me out of a profit?"

"Of course not. How about twenty?"

"No way, I'll give you twelve, and it's my final offer."

"Agreed." Raydoo took the credits, bowed to show his respect, and the boys left the store, grinning at each other. "I was only expecting ten credits. We'll split it three ways. And now that our pockets are full, let's find an eatery and spend some of it. I'm starving." Raydoo patted his stomach with one hand while pointing to a diner across the street with the other.

After feasting on miniature fruit pies, munching down candied dallups, and sipping endless cups of hot Azollie tea, they stopped at a food stand displaying maize and purchased twelve ears to feed their animals. Having finished their business in the village, they mounted up and rode west out of town. The trio passed a grove of half-dead trees.

"Why are these cottlepines shriveled up?" Seth asked Calrin.

"This is the boundary line for the Blighte. No one goes in there."

"If that's the case, it would be a great place for the hoverboard ride I promised you. No one will see us."

"I'm not sure it's a good idea, Seth. The Blighte is an unexplored wasteland. Not even hardy bush varmints can survive there. Kacks also avoid it. No one knows why. The only way to cross the blighted lands is on foot. And nobody has gone more than a league into the interior and survived to tell the story. Some say it's haunted like the Lost Forest. If we enter, we'll perish before we get a quarter league inside the boundary. If the heat doesn't get us, the cold will."

"Or the ghosts." Raydoo's voice quavered as he spoke.

"Ghosts?" Seth raised his eyes in skepticism.

"Yeah, according to the rumors, those who enter this waterless domain, never return. The handful of explorers who scouted the outer perimeters reported strange noises. I don't think—"

"That's bananas, Raydoo." Seth shook his head in disbelief. "So, you dudes can face flesh-eating tarkks, yet when it concerns a rumor or two about ghosts, you're scared?"

"Well, it's more than a few tales. Most Lower Realm residents believe the stories."

"What happened to Rule Number Two?" teased Seth. "Don't be scaredy-cats."

Unfamiliar with the cat reference, Raydoo and Calrin merely stared at each other in silence. Finally, Raydoo responded, "We're simply saying—"

"Hold on, guys. Hear me out. What if I told you I could travel so fast on my racing scooter that not even a ghost could bust us? Besides, I've outrun quawners many times, and they're scarier and more dangerous."

It took a little urging on Seth's part, but Calrin and Raydoo agreed to a short trip into the Blighte. While his fellow trekkers hobbled their three kacks and dropped maize for the animals to nibble on, Seth removed the hovercraft from his satchel, unfolded the four sections to assemble it, then motioned Raydoo and Calrin to hop on behind him.

"Should we bring torches?" Calrin asked.

"Nope, we're not gonna be gone long. Just in and out. Still, if it is hot as you say, we better snag a couple waterskins."

"I don't think two will be enough." Calrin withdrew a skin from his side carrier; Raydoo did likewise. Since the waterskins had straps, they hung them over their shoulders.

"If it's not, I have other options." Seth reached into his satchel and felt for the hydration and nutrition tablets he brought from Camayah. He counted twenty pills. "We'll be fine."

"How so?" Raydoo wondered.

"I'll explain later; let's dip." He balanced the board for his two passengers. "Hang on tight, bros—I'm gonna push it to the max this time—pedal to the metal." Seth pressed the accelerator all the way to the floorboard. Within moments, they were flying inches over the barren terrain, heading due west, chatting among themselves as they traveled.

As soon as they passed the last stand of dead trees and officially entered the Blighte, a stinky odor filled the air. The farther they traveled, the stronger the stench became. "Now I understand why kacks won't enter this area," Calrin said. "The whole place smells like rotten eggs from a homing flyer's nest."

Seth recognized the smell as burnt sulfur. "I think a volcanic eruption left this whole area uninhabitable."

"Are we going die from the fumes?" Raydoo covered his mouth and began coughing to accentuate the question.

"No, not unless it gets worse. If it does, I'll turn around, and we'll book out of here. I think we will be safe, though. I've encountered these smells before at geyser vents in Yellowstone. They're stinky yet breathable."

"Yellowstone?"

"It's a park in . . . Oh, never mind. Let's keep moving." In less than a quarter span, they covered several leagues. At the urging of his two worried friends, Seth started to turn around when he spotted ruins in the distance. He raced for it.

Up ahead, they discovered a dry lakebed, filled with sunken ships. A series of dilapidated structures littered the shoreline. Seth brought his hovercraft to an abrupt stop at the southernmost part of the lake. The boys climbed off and wandered over to inspect the remnants.

"This place looks ancient, as if abandoned eons ago." Calrin squinted an eye to see better through the glare.

"No doubt, something tragic occurred here that caused the inhabitants to depart," added Raydoo. "But what?"

"Who knows; maybe they were nuked."

"What's being nuked, Seth?"

"It's what happens when people disagree and resort to extreme violence to resolve their issues. However, with the burnt smell and the sulfur-colored sand, I'd say it was a natural disaster or release of underground toxic material. Maybe the gases forced them to leave. Let's circle the lake and see what else we can find."

"We better hydrate, first. I'm dying of thirst." Calrin opened his waterskin, followed by Raydoo; they both took long swigs. Afterwards, Calrin tossed his skin to Seth who downed several large gulps before returning it.

"Dudes, I think we better save a couple swallows for later." The teens nodded and slung the waterskins back across their shoulders.

The trio climbed aboard the craft and skirted the lake's edge, passing a crumbling dock. Not stopping, Seth steered left to follow a dry riverbed. They soon stumbled upon a seaport with broken-down pilings, pier ramps leading nowhere, and disintegrated launches. To the west, a vast ocean lay as far as the eye could see. The teens paused to investigate, but finding nothing other than rubble, they continued north, past another set of ruins, stopping at the third one. As Seth checked the power settings on his board, his buddies disembarked to survey the locale. Seeing caves in the distance, Raydoo and Calrin hiked toward them.

"Yo, dudes, those caverns might be unstable."

"We've come this far, might as well see them." Raydoo led the way.

Leaning his hoverboard against a tattered wall, Seth followed his friends, muttering to himself, "Caves and hollows. Why does it always have to be caves and hollows?"

"Hey Seth, these openings are manmade. Look at the wooden beams in the entrances." Raydoo pointed at the supports.

Calrin crept nearer. "And the interiors appear empty."

"Yeah, right, or filled with quawners."

The trio entered the first one and went fifteen paces before discovering that rocks blocked the way ahead. "A collapsed mine or perhaps somebody sealed it intentionally," noted Raydoo. "There's no way we can go further without a team of miners and digging tools. Let's try the second one."

"This cave appears intact." Calrin peered into the shadows. "Too bad we didn't bring a torch. It's dark in there."

"Maybe these will help." Seth seized three crystals from his satchel and handed one to each teen, keeping the third one for himself. "This is Criunite. I brought it from Camayah. The rocks give off a greenish glow and make great projectiles." He grabbed a fourth crystal and placed it in his sling, keeping it at the ready. "Alright, spelunkers, let's go explore this cave."

The second cave had a long tunnel-shaped entryway, braced with wooden timbers. After walking fifty paces, the tunnel opened into a high cavern. In the center, they found a hewn stone, four-hands high, with a flat, circular top. In the middle of the slab sat a small metal box. Without hesitating, Calrin unfastened the lid on the chest.

"I don't think . . ." Before Seth could finish, Calrin reached inside and snatched a black stone.

"What do you make of these symbols? It says *TREOW* on the front. Is that a word?" He passed the smooth rectangular stone to Raydoo, who in turn handed it to Seth.

"I have no idea. Maybe Lundy can discern the meaning . . . Hey, wait, there's more inside." Seth peeked in, removed a folded piece of paper and scroll tied with a crimson cord.

"Let's take our finds outside into the light and examine them closer. This place gives me the creeps." Seth returned his two items to the chest. Calrin placed the stone back inside and closed the lid. Raydoo grabbed the chest and hurried for the entrance, followed by Calrin and Seth.

Once they exited, the boys reexamined the contents. "This stone is too light to be a real rock. To me, it feels like plastic."

"What's *plastick*, Seth?"

"A synthetic material, not occurring naturally."

Raydoo untied the red cord and unrolled the scroll. "It's filled with strange words."

"Do you recognize any of them?" inquired Seth.

"A few. It might be the language of our ancestors. The Archives should study this." Raydoo rerolled the scroll, tied the cord, and replaced the document in the metal container.

Calrin unfolded the paper. "It's a map of Eskaonus, showing forests, mountains, rivers, and several wilderness areas. There are three places labeled Beay, Bria, and Gahn."

"Let me see the map." Raydoo stepped closer to study the legend. "Beay might denote Beayama in the Lower Realm. It's in the correct location for our city."

"And Bria could signify Briacap." Calrin slid his finger north to the area between two mountain ranges. "It's the same spot in the Upper Realm."

"I think you nailed it, dudes. If the other two names represent cities, then this one in the east, marked Gahn, probably does as well."

"And it lies past a vast desert, which appears to be the Nae Wilderness." Raydoo indicated a barren section on the map. "Guess what I'm thinking."

"Lay it on me, bro."

"Rumors of a civilization on the far side of the Nae might actually be true. Either way, we need to get this map and other items to Lady Saephira as soon as possible."

"First, pass me the waterskin." Seth made a choking motion with his hands. "My throat is so dry I can hardly talk."

Calrin slipped the water pouch from his shoulder and shook it. "My skin is bone dry."

Raydoo checked his. "Mine's empty, too. The extreme heat must have evaporated the water through the skins. If we don't hydrate soon or reach cooler weather, we'll perish like everyone else who attempted to enter the Blighte. No one will ever know about these discoveries unless we leave now."

"Squares with me. Okay, dudes, grab the steel box, follow me to my board, and let's scoot. And don't forget to watch out for ghosties." Seth smiled at his jest; the two boys did not.

They shuttled back to get their kacks, unhobbled the animals, galloped to the river, hurriedly dismounted, and scrambled to the bank. Kneeling by the edge, the thirsty teens gulped down handfuls of water until their bellies ached. Once their thirsts were quenched, they rode to camp. Forgoing a fire, they snacked on leftovers of roasted eel, fresh dallups, and slices of kin. The boys stayed awake for spans talking until twilight faded into darkout. They planned to seek out Jesse and Saephira on the morrow concerning their discoveries. With the approaching cold, they moved inside the tent and fell asleep, exhausted.

NAE WILDERNESS

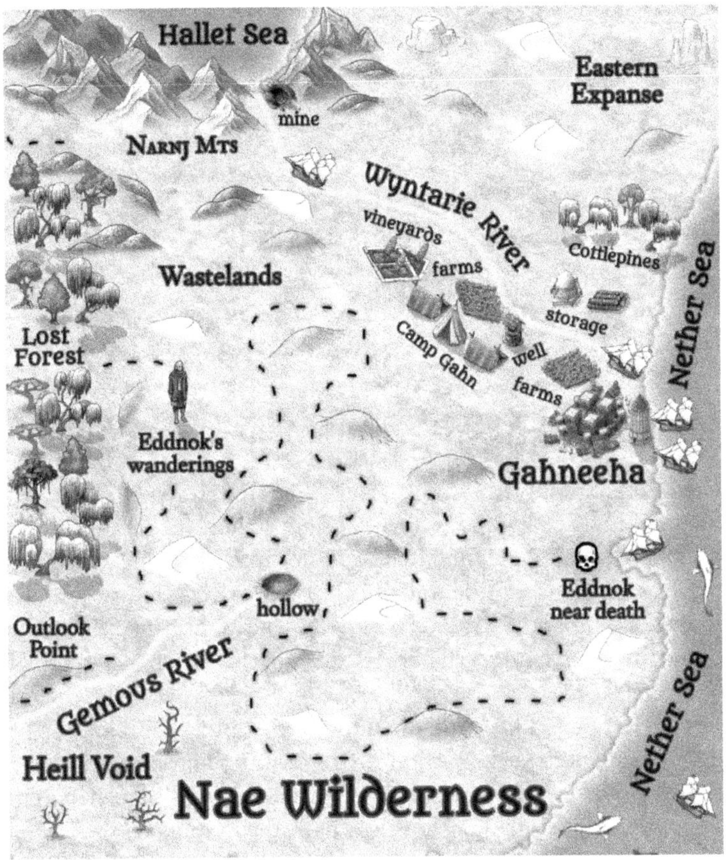

The Nae Wilderness is arid, lifeless, and desolate. It has no flowing water except in the southern part where the Gemous River intersects with the Heill Void. This massive desert borders the Lost Forest on the west. Settlements are rumored to exist in the east.

CHAPTER 13

EDDNOK'S WANDERINGS

After exiting the Lost Forest, Eddnok sat by a rock to catch his breath and think. He wondered how Briacap fared against Lady Saephira's forces. Surely her feeble militia had already been defeated, and she and her rebel friends, killed. That thought brought a smile to his face. Either way, victory or defeat, it was Commander Bolgog's problem now, not his. He had his own concerns; namely, where to go and how to survive in the Nae Wilderness.

He opened his satchel and took inventory. It contained his dagger, notes detailing a liquid-fire formula and catapult design, spare clothes, a fur-lined coat, his black stone, and a half-full container of kunakk. He also had the Tracker's saber and Preaverca's leaking waterskin, which the acidic, green slime had compromised. The predatory plants had devoured everything else. He had no rations and a limited supply of liquids.

His pocket contained a torn section of paper inferring he would become the Ruler of Fate. "Stupid poem! To blazes with this ancient rhyme and the fool who translated it. If I ever see Master Lundy or his friends again, I'll . . . I'll . . ." Rage consumed him, flushing his face red. "And where is my mystical knowledge fruit?" Angered to the point of hysteria, he nearly ripped the thing into pieces, but thought better of it, refolded the manuscript, and stuffed it back in his pocket.

Fortunately, Eddnok retained his torch and a striking stone to light it. If he conserved its usage, the torch could last a dozen spans. Making a fire to stay warm during darkouts was an option, too, assuming this wasteland contained kindling.

He removed the black talisman and rubbed it. "This ancient stone is worthless. Don't even know why I brought it." Eddnok stood and tossed it as far as he could. "Good riddance!" With the saber tucked into his belt and his satchel slung across his shoulder, he traveled south, searching for the headwaters of Gemous River. Before he covered sixty paces, Eddnok spotted the stone he'd thrown away, laying half-buried in the sand. He bent over, dusted off the talisman, slipped it inside his carrier, and kept walking. With the heat beating upon him, he stopped frequently to drink from Preaverca's waterskin, draining it to the last drop. During latecycle, he passed a tall white sand dune and turned left. As twilight neared, he sighted the Gemous River in the distance and stopped for the night. Figuring he could fill both containers with water on the morrow, Eddnok guzzled down the remainder of his kunakk, drinking himself into a mild stupor, and then bundled up in his coat to fall asleep.

At firstlight, he reached the riverbank. After taking several long drinks, he refilled the skins with silty water. Although drinkable, it had a mineral aftertaste. He realized that all Eskaonite watercourses followed the contours of the land. In the end, however, their currents always flowed upstream. Eddnok decided to trek east and see how far the river went into the Nae. He hiked for another span and came upon a giant hollow where the river entered and disappeared. Beyond the depression lay nothing except barren wastelands. His only apparent water source ended at the hollow.

Craving nourishment, he thought he'd try his luck fishing along the riverbank. Eddnok knew better than to wade out into the current. He presumed tarkks swam there, as they did in other waterways connected to the Nether Sea. He didn't survive the carnivorous plants only to have a predatory fish eat him. Slimy eels were the safer bet. Perhaps he could spear a smaller one with his saber.

Three tries later, he snagged a mid-sized elver and flung it onto the shore. He rushed over, cut off its head, and sliced six fillets. His mouth watered and his stomach growled in anticipation of the first meal since leaving Briacap. He popped the first piece in his mouth and began chewing it. The foul taste caused him to spit it out, gagging. He realized too late that a person had to cook river eels to make them edible.

Using his dagger, Eddnok shaved off strips of kindling from his torch and set them aside. He used the sword to cut the rest into smaller pieces. He dug a small pit, arranged the wood inside it, withdrew the striking stone from his satchel, and lit the firewood aflame. While the wood slowly caught fire, he threaded the remaining eel fillets onto his blade. Hurriedly, he roasted the slices over the fire before the flames died. When the last ember became ash, the slimy eel was barely half-cooked, the flesh still whitish-green. It would have to do. The meat tasted horrible, like rotten dallups, but at least he didn't puke. He quickly consumed each piece.

Eddnok spent the rest of dayrise exploring the area. As soon as twilight arrived, he donned his coat and waited for darkout. With no torch for light or fire for heat, he curled into a fetal positon to conserve warmth.

Next dayrise, he refilled his waterskins. Seeing no reason to linger there, he departed, heading north. Eddnok lost all sense of time and direction. He had no idea how many spans or cycles had passed—only that firstlight came, then unbearable heat, then darkout, and then the cold. The sequence continued, unending, unchanging. He wished he were dead, hoping the next dayrise would bring his demise, except it never did. For whatever reason, he lived on, longing to die, but too afraid to fall on his sword or slit his own throat to end it all. *I'm not a ruler of fate at all, just a coward.*

Eddnok wandered aimlessly. He emptied Preaverca's leaking waterskin and discarded it. Soon, the second skin was half-empty. Faint from a lack of food and extremely dehydrated, he began to hallucinate. A ten-foot-tall, non-existent bush varmint approached him from behind a sand dune. For the next several dayrises, the apparition shadowed him. Eddnok finally named him Commander Harvie.

"Well, Commander, which way should we go this dayrise?"

Silence.

"So, you're not talking to me again."

Silence.

"Fine! I guess you'll hafta follow me; howbeit, you won't get any of my water." Eddnok continued his trek, traveling in endless loops, sometimes covering the same terrain without realizing it. Conversations with Harvie were much the same, until one dayrise when the creature hopped away and vanished into a haze.

Searing heat baked Eddnok's brain during the days. On cold nights, he shivered, even though he wore his coat. Without a torch to see, he had to stop before twilight. To limit the loss of body heat after darkout, Eddnok dug a pit with his saber and crawled into it. Every nightrise, nightmares plagued him.

He dreamed of Preaverca and Menarbat rising from the dead to exact their revenge, plant creatures dragging him back into the Lost Forest to devour him, and Flissae binding him with cords to torture him for the way he treated her.

Severely weakened by the harsh elements, Eddnok stumbled on through the wilderness with swollen eyelids, a throat so parched he could hardly swallow, and lungs that ached with every breath. In the distance, he beheld a vast, blue sea, one of many such mirages he'd seen during his tragic desert passage. The Nae had played its final trick on him. At the point of near death and unable to take one more step, Eddnok blacked out and dropped to the ground.

As Eddnok lay unconscious, a brigantine with two masts approached the bay. An anchor dropped, making a loud splash, followed by two sets of white rectangular sails being tied to the yardarms.

"Alright, men, pull out the boats and make for the shore," ordered QuiQuot. "I need one crew to harvest rock clams and the other to scout for signs of antaloop." QuiQuot peered through his magnifier to the west. "Occasionally, these animals cross the Void and migrate up the coastline during this period of the yarn. Take your ropes and hunting gigs in case you sight any. I hope to finish here and return to Gahneeha prior to darkout. Now, shove off."

After the clamming crew loaded their catch into the skiff, two of the sailors decided to wander around while the hunters tarried. They climbed a nearby cliff, spotted a shape lying on the ground, and hiked over to investigate. "A corpse," said VieRook. "Another fool who tried to cross the Nae."

HieHoot inched forward to take a closer look. "Not decayed yet." He kicked the stranger's foot, and it moved, startling the first mate. HieHoot knelt, opened his waterskin, and sprinkled a couple drops of water into Eddnok's mouth. Slowly two eyelids opened, and Eddnok twisted his neck to stare at the man. "We better hail QuiQuot. Our shipmaster will want to see this." VieRook, the second mate, agreed, and he blew one long blast on his horn.

Ten moments later, the skipper arrived to find Eddnok lying on his back, marginally cognizant. "What's your name, traveler?"

"Edd . . . nok." The reply was broken and nearly inaudible.

"Did you understand him?" QuiQuot asked.

"Not sure, sir. I believe he said his name was EdNook." HieHoot poured more water down his throat, hoping to revive him further.

QuiQuot continued his queries. "Who are you, EdNook?"

"Ruler of fate . . ."

"And where do you hail from?"

"Bria . . . cap." Following his response, Eddnok slipped into unconscious.

"I think he's trying to say he's a Bria descendent," suggested HieHoot.

"Aren't they the ones who banished our ancestors?" VieRook asked.

"According to records in our archives, many of them incomplete and vague, both the Brias and Beays were traitors who tried to destroy us Gahns. However, that was eons ago, and no one actually knows for sure what transpired. Some believe—"

"Sorry for interrupting, sir." HieHoot stood with frustration showing on his face. "This man said he's a *cap*, probably meaning he is a captain."

"Not in our fleet, he ain't."

"He also has a curved sword strapped to his belt. It's bronze, not iron like our blades. Maybe he's a spy."

"Okay, HieHoot, let's search the man while he's still lethargic. Maybe we can glean more information. Start with his carrier but first remove his sword. We don't need any surprises if he becomes lucid again."

HieHoot quickly rifled through the bag. "He's got a dagger, a few tattered clothes, an empty waterskin, two scrolls, and this." He held up a black stone, engraved with the word *TREOW*. QuiQuot grabbed it, holding the rectangular amulet reverently as he examined it.

"Isn't that a sacred stone?" wondered VieRook.

"Indeed. Exactly like the one in our magistrate's office."

"How's it—"

"I have no idea. We better check his pockets."

VieRook rummaged through EdNook's coat. "I found a striking stone."

"And I located a folded piece of paper." HieHoot raised it up for his skipper to view.

"What are you waiting for, sailor, open the thing?"

HieHoot unfolded the paper and paused to study it. "Part of the document is missing, torn off; the rest reads like a poetic prophecy, ending with a line about *a rule of fate*."

"Hmm, maybe this guy really is the foretold leader. We have a scroll calling him a fated sovereign, and he possesses a sacred stone. No doubt, Magistrate RyeYook and the city elders will desire to talk with this person right away." The shipmaster paused to glance at the dimming horizon. "Okay, you two; haul EdNook to your boat, along with his carrier bag, while I signal the hunting party to return." QuiQuot unstrapped his horn and sounded three short blasts. "When everything's loaded on our ship, we'll set sail. I wish to make port by twilight."

During the fifty cycles that followed, Eddnok recovered his health and assumed the name of EdNook. He lied to Gahneeha's magistrate and city elders, convincing them he was their promised leader. Spouting falsehoods of witchcraft and imminent assault, he urged the elders to appoint him as Ruler EdNook. Afterwards, he ordered the skippers to deploy their fleets and the captains to lead their soldiers in an attack against Beayama and Briacap, telling them their real enemies were those who lived in the Lower and Upper Realms. At long last, he'd get his revenge on Lady Saephira who jilted him and Senior Commander Bolgog who betrayed him, even though the allegations were untrue. EdNook was amazed how easily he could deceive the inhabitants of Gahneeha. But then again, he excelled in deception.

CHAPTER 14

LOST SHIPS

The skippers had advised Maximus their three ships could be crewed and ready to depart by postcycle. Because of the urgency in locating the missing fleet, the seafarers rushed their preparations and finished a span earlier. Riding the outgoing currents, the rescuers set sail for open waters. Master Haleema's flagship, *The Baye*, took the lead. The other two vessels, both captained by experienced seamen, followed in line formation. The winds were favorable and the seas calm.

Once they cleared the shore, the ships divided into three groups to search the most common fisheries used by tarkk harpooners. If the vessels were within sight, the skippers raised colored banners on their masts to signal one another. When the field of vision changed, they sent homing flyers to deliver messages. During darkouts, their search efforts continued with the use of reflectors. Sailors made these innovative search lamps by placing normal torches inside mirrored, metal boxes with circular openings in the front, which projected a focused light beam up to forty paces.

The mariners searched the rest of that dayrise, all nightrise, and the following cycle, yet the hunt yielded no results. At firstlight on the third day since setting out, they rendezvoused northeast of Bayegulf in the dangerous waters of the Nether Sea. They set an easterly course up the coastline, trying to avoid running aground on rocky shallows or smashing into hidden reefs along the Heill Void. *The Baye* sailed point; the other two cruised on the port and starboard sides. Being in uncharted seas, the captains stayed within a hundred paces of the flagship, concerned that contrary winds or wayward currents might separate them.

Ten spans later, as the light faded into latecycle, they sighted floating debris in the water. Most of it appeared burnt. Haleema raised two green banners, signaling the adjacent crafts to lower their mainsails and launch service boats to investigate. Before the skippers could drop their boats over the rails, three headsails appeared on the eastern horizon, moving fast.

"There they are! We found our lost fleet!" yelled the watch mate. The deckhands on *The Baye* began to celebrate. Cheers echoed from crewmembers on the other ships as well.

Haleema hurried to the rail and focused her magnifier. "Not our sails. I've never seen this configuration. Those boats have two masts similar to ours, except the headsails aren't battened. Each mast carries a pair of high and low rectangular sailcloths with a smaller foresail jutting from the bow. They aren't Bayegulf crafts." With fear showing on her face, Master Haleema stared into the eyes of her first mate. "We need to change course and steer southwest. Raise the red banner to cancel my last order; then hoist the red-striped and yellow ones to signal the other captains to . . ."

Before she finished her command, the unidentified ships launched three projectiles high into the sky. Even from a distance, the things approached in a matter of moments, trailed by lines of thick black smoke. After reaching an apex, these strange objects arced downward, heading toward their targets. At thirty paces, they looked like flaming wooden barrels.

Two skyfire barrels struck the ships on the port and starboard sides of Haleema's flagship. The vessels burst into flames on impact. Unlike a normal fire that starts slowly and spreads, this blaze erupted all at once, covering the entire deck. Men scrambled to get out of the way. Crewmates tried to put out the flames but to no avail. With the fore and aft decks on fire, the mariners didn't have a chance to lower their lifeboats. Both crafts began listing heavily to their starboard sides. The skippers raised yellow-striped peril banners.

The third skyfire weapon dropped short of *The Baye,* hitting the water. Instead of sinking into the depths, the device exploded and spread like an avalanche of liquid fire. The water didn't extinguish the blaze; it increased it. The strange accelerant danced along the waves until it reached the flagship, where its flames climbed the hull.

Anticipating more attacks, Haleema decided to send a message. She quickly removed one of their two homing flyers from the pen and scribbled a note. She tucked it into the small leather carrier, strapped to the bird's back:

Found possible wreckage of missing ships. Being assaulted by unknown vessels hailing from eastern seas. Our crafts in peril. Trying to escape. Heading back to Bayegulf. —H

She released the bird and returned to help her mates raise the sails, so they could attempt a retreat. Before they could get their battened sails half raised, another streak of smoke appeared in the sky. The crew watched in horror as the fiery projectile flew toward their ship. Moments later, it hit the bow and erupted into a fireball. The flames spread quickly across the foredeck. Haleema ordered a lifeboat dropped. Five terrified sailors scrambled into the boat while the blaze enveloped the afterdeck. Her other crewmembers were unable to access additional lifeboats in time. Most had died at their posts. The few that survived were burned beyond recognition. Their screams echoed briefly—then silence—only the crackling of burning planks remained. As the flames raced toward her on the quarterdeck, Haleema wrote a second message and released her last homing flyer:

Two fleet vessels have sunk. Skyfire weapon hit flagship. We're going down. Launched one lifeboat with five survivors. Farewell. —H

CHAPTER 15

TRIP TO TABAHIR

On the next cycle, Saephira and Jesse left for Tabahir as planned. They met at the stables at forecycle. Saephira had everything packed for the trip: torches, one waterskin, a haversack of rations, and a gift for Nanlon's son. Jesse brought his satchel as usual. The two rode north, cutting across the farmlands, traveling at a gallop. Kacks were hardy animals with great stamina that could trek great distances without tiring or requiring water. In fact, they seemed to enjoy running, especially after being confined in the stables for cycles at a time, so Saephira and Jesse didn't hold them back. Besides, they hoped to cover the two leagues between Beayama and Tabahir by twilight.

They only paused twice on the way to Tabahir: Once at a field in the farmlands to pick a sack of fresh maize for Nanlon. She would reimburse the laborers on her return trip, giving them double their selling price. The second stop was at the southern boundary prior to entering the Neutral Lands. Because the mild climate in the southlands turned arid above the borderlines, Jesse and Saephira needed to shed their coats.

Tabahir was a nonaligned city in the Neutral Lands influenced by Briacap. Commerce came from taverns, lodging, and brothels. The city had a few honest merchants, but most of the traders were smugglers. Bush varmint hunting was good outside of town and throughout the borderlands. Sadly, the entire area was a lawless vicinity with no magistrate and no local mender—a treacherous place at best.

By latecycle, they approached the city limits. Before going to Nanlon's tavern, Saephira stopped at the Postal Tower and sent a message to Senior Commander Bolgog in Briacap. Being in the vicinity overnight, she wanted to invite him to meet with her at the Copper Rail on the morrow to break fast and discuss realm activities. Using homing flyers to deliver messages was faster than hiring Tabahir couriers. They were generally unreliable, spending most of the day at a tavern or brothel before delivering their assigned mail. Flyers, on the other hand, were fast-moving predatory birds with transitional vision, which enabled them to navigate at all spans, even during darkouts, and their flight path between Tabahir and Briacap took less than ten moments.

With the message sent, Jesse and Saephira rode to the Copper Rail, dismounted, and walked their rides to the rear of the building where the stables were located. The Copper Rail Tavern was a diner with second-floor housing units run by Nanlon, the sole proprietor, who served as barkeep, cook, and housekeeper. His son worked in the stables.

"I'z kno you be coming bac. Da be surpized you'r here." The stable boy bowed so low he almost fell over. "I'z tak care of yar kacks rel good, Great Lady."

"Thank you, young sir. If you don't mind me asking, I would like to know your name. Guess I never—"

"It be Natt." The boy grinned with his toothless smile. He approached the animals and petted them on their snouts. "I'z water and fed 'em. They be redy when you leav. I cares most for the white-striped one."

"Her name is Salie. She's loves to have her mane brushed." Natt immediately pulled a brush from his pocket and began grooming Saephira's kack. "What do we owe for the care of our mounts?"

"Nothin. I'z doez it for free."

"Very generous of you, Natt. Since you're not accepting payment, would you allow me to give you a present instead?"

"I'z don't get many tips these days. Things have been hard on da. Businss been rel slow."

"Sorry to hear that. What's the reason?"

"Da tell you more. He upstairs fixn varmint stew for dinnr."

"Okay, we'll ask him." Saephira reached into her satchel and withdrew a leather belt. "This is an official militia belt, which is awarded to soldiers when they finish their training. And because you have faithfully served me and the Lower Realm during our conflicts with the Upper Realm, I would like to reward you."

Natt rushed over and wrapped it around his waist. Although the belt was too large, he looped it twice and found a way to tie it securely. "Fits perfik." Jesse stood back and watched, smiling. "Sorry, sir, I'z forgot to hail you." He bowed again, offering Jesse the nightrise greeting.

"Not a problem. It's good to see you again," replied Jesse. "Seth couldn't be here today. He's gone fishing, but I'm sure he's wondering how the sling he gave you worked out?"

"Good. I'z a bettr shot now. Nail bush varmints at fiftie paces. And skn 'um with the knif Seth giv me."

"Excellent! Captain Maximus could probably use you in the Militia someday. Keep practicing with your sling."

"I'z will, sir." Natt clutched a rake and began cleaning the stalls to ready them for the two mounts.

"Jesse, we better check on room availability for nightrise." Saephira removed the haversack of maize from her side carrier, and the two climbed the rear passageway leading to the lobby.

Nanlon, who was standing behind the counter shuffling papers, glanced up. "What a surprise! You should have sent a flyer message to announce your arrival." Nanlon bowed. "Good nightrise, Lady Saephira and Sir Jesse. What brings you this far north? I pray there aren't lingering conflicts."

"Good nightrise, Nanlon." The two moved closer to the counter. "No, none," replied Saephira. "We're merely visiting for the cycle."

"And we need lodging for the night. What's the current rate?" Jesse leaned against the countertop, resting his elbows, and grinned.

"Unfortunately, I had to raise my prices due to recent developments and financial setbacks. It's three credits per person, paid in advance; in your case, though, no charge."

"What about stable fees?"

"Included."

"Knowing what the answer would be," Jesse asked, "should we sign the register?"

"Don't use one. We take no names, ask no questions." Nanlon chuckled at his familiar quips. "Should I ready a single room?"

"Make it two." Saephira placed her credit purse on the counter but didn't open it.

"Of course, my Lady, that's only proper."

"What are these recent developments and financial setbacks?" inquired Saephira.

"Well, for one, I've lost customers. A woman from Briacap, named Flissae, relocated to town sixty cycles ago. She purchased an existing establishment near the city center and renamed it Flissy's Place."

"Is it a tavern like yours?"

"In some ways, yes. They offer meals, serve drinks, and provide temporary housing. It's real popular with the miners and traveling merchants. According to those who frequent Flissy's Place, it's more of a brothel than anything else." Nanlon looked down and frowned. "Oh, I still get a little commerce from my regulars who aren't seeking Flissae's brand of comfort. However, my tavern business has dropped way off. Almost no overnighters. Hardly anybody eats here these cycles. In fact, I may have to shutter the Copper Rail."

"Please don't close. This is my favorite place."

"Thanks, but I cannot make a go of things with an occasional visitor. No offence, my Lady, but—"

"None taken. You mentioned other reasons for concern."

"Right. This whole town has become a den of crime. Several cycles ago, two men were stabbed across the street and left to die. Shop owners are reporting break-ins, vandalism, and thefts. Some thug assaulted and raped a teenager. Her parents are warning young girls to be careful if they venture outside during nightrise. Although the place has never been free of crime, it has gotten worse this last yarn. Something ought to be done."

"I agree. Therefore, I am appointing you as temporary magistrate to start dealing with these lawless issues. That is, if you're willing. You must hold a vote within a yarn to retain the position. All city magistrates in the Lower Realm earn a stipend of credits each period. Perhaps this will help with your shortage of funds and take the pressure off from trying to earn a living by running your tavern."

"How much is the stipend?"

"Two hundred credits, delivered by rider from Beayama or you can retrieve the funds in Briacap if you prefer. I will notify Senior Commander Bolgog if you choose the latter option. So, are you interested?"

"I believe so. Will the residents of Tabahir accept me as their magistrate?"

"They will have to. I'll sign an official authorization on the morrow, prior to my departure. In fact, I'm meeting Commander Bolgog at dayrise to break our fast, so I will have him sign it as well. You will have authorizations from both the Lower and Upper Realms. Furthermore, we will post notifications advising the townsfolk that law enforcement has returned to Tabahir and surrounding areas in the Neutral Lands."

"A couple more questions before I say yes."

"Ask them."

"Can I still run the Copper Rail Tavern?"

"Certainly, and I insist you do. Besides the tavern being your residence, it's the most respected establishment in this town. We need it open. And the second question?"

"Assuming I have the power to arrest lawbreakers, where do I detain them? We don't have a jail here."

"You'll have authority to detain wrongdoers and determine their penalty as long as it's not a death sentence. Those judgments are my decision, and I prefer not to employ execution as a punishment. I suggest you check with Midvill concerning their jailing protocols. Regarding detentions, for the time being, send your offenders to Briacap. They have guarded stockades. What will it be, Nanlon, yea or nay?"

"Okay, I'll do it."

"Wonderful. With those issues resolved, I have a surprise for you."

"What?"

Saephira placed a haversack on the countertop. "It's maize. Jesse and I picked it at a local farm."

"We seldom get fresh maize here. Most of it is either cycles old or dried ears. I'll fry a platter of fritters for the morrow."

"Hopefully, we won't have to wait that long to eat," teased Jesse. "I'm famished."

"Why don't you check into your chambers, rest, and wash up. There are water basins and soaproot in the units. And I'll have dinner ready," He clicked his fingers twice, "in a couple snaps."

"Good idea. It was a dusty ride after we crossed the boundary line and entered the barren lands." Saephira opened her purse, counted out twenty credits, stacked them on the counter, and returned the handbag to her satchel.

"No, no, no, I can't possibly take it." And Nanlon pushed it back to her.

"Fine, then it can sit there for a yarn." She smiled. As soon as the two climbed the stairs to their units, Nanlon grabbed the coins and tucked them away under the counter. Two spans later, the dinner bell rang, and Jesse and Saephira descended the stairs to the dining hall. They feasted on varmint stew, candied dallups, and fresh baked kin. When they finished, Nanlon brought out two bowls of yarm berry pudding.

"Why don't you and your son join us for dessert?"

"I would love to, except I promised to have dinner in the stables with Natt. And later, we best clean the kitchen and prepare the maize fritters for breaking your fast with Commander Bolgog. I wish to make a good impression."

"I'm sure you will. Although he's a stern military leader, I've found him to be a gracious man."

"Hope so. Before I take your leave, my Lady, I wanted to mention some concerning news."

"Go on . . ."

"Miners from the Pit and Dig come here on occasion to hoist a few drinks. They've reported strange lights coming from the Hallet Sea during darkouts."

"Does anyone know what these lights are?" asked Jesse.

"No, but the miners sounded afraid. At least one has considered quitting the mines and transferring elsewhere. I think these strange sights have them spooked."

"Hmm . . . I will mention it to the commander on the morrow and ask him to investigate."

"Thank you, my Lady. I didn't mean to be bothersome."

"You're not."

"Then, I bid you two, good nightrise." Nanlon bowed and headed for the kitchen.

While Jesse and Saephira finished their desserts, they speculated about the lights and discussed the positive changes a magistrate would make in town. And as she promised Jesse, there were no more inquiries, just a nice time with pleasant conversation. Afterwards, the two retired to their separate quarters for the night.

CHAPTER 16

REVELATIONS

In the morning, Saephira and Jesse arose at firstlight, packed their satchels, and headed downstairs to the dining area. The smell of something delicious wafted through the air. When they entered the hall, they found Senior Commander Bolgog already sitting at the table, drinking a cup of steaming hot tea while munching on an orangish-brown, battered pastry. The tabletop held a teakettle, a huge platter of maize fritters, and two more place settings. As soon as he saw Saephira and Jesse enter the room, he swallowed the last bite of his fritter, put his cup down, and rose to greet them.

He spread out his arms and bowed. "Good dayrise, Lady Saephira." Bolgog studied Jesse for a moment, then added, "And the same to you, good sir." Jesse and Saephira returned the dayrise greeting. Saephira offered a curtsy to show her respect for the de facto leader of the Upper Realm. Jesse followed her lead by bowing. With the pleasantries concluded, Bolgog said, "I don't believe I know your name, sir."

"It's Jesse, my Lord."

"I'm not a Lord, Jesse, just an appointed overseer. They asked me to assume leadership after the scoundrel, Eddnok, abandoned Briacap and escaped into the Lost Forest with Menarbat and Preaverca." He waited until Jesse and Saephira joined him at the table before he reseated himself. "Can you explain why you have summoned me?"

"I would be happy to. We haven't talked since the peace accord in Midvill, and I wanted to reconnect and see how things are going."

"Fine, but knowing you, Lady Saephira, I'm sure there's another reason or two."

"Why, yes, there is. I need to you to sign an authorization for Nanlon to serve as the magistrate for Tabahir. This place is without an official to oversee city matters. And as you and I are aware, this area is basically lawless." She passed the document over to him. He quickly read it and subsequently signed his name under hers.

"Is Nanlon a good man? Can he be trusted?"

"I have no doubts." As she spoke, Nanlon entered the dining hall bringing another platter with more fritters and tea. "Here, you can meet the person for yourself."

Nanlon put the platter on the table and bowed. "Good dayrise! I hope you have enjoyed my maize fritters."

"I did. They're very tasty. I've never eaten one quite like it. How do you make them?"

"We cut off the kernels, add them to kin batter, make rounded patties, and fry the mixture in varmint grease. It's topped off with yarm berry jelly."

"Perhaps you can visit Briacap some cycle and show our cooks how to make them."

"I'd be happy to, my Lord."

"As I was telling Jesse, I am not a Lord, simply a senior commander in the Guards. As for you, though, I understand you're considering a magistrate position for Tabahir and the surrounding areas."

"If you approve."

"I do, and here's your authorization, signed by both Lady Saephira and myself. Keep it in a safe place."

"Thank you, Lord, I mean Commander."

"While you're cleaning up this lawless place, if you care to jail a few ruffians, haul them over to our stockades. We have plenty of open cells. With a half yarn of confinement under their belts, they'll surely change their ways. And if they don't, we'll remand them there till they do." Bolgog chuckled at the thought.

"Until we can build holding cells here, it would be appreciated."

"Glad to help, especially if you turn this den of crime around." Nanlon bowed again and scurried out of the hall toward the kitchen.

Bolgog turned to face Saephira. "You indicated two reasons. What's the other one?"

"Nanlon told me the Dig and Pit miners who occasionally frequent his tavern have reported strange lights in the Hallet Sea during darkouts. Can you confirm?"

"I've heard nothing. On the morrow, I can send a guard detachment to investigate. If we learn more, I'll advise you by homing flyer."

"Good, thank you, Commander. It's a bit of a mystery." Saephira poured everyone another round of tea. "Since our business is done, let's finish breaking our fast. Please pass me the platter of fritters. I can hardly wait to taste one."

After the three had eaten to their heart's desire, Bolgog arose and excused himself from the table. "I'm sorry, Lady Saephira, but I must return to Briacap. I have realm business to deal with."

"And I should get back to Beayama for the same reason. I wish you well, Commander."

Bolgog nodded, exited the tavern, mounted his kack, and trotted down the street.

"You didn't say much, Jesse. Is there a problem?"

"Realm business doesn't involve me. Besides, I'm merely the escort for this little trip."

"You are much more than that. In fact, I would say—" Before she could finish her comment, the radio inside Jesse's satchel made a crackling sound, followed by a voice. It was Anna.

"Annabelle to Jess, come in please."

"Go ahead, Annie. Is there a problem?"

"No. However, the reverend and I have some important news from Onnie Passage."

"Only Lady Saephira and I are listening, talk freely."

"Well, first, an update on the life tree. It has grown to over fifteen feet tall. The limbs have multicolored leaves and purple blossoms exactly like the ones on the Tree of Life in heav . . . I mean the high realm. Small fruit sets have also appeared. At first, we thought there were no mature fruits, but Lundy spotted one between two limbs at the top. A safeguard climbed the tree and picked it. We all shared a bite. It tasted the same as the fruit from the place we hail from."

"Fantastic news, Annie."

"Lundy pondered why only one mature fruit had developed, whereas I felt it was providential, believing the tree knew what it was doing. He kept the pit to plant it elsewhere on Eskaonus. Prior to leaving, we picked leaves and filled two small totes. Ottaar plans to brew several different batches of healing tea, so when you arrive in town, you can try one and see if it resolves your nearsightedness. She thinks the healing properties in the leaves will cure almost anything. They did on Camayah, including the deadly Triverphol Disease. She may even try creating a medicinal salve from them."

"Incredible!"

"That's not the half of it. Lundy discovered a black, rectangular-shaped stone with the symbols, *TREOW,* engraved across the front. He thinks it's a religious artifact."

"Has he discerned the meaning?"

"He has a few ideas about—"

"Hold on a moment, Annie. Lady Saephira wishes to speak to you."

"Annabelle, please show the stone to my vice-leader. Once she's seen it, ask Lundy to take it to the Archives for the keepers to analyze. Our ancient records may mention these symbols. Perhaps with his language expertise, the archivists will be able to unlock its meaning."

"Yes, my Lady. The reverend already planned to go there and offer his assistance. I will be joining him."

"Good, keep me posted. Jesse and I are leaving soon for Beayama. We'll see you at latecycle. I look forward to hearing all about your trip and discoveries."

"Copy, Annabelle signing off." Saephira handed the transceiver to Jesse. No sooner had he dropped the device into his satchel than another call came in.

"Hey, JW, got your ears on?"

"Yeah, Seth. Is everything okay?"

"Totally cool. I'll skip the fishing trip and campout and get to the good part. After catching a ton of slimy river eels, I gave Calrin and Raydoo a ride on my hoverboard."

"I thought we agreed not to reveal the devices we brought with us, unless—"

"Don't blow a circuit, JW. My friends already saw the board. I had to use it save Calrin from drowning. They also heard me use the radio during a hail from Rauteira on Camayah."

"What? How's that—"

"I'll give you the entire lowdown on the flipside. Anywho, as I was saying, I promised to give the boys a short ride if they kept their mouths shut."

"And . . ."

"I didn't want anybody else to see my hoverboard, so we took a quick jaunt into the Blighte. Man, that place is desolate and stinks like sulfur. We were ready to dip out when we noticed ruins near a dry lake. We circled the vicinity, finding sunken ships, an old seaport, more abandoned structures, and several caves."

"Did you tell anyone?"

"Yeah, Narleen knows. Hang on to your bootstraps, JW. I haven't gotten to the gnarly stuff yet."

"There's more?"

"Correctamundo. Inside one of the caves we found a metal box containing a black stone with the phrase *TREOW*."

Saephira motioned for the communicator. "Seth, this is Lady Saephira; please describe the stone." She listened intently as he related the information. While Seth talked, Saephira turned to Jesse and whispered, "It sounds similar to the stone Lundy found at High Springs."

"And us dudes found two more things in the chest: a scroll with ancient writing and a map."

Saephira's eyebrows rose. "What kind of map?"

"Calrin believes it's an early map of Eskaonus. It indicates three settlements named Beay, Bria, and Gahn. The first two are the same location as Beayama and Briacap. The third lies past a forest, beyond a great wilderness, near an unnamed river."

"Really, are you sure it's Eskaonite territory?" asked

Saephira.

"Yep, pretty much. Calrin and Raydoo think the rumors of an eastern settlement on the other side of the Nae are true."

"You boys may be correct. Please turn the material over to Lady Narleen, and tell her I said to give it to the Archives. Perhaps they can decipher the scroll and confirm the map locations."

"I already did. Narleen sent all three items to the archivists by courier this morning, but she kept the chest at her residence for Max to see."

Saephira returned the transceiver to Jesse. "Thanks, Seth. Good job! I'll forgo the reprimand on using your hoverboard. You may have discovered important relics. Once Saephira and I get back, you can tell us the whole story. What are you doing for the rest of this cycle?"

"Not sure. Hang with Max, I guess. He's still conducting militia training. Maybe I can show the military dudes how to sling a stone."

"Alright, we'll catch you later." Jesse placed the unit on the table. No sooner had the conversation finished when he heard Narleen's voice.

"Narleen to Jesse. If you can hear me, please respond."

Jesse glanced at Saephira and shook his head in disbelief. "Wow, it's central station around here. These calls keep coming in. I wonder what it is this time." He picked up his walkie-talkie again. "Go for Jesse."

The two listened patiently as Narleen relayed the same information Anna and Seth just shared. The last bit of news, however, dismayed them. "A flyer message arrived in Bayegulf and was forwarded to me moments ago. Master Skipper Haleema believes the three missing fishing crafts have sunk. Her crews found floating wreckage. The message also states her vessels are under attack from unknown ships hailing from eastern waters. She's changing course for Bayegulf."

Saephira asked for the radio to respond. "Thank you, Narleen. A disheartening development if true. Please inform me the moment Haleema and her skippers reach port. And tell Maximus that I want a full report."

"Are you returning this dayrise, my Lady?"

"Not sure. Jesse and I may stay a little longer. We're waiting for an update from Commander Bolgog concerning another issue in the Hallet Sea."

"Understood. Narleen out."

After the call ended, Jesse and Saephira stared at one another in silence for serval moments before she said, "Jesse, we may need to change our plans."

MAP OF EAST ESKAONUS

The existence of East Eskaonus remained unconfirmed until recently. No one from the western provinces realized people inhabited this area or that the land contained farms, vineyards, a major river, and a city called Gahneeha. This eastern civilization has an army and fleet of sailing vessels. Residents mine and process iron for weapons and tools.

CHAPTER 17

EAST ESKAONUS

As Saephira and Jesse discussed their options, Nanlon entered the hall to clear table settings, pick up leftovers, and bring a fresh pot of tea. Seeing their bewildered faces, he asked, "What's wrong, my Lady?"

"We must travel into the Nae Wilderness. It appears the rumors of settlements in the east are true. And if so, we should investigate."

"There's nothing out there except arid wastelands. Early explorers searched for that fabled community and never located it. I don't think such a place exists."

"Recent documents discovered in the Blighte suggest it does."

"Excursions into the Nae are not recommended. It's hot during the days and cold during the nights. There's no water— nothing but sand dunes, rocky hills, and endless leagues of barren wilderness—all of it uncharted."

"If there are inhabitants there, we need to contact them. Jesse and I have already decided to enter the Wilderness for a cycle and look for signs of civilization. Can you supply us?"

"I can. However, I urge against it. Sojourning in this desert, even for a cycle, is dangerous."

"Nanlon, I appreciate your concern for our welfare and the warnings; nonetheless, we have to try. With Briacap's miners reporting strange lights in the skies east of the Hallet Sea and our fleet sighting unfamiliar ships from eastern waters, much could be at stake." Saephira declined to mention about their fleet being in peril.

"Alright, if it's just a cycle, I'll supply the shelter. Actually, what I have is more of a canopy."

"You mean like a tarp," probed Jesse.

"Not sure what a tarp is. A canopy tent is a simple overhead covering with no sides. It'll offer shade during dayrise but little relief from the extreme heat. There's enough space for two people and their rides to gather underneath it. A pole supports the middle, and even though you can stake the sides down, there's no privacy. You'll be in the open air."

After several more warnings trying to dissuade them, Nanlon provided Saephira and Jesse with his shelter, which included two pole sections for lashing together, cords, and four stakes. He packed a haversack with six ears of maize, a pouch of dried antaloop jerky, a loaf of kin, and the leftover fritters. Since his friends only brought one waterskin with them, Nanlon filled an extra and handed it to Jesse. By forecycle, the determined sojourners were packed and ready to depart. They bid farewell to Nanlon and Natt as they rode from the stables. Nanlon waved back, then turned to face his son, slowly shaking his head.

"Da, don't wory," Natt said as he placed a hand on his father's shoulder. "Great Lady be ok. Got Jesse to potect her."

Jesse and Saephira exited Tabahir and traveled east until reaching the leading edge of the Lost Forest, following it until they approached the Narnj Mountains. They turned right and took the eastern trail until it ended. The wayfarers stopped during latecycle at the entrance of the Nae and erected Nanlon's awning in a secluded area between the mountains and the forest. As twilight set in, they gathered their mounts and moved under the covering, trying to avoid the increasing temperatures.

According to Seth's report, the Blighte was an arid wasteland. The Nae seemed no better. Jesse hobbled their animals under the open tent and put out maize for them to nibble on. Saephira brushed their sweaty coats and long manes, trying to distract them from unfamiliar surroundings and uncomfortable heat. Once the kacks were settled, she distributed the rations Nanlon had packed. While eating, they chatted about the recent events and speculated on whether new settlements actually exist in the east. When darkout came, instead of using torches, Jesse opened his candle lamp for light. They sat quietly for a time, both lost in their thoughts. "Before we turn in for the night, do you mind if I write in my journal?" asked Jesse. "It helps me focus my thoughts."

"Fine with me. There's not much else to do right now."

Entry Nineteen

I had only planned for a short layover in Eskaonus, but circumstances have changed. Wreckage from Bayegulf's fishing fleet suggests their three crafts were lost at sea, and the crews sent to search for them are in jeopardy, under attack by unknown assailants.

Moreover, recent discoveries in the blighted lands: a map and other artifacts unearthed by Seth, indicates a settlement may lie in the east, past the Nae Wilderness. In light of the map, lost ships, and other developments, Saephira wants to unravel the mystery. I don't blame her; howbeit, I have concerns about surviving in this desert. This area is similar to Death Valley on earth. The temperatures are almost unbearable. Even though we have a tarp to provide a little shade for our mounts and us, it offers little relief. Our water supply is low. I'm hesitant about tomorrow's activities. Saephira and I will discuss those plans in the morning. Knowing her as I do, I don't think she will quit until she determines more.

Jesse tucked his pen away and closed the journal, planning to return it to his satchel, when Saephira asked, "May I see your entries?" Jesse realized she didn't read the earth language, yet he passed the diary over to Saephira anyway, trying to accommodate her curiosity.

"I doubt you can make sense of the words. It's written in English."

"Let me try." She began flipping through the pages. "To me, it looks like you wrote in Eskaonese." Jesse had forgotten the Holy Spirit had bridged language barrier with a miracle similar to what occurred on the Day of Pentecost, making it possible for him and his team to understand the Eskaonite vocabulary. Apparently, it also worked the other way around, allowing Saephira to read and comprehend English. Saephira kept scanning the entries, stopping occasionally to ponder the words. "This diary is interesting, and it raises lots of questions in my mind. However, due to the lateness of the span, I will ask just one."

Jesse began chewing on his lower lip, something he did unconsciously when nervous. "Alright, if it's not a hard one. I guess we're past keeping secrets from each other."

"What is *the day after always* mentioned in **Entry One**?"

"It's a cycle that never ends. It goes on forever and ever. Some call it eternity."

"Eternity?"

"Life doesn't end with death; our spirits live on."

"Is this true for all people?"

"I believe so."

"I'm not sure I understand, although it does sound reassuring to think there's more to life than a few short yarns."

"I agree. Eternity is more than floating on clouds and playing harps."

"What?"

"Oh, nothing, it's just a silly phrase."

"Well, you said one question, so for now my other queries can wait. Besides, we should focus on the matters at hand, and . . . I'm really tired. Let's get a couple spans of rest before firstlight." She returned the diary to Jesse. "We can decide our plans on the morrow." He stowed the journal, closed the lid on his candle lamp, and bundled up in his coat. Saephira donned her jacket, and the two fell fast asleep.

At firstlight, another radio hail awoke them. "Narleen to Jesse or Saephira. Please reply. This is urgent."

Jesse sat up and grabbed his communicator. "We're listening, Narleen. Is anything wrong?"

"Yes, we have depressing news. Let me put Maxie on the call."

"Sir, we received a second message from Skipper Haleema. Let me read it to you, word for word."

"Okay, both Lady Saephira and I are listening." Jesse stood while Saephira drew close and embraced his arm. She gazed at him with tearful eyes.

Two fleet vessels have sunk. Skyfire weapon hit flagship. We're going down. Launched one lifeboat with five survivors. Farewell. —H

"Oh, no! Are you sure? I thought our three search crafts were returning—in peril in some way—yet still heading to port."

"No, ma'am. They're all lost."

"What about the five survivors?"

"Unknown. I pray they escaped. We'll send mounted patrols along the coastlines to check for castaways, but we should assume these attackers also destroyed their lifeboat. Regarding our one remaining ship, I ordered it to safety."

"Where?"

"Upriver. In two spans, it'll sail out of Bayegulf, up the Lower Fork to the Gemous River, and then onto Outlook Point where the ship will be anchored. I've dispatched Phauch with a company of mounted militia, armed with longbows, to protect it. More militiamen are on their way to reinforce Bayegulf as a precaution. Six of the seven vessels in our fleet are gone. Experience suggests this may be a prelude to an invasion from a brutal enemy."

"Are you certain our cities and villages are in jeopardy?"

"No. Still, it's wise to be prepared. A lesson I learned the hard way from my days as a Roman centurion. Consequently, Narleen and I think you and Jesse should come back to Beayama immediately."

Saephira motioned to Jesse to take over the conversation. "Max, we need you to stand by while we confer." Several moments passed as Saephira and Jesse debated the matter. He agreed with Max. Saephira, though, felt it was prudent to continue their journey, locate this eastern settlement if it existed, and discern the situation.

"Captain, this is me, again."

"Yes, my Lady."

"Since we're already inside the Wilderness, we plan to press eastward for at least another cycle. Please inform me if there are any important updates."

"But ma'am—"

"You have your orders, Captain; carry on. I'll advise Lady

Narleen on our progress using this incredible talking device. Good dayrise." Saephira placed the radio into Jesse's hand.

"Well, Max, it appears we're moving east. I'll keep you posted on developments. Jesse out."

After packing, they broke their fast. With little water left, Jesse handed Saephira two pills. She studied the oval tablets. "What are these things?"

"They're supplement tabs. I brought them from Camayah. The greenish-blue one is Tyhydru; it will keep you hydrated for three cycles. In fact, you won't feel thirsty, even in this heat. The reddish-brown one is Dapferon; it does the same thing for nutrition. You'll not have a single hunger pang for cycles."

Saephira popped the tablets into her mouth and used a sip of water to swallow them. "I hope they're safe?"

"Our team found them to be so, effective too. Real lifesavers." Jesse ingested his two pills without liquid because his waterskin was already empty.

"If that's the case, let's give some to our rides. They are severely dehydrated, and we have no feed for them."

"Agreed. There's no reason it shouldn't work on the kacks as well." Jesse hid the tablets inside the last of their maize fritters, hoping their mounts would consume the supplements without spitting them out. The animals eyed Jesse, wary of the procedure. With a little coaxing from Saephira, their kacks finally ate the fritters.

They broke camp, mounted up, and rode eastward. The weather and terrain were much the same: arid and barren. With the horizon showing latecycle, Jesse and Saephira erected their shelter behind a giant sand dune. Since a few spans of light remained, they resumed their trek. One span later, their excursion led them to large river with brigantines sailing upstream. Following the river downstream, they observed vineyards, an encampment, and in the distance, a large city. Near the riverbank, a young girl skipped rocks across the waves. Concerned she might spot them, the duo reversed course to flee to their campsite. Before retreating ten paces, the girl yelled, "Don't leave!" and beckoned them to approach.

CHAPTER 18

THE ARCHIVES

When Lundy and Annabelle entered the Archives, they found the curators bustling around the facility, running over to shelves and removing cataloged material, then returning to a large oblong table in the middle of the room. Caretakers placed some documents on a nearby desk where a scribe sat. They scattered the remaining items across their central table. The left corner held two black stones; the middle section displayed an open scroll, weighted down on the ends; and the right corner bore an antique map.

"Well, laddies, any progress yet?"

"A little," replied Taula, an older woman with long, braided, white hair. Taula was the senior curator who oversaw a team of four researchers. "We have been communicating with the Archives in Briacap via homing flyers."

"Were the lads helpful?"

"Not with the scroll translation, howbeit, they provided interesting information about the rocks with the *TREOW* symbols."

"What did they say," Anna asked.

"The keepers had one of those objects in their collection, except it went missing a yarn ago after a visit by Lord Eddnok. They believe he took it, which Eddnok denied. At any rate, they have no idea of the item's purpose or the meaning of the symbols.

Their recorders only kept a sketch of it."

"Stealing it sounds like Eddnok's modus operandi." Lundy picked up one of the stones. "Concerning this engraving, I don't think it's a symbol. According to me memory of Old English, *treow* is the word for tree."

"You mean like a cottlepine?"

"Perhaps, or it might refer to a family tree."

"Our ancestors?"

"Me thinks so, Taula. Even more interesting than a tree reference, the word could represent trust or promise. And more specifically, something that's true or accurate. If this is the case, then the word could also indicate loyalty, faithfulness, favor, or a covenant of faith."

"It has all those connotations?"

"Aye, could be, unless you have another meaning."

"No, we got nothing. Therefore, we'll go with your interpretations until we know more." Taula turned to a scribe. "Put Master Lundy's comments into our report."

Annabelle wandered over to the right side of the table and glanced down. "What about the map Seth found?"

"Ah, yes. It appears to be a chart of Eskaonus, revealing a settlement in the east, past the Nae. Although it's vague, we made a copy of it for our report. However, the scroll is a mystery. It seems to have a few words in ancient Eskaonese. Unfortunately, our team has been unable to understand it."

"Let me take a gander." Lundy approached the table, leaned in for a closer look, and studied the page of codex. "It seems to be using ciphers or codes, maybe both."

"I'm unfamiliar with those terms."

"Codes and ciphers are used to keep information hidden. When a person mixes or substitutes existing letters, they're employing a cipher. If they substitute one word for another word or replace it with a foreign phrase, it's a code. Where I hail from, deciphering and decoding is termed cryptography."

"Interesting. Can you decode this scroll?" Taula gazed at Lundy with hopeful eyes.

"Maybe if I understood your language better or had ten yarns to study it. Even then, me doubts it. It's very complex."

"I have an idea," interjected Anna.

"We're open for suggestions, Annabel."

"One of my nyeflute tunes might help you guys. According to the angel, I mean mystic, who gave me the instrument, songs played on nyeflute cause certain effects, such as sleepiness, confusion, and invisibility. Other tunes impart confidence, encouragement, and enlightenment."

Anna pulled the flute and tablature from her satchel, glanced through the various arrangements, picked the tune for discernment, and began to play. The music was soft and sweet, like a whisper.

Almost immediately, Lundy exclaimed, "I think me figured out the cipher!" Lundy pointed to a line of text. "If you move this letter here and eliminate the other one, it begins to make sense. And here, I believe this one is coded." He indicated a different passage. "Just replace this sentence with the previous passage, and we'll discover the intended meaning."

"Ahh, I see it now," replied Taula. "It's so simple. I don't know why I didn't catch it before." Anna merely smiled as she returned her flute to its carrier. During the next several spans, Lundy and Taula made notes and translated sentences. Afterwards, she handed their notes to the scribe who placed the information into the report:

Archive Analyst Report
Attention: Lady Narleen
Dear Vice-leader,

After much deliberation, we were able to decipher and translate the ancient scroll. According to Master Lundy, the writer used codes and ciphers to keep the information confidential. We are sending this report to you because Lady Saephira is away traveling. The Archives will retain a copy. Here are our findings:

The Early Inhabitants or Ancestors of Eskaonus

The early inhabitants or ancestors of Eskaonus referred to their land as ***Eskaon***. It was located in the territory we now call the Blighte. Their realm had three great leaders: a woman named Beay and two men named Bria and Gahn. They led families or clans who had similar interests and worshiped a deity called the *Unseen One.*

Beays were farmers and gatherers. Their clan sought peace and harmony, enjoyed meditation, planted vineyards, and grew crops.

Brias were hunters and miners. The group hunted animal herds, dug caves, mined minerals, and forged tools and weapons.

Gahns were sailors and explorers. They excelled in fishing, making continental maps, cutting timber from forests, and building ships.

Eskaon: One yarn, long ago, the land changed. It slowly became a wasteland: the lake dried up, crops quit producing, temperatures rose, and water supplies dwindled. No one understood the reason for the calamities. Around this time, darkouts began. The inhabitants needed torches to see after nightrise. The factions blamed one another for the disasters. The Gahns believed the Beays had used sorcery or that their unseen deity had cursed them. Angered at the thought, the Gahns and Brias no longer revered this god, labeling him or her a fable. Most Beays retained faith in their *Unseen One*, made a book of records with their teachings and other histories, and hid it in a cave before departing the area.

Apparently, all three groups had no choice but to leave their blighted land in order to survive:

Beays packed up and traveled southeast to establish a farming society near a large river. We speculate their settlement became Beayama, the capital city of the Lower Realm.

Brias traveled northeast and established a fortress, mined the hills and hunted the northern lands for wild game. We believe they settled in the area near Briacap of the Upper Realm.

Gahns took their remaining ships and sailed west, rounding the landmass, and established a distant colony in the east.

We don't know if these collectives communicated with each other after the catastrophe.

Map of Eskaon: Please see the attached map for the locations mentioned above. We are keeping a copy in our files.

Black Stones: These smooth rectangular objects come from an unknown material. As a result of translating the document, we gleaned additional information relating to the black stones. They are some type of sacred token or marker. We believe our ancestors made four. The one Seth found in a cave in the Blighte is the master token of ***Eskaon***. The other three were given to the Beays, Brias, and Gahns prior to their departure. We speculate the one Lundy and Anna uncovered at the ruins on Onnie Passage once belonged to the Beays. The artifact library in Briacap confirmed they had a similar talisman, but it disappeared. The custodians think Lord Eddnok stole it. As for the fourth one, if the eastern settlement of the Gahns still exists, we think they probably possess it.

TREOW: Concerning this symbol or word, Lundy, a master linguist, believes it signifies or represents a tree and may refer to several related concepts, including truth. These are our best guesses on the meaning or meanings at this time. We included Lundy's entire analysis in a separate attachment.

Lastly, the scroll ended with a prophecy regarding an emerging ruler of fate who would gather the four *TREOW* stones and join them together. And afterwards, all the clans of ***Eskaon*** would reunite in unity, truth, and never again be separate.

Respectfully submitted,
Taula
Senior Curator

As soon as the Vice-leader received the report, she summoned Captain Gelr and Captain Maximus to the Great Hall for a conference. Later, Narleen asked scribes to make copies, which she sent by couriers to Commander Bolgog and the archivists at Briacap. Additional transcripts were dispatched to the magistrates at Bayegulf, Tabahir, and Midvill, as well as the elders at Ritwell, Cali, Falein, and Nakk villages.

ALIROOT

AliRoot lives in Camp Gahn with her mother, MiaRoot, who is a strict yet loving parent. The child is highly curious, often impetuous, and loves to play games. She is friendly, helpful to her friends, mischievous at times, and very perceptive for a nine-year-old.

CHAPTER 19

ALIROOT

"Don't leave yet," urged the young girl. "Come play with me." Realizing this might be an opportunity to discover more about her settlement, Jesse and Saephira rode closer, stopping in front of the child. She was about nine yarns old, maybe older, and dressed in a pink smock with yellow boots. She tied her dark hair, which had reflective undertones, in ponytails, using pink ribbons. Freckles covered her face. To Jesse, she seemed friendly and harmless enough.

"Bet I can skip a stone farther than you," said the girl. Saephira climbed off her kack, walked to the riverbank, seized a smooth, flat stone, and flung it across the water. "Not bad. My turn now." She swung her arm way back and tossed one, besting Saephira's mark. "You wanna to try again?"

"No, I think you're a better rock flinger than me." Saephira glanced at Jesse. "Do you want to fling a stone?"

"Sure, I'll give it a go." Jesse's throw hit the first wave and sunk.

"Ha, ha!" laughed the little girl. "You need more practice and a flatter stone." Embarrassed more than disappointed, Jesse simply shrugged his shoulders.

"If you don't mind me asking . . ." Saephira bent down on one knee. "What are you doing here all alone?"

"None of my friends will play with me."

"Why is that?"

"Cause I know things."

"What kind of things?"

"What people are thinking, whether they're good or naughty, what they've been doing, and sometimes, where they've been. The other cycle, one of my playmates didn't think I knew he had cheated on dice. When I told him, the nasty boy called me a kack, and said he'd never talk to me again."

"Did you see him cheat?"

"No, I just knew it. And last period, a playmate lied to her parents concerning where she had been. When I said she fibbed, she pulled my ponytails and ran off to tell her daddy."

"That wasn't nice of her. Are the things you know revealed in dreams?"

"No, dreams are how *you* see things." Saephira's eyes widened, wondering how a stranger could discern she had premonitions while asleep. "I close my eyes and things appear in my mind. The longer I'm around people, the more I know. I suppose you don't like me now?"

"We like you fine. You have an interesting gift. Do you know stuff about us, too?"

"Uh huh. Wanna know what?" Her greyish-blue eyes sparkled as she spoke.

Saephira glanced at Jesse who shook his head no. Disregarding his reaction, she replied, "Why yes, please enlighten us."

The girl closed her eyelids for a few moments and then reopened them. "You are noble and kind like my momma. Your friend is brave yet hiding his feelings. You're both good persons who mean me no harm."

"We surely don't. We're merely neighbors who desire to understand this place."

"Of course you do, except you're not from here, are you? You live past the Wilderness in the west. As for your friend, he comes from even farther away."

"You are quite perceptive, young lady. May I ask your name?"

"I'm AliRoot." She scurried over and petted Saephira's kack. "Pretty colors. I've never seen a white-striped one before."

"Her name is Salie."

"You love Salie, don't you?"

"Much. She's special. I've owned her for many yarns."

"If you let me ride her on the morrow, I will show you around Gahneeha. Meet me here during forecycle."

"Don't you care to learn our names?"

"No, you can tell me later. I gotta run now. Told my momma I'd be home prior to twilight."

"Do you and your mother live close by?"

"We live in a small tent at Camp Gahn. Momma and I had to move there after my father detached us and took up with one of those comfort ladies in the city. Because he works in the iron mine at the mouth of the Hallet Sea, I hardly ever see him. Anytime I do, father ignores me." Her greyish-blue eyes turned green as she cried. "He kicked us out of his house two yarns ago, so Momma has to work long spans in the vineyards and farms to earn our keep." She wiped away the last of her teardrops. "Momma made these playclothes for me. See." AliRoot spun in a circle, smiling. "What do you think?"

"Very nice! Your mother sounds like a wonderful woman. I'd love to meet her. However, I'm not sure we're able to return here next cycle."

"You will." AliRoot grinned and scurried off toward a group   of   tents.

As soon as AliRoot left, Jesse and Saephira mounted up and headed for their shelter, discussing the encounter as they rode. "I think we should go back on the morrow, Jesse. This child may be a helpful ally."

"I have a few reservations, but yeah, you're probably right. AliRoot seems very intuitive. And she sure pegged who we are. I wonder how much she really perceives."

"No doubt, we'll find out next cycle."

"That's what worries me. Oh, by the way, what does detached mean?"

"Unwedded."

"You mean divorced?"

"I'm not familiar with that word. Being detached is ending a betrothal or spousal union."

"You know, Saephira, it breaks my heart to think—"

"Mine too. I feel sad for her and her mother's situation. Although they may not accept credits in this place, I plan to leave her a handful on the morrow. If the people don't use them, her mother can turn the bronze and silver coins over to a smith to be melted down. The metal must be worth something, even if Gahneeha's system is just bartering."

They ended their conversation, and raced their mounts to their shelter, hoping to reach it by twilight. No sooner had they arrived and hobbled their animals, than a radio hail came in from Narleen.

"Narleen to Jesse, please answer."

Jesse withdrew the communicator from his satchel while Saephira rushed over and grabbed his arm, expecting the worse. "Go for Jesse."

"Lady Saephira said to keep her advised. Is she there?"

"Yes, we're both on the call."

Reading it word for word, Narleen shared the *Archive Analyst Report*. After listening for a quarter span, Saephira responded, "Well, this makes more sense now: three ancestor families, an ancient land in the Blighte called *Eskaon*, and four mysterious *TREOW* stones. Please thank the archivists and Master Lundy for their efforts in translating everything. Concerning the Gahns, I believe we've located their eastern settlement. Jesse and I plan to visit a city named Gahneeha on the morrow, which may be the one they established eons ago."

"Is this wise?"

"It may be our only way to get to the bottom of things. We met a friendly little girl who offered to show us the sights. Hopefully, we can confirm some of the information in the archive report by next cycle."

"Maxie and I think you should return now. Seth said he can shuttle you home before you snap your fingers twice."

"One of Seth's sayings; you know how he exaggerates. We may request a ride, however, once we ascertain the facts or if we face hostility and need to escape. Please tell him to stand ready."

"But, my Lady, we feel—"

"I'm sorry to cut you off, Narleen. This is my decision. We

will take precautions. And now, can you put Captain Maximus on the line? Jesse wants to talk with him."

"I'm here, sir. How can I be of service?"

"Please update me on what our colleagues have been doing."

"Seth practices longbow and sling with the Militia. Lundy and Miss Anna assist the Archives with research and translation. Holley spends much of her time with Mender Ottaar. They have brewed several batches of healing tea and bottled it. The reverend drank the mixture and recovered his stamina and strength; even his stiff joints feel better. Ottaar saved a small flask for you. She believes it will resolve your nearsightedness and leg issue."

"I would welcome the relief. I'm running low on Helixzon salve for my injured knee, and my eyesight seems to be getting worse every cycle. Please have her put the cure in my room."

"Already done."

"Anything else of importance?"

"Only that Commander Bolgog dispatched guards to the Dig and Pit to check on the miners' stories about lights and noises coming from the Hallet Sea during darkouts. His men never reported in. It's disconcerting. Therefore, I urge caution on the morrow. Don't take chances, especially with the life of our leader at stake. Contact us, and I'll send the kid to the rescue."

"Understood. Thank you, Max. We will keep you and Narleen posted on our progress and anything we uncover. Jesse out."

When the call ended, Jesse and Saephira discussed how the new information correlated with what AliRoot told them. They made plans to rise early and travel back to the river. Jesse looked forward to scoping things out. As a former police chief, he loved doing investigations, gathering facts, being on the hunt for clues, and solving cases.

Before turning in for the night, Jesse gave Saephira additional supplement pills, two Tyhydru and two Dapferon, which she placed in her credit purse for safekeeping. Although the tablets they consumed at firstlight would provide hydration and nourishment for two more cycles, he felt it best to divvy up the pills in case they were separated or if tomorrow's circumstances turned contrary.

CHAPTER 20

GAHNEEHA

The next cycle, Saephira and Jesse arose at firstlight, packed their canopy tent, and rode to the river location where they first met AliRoot, arriving during forecycle. Even at this early span, the heat felt unbearable. They found the young girl at the river, skipping rocks across the waves, wearing the same outfit as yestercycle. She waved them over. They dismounted and approached the riverbank. After going through another ritual of stone flinging, where Saephira's toss nearly matched AliRoot's throw and Jesse's distance had improved, the three gathered around the kacks. AliRoot gave each an ear of maize, but the animals turned aside their heads as if they weren't hungry.

"What's wrong with your rides? They are not eating. Kacks are always hungry."

"Perhaps we fed them earlier."

"I don't think so." She closed her eyelids for a moment and then reopened them with a knowing smile on her face. "You gave them something yestercycle, and now they are not hungry or thirsty."

"How did you determine that?" Saephira asked.

"As I said, I know things."

"Did you read our minds?"

"No, not yours, Salie's. She thinks you put two objects in the fritter you fed her."

"So, you can talk to animals?"

"No, not exactly, I just discern things. What did you give her?"

Wanting to keep the rapport open, especially since they sought information regarding East Eskaonus, Jesse reached into his satchel and removed two supplement tablets. He held them in his hand for her to view. "The greenish-blue tab is Tyhydru and the reddish-brown one is Dapferon. They work for three cycles to keep us and our rides hydrated and nourished."

AliRoot gazed at the tablets, seemingly uninterested, so Jesse returned them to his carrier. "You wanna know what else the kacks think?" AliRoot looked at Saephira and giggled. "Salie likes you and loves it when you brush her mane."

"What about my mount?" Jesse asked, wondering if the little girl was making up stories or actually knew.

"He enjoys racing and wishes to swim in the river."

"Maybe later we can take them for a dip," suggested Saephira. "Right now, we're anxious to see your city."

"Before we leave, though, you need to tell me your names."

"We thought you'd know them."

"I never perceive names, only things concerning people."

"And apparently, certain creatures." Saephira grinned. "Well, young lady, my name is Saephira and my friend is Jesse."

"Odd-sounding names. They'll never work in town. Residents will assume you're outsiders. Therefore, I will call you SaeFear and him, JayEsse. Those won't draw attention, but your hairstyles will. They're all wrong."

"How so?"

"Women wear double ponytails like mine, not a single braid, draped over the shoulder as you do. Please don't be mad at me. Although your hair is really pretty and the length okay, it needs fixing."

"Please do." Saephira took a knee while AliRoot unbraided her hair and wove it into double ponytails. She tied the ends with blue ribbons from her carryall bag.

"These will match your light-blue eyes. I found the scraps in my momma's mending basket, so I brought them from home, figuring you'd be pleased."

"I am. Thank you. What about Jesse, I mean JayEsse's

hair?"

"His may be a problem. JayEsse's dark brown hair is thick enough yet too short for a ponytail. Gahneeha men wear them in long tails behind their backs. Seamen, however, usually prefer shorter ones called sailor buns."

"I'm an old Navy man; give me one of those." Jesse knelt on both knees as AliRoot bunched his hair and tied it with a black cord from her pocket. "Hmm, and you just happened to have a black hairband with you." She blushed, using her hand to hide a half-smile.

"You promised I could ride Salie."

"I did. We'll double up on the other kack." Saephira motioned for Jesse to take the steering position in front. She climbed on behind him, wrapped her arms around his waist, and snuggled close.

"Where are we going first?" questioned Jesse.

"To my home. Momma is already working in the fields. Maybe we will see her when we pass the vineyards."

AliRoot led them down the Wyntarie River past a series of kunakk vineyards. Kunakk was a dark, frothy liquor produced from vine-ripened grain pods grown on trellises. The distilling process made the drink highly intoxicating.

The party turned left at the first farm, which contained tall stalks of maize. Nearby fields featured a variety of vegetables, edible gourds, and yellowish fruits, but no pink yarm berries. After weaving through the farms, they finally entered Camp Gahn.

"This is my place. Wanna go inside?"

Before they could answer, a man rode by on a kack and yelled, "You can't hobble your rides here. Take them to the stable master."

"I'm sorry, SiaVoot. My friends cannot afford the barter price."

"Not my problem," replied the Gahn camp manager. "If your friends don't relocate them by the time I return, I'll confiscate the animals for MiaRoot's past due rent barter. Your mother owes me for ten cycles. And by the way, who are these people? Don't believe I've ever seen them." SiaVoot climbed off his ride, trudged up to Saephira, and walked behind her, glaring at her slender figure.

"Her name is SaeFear and her companion is JayEsse."

"We don't have vacancies. If your acquaintances plan on staying in my camp, they'll have to share sheets with another family." He continued to circle Saephira. "You're a fine looker. Our comfort tent might be interested in offering you a good barter price if you work for them."

"I'm sorry, sir, I'm not interested."

"Fine, go labor in the fields for all I care." Sneering at Jesse, he added, "You got a problem with that, sailor boy?"

"No, sir, we simply wanted to ask a few questions regarding—"

"Got no time for your stupid inquiries." The camp manager remounted his kack. "If you associate with this child mage, you must be diviners yourselves, and I don't care for your kind here. Move along. Remember what I told you, AliRoot. Ten cycles, and if there's no barter, then you and your mother are out on your ears." SiaVoot gave Saephira one last lustful stare, then turned his mount toward the vineyards and rode away.

"What is this barter system?"

"I'm surprised you don't know, JayEsse. We don't use tokens for payments. People barter everything: crops, products, labor, even comfort. Momma's labors are paid with a portion of the vineyard or farm crop, and she barters it for rent and other needs."

"Thanks for confirming the particulars."

"I guess you don't use this system." AliRoot closed her eyes to focus. "In the high realm." Jesse stared at Saephira and nervously cleared his throat. "Are you mad at me, JayEsse?"

"No, of course not. I'm merely taken back by what—"

"Our camp manager is a bad man."

Relieved for a change in topic, Jesse replied, "One doesn't require special discernment to conclude that."

"He's almost as bad as Ruler EdNook." At the mention of that name, Saephira let out a sigh, then glanced at Jesse, whose lips were pressed tightly together. Although neither of them said anything, AliRoot could sense distress on their faces. "I better grab a waterskin since I still get thirsty."

As soon as AliRoot entered her tent, Jesse whispered, "EdNook sounds similar to . . ."

Saephira raised her hand to silence him. "We'll talk later."

Several moments passed before AliRoot returned. "It's getting late. I'll race you to Gahneeha. If we get there by midcycle, you can meet QuiQuot. He's probably at the port getting his crew and ship ready to cast off. The shipmaster is a good man, honest, and my only true friend . . . other than you two. He'll answer your queries without making you feel like slimy river eels."

On the way, they passed a watering well and another farm before arriving in the city. AliRoot led them through numerous streets until they arrived at a town square. Merchant and smith shops lined the plaza. Street vendors displayed their wares, calling out their best barter prices. Food carts rolled past, offering samples from their menus. To Jesse, it reminded him of a flea market from his hometown in Dayton, where shoppers haggled over prices and made deals. The party continued on to the port facilities and stopped near a pier. "There's QuiQuot, standing on the second ramp. Come on; let's go meet him."

When the shipmaster noticed AliRoot, he shouted, "Hail, little one. What are you doing here? And where did you get a kack? I hope you didn't steal it." QuiQuot drew nearer, chuckling to himself.

"Salie isn't mine. She belongs to SaeFear. Her companion, JayEsse, owns the other one. QuiQuot studied the couple with a wary eye. "These are my new friends. They have questions, except SiaVoot wasn't very helpful." The party dismounted and stood by their rides.

"He never is. Your selfish camp manager is a pain in the . . . well, never mind. Are your companions seeking work? It appears one of them is a sailor." He stepped closer to Jesse. "I admire your haircut, JayEsse. Your bun is regulation; the way we skippers prefer it. If you're trying to impress me, you just did. Tell me how much experience you have on the sails?"

"Enough to recognize a port side from the starboard. I can tie a boom, lean the rails, swab the decks with the best of them, and then hoist a cup or two with crew afterwards."

"Sounds like you know sailoring. I'm short four men. Interested in a job? We're doing a cargo run on the morrow."

"Let me think on it."

"Fair enough. We pay top barter. And you receive your

portion after each run, so give it a good think." QuiQuot leaned against a piling and crossed his arms. "Alright, ask your questions?"

"I'm wondering about all this port activity. I count ten ships."

"Actually, there are fifty in our fleet. Twenty of those have already set sail for the Hallet Sea. The other twenty are headed southwest along the coast. My ship and a few others are cargo haulers. As for my crew, we're sailing the Wyntarie River to collect a load of iron at the mine. We have five fishing vessels in port, offloading their catches. The remaining crafts are military supply transports. We're in the middle of an invasion campaign."

"We didn't realize you're at war," replied Jesse.

"Most residents don't yet. I'm torn about the decision. However, Ruler EdNook sidestepped the elders' advice and ordered the attack. We had little choice but to comply."

"What attack?" Where?" Saephira gasped as blood drained from her complexion, turning it white as the desert sands. "Who is this EdNook?"

CHAPTER 21

EdNook

"**Who is EdNook?** I'm not really sure myself." QuiQuot motioned for the three to follow him a few paces down the landing, away from the listening ears of his crew.

"Where can we hobble our kacks?"

"Just leave the animals here, JayEsse. No one will bother them." After they passed the second pier, he continued talking in a low whisper. "It's odd how a total stranger emerged as our supreme ruler. Even so, I probably know the story better than most." He peered around to see if anyone stood nearby.

"It happened about fifty cycles ago. My ship had stopped in a cove to dig for rock clams and search the area for signs of migrating antaloops. This is where my crew discovered him. At first, we thought him dead, another fool who tried to traverse the desert."

"You mean the Wilderness?"

"Yeah, the Nae. At any rate, when my first mate provided water and revived the outsider, I interrogated him. We finally determined his name was EdNook. The guy was dehydrated and incoherent, spouting foolishness about being a ruler of fate."

"What did he look like?" Saephira asked.

"A corpse with a span left to live." QuiQuot laughed at his wisecrack. "Sorry for being insensitive; I assume you want an actual description. Well, he was short, stocky, no ponytail and mostly bald. Instead of an iron sword, such as our military carry, he had a curved, bronze blade. Strange, huh? I half-considered leaving him there to die but felt it wise to search his belongings. His bag contained a dagger, scraps of clothing, an empty waterskin, and two scrolls: one described how to build a launching platform and the other listed the ingredients required to produce liquid fire." Jesse stared at Saephira knowingly, yet neither gave the slightest indication they knew such weapons existed or that Lord Eddnok previously used them against Falein Village. "Those documents made no sense to me; therefore, I handed them over to the military to decipher. However, the last item surprised all of us. His bag contained one of the sacred, black stones. The *TREOW* was an exact copy of the one in our magistrate's office. In his pocket, we found part of a poem, mentioning a mystical treasure and fated ruler."

"Mysterious treasure? Ruler of fate? Sounds interesting." Jesse wanted to inquire concerning the black stones but decided to wait and see if QuiQuot mentioned them again.

"Yeah, I thought so. Once EdNook recovered his health, we brought him in front of the elder council to answer questions. He told a tale regarding a witch named Saephira who seduced her residents with magic. She could make pointed sticks fly and rocks float, so he escaped to warn our citizens that she intended to invade our land and destroy us unless we acted first. EdNook bade our woodsmiths to construct his catapult launchers and provided our chemist with the formula to make their fire-laden projectiles. Soon thereafter, our magistrate lay dead in his quarters. Someone had slit his throat during darkout."

"Do you know who murdered him?"

"No, JayEsse, not with certainty, but my crewmates suspect EdNook. The man talks a good tale; I'll give him that. He impressed some and frightened others. In the end, though, the elders promoted him to supreme leader. That's how he became Ruler EdNook."

"EdNook is . . ." The words stuck in AliRoot's dry throat. She opened her waterskin and guzzled half the contents in three gulps. "A bad man."

"I agree, AliRoot. There's little I can do. His campaign to destroy the Beays and Brias has already begun." He frowned and shook his head, seeming more angry than frustrated. "Hey, would you three like to see the *TREOW* stones. Although they are guarded, I think I can talk my way in."

Saephira paused, glanced at Jesse, trying not to appear overanxious. Before she could answer, AliRoot replied, "Yes, we wanna go."

"Works for me. I need a break anyway." He yelled to HieHoot, his first mate. "I'll be gone for a span. Oversee the loading. I'm showing AliRoot and her friends the sacred tokens." He took AliRoot by the hand. "Alright, folks, follow me. The annex is a couple streets over and four blocks this way."

The building's egress had an arm gate, which swiveled up and down to allow entry. The barrier rested in the closed position. Two guards stood on either side of it. They wore iron half-plate armor with leather greaves on their shins, albeit no helmets. Both men donned long ponytails and held oval shields covered with tanned leather, lettered with GN across the front. Double-edged swords hung unsheathed from their belts. Two twelve-foot wooden pikes with iron points leaned against the wall behind them.

One of the sentries shouted, "No entrance without permission from Ruler EdNook or the elder council."

"I am on the council, you idiot. Didn't your commander tell you? I was appointed temporary magistrate of Gahneeha following the unfortunate demise of RyeYook."

"Our apologies, Magistrate QuiQuot, we didn't realize you were the replacement."

"Well, nobody else sought the position. Too afraid of having their throats slit in the middle of the night. Feel free to apply for the job. I'd be happy to step aside."

"No thank you, sir. My cohort and I value our necks. So, how may we assist you?"

"Let my friends and I see the sacred tokens."

"Of course." The guards raised the arm gate. "Come on in, except don't touch the talismans."

"We're merely viewing them, nothing more." And the three climbed the steps to enter the building. A tall pedestal sat in the middle of the room. On top were two rectangular-shaped, black stones. The group approached and slowly circled the stand to examine the objects.

"Our archives have little information on these artifacts or the meaning of *TREOW*. The one on the right is ours; explorers discovered it long ago in ruins near the Narnj foothills. The other belongs to EdNook, or so he says. We think there might be more due to an obscure prophecy that says whoever possesses all of them will bring unity to the land."

"What does it mean?" Jesse asked.

"I have no idea. Probably just a foolish fable." QuiQuot mumbled a few words to himself before adding, "EdNook thinks it means he's the destined ruler this prophecy describes."

"Is he?"

"I doubt it, JayEsse. Don't get me started. I don't care to be cussing in front of the little one. Still, she probably already read my mind since she seems to discern what others are thinking." AliRoot sheepishly covered her mouth as he spoke, trying to hide her grin. "Okay, this tour is finished. I best get back to the docks. Can you make sure AliRoot gets home without incident?"

"We will, QuiQuot, and I'm grateful for the forthright answers to our questions. They were most informative." Saephira curtsied, showing her respect to the pro tem magistrate, thinking to herself, *informative and distressing.*

"You're both welcome. And if you seek a sailor job, JayEsse, come and see me on the morrow. We cast off at firstlight."

"Thank you, sir, I appreciate the offer. I have much to think on."

"Don't we all." Once outside, QuiQuot wished Jesse and Saephira fair sailing and gave AliRoot a pat on her head. "Tell your mother I'll stop by and see her soon." And he dashed off for the docks.

The three returned to the wharf area, mounted their rides, and rode away, winding through a maze of streets, past the town square, moving west. Saephira and Jesse whispered to each other as they traveled along, discussing the information they'd uncovered. AliRoot appeared uninterested in their conversation as she viewed the sights of Gahneeha. As soon as they were out of the city limits, Jesse stopped, slipped off his kack, and helped Saephira dismount.

"I'm sorry, dear one; Jesse and I must depart now."

"You're gonna ask a cute boy to pick you up on his flying board."

"Obviously, we cannot hide anything from you, can we?"

"Are you mad at me because I know things?"

"No, not in the least, but I need to ask a special favor."

"Please. Whatever it is, I'll do it."

"Can you take care of Salie for me? In fact, I'm giving her to you in appreciation for your assistance. Your mother can have the second animal and our canopy tent. Perhaps she can barter them to pay for her rent and other needs. I'm also leaving my purse of credits." She withdrew a small pouch from the hiding place inside her garment. "I realize you don't use currency, but the silver and bronze coins should make good barter. Maybe there's enough to move away from Camp Gahn and into the city."

Without looking inside, AliRoot added the credit purse to her carryall. "Really? No one ever aids Momma and me. Most people hate us because I perceive their intentions."

"We don't. Howbeit, with the lateness of the span, we believe you should head to Camp Gahn. The other mount will follow Salie."

"I can wait for a while. Besides, I'd enjoy meeting this cute boy."

"I'm sure you would. From the things I've heard, most girls think he's charming. However, we promised QuiQuot to get you safely home, and twilight is fast approaching. It's best if you run along. We'll both be fine. After we call him, Seth will arrive in less than a span. His hoverboard is faster than a homing flyer."

Half pouting, she asked, "Can't you stay a few more cycles and play with me?"

"Regrettably, we need to leave, and I think you realize why."

"If you gotta go, let me give out farewell hugs first." She skipped over to Jesse. He bent down, allowing her to embrace him around the neck. When she released him, she whispered into his ear, "SaeFear likes you." Next, she hugged Saephira's neck, holding on tight, not wanting to let go. "I will miss you most of all."

"And I will miss you; we both will. You're a gifted little girl."

AliRoot leaned in closer and whispered, "JayEsse cares for you."

Saephira furrowed her brow. "Are you sure?"

The young seer closed her eyes for a moment before reopening them, then nodded and giggled. As AliRoot slowly released her grip, she spoke softly into Saephira's ear. "EdNook is not the promised ruler . . . you are."

Not waiting for a response, AliRoot, rushed to Salie, jumped on, and rode away, not looking back. Bewildered by her last comment, Saephira simply watched in silence as she galloped north toward Camp Gahn. Since kacks have herd instinct, Jesse's mount followed close behind.

"What were you two ladies talking about?"

"Oh, nothing much, just girl talk."

"Hmm . . ." Jesse removed the radio from his satchel. "I better contact Seth so we can get a ride out of here prior to darkout."

"Jesse to Seth, do you copy?"

"I sure do, JW; been waiting for your jingle. Max suggested I be ready to shuttle you guys to safety."

"Where are you?"

"Out past Outlook Point. I dropped Holley off at Ritwell Village to assist a family with a medical emergency. A child with a broken arm or was it a leg? Anywho, Holley is a mender now. She even wears a purple sash with tassels. Oh, yeah, after Ritwell, I continued on to the Gemous River where our sole surviving ship is anchored. Max tasked me with delivering a tote of supplies to the company of militia protecting it."

"Does everybody know about your hoverboard?"

"Pretty much."

"I guess it was inevitable. What's your current 10-20?"

"I'm hanging at the boundary of the Nae by the Gemous River."

"You're almost halfway to our location."

"Which is?"

"We're outside a huge city named Gahneeha in a land called East Eskaonus."

"Sounds familiar. The map we discovered inside the Blighte cave showed an eastern settlement."

"That's it. Travel east until you reach the coastline, then turn north."

"I don't mean to cause a downer, but you're in a massive wilderness. How will I find you, I mean specifically?"

"I've been experimenting with our communicators. They appear to have a homing signal option. Instead of turning the selector to access a channel, push the dial in. It will allow you to track my transceiver signal. The closer you get, the louder the beeps resonate."

"Cool. Let me try it. Yep, it's beeping. I'm on my way."

"You better hurry. It'll be dark soon, and we don't have torches."

"Don't worry, JW. I'll be there for the crew in a few." Jesse grinned at Seth's constant use of clichés. For Saephira's sake, he hoped the kid's quip was correct.

Even gunning it the whole way, it took Seth over a span to arrive. By then, the light had begun to fade. Realizing the time urgency, he hurried Jesse and Saephira aboard, balanced his hovercraft for the extra passengers, and engaged the floor pedals. Seth flew across the terrain like an Indy racer, bobbing around sand dunes, past where the Gemous River disappeared into a giant hollow, arriving at Outlook Point by nightrise. Unable to go any further in the darkness, Seth parked his board, and the three of them boarded the anchored ship.

They decided to spend the night on the vessel and continue to Beayama at firstlight. Once they settled in for the evening, Saephira used Jesse's radio to reach Lady Narleen. She asked her vice-leader to arrange for a meeting in the Great Hall on the morrow with Captain Gelr, Captain Maximus, and her entire leadership council. She also instructed her to send homing flyers to all city magistrates and every senior village elder, summoning them to an emergency assembly at nightrise on the following cycle. Although Narleen asked concerning the urgency, Saephira decided to wait to share the tragic news of an impending invasion from the east.

Eddnok had abandoned Briacap, survived the Lost Forest, traversed the Nae Wilderness, and now wanted to extract his vengeance on those who opposed his wicked regime. The situation couldn't be worse.

CHAPTER 22

DECISIONS

AliRoot raced for Camp Gahn, arriving at twilight. She immediately opened her waterskin and emptied the contents, savoring every gulp. "You may not require water, Salie, but my mouth is so dry I can hardly talk. Those pills JayEsse gave you must work really well. You weren't sweating even though you ran the entire way here." Salie only neighed. "Would you like to have your mane brushed?" More neighs. "Let me check SaeFear's side carrier. Maybe she has a comb in there." A quick search of the carrier revealed a small wire brush, a nearly depleted waterskin, one used torch, and a striking stone. She removed the brush and began grooming Salie's mane. When the second kack arrived, she also brushed his mane. "Alright, you two, let's go find a home for the night."

She walked her mounts to the southern stable. "What are you doing with those, little girl?" asked the stable master. "Did you steal them?"

"No, they're mine, a gift."

"Doubtful. However, if you want to board your rides here, you'll have to barter for their care. What ya got to trade?"

"Something valuable." She reached inside her carryall, located SaeFear's credit purse, and withdrew a token.

"I don't take children's toys. Move along."

"Fine, I'll try the northern stable. Perhaps they'll be

interested in silver."

"Let me see that thing." He flipped it over in his hand twice, placed the object in his mouth, and bit into it. "Yeah, it's silver. Your barter is accepted. It'll pay for thirty cycles of storage for one animal, including feed."

"What about the other?"

"Got another silver token in your handbag?"

AliRoot knew better than to reveal how much she actually carried; therefore, she offered a different deal. "You can have the canopy tent for stabling my second ride for thirty cycles."

"Twenty."

"I'll throw in one side carrier, except I need thirty cycles of care for both mounts."

"Done." He reached for his ledger and recorded the transaction. "What name do you request on their stalls?"

"AliRoot for the white-striped kack, named Salie, and MiaRoot for the gray one."

She petted the animals and kissed their foreheads. "I'll visit you on the morrow. Don't mind the mean man. He'll honor the barter." And she dashed off, heading for her tent, holding her empty waterskin in one hand and the carryall containing SaeFear's purse in the other.

"Where have you been, AliRoot? I've been worried sick. You've never been this late before. It's almost nightrise."

"Sorry, Momma, I guess time got away from me." She hung her waterskin on a pole hook and tossed her carrying bag in the corner. "I met two new playmates who actually liked me. We skipped rocks, had fun, and—"

"That's nice, dear. Sorry to cut you off. I'm tired and fatigued. It's been a hard cycle at the farms. I left a bowl of maize soup for you, but it's probably cold by now. I regret not having extra barter to purchase proper food for us to eat." Tears formed in MiaRoot's eyes. Although she tried to wipe them away, they kept flowing. "My boss ordered our crew to start working the fields at firstlight, so I'm going to bed early. I love you, dear."

"I know, Momma. I love you, too. Things will get better for us."

MiaRoot sighed as she climbed onto her sleeping pad and

pulled up the covers. "I hope so."

While AliRoot sipped her bowl of soup, MiaRoot fell asleep and began snoring. Before the light totally faded, she retrieved SaeFear's credit purse and emptied the contents on her sleeping pad. It contained fifty coins—twenty bronze, thirty silver—and four supplement tablets. Two pills were greenish-blue; the other pair, reddish-brown. *I wonder if SaeFear forgot these things were in here or did she mean for me to have them?* She placed the pills in the side pocket of her carrier bag, returned the coins to their holding pouch, and hid it under her pillow. Feeling exhausted herself, she slipped under the covers and drifted off to sleep. A dream unfolded in her mind. Several images seemed familiar; others were strangely beautiful; three frightened her:

Vast desert, empty hollow, missing river

Four black stones joined together

Worms entering a hole, flying ships, reddish lights

Cities in ruins, burnt faces, children crying

MiaRoot arose one span prior to firstlight, checked on her daughter who was still sleeping, and departed for the fields. No sooner had her mother closed the tent flap, AliRoot climbed out of bed. She no longer needed to pretend being asleep. Whether it was the dream during nightrise or discernment, she understood what she had to do. AliRoot lit a candle to see. She unzipped her drawing pouch, located a scrap of paper and a stick of red chalk, and began writing:

Dear Momma,

I must go away for a while to help my new friends. I'll return as soon as I can. Under my pillow is a handbag of silver and bronze tokens. Barter with them to get what you require. There should be enough to find a nice place in the city. You also own a gray kack at the southern stables. I hope you'll keep the animal for riding, but feel free to trade him if you think it best. I already paid the stable rent for thirty cycles.

Please don't worry. I'll be safe. And don't be angry with me. If you get in trouble, contact QuiQuot. He will protect you. I think he desires an attachment. If he asks, say yes. He's a good man. EdNook is not. I'm leaving now. I'll explain everything when I come home.

Love you,
AliRoot

She pulled on her yellow boots and packed a coat in her carryall. AliRoot took one last look around the tent, blew out the candle, and went outside. Since darkness still lingered, she struck a spare torch aflame and hurried to the stables, finding the stable master raking the stalls. "Oh, it's you. What do you want?"

"To release Salie."

"Don't recall such a name." The man scratched his chin, covering a half smirk on his face.

"She's my white-striped kack."

"Aha. And where ya going so early? It's a span away from firstlight."

"I have business."

"Yeah, don't we all. Oh, by the way, what kind of transactions does a child have at this span?" The man waited several moments for her to answer, then lost patience and bellowed, "Ah, forget it. It's not worth the aggravation. I'll retrieve your pet." He unbarred the stall and Salie trotted out and nuzzled AliRoot's shoulder. "Are you aware your mounts haven't been eating or drinking? If they're sick, I'll have to vacate them."

"Please don't." She remembered JayEsse saying the supplement tablets worked for three cycles. "They'll probably be hungry by nightrise."

"Guess I'll hafta trust you on that." He grabbed his forked tool and continued raking the front stalls. "Have a nice outing, little one. And if you find any more riding creatures, remember, we have the best stable rates in Camp Gahn."

AliRoot glanced at the horizon and noticed the glow of firstlight had begun. She stowed the torch in her side carrier, placing it next to the other one. After petting Salie on the forehead, she adjusted the carryall strap across her shoulder, mounted up, and galloped south toward Gahneeha. Other than a few street vendors setting up their wares, she traveled through mostly empty streets until arriving at the annex where the black stones were stored.

AliRoot dismounted and surveyed the area. Streets on both sides of the annex were vacant. Two armed guards were asleep on the landing. One leaned against the rear wall, snoring, with one knee bent awkwardly in front of him; his neck tilted to the left. The second sentry lay on his right shoulder, legs curled up, with the flat of his face against the upper step. Between the men, a tipped-over container slowly leaked its contents. The smell of kunakk filled the air. Two drinking cups sat on the first step. Apparently, the guards had overindulged and passed out.

"Okay, Salie, you gotta be quiet. We don't want to wake the sentries." The animal just stared at her. "I'll be back shortly." AliRoot gingerly approached the stairway leading to the landing. She took three tiny footsteps, then paused, followed by three more until she stood in front of the closed arm gate. Small enough to slip underneath it, she dipped down, hurried over to the pedestal, and seized one of *TREOW* artifacts. She rubbed the smooth surface, running her finger along the symbols, and then tucked it into her carrying bag. AliRoot clutched the second one in her right hand, tiptoed to the exit, and stopped. She checked to see if the route remained clear prior to ducking under the arm gate to descend the stairs. On the bottom rung, she misjudged her stride, stepped on a drinking cup, tripped and fell, jarring the stone loose from her fingers.

The noise awakened both guards who rose unsteadily to their feet. "Hey, what are you doing?" AliRoot sprung up, snatched the item from the ground, and ran to her kack. "She has one of the sacred talismans. Stop!" yelled the guard. She ignored the command.

"Let's go after her," responded the other. Still inebriated from drinking too much kunakk, they had trouble navigating the stairsteps, and both landed face down in the middle of the street.

"Time to go, Salie." She stuffed the second *TREOW* into her bag, jumped upon the back of Salie, and galloped west. Once they cleared the city limits, she stopped, climbed off, and stood facing her ride. "Well, that didn't go as planned." Salie made a snorting sound. "You think I stole those two black stones, don't you?" She whinnied. "Alright, I did, kind of, but only because they don't belong here. I had a dream concerning those objects. Four exist, and someone must join them together. I'm not sure how yet; I think SaeFear knows . . ." In the distance, an alarm bell rang out.

"We have choices to make. Stay here and be arrested or

escape into the Wilderness. Can you lead the way to the Beay settlement?" Salie wiggled her ears. "I'll take that for a yes." More alarm bells began to toll. "We'll never survive the desert unless we're hydrated. All we have is SaeFear's waterskin, and it barely has a swallow left." She reached into her carryall and withdrew four supplement tablets. She popped two in her mouth, one of each kind. With a dry throat, they were difficult to ingest, so she removed the waterskin from Salie's side carrier and drained the last couple of drops, which helped the pills slide down her throat.

AliRoot held the other two pills in her open palm and placed them in front of the Salie's mouth. The kack turned away. "I think SaeFear left them for us. You saw me swallow mine; now it's your turn." Salie snorted and shook her head. "I'll brush your mane later, even braid it." AliRoot held the tablets out again. This time, the animal nibbled at her hand, removing the pills. "See, they weren't so bad." Hearing shouts, she turned about to see a company of guards approaching on foot. She placed the empty waterskin in the side carrier and remounted her ride. "Okay, let's go find SaeFear." And the two trekked west into the wilderness. The guards didn't follow. They knew the danger of traveling the Nae. Those who tried usually perished.

CHAPTER 23

WESTWARD BOUND

Holding on to Salie's long striped mane, AliRoot raced across the desert wilderness. Endless leagues of barren land lay before them, most of it consisting of sandy terrain, dotted with buff-colored hills and yellowish sand dunes. No vegetation anywhere. After four spans, she pulled gently on the animal's mane and brought her to slow stop. AliRoot glanced at the sky, guessing it was around midcycle.

"Sorry, Salie, I gotta have a break. We've been running for half a dayrise, and my bottom is sore from sitting on your back." She slid down and stood awkwardly. "Don't be mad at me for telling you my legs are bowed. I've never ridden a kack this long. Look, I can hardly walk." She took a couple steps and began giggling. "My thighs feel like bent cottlepines." Her giggles turned into laughter. "So, how are you doing?"

She felt Salie's fur. "You're not even sweating. Your coat is dry, and you don't seem dehydrated, even in this scorching heat. Apparently, those supplement tablets really work." Salie simply neighed. "I'm not a bit hungry or thirsty. What about you?" Salie shook her neck from side to side. "Good, then we better keep going."

AliRoot petted Salie's forehead and gave her a kiss on the snout. "I'm glad you're my friend. Most people don't like me 'cause I know things about them. But you do, right?" Salie blinked her eyes several times in a row. "Hmm, I assume that means yes. QuiQuot once told me kacks could run for long periods of time. If you're getting tired, though, we can slow our pace." Salie pawed the ground three times with her front left hoof. "I agree. Since we're not tired and don't need to break our fast, let's mount up and fly like a windblower." AliRoot climbed upon her friend, and the duo sped away at a gallop, continuing west.

At twilight, they stopped again. This time it only required a few moments for AliRoot's bowed legs to straighten out. "It will be nightrise soon, so we should decide what to do." Salie sniffed the air and snorted. "Yeah, it's getting cold; I better get my coat." She reached into the side carrier, withdrew a tan pullover lined with varmint fur, and slipped it on. Then she grabbed one of the torches and struck it aflame.

"Well, there are two options: We can remain here through darkout or keep traveling. If we take it slow, this torch will help light our path. If we stay, I can use the spare torch to build a fire to stay warm. Which do you prefer?" Salie whinnied and swatted her tail against her hindquarters.

"I know, I know, it's a hard decision. I wish Momma were here to advise me. I understand kacks can see during the dark, not as well as homing flyers, but better than us two-legged creatures. Is this true?" Salie bobbed her head.

"The ground seems fairly clear; I mean no rocks or holes, just sand. You can choose a safe pace, maybe a slow trot, and I will hold the torch. What do you think?"

Salie pawed the ground with her hoofs. "Okay, it's decided; we go." She climbed back on and the two continued west until the light faded into darkness. Salie started with a walk and later switched to a trot. By the time darkout covered the land, Salie was galloping ahead while her rider hung on to her mane with one hand and a burning torch in the other. The faster speed created air resistance that ultimately extinguished the light's flame. AliRoot couldn't see anything in the pitch darkness. She hoped her mount could.

Sometime during darkout, AliRoot leaned forward against the animal's withers and fell asleep, still holding on to the kack's mane; the unlit torch, however, slipped from her tired hand and plummeted to the ground. Salie felt a slight change in her rider's positon and weight distribution after the torch dropped. Instinctively, the animal slowed down, yet continued a steady pace until the darkness ended. At firstlight, Salie stopped and waited for her companion to awake. Finally, AliRoot opened her eyes, yawned, and sat up. She beheld a great river flowing into a huge hollow.

AliRoot slid off her mount and rubbed her weary eyes, trying to remember what happened. "I'm sorry, Salie, I must have fallen asleep and dropped our torch. Are you mad at me?" Salie neighed softly. "Do you know where we are?" More neighing. "This place seems strange, and there's a hole in the river. I'm gonna scout the area."

She explored the shoreline and discovered a fire pit with ashes. "Somebody camped here before, but why? This place is in the middle of nowhere." She kicked the ashes with her foot and uncovered small bones. "I wonder if these are slimy eel remains. They sure aren't tarkk bones; those would be much larger." Salie wandered closer, sniffed the ashes, and began snorting and bucking violently. "Settle down; there's nothing to worry about. Whoever was here is long gone." AliRoot led her away from the pit to the riverbank. "Hey, I have an idea. Let's go for a swim." Salie shook her head. "Oh, come on, you're acting like scared bush varmint. I'm going in for a dip." AliRoot unstrapped the side carrier and placed it on the ground. She removed her clothing and placed them in a pile. "I'm sure you want to. Remember, I discern your thoughts." She waded into the current and motioned for her ride to follow her. "If you try, I'll brush your mane like I promised yestercycle." Carefully, step by step, Salie entered the water. "See, I told you, nice, huh? We better not wander out too far 'cause we don't wanna get eaten by a tarkk or sucked into that hollow."

The two began to play. Salie pranced around, splashing water everywhere. AliRoot responded by cupping her hands and throwing water back at her playmate. Salie snorted, shaking her mane, flinging even more droplets at AliRoot. Unknowingly, the two drifted farther into the river. Their playfulness continued for a span until AliRoot noticed a large dorsal fin approaching. She bolted for the shoreline, followed by her ride. Missing its chance for a meal, the tarkk turned, swam toward the hollow, and dove under the surface before vanishing. "Wow, that was close, yet fun, huh, Salie?" By the time AliRoot walked over to get her clothes, her body had dried in the morning heat. She quickly dressed. The kack waited, then shook the remaining water from her furry coat, wetting AliRoot's clothes. "Not funny! Because you soaked my clothing, I may not brush your mane. Bad girl!" The animal lowered her head. "If this means you're sorry, I'll recant." AliRoot chortled to herself. "I knew you were merely teasing me. You're a good mount. Come here and let me comb your coat."

For the next span, AliRoot groomed her furry friend, first combing her coat and then brushing her long mane. Afterwards, she braided it into two sections, tying the braids with straps from the side carrier. "Now we have the same hairstyle." She fluffed out her ponytails and spun in a circle. "See, we're lookalikes."

Suddenly, AliRoot glanced at the horizon with a frown on her face. "It's forecycle already. We better keep moving." She refitted the side carrier to Salie's croup. "Wait a moment, I better fill our waterskin. We may need it when the hydration tablets wear off." She rushed to the river, dipped the skin into the current, returned with a full container, and tucked it into the carrier flap. "Alright, we're ready. I say we follow the river downstream and see where it leads."

The friends traveled nonstop for many spans until they encountered a trail. They followed the path until the pair approached a battened-sail vessel anchored in the middle of the river. Three soldiers, holding sticks bowed by strings, appeared from behind a makeshift shelter, and blocked her path forward. "Halt or we'll fire!" AliRoot yanked on the mane, causing the kack to come to a screeching stop, throwing her over its head. She landed on her back, face up. The men laughed. "Well, little girl, what are you doing out here all alone?"

She stood and straightened her pink dress. "I am not a little girl, and I'm not alone. I have my friend with me."

"Isn't that Lady Saephira's white-striped mount? I'd recognize it anywhere," said one of the militiamen.

"I believe you're correct." Phauch inspected the animal. "Sure looks like hers, and it's fitted with one of our side carriers. "Better tell me, young lady, did you steal it?"

"No, SaeFear gave it to me."

"If you mean, Saephira, that's doubtful. May I ask where you're headed in such a hurry, nameless one?"

"I'm AliRoot, and Salie and I are journeying to Beay to find SaeFear."

"If you're referring to Beayama, the place is at least two leagues away." He glanced skyward. "It's latecycle; you'll never reach the city prior to darkout."

"Yes, I will. Salie is fast." She remounted her ride. "Now, get out of my way. I'm on a secret mission."

"Secret, huh? Okay, my ladyship, you may continue your journey, but you'll need a military escort. There's trouble afoot." Phauch pointed at one of his men. "See this determined young woman safely to the city."

AliRoot closed her eyelids for moment. When she reopened them, she said, "Thank you, Militia Chief. You're a good man."

Before Phauch could ask how she knew his rank in the Militia, she galloped off. Her escort trailed behind her, endeavoring to catch up.

CHAPTER 24

MEETING IN BEAYAMA

Saephira's meeting with her vice-leader, captains, and leadership team was informative yet disturbing. She explained in detail the events that occurred in East Eskaonus during the last three cycles. Even though Saephira's advisors agreed with her concerns about a possible invasion, most were unsure how to counter it. The group decided to table their discussion until the morrow when the city magistrates and village elders arrived for a realm-wide meeting. Saephira asked her leadership to be ready with military recommendations and other suggestions, urging them to hold off sharing those particulars with local residents. Once the meeting broke up, servers brought out tea and desserts. No one partook. Hearing her dire report spoiled their appetites. For the rest of the cycle, realm business went on as usual, howbeit with trepidation and somber hearts.

The following forecycle, those whom Saephira summoned began congregating in Beayama. The elders from Ritwell were the first to arrive, followed by representatives from Falein and Cali. Being closer to the capital city had advantages for the Lower Realm villages, not only for trade but also for administrative purposes such as this meeting. Hyneil, the magistrate from Bayegulf, came next. The newly appointed magistrate from Tabahir, Nanlon, rode in at postcycle. He pushed his ride at a full run to get there in time for the gathering. Yosah, the official from

Midvill, arrived at twilight. Due to a lame kack, she had detoured to Falein for a replacement.

Having also received a summons from Saephira, Jesse and his associates likewise planned on attending, except Holley, who remained in Ritwell Village to help with a backlog of mender issues. Earlier in the cycle, Nakk Village sent their regrets. Due to the short notice, harvest time, and distance involved, Leeda, the senior elder from Nakk, had declined. She asked Lurah to notify her by homing flyer of the meeting's agenda. Commander Bolgog from Briacap was a no show.

By nightrise, Bolgog still hadn't arrived. Feeling she'd waited long enough, Saephira called the meeting to order, starting with general announcements. "Since it is well-past banquet time, I've asked our servers to place kin rolls, hot Azollie tea, and yarm on the tables. Please feel free to partake. Those who arrived late probably didn't have time to eat, so I hope these refreshments will suffice. Because this meeting is confidential, I've dismissed the attendants and posted safeguards at the exits."

The magistrate from Midvill raised her hand. "Yosah, do you have a question?"

"Yes, my Lady. A few of us are wondering why Jesse and his friends are here, being this is a confidential meeting."

"Good question. Jesse and I recently sojourned in the east, so I felt his presence and advice would be beneficial. Besides, he can confirm my account and our findings. If you remember, he was instrumental in saving the Lower Realm and bringing peace to the provinces. Therefore, I felt it prudent for both he and his colleagues to be present. Many of us consider Lundy, Annabelle, and others in his collective as heroes." She waited for dissents yet only observed smiles and nods. "Before I continue, does anyone have information on the whereabouts of Senior Commander Bolgog? He never answered my summons."

Nanlon rose. "I do, Great Lady." Seeing puzzled faces at the title he used for Lady Saephira, he added, "I mean, my Lady. Commander Bolgog begs your forgiveness for his absence. The commander is dealing with issues at the Dig and Pit mines. He sent a guard company to investigate, but neither the guards nor his miners have contacted him. Since those circumstances are his first priority, he declined your summons and asked me to report the outcome and decisions of this meeting when I return on the morrow."

"Thank you, Nanlon. Unless there are more questions or comments, I'd like to begin with the *Archive Analyst Report* compiled by Taula, our senior curator. Did everyone receive a copy of the document?" Jesse, Seth, and two elders shook their heads no. "Fortunately, I brought extra copies with me." Glancing at Lundy, she asked, "Would you please pass these out to those who need a copy?"

Saephira gave them several moments to review the handouts, then read the entire report out loud. As soon as she finished, hands rose throughout the hall. "I realize you have questions, but I am asking you to hold those queries until I summarize the most important findings in Taula's report, their implications, and what Jesse and I discovered in the east." The hands dropped.

"The greatest surprise is that the Nae is actually the Realm of East Eskaonus, and a civilization resides there. We traveled through the Wilderness and—"

"Impossible!" shouted Yosah. "With all due respect, my Lady, nobody has ever survived the Nae Wilderness and lived to tell the story. It's an endless wasteland with little food or water. They say the heat can even suck the water out of waterskins. You and Jesse would have dehydrated by the first or second cycle."

"Not so!" Seth jumped from his seat and withdrew two pills from his satchel. "Listen up, leadership dudes. They could have survived on these nourishment tablets." Using his index fingers and thumbs, he held a greenish-blue and reddish-brown tab in each hand. "We brought these with us from . . ." In the corner, he spotted Jesse patting his mouth with his hand, trying to shush him. "From a recent journey, and they work really well."

"I can validate what the kid said is true." Maximus stood and rubbed his chiseled jaw. "Anybody care to disagree with me?" He waited. "No takers, huh?" He grinned. "I didn't think so. Continue on, Seth."

"One pill lasts three days or is it dawns?" The attendees seemed confused at his calendar terms. Seth's face flushed red, showing his frustration. "I meant to say cycles. Anywho, that's the skinny of it. I'm not psyching you, either. After swallowing them, you're not the least bit hungry or thirsty. We survived seventeen . . ." Seth paused again as Jesse tapped a make-believe wristwatch. "Well, a long time, and I'm giving you dudes the square deal." Feeling embarrassed, Seth sat back down. "Sorry for interrupting."

"I'm glad you did, Seth. Those pills are exactly how Jesse and I tolerated the Nae's harsh conditions, as did our kacks. If I may continue . . ." Saephira took a deep breath and released it slowly. "The early inhabitants or ancestors of Eskaonus called their land, *Eskaon*. It was located in the territory we know as the Blighte. Their realm had three great leaders: a woman who hailed as Beay and two men named Bria and Gahn."

"How did you learn these things?" inquired an elder from Cali.

"From a recently unearthed scroll that Lundy and Taula translated."

"Aye, we did. No havers in our work. And we weren't feeling peely-wally, neither."

"Thanks, Reverend. According to the document, an undetermined calamity blighted their land, so the three families had to evacuate. The Beays moved here, the place we now call Beayama. The Brias traveled to the Briacap area, and the Gahns sailed away and established Gahneeha in the east. Jesse and I searched for several cycles and found this city by an unfamiliar river, called the Wyntarie. Their settlement had farms, vineyards, and a large port with dozens of ships. It's a realm of its own. Herein lies part of the problem."

"Which is what?" Yosah asked.

"We have brothers and sisters who we never knew existed."

"And the other part?"

"They are on their way here to invade us with a huge flotilla of ships."

The audience grew silent.

"Apparently, Lord Eddnok is alive. After he escaped Briacap and disappeared into the Lost Forest, he ended up in Gahneeha. The details are sketchy. However, two people we met while scouting East Eskaonus verified it was him. He had changed his name to EdNook and proclaimed himself as their ruler of destiny. Most of you have already heard about his evil deeds, deceitfulness, hatred toward me, and how his mind became corrupted by eating fruit from the knowledge tree."

Scowling faces revealed the group was sickened at Eddnok's actions. Saephira allowed a moment for the upsetting news to sink in and then continued. "Taking advantage of an ancient distrust between the Gahns, Beays, and Brias, who are all our ancestors, it was easy for Eddnok to convince the city elders that we were the enemies. Then, as absolute ruler, he ordered an invasion."

The representative from Falein loudly cleared his throat. "Excuse me, ma'am, are you sure we're being attacked?"

"No, nothing is certain at this point. I've asked Captain Maximus to address those concerns when I finish my presentation." She withdrew two rectangular black stones from a metal box and placed them side by side on the table in front of her. "These are the sacred *TREOW* tokens mentioned in Taula's archive report. Based on the translation, we believe there are four of them. Lundy uncovered one in the ruins on Onnie Passage, and Seth and his friends found the other inside the Blighte. The archivists have tagged them *A* and *B* on the back for identification. I can confirm the existence of two more in Gahneeha, having seen them myself. Jesse viewed them as well. The reason our ancestors made four and their purpose remains unclear."

She withdrew another document from the box, unfolded it, and held it up for everyone to see. "This is the original map discovered at a cave in the Blighte. It reveals the eastern settlement Jesse and I visited." She placed it next to the stones. "Later, you are welcome to take a closer look at these relics." She motioned Max to come forward. "Captain Maximus will continue this briefing."

Max gave a blunt assessment of the situation with one exception. He didn't comment on the possible threat of catapults using liquid-fire projectiles. Eddnok had used such a weapon against Falein Village. With the memory of the Falein attack still fresh in the minds of the villagers, Lady Saephira felt it might cause a panic if Max repeated information, based solely on hearsay from QuiQuot in Gahneeha.

Following his initial remarks, Maximus added, "Don't dwell on the unknown. Any attack, if it comes, may be cycles or longer away. Even so, we should stay vigilant. This is why I sent Lead Chepho to Bayegulf with a company of militiamen to reinforce our port facilities and asked Seth to train more archers. Because we must increase the size of our militia, I'll be at the practice field on the morrow to enlist volunteers. I'm requesting other places with military outposts to also conduct open enlistments."

"Captain Gelr is doubling the guard presence at our towers and city gates. Those who are willing to serve as safeguards, please see him. Miss Anna, an experienced slinger, has offered to train those interested in sling usage and tactics." Although Max didn't mention it, he realized her nyeflute would be an additional asset. "If we must defend our realm, a good defense is our best offense." Nanlon raised his hand. "Do you have something to add, sir?"

"Yes, Captain Maximus. Before I departed Tabahir for this meeting, Commander Bolgog advised me he had fifty guardsmen who could be posted wherever needed."

"Good, I will message him at firstlight." Max unsheathed his Gladius and raised it high over his head. "And one more thing . . ." He paused for effect. "Regardless of the situation or outcome, we will *stand our ground*. This is Rule Number Five." Affirmations and clapping filled the room. When the applause tapered off, Max returned to his seat.

Narleen spoke next. "As the Vice-leader, I recommend all city and village heads make preparations. Those who have fulltime menders, please ask them to organize their aid supplies. They can coordinate with our lead mender, Ottaar, for the specifics. Moreover, each locale should setup escape routes in case we deem evacuations necessary. Lastly, have your residents stockpile provisions in case of a siege."

In the outer hall, AliRoot and her militiaman escort waited for the meeting to end. Growing inpatient, she stomped around the hallway, shouting, "I must see SaeFear!"

"Be quiet, little girl. There's a meeting going on."

"I am not a little girl!"

"Stop hollering." The militia escort grabbed her arm to take her outside.

"Let me go!" AliRoot kicked him in the shin, distracting him long enough to escape his grip. She dashed through the main entrance, yelling, "SaeFear, SaeFear!"

CHAPTER 25

SaeFear, SaeFear

Two safeguards at the entry grabbed AliRoot by the arms before she could get any farther. They lifted her off the ground, but her feet kept running. "Let go of me. I need to see SaeFear."

"Release her!" Saephira shouted. "You're detaining a young lady who's my friend and our benefactor." The guards immediately dropped her. As soon as AliRoot's yellow boots hit the floor, she ran toward the platform where Saephira and her leadership team sat. She passed Jesse and his colleagues who were sitting at a corner table, stopped abruptly, and turned to face him.

"JayEsse." She curtsied. "Are you surprised to see me?"

"Nothing surprises me about you."

"You're not mad at me, are you?"

"Not in the least. Still, I didn't expect we'd see you this soon."

She noticed the teen who sat next to Jesse. "SaeFear told the truth; you are cute." Seth's face flushed red. AliRoot stepped one pace sideways and stood in front of Annabelle. She closed her eyes, paused for a moment, and opened them again. "You're a singer of sacred songs." The girl smiled, then added, "And a seer of hidden things, like me."

"Who are you, precious one?"

"I am AliRoot from Camp Gahn."

"You were in one of my dreams, Miss Root."

"Yes, I know." She grinned at Anna, moved to stand in front of Lundy, and momentarily closed her eyes. When she reopened them, she said, "You, sir, are a teller of truth and very wise."

"How did you come to these wee assessments?"

"I discern things. Most of my playmates hate me because of it. Are you mad at me?"

"Far from it, little one. Old Lundy is intrigued."

"You're not old. No one ages in the realm you call home."

Lundy winked an eye. "Aye, it be true."

AliRoot curtsied again, covered her mouth trying to hide a giggle, and then skipped to the platform where she leaped into Saephira's open arms and hugged her neck. "How did you get here, AliRoot?"

"I used the supplement tablets you left in your credit purse and rode day and night, including through a darkout, to arrive in Beay."

"Did you sojourn this great distance by yourself?"

"Nope, wasn't alone. Salie came with me. I told her to find you, and she did."

"I see. Is Salie okay?"

AliRoot nodded. "The militiaman put her in the stable. She's resting now. I promised to brush her mane later."

"I'm sure she would relish it. I always groomed her each dayrise. Did you feed her, too?"

"She's not hungry or thirsty yet. Salie ate the same supplement tablets as me."

"No doubt, it's how you both survived the Nae Wilderness. Thank you for taking care of her. So, what was the rush to get here?"

"To give you these." AliRoot pulled out the black stones from her carryall and placed them next to the other two on the table. Immediately, all four turned white.

Saephira grabbed one in her hand, removed it, and the stone turned black again, as did the three on the table. "Hmm, we need to study this phenomenon and determine the connection." Looking at Lady Narleen, she added, "AliRoot will be staying with me in my quarters for nightrise. We have much to discuss."

"What about this meeting?" asked Narleen.

"The meeting is yours, Vice-leader. Once everyone has had an opportunity to view the artifacts, I want these four stones, the map, original scroll, and its translation locked in my personal vault." She curtsied to the crowd and departed the hall with AliRoot. Two militiamen met Lady Saephira and AliRoot at the exit and followed them until they were safely inside Residential Hall.

When the onlookers had finished viewing the artifacts, Narleen gathered the items, placed them into the metal box, and tucked it under her arm. "This concludes our assembly. The Militia and Safeguards are dismissed. As for our visiting envoys, we have housing prepared in Residential Hall for the coming darkout. Grab a torch outside and follow me. The rest of you I bid, good nightrise."

While Narleen guided the envoys to their quarters, Jesse and his party returned to Ottaar's place. Being late, the tired group settled into their rooms. Jesse decided to write in his journal before calling it a night.

Entry Twenty

I never gave much credence to Murphy's Law, but whoever coined the phrase—anything that can go wrong, will go wrong—may have been correct. This seems to be the situation here on Eskaonus. Each day, more things go wrong. First, Bayegulf's fishing ships vanish. Then the vessels searching for them are attacked and presumed lost at sea. Next, we discover Lord Eddnok survived the Lost Forest, endured the Nae Wilderness, and ended up in East Eskaonus, which was a place no one believed existed. Somehow, he tricked their inhabitants into believing lies concerning Saephira; murdered the magistrate of Gahneeha, and built catapults capable of launching firebombs. Similar weapons previously devastated the Falein Village area. Worse yet, Eddnok proclaimed himself as supreme ruler and is on his way here to exact revenge by destroying his rivals.

We can't return now and leave our friends to face this threat alone. A Scripture from Ephesians 6:12 comes to mind:

"For we wrestle not against flesh and blood, but against principalities, against powers, against the rulers of the darkness of this world, against spiritual wickedness in high places."

As I recall, the next verse exhorts us to wear spiritual

armament to withstand evil. Unfortunately, my armor has become a bit rusty. Even so, I think this passage means more than simply praying. We must offer practical assistance as well. If the Eskaonites are facing a superior force with plated shielding and iron weapons, I don't think God wants us to turn tail and portal back to the safety of heaven while our friends perish. After everything we've been through, can this be eternity's grand purpose for Eskaonus or other places like Camayah? I sure hope not. Either way, the passage ends by saying that having done all, to stand. Not surprisingly, Max's Rule Number Five to stand our ground hits home for me. I feel obligated to put my life on the line to save this world. Did not Jesus do likewise for us?

Seth had just climbed into bed when he heard a familiar voice on his radio. "Seth, do you hear me?"

He arose and withdrew the walkie-talkie from his satchel. "Yeah, Rauteira, I copy ya loud and clear. How are things in Camayah?"

"Exceptional. Terraforming procedures are working. Each phase, additional wells bring more hydrew to the surface. Flora has rebounded and soreseed crops produce enough food for all the sectors. In fact, I heard the Council of Twelve recommends switching from nourishment tabs to real nutrition."

"That's nice."

"We have you and the *sent ones* to thank for it."

"Yeah, I guess." Seth's short replies indicated a lack of interest, as if his thoughts were focused elsewhere.

"I'm a little bit mad at you, Seth. Last time we talked, you promised to call me back. That was over 130 dawns ago; nearly five phases have passed."

"Five months, no way! It's hardly been eights cycles, I mean dawns."

"I've logged the dates on my datatop. It was exactly 136."

Apparently, JW was right; time is relative. "I'm sorry, Rauteira, I've lost track of the calendar. My mind has been in the clouds, lately. We've got problems on Eskaonus."

"Cloud problems?"

"No, something more serious. We're about to be wiped out by an evil Lord Eddnok. A huge fleet is on their way to invade the western lands. They plan to annihilate every settlement in the Upper and Lower Realm. Things look grim. Maximus exudes confidence, but privately, he told me our cities and villages have no defense against weapons capable of launching firebombs."

"Are there no options?"

"Only one. Stand our ground. It's Max's Rule Number Five. However, unless a miracle happens, we're probably toast."

"Oh, Seth. I don't want you to—"

"Don't worry. I've died before and survived."

"What does that mean?"

"Never mind, just rambling. I can tell you this, though; I'm not going down without a fight."

"What can I do?"

"From Camayah or whatever dimension you're in? Not much. Too bad I didn't bring a trispike stunner with me."

"Now, I'm really worried."

"Yeah, ditto for me." A long pause ensued, followed by static. "Hey, Rauteira, I gotta crash and get some sleep. Our leadership meeting went past nightrise, and my body feels totaled. If I survive this upcoming turkey shoot, I'll try to contact you. Luv ya much." As soon as the conversation ended, Seth smacked himself on the forehead. "Oh, man, I can't believe I said that. Dude, you must be beyond tired." He returned the radio to his satchel, blew out the candle on his dresser, crawled back into bed, and pulled up the covers. Soon, he was fast asleep.

In an adjacent room, Anna played her nyeflute, practicing a new tune. She finally slid under the sheets and drifted off to sleep. Slowly, a vivid dream sequence unfolded. Several images seemed familiar, others disturbing:

Children riding quawners, airships, rivers of hydrew

Worms entering a hole, silvery moon, reddish light beams

Fireballs, iron soldiers, long spears, a white glowing cross

After staying nightrise in Residential Hall, the visiting magistrates and elders arose early and walked to the Great Hall to break their fast with refreshments set out the prior night. Having eaten their fill of yarm berry tarts provided by Ellee's Place, they hurried to the stables, mounted their kacks, and departed Beayama for the return trip to their cities and villages, anxious to share what they had learned at the meeting and make preparations. As they rode off, they were unaware that two eastern armadas had already arrived. One sat off the coast of Bayegulf, hidden in the mist, and the other floated along the western shoreline of the Hallet Sea behind the Narnj Mountains. The span following firstlight, their invasion began.

CHAPTER 26

INVASION

A heavy mist crept in along the Nether Sea coast near Bayegulf. Because the southern areas in the Lower Realm had cooler climates, the coastlands were often foggy before firstlight. The skies generally cleared when the yellow bands of light appeared. This day, however, the mist hung around for several spans, limiting visibility.

Lead Chepho, the senior-most officer in the Militia, was in charge of the twenty militiamen Captain Maximus assigned to protect Bayegulf in case of invasion. Chepho had deployed ten soldiers along the docks and the remainder inside the city limits. Other than the sole vessel hidden on the river by Outlook Point, the Lower Realm had no ships. Six had been lost at sea under mysterious circumstances. With none to sail, the sailors who would normally be tending those vessels were at home with their families.

During nightrise, Chepho only needed a few sentries per span, so his men alternated shifts between watch duty and sleeping. He stayed awake and patrolled the area with a wary eye, occasionally kicking a dozing sentry to rouse him. Elsewhere, shop owners had started setting out their wares in the town square. Most of the residents, though, were still in their homes, asleep. He noticed smoke from several chimneys as people prepared food to break their fasts. All seemed normal for this early span. The thick mist lingered as dayrise dawned.

The armada from East Eskaonus moved closer to the coastline, their sails obscured by the mist. EdNook released a homing flyer to the northern armada in the Hallet Sea. He didn't wait for a reply, knowing JaeLuet, the flagship skipper, already had her orders to attack Briacap one span following firstlight. Gleeful their approach had surprised his enemy, EdNook ordered TaeVook, the flagship skipper of the southern armada, to contact his three catapult-equipped crafts to begin their assault. TaeVook hurried to the foremast and raised a green-striped banner, signaling the under-skippers to launch their first volley of firebombs. Hardly able to contain his excitement, EdNook walked to the bow, peered through his magnifier, and waited.

Soon, flaming barrels rose high into the air, leaving a trail of black smoke in their wake. Upon impact, the projectiles exploded, spreading liquefied accelerant in all directions. Anything the flames touched—erupted into fireballs—shops, homes, docks, even the streets burned. The flames ran like rivers, destroying everything in its path.

Hearing the explosions, residents bolted from their dwellings to investigate. Individuals who stepped outside their doors, died on the spot, burnt beyond recognition. Then a second volley of fire-laden objects landed. More structures burst into flames. As confusion and mayhem spread, families dashed from place to place, trying to avoid the onslaught. Many were unsuccessful. Parents carried injured children in their arms. Husbands embraced their spouses: some already deceased, others crying hysterically. Bodies lay in the streets; their mournful cries filled the air. A third volley followed, delivering even more flames and death. The carnage was unimaginable. The entire city of Bayegulf seemed to disappear under a cloud of smoke.

"Report!" shouted Chepho. "What's our status?" He looked at Bonarb, his younger brother, whom he had promoted to squad leader after rescuing him from Eddnok's prison-labor camp at the Dig.

"We lost five men; several are wounded. The city's in chaos." His voice faltered as he spoke. "What are those things flying through the air? Whatever they touch, burns."

"I have no idea, brother. Captain Maximus would probably know. We better—"

"Incoming ball of fire!" screamed one of the militiamen. "Take cover."

"Where?" asked another. "There's no place safe."

"Behind a wall or building; any spot is better than standing here exposed." Chepho pointed at an unburned area near the docks. The militiamen dashed for safety as three more flaming objects flew overhead; one landed nearby, barely missing them.

"Wow! That was close."

"We cannot stay here. Use your horn, Bonarb, and rally the men we have left. Let's move the wounded to the city mender's place."

"There is none, not anymore. According to a fleeing neighbor, the first strike hit Bayegulf's only aid station. It's nothing but cinders. He doubts the mender survived."

Chepho took a deep breath, slowly exhaling it in an anguished sigh. "I'm open to suggestions, squad leader?"

"I understand Ritwell Village has a visiting mender. Holley is there."

"Okay, have the surviving residents flee to Ritwell. We'll carry the injured with us. I sure hope these skyfire projectiles have a limited range." Chepho scanned the area. "Did any of our kacks survive?"

"Most did," advised Bonarb, "although they're scattered. We'll have to round them up."

"Alright, do that first, and then we'll evacuate as many as we can. Bayegulf is lost. Once we get the injured to safety, we'll establish a defensive perimeter around the village. We can only assume their foot soldiers will be next."

The northern armada sat anchored off the shoreline in the Hallet Sea. At the agreed upon time, Skipper JaeLuet signaled her three catapult-equipped crafts to launch their projectiles. The first volley arced across the horizon, soared over the Narnj Mountains, flying toward the fortress at Briacap. Gahn spotters, who had infiltrated the Dig and captured their miners, tracked the flight. The bombs fell short of their intended target, hitting an old well.

The liquid fire spread everywhere yet did little damage. A spotter released a homing flyer to the flagship. The messenger bird arrived within a few moments.

Load too heavy. Launches are short of target. Use half barrels to increase range. Trajectory is fine. —Spotter

The crews switched from full to half-sized barrels and released a second volley. Two firebombs landed inside the compound. Smoke billowed high into the sky. The third crashed into the rampart, sending flames over the parapet.

The spotter sent a second flyer: *Direct hits. Great aim. Proceed.*

JaeLuet raised two more green-striped pennants. Her catapult ships launched two more volleys at Briacap and then stopped. Of the six firebombs released, one smacked against the main entry, five landed inside the city.

"What was that?" Brappt asked. "Did you see where those things came from?"

"The Hallet Sea area," replied Bolgog. "The explosions are probably caused by liquid-fire contraptions. They're the same type of projectiles Lord Eddnok used against Falein Village three periods ago. His attack devastated the village, local farms, and docks at the lake."

"Well, it's a good thing these large flaming buckets landed short of the city by the dry well. It's worthless."

Bolgog focused his magnifier to scan the skyline. "I assume they're adjusting the range even as we speak. We won't be so fortunate next time. Better sound the general alarm and wake the guardsmen. I need every available man on the walkways." As the bell rang, the guards scrambled from their barracks into the courtyard, heading for the armory to gather their weapons. Before they could arm themselves, a second volley dropped two skyfire devices in their compound, catching the men in the open. A third blazing barrel struck the battlement. The flames took most of the guardsmen.

Two more volleys followed: One projectile hit the entry, setting the gates aflame. Five more landed inside the citadel. As Briacap burned out of control, Bolgog raced to the mail tower and sent three flyers: one to Nakk, the others to Tabahir and Beayama.

Being attacked. Skyfire weapons. Expect siege next. Send troops if you can. —Bolgog

During the aerial assaults, EdNook's dispatch to Skipper JaeLuet finally arrived, and a deckhand rushed the note to her: *Set Briacap aflame. Siege and occupy city. Capture traitor Bolgog and officers. Hold for execution. —EdNook*

After JaeLuet read the message, she mumbled to herself. "Already accomplished the first part." She went to the foredeck and raised the black banner. As soon as NiaLuck, an under commander in the northern battalion noticed it waving in the wind, she hoisted a black-striped pennant to signal the brigantines under her command. The sixteen brigs sailed closer to shore, dropped boats, and began disembarking their army. JaeLuet's flagship and her three catapult transports stayed anchored offshore in the Hallet Sea.

Meanwhile, the southern armada paused their aerial attack on Bayegulf.

"Can we reach Ritwell Village from here?" EdNook asked.

"Easily," replied Skipper TaeVook.

"What about Beayama?"

"Not with full barrel projectiles. Our catapult vessels didn't stock the smaller half-sized ones. Those were loaded on the northern fleet. We must be closer to the target for an accurate strike."

"Who's to blame for that? Never mind. I want one more volley aimed at Ritwell Village. Afterwards, send our three catapult transports up the Lower Fork River. Have them anchor in range of Beayama. In the meantime, signal Commander LyeDuek to reposition his sixteen brigantines and begin disembarking his forces. I expect our army to occupy whatever's left of Bayegulf by forecycle. From there we can march on Ritwell."

"Shall we follow the brigs?"

"No, we're staying anchored offshore in *The Gahnatine*. You and I can monitor the situation from our flagship. Now get going and carry out my orders."

CHAPTER 27

UNDER SIEGE

"It seems as if the aerial assault has stopped." Commander Rennard looked around at the carnage inside Briacap.

"Yeah, but for how long?" Sub-Commander Brappt scanned the eastern horizon over the Hallet Sea where the skyfire projectiles first appeared.

"Unknown. Let's use whatever time we have to our advantage." Bolgog tromped across the alure, cursing under his breath, pounding his fists against the merlons. "This attack has all the earmarks of Lord Eddnok. How did that deserter survive the Lost Forest? Those liquid-fire projectiles are his doing. I'm sure of it. The man is evil, through and through." The senior commander surveyed their courtyard, noting the damage. "What's our defensive status? How many reserve guardsmen do we have?"

"Maybe fifty survived," replied Rennard.

"Out of two hundred guys?"

"Sorry, sir. Most of the guards from the barracks that responded to the alarm bell are either dead or severely wounded. Being in an exposed plaza, they didn't stand a chance."

"Okay, add those fifty men to the battlements. What about our sentinels?"

"They're already on the towers."

"And the warders?"

"Since they were stationed inside our stone-walled

stockades, they survived the assault."

"Good, have them release the incarcerated. If their prisoners assist with the defense of the city, they'll all receive full pardons for past crimes."

"What's the status of our two menders?"

Staring at the ground with downcast eyes, Brappt replied, "One dead, the other alive. By now, she's likely overwhelmed caring for the injured."

"Alright, have our warders help her set up a triage inside a stone enclosure. Make it the kitchen. They're under her command now."

"Is that all, sir?" asked Brappt.

"No, I want every able-bodied citizen to work on extinguishing fires; give priority to the city gates. We can ill afford to lose their integrity in case of a siege. A land attack is probably forthcoming. You and Rennard split those duties. Get going. I'll expect a report every half span."

The officers raced off while Bolgog stayed on the battlement to keep watch. He paced along the wallwalk, stopping occasionally to view the eastward landscape through his magnifier, expecting to see an army marching through the pass at Narnj. A span later, the invading force appeared.

By midcycle, three hundred enemy soldiers had surrounded Briacap. The troops were on foot, fitted with breastplate armor, carrying shields. Half of them held double-length spears; the others brandished swords. Several wore helmets with red or yellow plumes, which Bolgog assumed were officers. The invaders formed into six units and began erecting tents behind their front lines.

Bolgog turned to a sentinel. "Sound the call-to-arms." As the bell rang out, guards not already on the ramparts, rushed to the battlements. "I sure wish we had bowmen and slingers like the Lower Realm. We could drop a few before they get any closer."

"Perhaps we should have accepted the Militia's offer to train us in those weapons," replied the sentinel.

"Regrettable decision on my part, one I now lament." Bolgog pursed his lips and stared into the distance. "Better raise the blue banner."

Seeing a truce pennant, three individuals wearing plumed

helmets approached, staying out of spear range. "Ho there in the tower," hailed the woman in a red plume. "I would speak to your leader."

"You're talking to him!" exclaimed Bolgog in an angry voice. "Who are you to attack our citadel?"

"I presume you're Leader Bolgog, the traitor." Bolgog said nothing. "I'm NiaLuck, Under Commander of the Northern Gahn Battalion."

"I'm sure you noticed our truce banner, Commander. We request a parley."

"Denied! You have only one option."

"So you say." Bolgog realized they had few desirable choices but wanted to draw out the conversation, hoping for more negotiations. "What do you propose?"

"Full capitulation."

"And if we don't?"

"We will withdraw our troops to a safe distance and continue with our firebomb launches until your ill-fortified citadel burns to the ground. Do you wish all your Bria inhabitants to die?"

"Suppose we were to yield, then what?"

"We will occupy your city, spare further destruction, instruct our two menders to care for your wounded, and guarantee the safety of your citizens. However, all fighters must surrender their weapons. Moreover, you and your officers will submit to arrest and face judgement for your traitorous deeds against our noble ruler, EdNook. You have one span to decide your fate." NiaLuck withdrew, followed by her two cohorts in yellow plumes.

Bolgog motioned for Rennard and Brappt to join him for a consultation. "Well, commanders, you heard the lady general. I see no way to avoid this mess. We could probably outlast a normal siege but not these skyfire weapons. If we don't surrender, they will likely burn Briacap to ashes and kill us all. If anyone has a suggestion, tactical or otherwise, now is the time to speak." The men glanced at each other and slowly shook their heads no. "I never thought I would give these orders: Rennard, lower the blue banner from the tower and raise the white one. When you're finished, send a final flyer message to Beayama."

"What shall it say?"

"Briacap has fallen."

"What about me, sir?"

"Brappt, I want you to instruct the guards to open our city gates. I'll meet you both there in ten moments after I say farewell to my children, assuming they're still alive."

"Sir, there must be some other way."

"There isn't. Go offer goodbyes to your own family members. Afterwards, join me at the gates. And commanders . . ." As Rennard and Brappt waited for Bolgog to finish his statement, they gazed at him with sorrowful eyes. "It's been an honor, gentlemen." With a tear-laden face, Bolgog embraced both officers, arm to arm, in the comrade farewell.

A quarter span later, the main gates were unbarred and Bolgog with his two lieutenants marched out, heading for the enemy's positon. Soldiers bound the three immediately and hauled them to a detention tent. After the invaders controlled the city, they placed Bolgog and his comrades in Briacap's own stockade, guarded by Gahn warders.

Commander NiaLuck kept fifty warriors at Briacap and ordered the remaining units to surround Tabahir, Nakk Village, and Midvill. She sent a homing flyer message to Skipper JaeLuet on the flagship in the Hallet Sea, advising her of their great victory over the Brias. The next flyer went to Ruler EdNook in the south, advising him she had captured Bolgog and taken Briacap.

Meanwhile, a volley of firebombs, launched from catapult vessels in the Nether Sea, flew toward Ritwell. Two dropped short of the village. The third landed near a row of huts on the eastern boundary of the village, sending liquid fire down the paths. Although the flames destroyed several outbuildings, most villagers were able to escape in time.

"I guess their aim is off. Encouraging news, right, Chepho? Do you think the aerial onslaught has ended?"

"We can only hope, Bonarb. Are the Bayegulf refugees secured?"

"As far as I know, a few stragglers are still evacuating."

"Direct them to the northern part of the village."

"Did you locate Holley?"

"She's in an elder's hut, mending the injured. Family members are helping her."

"We did what we could, brother. Time to establish defensible positions around Ritwell."

Bonarb sounded the rally call on his horn. "Should we hobble our kacks, first?"

"No, if the villagers decide to evacuate to Beayama, they'll need them more than us. Let them roam free."

"What if we have to retreat?"

"I doubt we'll have that option, little brother. We are here to defend the village."

When the remaining militiamen responded to Bonarb's rally call, Chepho gathered the men around him. "If any of you with a spouse desire to leave, you are free to do so, no questions asked, except you had better depart soon. I anticipate their invasion force any span now."

Bonarb viewed his squad, seeing agreement on fifteen faces. "The Militia will stand, sir."

"Okay, men. Get your longbows strung and arrows ready."

A span before aftercycle, Chepho sighted the invaders marching toward Ritwell. He estimated three hundred combatants. They wore half-plate armor, no helmets, other than the officers who donned decorative ones. The troops carried medium-sized oval shields, silvery swords, and long wooden spears with metal points. Most wore leather greaves. None had javelins, bows, or slings. Chepho counted six detachments, five ranks deep containing fifty men. Three of the units held spears; the other three wielded swords. Behind their advance, a thick cloud of black smoke enshrouded Bayegulf.

"Alright, militia, let's notch a couple arrows and see if we can slow them down."

"Sir, they're wearing metal armor," noted a nearby militiaman.

"All armor has weak spots. Let's pray our arrows can find an opening." The first volley dropped a dozen to the ground. "Great aim, militia; keep firing at will." Subsequent arrows, however, were less effective. The advancing soldiers would place their shields over the person next to them, forming a type of shell. Most bounced off. When the Militia exhausted their supply of arrows, they drew swords.

"This is it, guys. Form two ranks and follow me. Stay away from those long spears. There is no way to engage them with our blades. Our best chance is to confront their swordsmen units. The one on the right flank looks a bit degraded from our arrows. Charge!"

Sword clashed against sword. Whenever the enemy lunged forward with a stabbing motion, the militiamen would counter with a parry, using a block or deflect, and respond with a sweeping slash. If the enemy tried a thrust, the militiamen would dodge to evade, employ a feint maneuver or forward stab, then rebound with a downward chop, tricking the enemy and catching him off guard. Captain Maximus had taught his militia well. The enemy seemed bewildered by their tactics.

Even though the Militia was better at swordsmanship and tactics, one by one they fell. Finally, only Chepho and Bonarb remained standing. They battled side by side, shadowing one another. Both were bleeding from cuts. Outnumbered, facing superior weapons and armor, Chepho realized they would soon join their dead comrades. As the enemy pressed their advantage, Chepho yelled, "We cannot prevail, brother. Run!"

"No way! We go down together."

"Report to Maximus. Tell him what we're up against."

"I'm not abandoning you."

"It's an order, squad leader. Move out! Ritwell is lost."

"Then come with me."

"No! Take a mount and ride. I'll cover your retreat."

"Brother, I . . ."

"Go!"

Bonarb sheathed his sword, located a kack, and galloped away. He glanced to the rear as he rode, catching a glimpse of five warriors surrounding his brother. A moment later, Chepho lay in the dirt, unmoving. Bonarb wanted to turn around and go back, yet didn't. He crossed the Gemous River ford, veered left, and steered for Beayama. Blood ran down his arms and legs from numerous lacerations. A stab injury to his left shoulder ached, but the emotional wound in his heart felt worst of all.

After the Ritwell village resistance had been defeated, LyeDuek, the southern battalion's high commander, dispatched a junior officer and twenty pikemen with orders to secure the village and detain discontents. He moved the remainder of his contingent across the Gemous River, stopping in a vacant area between Yarm Vineyards and Beayama. While his forces organized their camp, he sent a flyer message to EdNook on *The Gahnatine.*

Bayegulf is ours. Ritwell under occupation. Battalion awaiting your orders for the assault on Beayama. —LyeDuek

Pushing his kack at a full run, Nanlon arrived in Tabahir during latecycle and discovered his city occupied by foreign troops. In the distance, he noticed smoke rising from Briacap.

He entered the town from the south and rode to the Copper Rail. As soon as he crossed the street to his tavern, five soldiers appeared and one shouted, "Halt! Who are you, and what's your business here?" The warriors were dressed in plated armor and holding double-edged swords at their sides.

"I'm Nanlon. The Copper Rail over there is my tavern."

"Why is it locked?" asked the apparent officer. "Shouldn't the place be open for business at this span?"

"Normally, it would be, except I was away traveling."

"Where?"

"The southlands. I'm a merchant." Nanlon dismounted from his ride. "What can I do for you and your crew? Need a room for darkout? We have the fairest rates in town and the best kunakk."

"We are searching for the city magistrate. They say he's new, yet no one seems to recall where he lives. We want to arrest him for treason."

"Understandable. Nobody cares for a traitor." Nanlon wiped away the sweat forming on his brow. "If I come across the person, I'll advise you."

"See that you do. This place is under martial law by the Gahn military. Are you a Bria or Beay city?"

"Neither, we're a neutral settlement. Why don't you come inside and let me pour a few jars of kunakk? My son can take care of your mounts in our stables."

"We don't have kacks. Our detachments just use footmen. However, we will return later to drink your kunakk. Right now, we're heading to Flissy's Place. They say she has the best comfort women in—"

"Sorry to interrupt you, sir, but I gotta send a flyer message prior to opening the Copper Rail."

"No flyer correspondence by order of NiaLuck, the under commander from our northern battalion."

"Really. How then will I order more kunakk for your warriors? I'm a merchant, remember, and my supply is running low."

"Fine, send your message, then hurry back to your tavern. We have a bunch of thirsty men."

"Yes, sir, commander, sir."

"I'm not a commander, just a squad leader, but I have full authority in this section of town. Therefore, if you're not here by the time we finish at Flissy's establishment, you'll be arrested and transported to Briacap to await execution with the other traitors?"

"What traitors?"

"Somebody called Bolgog, along with two of his treasonous officers."

"When is the execution date?"

"Not sure. Three spans maybe. They're currently building their gallows."

"Thanks, nice to be informed. When I see you guys next, all drinks will be on the house."

"Good, cause we don't pay for nothing." And the men trotted down the street.

Once they were out of sight, Nanlon led his ride to the stables, checked on his son's welfare, and asked him to feed and hydrate the animal. "Hey, Natt, I'll be back shortly. Got an errand to run. I'm making varmint stew for dinner. Hope you're as hungry as I am."

"I'z starvin. Varmint stew my favorite." The boy smiled and smacked his lips together in anticipation. "Da, can I help with the fixins?"

"Of course, I hoped you would." Nanlon grabbed his satchel from the side carrier and walked outside, trying to act nonchalant, pretending things were normal. He rounded the corner and jogged up the street to the Postal Tower. "Whew, no guards." He scribbled a message and handed it to the mail clerk.

Tabahir under occupation. Briacap burning. Bolgog and officers captured, pending execution. Enemy surveillance everywhere. Don't reply to message. —Nanlon

"Sir, I've been ordered by the military not to send messages."

"Just do it. I'll take responsibility." He watched as the young woman placed his message inside a small leather carrier pouch attached to the back of a homing flyer. Following the bird's release, Nanlon returned to the Copper Rail. Before he entered the stables to explain to Natt about the situation in Tabahir, he wiped more sweat from his brow.

CHAPTER 28

COMPLICATED SITUATION

Squad Leader Bonarb arrived in Beayama during postcycle. Seeing his distress, the safeguards opened their main city gate and rushed down the tower steps to assist him. By the time the guards approached, he had fallen off his kack and was lying on his face in the dirt. His torn clothing and bloodied body indicated he had endured a tragic event. They carried him to the mender's home and summoned Lady Saephira and Captain Maximus. While Ottaar cleaned his wounds and applied healing salve, Saephira and Max arrived.

"Can I question him?" asked Max.

"It would be better if he rested until he recovers his health," advised Ottaar. "He needs—"

"I'll talk." Bonarb's reply was barely audible. "I have to tell . . . what happened."

Max raised a finger to his mouth and shushed those in the room. "Go on, Bonarb."

The colleagues listened intently as Bonarb described the flashes of fire in the skyline, the aggressor's approach, how their twenty men were outnumbered fifteen to one, and about the Militia's valiant efforts in defending Ritwell. "Chepho and I were the last two resisting the horde when he ordered me to retreat and give our captain the battlefield report." He stared at Max with sadness in his eyes. "The last view I had of my brother was of him lying on the ground, surrounded by the enemy." Bonarb began to weep.

Max waited for a moment as the squad leader composed himself, and then asked, "Are there militia . . ."

The mender put up her hand to stop him. "Captain, I think we should allow Bonarb to—"

"No, I promised my brother. Ask your questions." Bonarb's voice seemed to grow stronger, more determined.

"Are there militia survivors?"

"Only me, sir."

"And Bayegulf's residents?"

"Many died during the skyfire assault. We helped some of the wounded evacuate to Ritwell before the enemy battalion marched on the village. Their contingent contained three hundred warriors or more, all wearing silver breastplate armor."

Max glanced at the gathering group of onlookers, confirming, "It's probably iron half-plate."

"Whenever we released a volley of arrows, they covered their heads with shields, one person holding it over the soldier next to him, creating a shell. Very few arrows hit their marks. Most just bounced off."

"Sounds like a Roman turtle formation. I've seen it in action. Very effective. What else can you tell me?"

"Half of them carried double-length spears and marched in units of fifty. The spears were layered one upon the other, similar to overlapping combs."

"Pike phalanx. I've encountered those as well. The Greeks used them. They're almost impenetrable."

"Our spears were too short to engage the pikemen, so we unsheathed our blades and attacked their sword units instead. The enemy's blades were not bronze. Theirs were silver-colored, stronger, and superior. During the sword battles, several of our bronze blades bent or broke on impact."

"Iron swords, no doubt." Max patted his Gladius. "Were their blades comparable to mine?"

"Similar. Their forces didn't use bows or slings. Don't think they had any."

"I have to insist, Captain Maximus," implored Ottaar, "Bonarb must rest now. No more questions."

Max turned to face Mender Ottaar. "Yes, ma'am, I'm sorry, but learning this intel is vital for our defense, assuming we can even mount one against such overwhelming odds." When Max glanced back at Bonarb, he had closed his eyes. Max gently rubbed his shoulder. "Ya done well, recruit."

After Bonarb arrived, other survivors and escapees filtered into Beayama from Bayegulf and Ritwell Village. The injured were directed to the mender's home for treatment. Most had identical stories of horror. Jesse remained silent as they shared their accounts. Once the last individual finished describing the destruction, he asked regarding Holley's whereabouts. The women replied, "We believe she was captured, along with others, and taken to one of the village huts."

Unconcerned about residents fleeing Bayegulf and Ritwell, the southern battlegroup continued their march and repositioned north of Beayama. EdNook had ordered the three catapult transports to relocate as well. They sailed up the Lower Fork and down the Gemous River. One vessel anchored a quarter league south of Beayama. The crew offloaded their launcher and wheeled it within range of the city. They waited there for additional instructions from EdNook.

The other two transports entered the Cali River tributary. One ship stopped near the entrance to Onnie Passage and set anchor in the river. Firebombs from its hurler could reach Cali Village. The second vessel continued up the Cali River, navigating through small channels in the fords to enter Mista Lake where the crew moored at the mouth of the Upper Fork. Their catapult was in range of Falein Village and Midvill. Both ships awaited launch orders from Ruler EdNook.

Meanwhile, the two flyer messages sent from Briacap arrived in Beayama. The first one read: *Being attacked. Skyfire weapons. Expect siege next. Send troops if you can. —Bolgog.* The second simply said *Briacap has fallen.*

Understanding more about the unfolding crisis from the flyer messages and Bonarb's battlefield report, Lady Saephira called for an emergency meeting at the Great Hall. She summoned Vice-leader Narleen, the entire leadership council, Captain Gelr,

Captain Maximus, and Jesse, who asked if his associates could also attend. AliRoot tagged along with Saephira. Although childlike in her behavior, she knew the East Eskaonus Gahns better than anyone else did, and Saephira felt her unique gift of knowing things might prove helpful.

Saephira thanked everybody for coming on short notice, then turned the meeting over to Max. He read the last two flyer messages from Briacap and shared what Bonarb and the other evacuees had reported. "We need to respond to this enemy."

"Maximus is right, but let's not forget these people are distant relatives," reminded Saephira. "They were misled by Eddnok yet are still our brothers and sisters."

"Agreed, it's a complicated situation. Notwithstanding, they have invaded our lands and killed many of our residents, including twenty of my best militiamen." Max's voice became gruffer as he spoke. "We must determine the location of these skyfire launchers, which I assume are trebuchets, and the actual size of their warbands."

Narleen chimed in. "Excuse me, Maxie, I mean Captain Maximus. If Holley survived the attack on Ritwell, we need to save her and those held against their will. I think that should be our top priority." The collective voiced their agreement.

"All the more reason we ought to scout the area," Max replied. "Being a likely suicide mission, I can't order another person to risk their life. I've already lost a quarter of my militia, not to mention my friend and comrade, Chepho."

"Hey, bro, I'll do it." The room went silent.

"Sorry, kid, too dangerous."

"Not for me. I can fly fast as Superman." Jesse and Anna smiled, realizing Seth referred to a superhero character from earth comic books. Those from Eskaonus seemed puzzled by the comment.

"In the air?" questioned Saephira.

"Actually, I've never attempted to go higher. Might try it someday, dawn, I mean cycle. Arrgh, these various calendar dates get confusing. Anywho, my board hovers a few feet above the ground, and it's faster than a speeding bullet."

Saephira wanted to inquire on the subject of speeding bullets, then decided it didn't matter. She surmised his meaning, having ridden on his swift-moving hoverboard through the Nae Wilderness.

"I'll be traveling quicker than the Flash. The bad dudes will never see me coming. And even if they do, they can't pick me off because their forces don't carry bows or slings."

"And I volunteer to go with Seth. My nyeflute will keep us safe. I can play the invisibility tune."

"Much too risky, my friends, I'm afraid you'll—"

"Bro, me and Anna can do it. Rule Number Two, remember? Face your fears to overcome them."

"Max, I share your concerns," interjected Jesse, "but we both know they are the only ones who could pull this off. You and I have seen what a hoverboard and nyeflute can do."

"Bro, somebody has to search the area, right?"

AliRoot began laughing. When all eyes turned to her, she said, "Quit acting like frightened bush varmints. The cute boy and Annabelle will be fine."

"How do you know?" Max asked.

"I just do." She closed her eyelids for a moment and reopened them. "And they will return unharmed with important information."

Jesse rose to his feet. "Max, I believe we should trust the kid's insigh—"

"I'm not a kid!"

"My apologies. We should trust the young lady's insights. I've found them to be amazingly credible."

"As have I," confirmed Lady Saephira.

Max paced around the table, scratching his jaw as he considered Seth's offer. "It's almost latecycle. How long will your reconnaissance take?"

"To circle each area and check on our villages and cities?" Seth gazed at the ceiling as he calculated the timeframe. "A span, maybe two. However, we should leave now. If you gotta contact us, we both carry communicators."

Everyone looked at Max to see if he'd approve Seth's plan. "I remain unsettled with respect to this operation, howbeit, you have the go-ahead. Stay safe out there, don't take chances, and give Jesse or me radio updates as you go along. At the first sight of trouble, return immediately."

"I got it, boss! We'll check on Ritwell first and call with the lowdown." Seth stood and bowed to Ladies Saephira and Narleen, "Okay, Anna, let's dip. We're burning dayrise." And he and Annabelle raced for the exit.

The group stayed at the Great Hall, except Lurah the Postal Overseer, who walked to the mail tower to check on flyer messages. Since her summoned guests had missed the banquet, Saephira instructed kitchen servers to bring out an assortment of entrees. After enjoying the refreshments, the leadership council sat alone, pondering recent developments. Max huddled with Gelr and Saephira to talk strategy. Jesse taught the earth game of Tic-Tac-Toe to Mender Ottaar and AliRoot. With her discerning abilities, the youngster always seemed to win. Lundy knelt by a chair, clasped his hands, and prayed for divine intervention. To bide the time, Narleen quietly strummed a tune on Anna's glifstring. Even though no one noticed it, a misty cloud formed across the ceiling as she played. The mood in the building stayed somber as they waited for Seth and Anna's return.

CHAPTER 29

KACK PATROL

After exiting the Great Hall, Seth assembled his hoverboard and beckoned Anna to climb on behind him. He balanced the shuttle for two riders and took off for the city gate. "Unlock the door, dudes. We're leaving on a secret mission by order of Captain Maximus." As soon as the safeguards cracked open the gate, Seth leaned right, engaged the foot pedals, and the two flew out the exit, racing toward Ritwell Village. The dimming sky indicated latecycle had begun.

When Seth approached Ritwell, Anna began piping the invisibility tune. Seth brought his hovercraft to a slow stop, and the two disembarked. Anna continued playing her nyeflute as Seth folded his board and tucked it into his satchel. They noticed twenty soldiers in plated armor milling about. Their pikes were stacked together forming a tripod. Two of the men circled a large hut, stopping occasionally to drink from their skins. Anna and Seth inched nearer. She could smell the strong odor of kunakk on their breaths as they passed by. The song worked perfectly, and the guards had no idea two people stood merely a pace away. They waited for guards to walk behind the hut before Seth slowly drew the entrance flap aside, and the duo snuck inside, finding approximately thirty villagers.

Holley was kneeling in front of a badly burnt woman, trying to comfort her. Others sat motionless with blank stares on their faces. Some were lying down, moaning in pain. In the corner, a militiaman leaned against a rear wall, bound and gagged, his clothes soaked with blood. The man's eyes were closed, and his head bent awkwardly to one side. Seth recognized him immediately as Chepho, the Militia Lead. As Anna steadily piped on her flute, Seth stalked over to Holley and whispered into her ear, "Rule Number One." Startled, she rose and glanced around, seeing nothing. A moment later, she smiled. Seth knew then that Holley had discerned the message to expect the unexpected. The two exited the hut, still veiled by the invisibility tune. Holley noticed the entrance flap open and close by itself. She concealed a grin, knelt back down by the injured woman, and continued bandaging her wounds.

Anna kept playing the song until they were outside the village where she stopped. "That's the longest arrangement I've ever attempted. My lips are getting dry."

"Yeah, but it kept us hidden. Grab a drink from your waterskin and wet your lips while I make a report."

"Who are you calling?"

"I'll try JW first; he's on channel five. Max uses channel three, except he usually lets Narleen hold and operate his device. I think he's more of a pony express kind of guy."

"Funny, although I'm not sure Max would think so." Anna loaded a stone in her sling, "I'll stand guard in case a sentry spots us, and we need to defend ourselves."

"Kack Patrol to headquarters."

Jesse chuckled at Seth's constant use of clichés adapted from TV programs. He recognized the play on words. Rat Patrol was a show about an elite squad of comrades who traveled through treacherous enemy territory to conduct operations. *I guess Seth's mission does have similarities.* "Go ahead, Seth. I'll turn up the volume so everyone can hear."

Seth reported the situation in Ritwell and ended the update by saying, "Tell Bonarb his brother is alive."

"Hold on a moment. Max wants to talk to you." Jesse passed Captain Maximus the radio.

"You saw Chepho? Is he okay?"

"No, the dude's in pretty bad shape. We oughta get him out of there, along with the other captives."

"Understood. Captain Gelr and I have been talking, and we may have a way to rescue them."

"Cool, what's the plan?"

"It involves Chief Phauch and his company of militia guarding our ship anchored near Outlook Point. At this point, it's tentative. I'll fill in the details after you finish your observations. Right now, I need you or Anna to give the chief one of your walkie-talkies. Do you have time for an extra stop?"

"No problemo. However, Anna and I had better scoot out of here if we hope to stay ahead of the coppers. Kack Patrol signing off."

Seth and Anna mounted the hovercraft and sped toward Outlook Point. As they approached the ship, Phauch hailed them. "What are you two doing out here? Taking a little sightseeing tour on your flying wheelbarrow?" Phauch laughed as he descended the boat ramp to talk face to face with his visitors. "You know, we haven't heard anything for cycles. What's the good word from town?"

"There is none," replied Seth. "I don't have time to explain. Max wanted you to have a radio." Anna handed Phauch her unit. "I'll show you how to use it; then we gotta dip. Anna and I are on special assignment."

"Is this one of those talking things Raydoo and Calrin told me about?"

"Apparently, no one keeps their mouth shut anymore. Yeah, we have five of them. Each one dialed to a certain frequency. I'm on channel one. You're holding Anna's communicator; it's set to channel two. Max and Lady Narleen's transceiver uses channel three, and Jesse can be reached on channel five."

"You said five radios. Who operates the fourth one?"

"Lundy, before he gave it to . . . ah, never mind. It's a long story. Just don't use channel four."

"Alright, I'll try to remember who has what."

"Don't let the details bury ya. Max said he'd be calling soon regarding a military objective. To answer the call, talk into the little screen on the front. He'll explain everything. The bottom line is . . . some bad dudes have invaded us. Well, Anna and me gotta book it. More places to reconnoiter. Later gator!"

Seth and Anna sped south to Bayegulf. They stopped for a moment to view the devastation and count the vessels along the coastline. "Kack Patrol to Headquarters. Seventeen sailing crafts docked at the port. One is flying a gold-striped banner. It's probably the flagship. We're moving on. I'll give my final report when we return. Patrol out."

Max related the reconnaissance report to the gathered leaders. Even though he tried to sound upbeat, downcast eyes indicated their despair. One leader stated the obvious. "We have one ship and this enemy has almost twenty. If they have the same amount in the Hallet Sea, we're outnumbered forty-to-one in ships alone. And if we add in the battlegroups they landed, it seems to me we are already defeated."

"You're only defeated if you think you are," Maximus replied.

Still distraught, the leader responded, "I assume this is Rule Number Six."

"If it isn't, it should be. Either way, take it to heart."

"I agree," enjoined Jesse. "Panicking doesn't help the situation; let's wait on the full scouting report. In the meantime, I suggest we think on positive things."

"Aye, good advice. Whenever old Lundy feels defeated, I remembers a saying from me favorite book. For those who are interested, it's found in Philippians 4:8: 'Finally, brethren, whatsoever things are true, whatsoever things *are* honest, whatsoever things *are* just, whatsoever things *are* pure, whatsoever things *are* lovely, whatsoever things *are* of good report; if *there be* any virtue, and if *there be* any praise, think on these things.'" The encouragements from Maximus, Jesse, and Lundy seemed to quell the doubts, at least for now.

Meanwhile, Seth and Anna crossed the Lower Fork and approached the Gemous River, finding a transport anchored in the river directly south of Beayama. Nearby on the riverbank, a crew had set up their catapult. The sailors spotted them as they whizzed past but did nothing more than look, probably thinking they had seen an apparition.

They followed the Cali River and noted a second vessel anchored near the ford at Onnie Passage and a third at the mouth of the Upper Fork, both armed with launchers. They circled Falein Village, entered the Neutral Lands, and passed by Tabahir. The city was guarded by foreign troops. Since twilight was upon them, they veered south to Yarm Vineyards, finding no enemy presence. Seth turned right and followed the road back to Beayama. The way appeared clear other than a large battlegroup, which had erected tents north of the city. He moved closer so Anna could conduct a quick count. She estimated the force to be three hundred soldiers. Before sentries spotted them, Seth turned his hoverboard around and raced for the city, arriving at nightrise.

No sooner had Seth and Anna entered the Great Hall, than a flyer from Tabahir arrived. Lurah rushed over to deliver the message:

Tabahir under occupation. Briacap burning. Bolgog and officers captured, pending execution. Enemy surveillance everywhere. Don't reply to message. —Nanlon

After digesting the message from Tabahir, the group listened to Seth and Anna's report. Although both were discouraging, they tried to stay optimistic. Subsequently, a discussion of all relevant intel yielded results, and Beayama's leadership hatched a strategy to rescue Holley and the prisoners held in Ritwell. Sadly, the leaders deemed any attempt to reach Briacap and save the commanders from execution as impossible. Saephira dismissed the meeting. Max instructed those involved in the rescue operation at Ritwell to report one span prior to firstlight for a final briefing.

CHAPTER 30

RESCUE THE CAPTIVES

Darkness still lingered a span before firstlight. Holding torches, Jesse, Annabelle, and Seth made their way to the Great Hall from Ottaar's home where they had been staying. Two safeguards stood at the entrance, spears in hand, guarding the hall's entryway. Maximus and Narleen were already inside. Max sat at the central table, holding a communicator as he studied an unfolded map. Narleen rushed around, helping kitchen staff set out platters with kin rolls, bowls of fresh yarm berries, and pots of Azollie tea for those who would be attending later. Saephira, her leadership council, and Captain Gelr were due to arrive at forecycle.

Max had decided to use the Hall as a command and control center for this cycle's rescue attempt at Ritwell. Max stood when he noticed his three colleagues and motioned for them to join him at the table for the briefing.

"Thanks for coming early. The rescue will take part in three phases: first, our ship decoy; second, a militia raid; and third, the retrieval of hostages. If all goes well, we should have everyone safely home by twilight. I've already talked with Chief Phauch and discussed his part of the operation. His militia company will be on the move at firstlight. As for you, Jesse, I mean team leader, sir, I wish for you to stay here and monitor calls from Seth's newly formed Kack Patrol."

"Come on, bro, don't be jiving me."

"I'm not, Seth. According to Jesse, your mobile recon unit is aptly named. It's critical to the success of our rescue mission. Therefore, I'm asking you and Miss Anna to patrol certain areas on your hoverboard and conduct reconnaissance." He pointed to the map, indicating the city's storage area by Onnie Passage, Mista Lake, the farmlands north of the enemy's main contingent, Yarm Vineyards, and the road running between Outlook Point and Beayama. "If you notice troop movements in any of these places, contact Jesse immediately. We can ill afford to be caught unaware. And try to avoid detection until your rendezvous with the Militia in Ritwell."

"What span is that?"

"Midcycle. The timeframe could change depending on circumstances; therefore, stay alert. One or more of Annabelle's nyeflute songs will probably be required for cover."

"I'm ready, Max. I memorized the invisibility, confusion, and sleeping tunes."

"Thanks, Miss Anna. As for us, Nar and I will handle communications from the Militia. Lady Saephira will arrive once the operation is under way. I understand she is taking AliRoot to Ellee's Place to break their fast with her famous yarm berry tarts."

"I'll conduct a second briefing for those not participating in the actual rescue. During the foray, we'll monitor the progress using radios. At first, I wasn't too keen on using them. Now I see their advantage over homing flyers. No doubt, there will be unknowns to deal with." Max released a deep sigh. "There always are in such endeavors. Hopefully, our surprise raid will catch the enemy off guard. This may be our only opportunity to rescue the prisoners before the aggressors besiege Beayama or launch a fiery catapult assault."

"Any questions?" The three shook their heads no. "Good, then we're ready. May God grant us favor."

At firstlight, Phauch and his company of twenty militiamen mounted their kacks, crossed the Gemous River, and rode toward Heill Void. Immediately following their departure, the skipper of Beayama's lone surviving ship, and his five sailors, pulled out their quant poles and began pushing their vessel down the Gemous

River toward the first ford. They navigated through a small channel in the waterway and continued. As their vessel approached the Ritwell area, the sailors hauled a barrel of yarm from the hold, placed it on the deck, and cracked open the lid. They spread partially eaten loaves of kin across the mess table and dropped half-full skins of yarm on the benches and floor, hoping to leave the impression their crew had left in a hurry. Once the vessel was directly north of the village, the crew stowed the quants and raised their two battened sails. After double-checking his ruse, the skipper sounded three long blasts on his horn. He knew the occupation force would hear the noise and see the raised sails. Having accomplished their part of the plan, the sailors abandoned ship and raced for Yarm Vineyards to hide among the rows of berry bushes.

The horn blasts and appearance of the Beay craft drew the attention of the soldiers guarding Ritwell Village. The occupiers decided to leave their pikes behind and hike to the river to investigate. The junior officer took sixteen cohorts with him, leaving four sentries to secure the village. Two watched the entrance while two guarded the hut holding their captives.

With swords drawn, the warriors approached the vessel with caution. The officer snapped his fingers at the bunch on his left. "I want you five to swim out, board her, and conduct a search."

A few moments passed. Suddenly, one of the men leaned over the rail and yelled, "It's abandoned, sir. The crew must have left in a hurry because food and drink is scattered everywhere."

"Check the hold."

"I did already. It's empty."

"Well, men, it looks like we have a free meal." The officer sheathed his sword and ordered his unit to do the same. "I don't know about you guys, but I haven't eaten a thing since we landed, and I'm starving. Let's go enjoy the bounty. Afterwards, we'll burn the old scow. The Beays won't miss it . . . much." Enjoying the sarcasm, the detachment joined their leader in a burst of hardy laughter.

From a secure vantage point west of Ritwell, Seth spoke into his walkie-talkie. "Kack Patrol to JW. The dudes have taken the bait. Other than a handful of soldiers, Ritwell Village is unguarded. Main roadway is clear, too. The battlegroup hasn't budged since firstlight. Standing by for orders."

"Good job, guys. Hold a moment while Max and I confer." A short pause followed. "Okay, the rescue is a go. Max just radioed Phauch with your report. The Militia has been hiding near the western edge of the Heill Void, waiting for the order to advance. They're on the move now and should reach Ritwell by midcycle. You're to rendezvous with them but stay hidden until needed. Wait for our militia to eliminate the remaining guards and then assist them with the prisoner extraction."

"Got it. Seth and Anna out."

After Phauch received the call to begin the raid, the Militia climbed on their animals and swooped into the village from the Void. Other than the four sentries who drew their swords, the village appeared empty. It took less than a moment of swordplay before the Militia outmatched the guards. The defeated foes surrendered and tossed aside their weapons. Four militiamen stripped the Gahns of their armor and stacked it in a pile, then marched them behind an outbuilding and bound their hands and feet. Concerned about their cuts and wounds, Phauch asked one of his men to bandage them. "And I need two more guys to gather stray rides. According to the scouting report, we have thirty people to transport. We'll require at least five more mounts."

While the militiamen searched for additional kacks, Seth and Anna appeared out of nowhere. Still holding her nyeflute, Anna jumped off the hovercraft and sprinted to the hut detaining Holley and the villagers. Seth followed behind her. The frightened hostages were huddled together in the rear of the shanty. As soon as Seth raised the entrance flap, Holley scurried over, kissed him on the cheek, and then hugged Anna. "I'd given up hope of being rescued. We all had. Then yestercycle, I heard a voice whisper in my ear, Rule Number One. I didn't see anyone and thought I'd imagined it, yet when the shelter flap opened and closed by itself, I knew you would rescue us. Thank you, Seth."

"It wasn't just me. Anna kept us hidden with her amazing nyeflute."

Annabelle smiled. "I used the invisibility tune. It allowed us to sneak into Ritwell and search for survivors."

"We have about thirty individuals. A few are from Bayegulf; the rest are from the village."

"Can they travel?" inquired Anna.

"The majority can. Some of the injured require assistance."

"Hunky-dory. The Militia is outside, ready to transport them to safety. Everybody will have to ride double. As for you, Jesse instructed us to bring you directly to Beayama on my hoverboard."

"I can't leave with you; the villagers are counting on me. With their elders either dead or missing, I'm their only leader. Besides, they consider me as their mender." Holley showed them the purple-tasseled sash wrapped around her waist. "However, you can transport Lead Chepho. He's badly injured and should have immediate mending by Ottaar."

"I'll be okay." Chepho tried to rise, stumbled, and dropped back on the floor mat.

"Lay still or you'll reopen your wounds. That's an order from your doctor."

"Yes, mender, I only meant to—"

"Shush . . . close your eyes and try to rest. You must save your strength. Seth and Anna will take you to town shortly." No sooner had she finished speaking when Chepho began to snore. "Good, he's sleeping." Holley motioned to the others. "The rest of you follow me outside. Hurry, hurry, no time to waste."

First, they loaded the injured, one behind each militiaman; the remaining captives doubled up on the five extra animals. Prior to departing, Phauch called Maximus on the radio and reported their rescue mission was a success. The Militia, along with the freed villagers, retreated into Heill Void, and then turned north toward Yarm Vineyards. The plan was to hide in the vineyards until postcycle.

The seventeen Gahns feasted until they could eat no more. They enjoyed the sweet-tart taste of the strange liquid in the waterskins. After plundering the supplies, the men confiscated the rest of the bounty to share with those guarding the village. In a final act of spite, the troops set the ship on fire and then returned to Ritwell. Not having immunity to yarm berries, the soldiers began feeling sick to their stomachs. By the time they reached the outskirts of the village, small pink rashes had broken out on their faces. The junior officer put those concerns aside when he noticed the village entrance and prisoner hut were unguarded. "Go find those fools. I'll discipline them myself." The unit dropped their bounty and began scouring the area.

Anna kept watch, peeking through a gap in the wall. As the detachment drew nearer, she readied her nyeflute. "Alright, Seth, time to plug your ears. Trust me; you don't want to hear this melody."

"What about Chepho?"

"He's sound asleep, so he won't suffer the effects." She stepped outside the hut and yelled, "Over here, gentlemen!"

Seth followed behind her and shouted, "Yeah, come get us!" The men drew their swords and charged forward. When Anna felt they were close enough, she began playing the confusion tune. Blank stares appeared on the soldier's faces. Some walked forward, then backwards. Several spun in circles. Others bounced off one another like pinballs.

She lowered her flute and motioned Seth to unplug his ears. "Time to go. I don't know how long these effects last."

"Long enough for us to escape I hope. And if not, the yarm left on the ship may slow them down to a crawl."

"You think they have yarm berry poisoning?"

"Correctamundo. It was part of the plan. Apparently, these guys don't grow yarm berry plants in East Eskaonus, so their residents have never developed a resistance. Don't worry, though, the sailors diluted the yarm with water. The dudes won't die, at least not from pink berry juice, but they'll sure feel sicker than a dog for a couple cycles. According to Max, we need every advantage if we're gonna save our realm."

Seth assembled his hovercraft and helped Chepho aboard. Anna held on to him as they weaved their way past seventeen confused soldiers and exited the village. Ten moments later, they arrived at Beayama and hailed a safeguard to unlock the city gate. They took Chepho to Ottaar's home and settled him into an upstairs room. The mender removed his torn clothing, applied Helixzon salve to his cuts and wounds, wrapped them in fresh bandages, and gave Chepho clean garments to wear. Prior to tucking him into bed for nightrise, she poured him a cup of healing-leaf tea.

CHAPTER 31

GRATITUDES AND REALITIES

Phauch's scouting patrols reported no troop movements, so during postcycle, the chief and his company of militiamen left their hiding spots in the Yarm Vineyards and galloped down the road to Beayama, arriving at twilight. On the way, he noticed their last ship, the one they had protected at Outlook Point, smoldering in the river across from Ritwell. Sadness gripped his heart. *Why did they have to burn it?* Lower Realm's entire fleet was now lost at sea or destroyed.

When he arrived in the city, Phauch dropped the severely injured at Ottaar's home to receive mending and delivered the remaining captives to housing locations reserved for the refugees. He thanked his men for a mission well done, dismissed them to see to their families, dropped his kack off at the stables, and headed for the command center in the Great Hall.

Lady Saephira had called for a leadership meeting to update her colleagues on recent events. Seth and Anna arrived earlier and were sharing with Lurah about the successful rescue. Phauch joined the discussion, adding in subsequent details. Assuming a long nightrise lay ahead, Narleen asked her kitchen servers to set out a special banquet fare. The individuals present included both military captains, their leadership council, Jesse, his associates, and AliRoot who hung close by Saephira's side. Ottaar and Holley couldn't attend because they were treating those injured during the recent attacks.

After everyone had dined, Lady Saephira rose to address the group. "Thank you for being here at this late span. We have endured several trying cycles. This gathering tonight is part celebration, part memorial. Due to limited seating, I was unable to invite our residents. However, I have scheduled a communitywide break-the-fast assembly for the morrow in the town square. Due to the circumstances and the number of people lost, we will not display our normal memorial tables at this event; therefore, don't bring keepsakes. Instead, we'll have a quiet time of reflection for those who have forfeited their lives. Ellee has agreed to host the meal and provide her famous yarm berry tarts. There will be no service, just a period of mourning for our loved ones. Right now, though, we want to mention a few of those who participated in the rescue operation. Lady Narleen, if you will." And Saephira sat down.

Narleen moved to the front of the table, glanced at Max for assurance, then began: "Seth, Annabelle, and Phauch were instrumental in saving the captives at Ritwell. Sadly, many others perished in service of the realm. We need to honor them, if not by name, at least by their heroic deeds. Let us remember the militiamen who made the ultimate sacrifice defending Bayegulf and Ritwell, our displaced residents who resisted the enemy, those in Briacap and Tabahir under occupation, and Bolgog and his commanders whose lives are in jeopardy." She stopped suddenly; her cheeks turned red. "This invasion is so senseless . . ." A moan erupted and Narleen began to cry. Max rushed over to hold her as she sobbed. "Sorry, I am too upset to say more."

Max escorted his spouse to her seat and waited, not sure what to do, realizing he was next on the agenda to speak. Lady Saephira rose to address the gathering once more. "As you can see, these are difficult times, filled with much heartache. Please make plans to attend the dayrise memorial and remember what your vice-leader said about honoring our heroes. I urge you to spread the word." She gestured to Max. "I've asked Captain Maximus to give us a strategic update." After Max strode to the front, Saephira hurried to Narleen's seat, wrapped arms around her distressed friend, and tried to console her.

Captain Maximus started by thanking Phauch and the

Militia for a successful raid. Subdued cheers echoed throughout the hall. Several approached Phauch and patted him on the back, sharing their appreciation. When the acclamations subsided, Max gave his military assessment of their current situation. "We have lost a quarter of our militia at Ritwell. Only Chepho and his brother survived. At most, we have forty militiamen left. With twenty safeguards, this makes a defensive force of sixty. We are facing three hundred highly trained soldiers, wearing plated armor, and carrying superior iron swords. Half their forces are fielding pikes, organized into phalanxes. We have the advantage with bows and slings, whereas they have catapults. The three launchers we know about are within range of our local cities and villages. I assume our adversaries have the same number catapults in Upper Realm, which they've already used against Briacap. More such skyfire attacks would be devastating. Although we can field mounted troops, they would have little success against their pike units. These are the hard truths."

"Being outnumbered, a counter offensive is out of the question. It would likely fail. Defending the city is our best option. Accordingly, we should prepare for a frontal assault, an extended siege, or both. What say ye?"

The group responded, "Rule Number Five, Rule Number Five."

"Okay, then we will stand our ground."

More shouts erupted. "Rule Number Six, Rule Number Six."

"Correct. We are only defeated if we think we are. Therefore, be encouraged. The battle is not yet lost." While Max recommended defensive postures at the gates and took questions from the leadership council, Jesse withdrew his journal and began an entry:

Entry Twenty-One

I already knew the situation in Eskaonus wasn't wonderful. Now that I hear firsthand reports regarding the invasion, I'm brokenhearted. It seems all the good we did here may be for naught. In the last few days, two huge battlegroups from the east have landed and are massing for battles. Fire-laden bombardments have burned the port city of Bayegulf to the ground. Tabahir and Ritwell Village are under occupation by hostile forces. Briacap has surrendered. Opposition forces have captured their military leaders and according to reports, plan to hang them on the gallows soon.

Seven ships in our fleet are gone. This enemy has at least forty sailing vessels, half of those anchored off the coast of Bayegulf in the Nether Sea. Three transports in this group carry catapults. According to QuiQuot, a person I met while scouting Gahneeha, the other twenty are in the Hallet Sea. Some of those are also equipped with catapults that the aggressors employed against Briacap.

These catapults launch projectiles that burn like napalm, destroying everything they touch. Perhaps we can outlast a land siege at Beayama but not their firepower. As for the local villages, they don't have a snowball's chance in Hades of surviving an aerial strike. The only good news is that we freed thirty residents held captive in Ritwell.

It appears the meeting is breaking up. Time to end this log. I'll write more later.

Narleen had gained her composure by the time Max finished answering the last query. She rose and walked over to the next table where Annabelle sat. "Anna, would you sing us a song?" Narleen unstrapped the glifstring from her shoulder. "Hoping you might say yes, I brought it with me. It's more yours than mine. I've enjoyed the instrument and its unique music. Even so, I never learned how to play it properly—not like you, anyway. I think it responds better to the touch of the original owner." Narleen smiled, handed Anna the glifstring, and retook her seat.

Annabelle held the eight-stringed instrument in a respectful manner, almost caressing it. Her eyes grew misty. She wiped the moisture away, adjusted her shoulder strap, and began picking a sweet, harmonious melody. "This hymn is one of my favorites. An Irish poet from a faraway land wrote it. Whenever I'm discouraged, I sing the words to focus my vision on eternal things."

> *Be Thou my Vision, O Lord of my heart;*
> *Naught be all else to me, save that Thou art.*
> *Thou my best Thought, by day or by night,*
> *Waking or sleeping, Thy presence my light.*

Be Thou my battle Shield, Sword for the fight;
Be Thou my Dignity, Thou my Delight;
Thou my soul's Shelter, Thou my high Tower:
Raise Thou me heavenward, O Power of my power.

High King of Heaven, my victory won,
May I reach Heavens joys, O bright Heaven's Sun!
Heart of my own heart, whatever befall,
Still be my Vision, O Ruler of all.

The words were mesmerizing, Anna's voice refreshing, like the morning dew. During the song, a misty cloud formed above them. No one asked for an explanation. They knew the mystical phenomenon as the anointing.

Once the song ended, Lady Saephira dismissed the meeting. With renewed vision in their hearts, the group gradually dispersed to their homes. Max caught up to Jesse before he left the room. "Sir, can I have a word?"

"Sure Max, what is it?"

Maximus hesitated until they were the last two in the hallway. "With your former military experience in the Navy back on earth, I'm sure you've already discerned that our options are limited. In fact . . ." He glanced around to make sure nobody else was listening, "there are none."

"You once told me there were always options."

"Not this time, sir. Not for us. We might be able to resist a siege for a week, but if our adversaries launch more of those liquid-fire projectiles, we will not survive." He drew in a deep breath, held it, and then released it slowly. "However, you might."

"How so?"

"You can gather the collective and portal back to heaven before the final attack, which we both know is merely a matter of time."

"Not an alternative for me, Max. I'm staying. I'll check with the others. Knowing them, I don't think they'll leave either. The Eskaonites are our friends. We are not turning tail to run home simply because times are difficult. Besides, I believe in your Rule

Number Six."

"Sir, I can no longer guarantee anyone's safety."

"Do you remember when my soul became discouraged after the disaster on Onnie Passage? I blamed myself for the tragedy and no longer wanted to lead the team."

"I do. You nearly scuttled our outreach."

"You said if I didn't quit, you'd follow me through the fiery abyss. Well, it sounds as if we're facing one. You didn't forsake me then, and I'm not going to abandon you or the Eskaonite people now."

"Jesse, I . . ." Max's eyes teared up as he grabbed his friend's arms in the comrade's embrace. Nothing more was said. The two left the building, struck torches, and walked home: Max to Residential Hall and Jesse to the mender's home. Outside, darkout covered the land.

The next cycle, as promised, Saephira held her dayrise assembly in the town square for the entire city. No sooner had the meal started, than alarm bells began to ring. Assault forces moved into positions surrounding Beayama. They carried battering rams.

CHAPTER 32

WAR IN HEAVEN AND EARTH

While Eddnok's forces invaded the Upper and Lower Realms of Eskaonus, Satan, the great dragon, declared war on heaven. He had gathered his demons and devils in a final attempt to overthrow God. In a coordinated response, Archangel Michael summoned his warrior angels to defend against the dragon's onslaught of evil. From Central Heaven, the seventh trumpet sounded its warning (Revelation 11:15). The last woe had begun. The events that followed would impact all of eternity.

As soon as elChesed heard the seventh trumpet, he transported to the Throne Room, hoping to catch Uzziel and volunteer for the upcoming battle. He knew this conflict was one that heaven must win, or all might be lost. Noticing the high cherub with his wings unfolded as if he were ready to take flight, he hurried over. "Excuse me, Uzziel." Chesedel bowed, showing respect for a higher-ranked angel. "May I have a word?"

"Of course, Chesedel, except you'll need to be quick. Michael has ordered our first-order cherubim to set defensive lines around each portal. I'm heading to the White Pearl Gate to guard it. Satan has gathered his forces from the unseen realms, and he's on the attack. The devil has threatened to do this for ages—and now it's happening—as foretold in prophecies from Revelation."

"Yes, I know. That's why I'd like to add my sword to the battle."

"Normally, we would welcome it. Your priority, however, is Jesse Walt and our off-realm envoys. If things on Eskaonus remain tenable, then indeed, you may add your blade to this fight. On the subject of brands, please unsheathe yours."

Chesedel removed his heavenly Gladius and held it at his side. "I'm not sure why—"

"Extend it toward me." Uzziel withdrew his sword from its scabbard. Flaming bursts of light erupted in every direction. Holding it in his left hand, *the Cherubim* raised his fiery weapon high overhead and in one swift motion, swung it downwards, hitting Chesedel's blade. Immediately, it caught fire and began to glow. The guardian's eyes widened as he watched his brand transform.

"Congratulations, elChesed! Because of your faithfulness, the Alpha and Omega has promoted you. You'll join the legions of the cherubim. You are a third-order cherub. It's an honored position in the kingdom of God—not an archangel status or first-order cherubim such as myself—albeit, a very high rank, nonetheless. You will no longer be a guardian angel. Instead, you'll oversee other protectors, including sentinels and winged ones. Moreover, I have removed the obligation to report to me concerning outreaches in the outer realms. From now on, you have the authority to make your own decisions. Still, I'd appreciate being kept apprised about such matters, especially the ones relating to Jesse and his associates, but I'll leave those choices to you."

"I don't know what to say."

"You need say nothing. You have earned this rank through God's favor. And when He feels you're ready, you'll be promoted to our second order."

"Will I have wings like other cherubim?"

"In time, yes. You'll also notice an increase in wisdom and spiritual discernment."

"What do you recommend I do, I mean, as my first action?"

"I suggest sheathing your glowing blade." Uzziel smiled, enjoying the jest. "Your brand is the same as mine; strong enough to defeat any demonic adversary. In fact, it can slice an opening in space-time itself, creating portals to multiple worlds and dimensions."

"I will use the weapon wisely."

"I'm sure you will. That's why you have one. I have a feeling it will soon come in handy."

Overwhelmed, tears flowed down Chesedel's cheeks. "Please accept my sincere—"

"You are welcome, brother." Uzziel sheathed his sword. Even in the scabbard, it radiated light. "I wish you Godspeed. I have full confidence in your decisions regarding the outcome on Eskaonus and elsewhere. Sorry to rush this conversation. With the battle for the soul of heaven looming, I must take my leave." And Uzziel vanished, slipping into the unseen realm.

Chesedel had already read Jesse's recent logs. ***Entry Nineteen*** mentioned the missing fleet, unfamiliar sailing vessels, and an ancient map showing a settlement in the east. ***Entry Twenty*** reported Eddnok survived the Lost Forest, escaped to a place called Gahneeha, and had tricked the city's elders into believing he was their promised messiah. Even worse, Eddnok planned to exact his revenge on Lady Saephira and Commander Bolgog whom he considered as traitors. The news was quite disconcerting. Chesedel wondered if Jesse had written a subsequent entry. He zipped across to the Hall of Records and discovered ***Entry Twenty-One*** had just arrived in the scroll room.

This latest log alarmed him the most. Eddnok's battlegroups had already landed in the Upper and Lower Realms, devastated two cities with firebombs, defeated the resistance, occupied settlements, and were currently massing for a final attack on Beayama. Unless there was intervention, the whole land would be conquered or destroyed.

With his flaming brand, Chesedel could easily route the entire invading force, but such actions would be contrary to the angelic code. Although there were certain exceptions, non-interference was the role angels had played through countless wars and holocausts. They could only take matters into their own hands when directed by the Spirit of God. As far as the conflict on Eskaonus, the Spirit had not given elChesed such authority. Indirect intervention, however, might be allowed.

He flew to the Supplication Garden and knelt down to seek a solution. Like lightening, an idea flashed through his mind.

Perhaps it came from the advanced discernment Uzziel mentioned. If the plan worked, it would be a way to aid his envoys without breaking the code that restricted direct involvement.

Chesedel raced over to the Rose Pearl Gate, pictured Camayah in his mind, and instantly disappeared into the unseen realm. Moments later, he arrived in the Camayah system. He flew past Moon Ethade and stopped. Unsheathing his sword, he sliced a rift in the outer atmosphere, creating a time-displacement window in space. God's newly appointed cherub entered the tunnel, bending it one way then the other, until he arrived in the skies above Beayama in Eskaonus.

Even though darkout covered the land, his angelic sight allowed him to observe the invasion forces surrounding the city and nearby villages. An attack seemed imminent. Knowing the envoys stayed at Mender Ottaar's place, he flew to her house and passed through the roof. Staying in the unseen realm, he entered Annabelle's bedroom. She was asleep, dreaming about worms tunneling through a silvery hole. Since angels must take solid form in order to minister, he materialized. He gently placed a hand on her shoulder; his fingers glowed with a bright golden light as encouragement infused her soul. She awoke and grinned. "Oh, Chesedel, it's you. I was just . . ."

The angelic messenger quickly touched Anna's forehead, causing her to fall into a deep sleep. He leaned over and whispered into her ear, "Continue your dream, Annie. It will make sense later."

Taking care to remain hidden, he slipped into the adjacent guestrooms. After administering encouragement to Jesse, Seth, Lundy, and Holley, he reentered the unseen realm.

Next, elChesed stopped by Residential Hall, finding Max and Narleen huddled together in bed. He could sense the child growing in her belly. He materialized and touched her slightly rounded stomach. The baby moved inside her womb. *It would be a girl.* He smiled, then slipped into the invisible realm and departed.

Finally, he approached Saephira's chambers. Passing through the wall, he found her asleep on the bed with AliRoot snoozing on a nearby settee. They were both having the same dream as Annabelle. Chesedel felt the Spirit's presence in

Saephira's quarters. *Hmm, that's interesting. I guess I'm not the only one out ministering this night, am I, Lord?* Staying in the unseen realm, he simply waved his hand, releasing an anointing. With the first part of his plan completed, he left the city, flew upwards and reentered the wormhole, arriving back in the Camayah system. Chesedel soared past the three moons, reaching Sector One during dusk.

First, he visited Runess at the Airship Dock, and second, Cndrek at RIFT I. Still veiled in the invisible realm, he whispered into their dreams. "Fly past the second moon, towards the new dawn. A portal to save your friends lies there." Chesedel planted an image in their minds of a flaming sword opening a silvery gap in space. Feeling he had accomplished his task without breaking the angelic code, the cherub returned to help fight the war in heaven.

War in Heaven

"And there was war in heaven: Michael and his angels fought against the dragon; and the dragon fought and his angels, And prevailed not; neither was their place found any more in heaven. And the great dragon was cast out, that old serpent, called the Devil, and Satan, which deceiveth the whole world: he was cast out into the earth, and his angels were cast out with him. And I heard a loud voice saying in heaven, Now is come salvation, and strength, and the kingdom of our God, and the power of his Christ: for the accuser of our brethren is cast down, which accused them before our God day and night. And they overcame him by the blood of the Lamb, and by the word of their testimony; and they loved not their lives unto the death. Therefore rejoice, *ye* heavens, and ye that dwell in them. Woe to the inhabiters of the earth and of the sea! for the devil is come down unto you, having great wrath, because he knoweth that he hath but a short time" (Revelation 12:7–12).

War on Earth

"And when the dragon saw that he was cast unto the earth, he persecuted the woman which brought forth the man *child*. And to the woman were given two wings of a great eagle, that she might fly into the wilderness, into her place, where she is nourished for a time, and times, and half a time, from the face of the serpent. And the serpent cast out of his mouth water as a flood after the woman, that he might cause her to be carried away of the flood. And the earth helped the woman, and the earth opened her mouth, and swallowed up the flood which the dragon cast out of his mouth. And the dragon was wroth with the woman, and went to make war with the remnant of her seed, which keep the commandments of God, and have the testimony of Jesus Christ" (Revelation 12:13–17).

MAP OF CAMAYAH

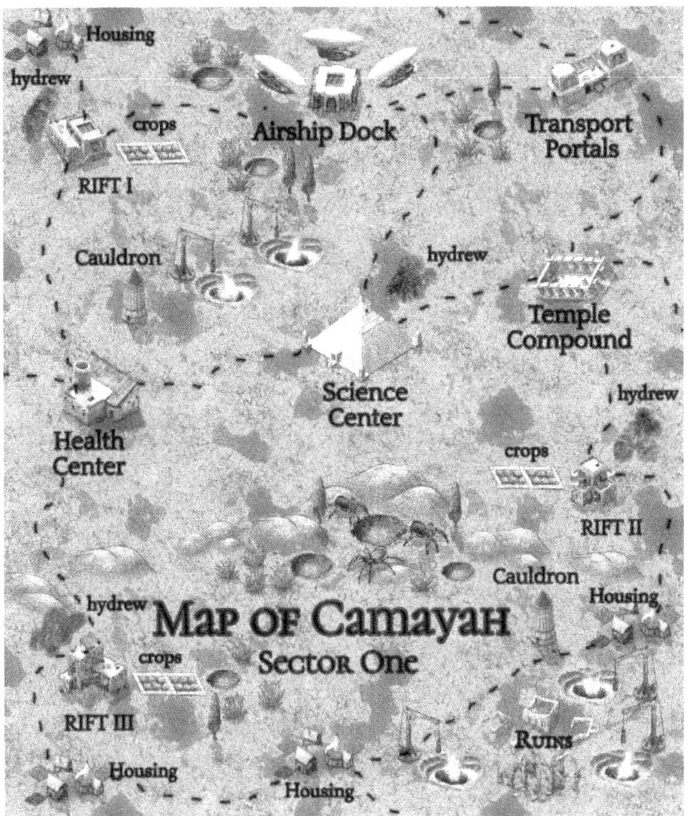

Camayah orbits a red dwarf sun, along with its three moons. The planet is slowly being terraformed after suffering a cataclysm called the Burning. The landmass is divided into Five Sectors. Flaming Triverphol pits dot the landscape. Daily activities revolve around the RIFTs.

CHAPTER 33

HAPPENINGS ON CAMAYAH

Prior to departing Camayah, Jesse's team left the Council of Twelve with two important choices. The Camayahnites could either have a better world, espousing faith, hope, and compassion, or return to a dystopian society. Fortunately, the Council chose the former and implemented the necessary changes.

Yah worshipers could now follow their religion without the threat of imprisonment or termination. The practice of reprogramming a person's mind had been halted, and the restoration process begun. Deceptions were exposed, and the cure for Triverphol Disease distributed to the populace. Terraforming of the planet had largely been successful. Trees grew around hollows; crops flourished by the RIFTs. Even the morning dew had started forming on plants for the first time since the Burning. Large underground hydrew deposits were located, pumped to the surface, and stored in ponds near the RIFTs. And the Council of Twelve met each phase at the Science Center.

At this phase's council, Layshura estimated that most sectors would be able to switch from hydration and nutrition tablets to real food in one stage. Cndrek noted the local quawners seemed less aggressive after planting soreseeds in the deep hollows. Runess reported airships had begun transporting small groups of animals to the northern sectors in an effort to repopulate the land. When all the reports were finished, Malmach offered a short prayer, set the schedule for the next meeting, and dismissed the gathering.

As the twelve councilmembers filed out, Rauteira approached Runess and Cndrek. "Fair dawn to you." Rauteira added the open-palms greeting. "Can we talk privately?"

Both men reciprocated with open-hand gestures. "Of course, Rauteira, what's on your mind?" Runess asked.

"I'm worried about Seth and his friends."

"You mean the *sent ones*?"

"Yes. I created a way to communicate with them after they left our planet."

"How?"

"By using Papa Lun's radio parts in my datatop."

"You mean Lundy?"

"Correct. I used his transmitter component as my datacomm to connect to the dataflow. Once I adapted the band frequency to our datastream, I was able to access their transceivers. I remembered Seth's talkie was set to channel one, so I tried his device, and it worked. Apparently, these units have an extremely long range."

"All the way to the high realm?"

"No, they didn't go there. Seth said they journeyed to place called Eskaonus."

"You never cease to amaze me, Rauteira. Your programming ability is par to none. So, what did Seth say that concerned you?"

"Nothing on first contact. However, I learned of a discrepancy in calendar dates. According to my calculations, for every day on Eskaonus, which they call a cycle, seventeen dawns pass here."

"Sounds like a time-placement distortion. Although never factually proven, such occurrences are rumored to exist."

Cndrek, who had remained silent while Runess and Rauteira visited, finally joined the conversation. "Forget the time theories. You said you were worried, Rauteira. What's the alarm?"

"On second contact, I found out that the inhabitants of Eskaonus are in peril. They're facing an evil lord who developed a fire weapon able to annihilate any settlement in their Upper and Lower Realms. According to Maximus, they have no defense against such weapons. Seth said if relief doesn't arrive soon, they will be toast, which I assume means dead."

"If the big guy is in trouble, we gotta do something, Runess."

"I concur. They came here to help us in our time of need. Can we do less? I feel we have an obligation to aid those in jeopardy, even if it means putting our lives at risk. Maybe it's time we become the *sent ones*."

"And how do we do that?" Cndrek wondered. "We have no idea where this place is located or how to travel there. We can't simply disappear into thin air as they did."

"I may know a way. Last dusk, I had a dream. It began somewhat strange. I was giving a ride to three children on a large quawner. We were laughing and having a good time. Suddenly, the scene changed, and I stood alone on Moon Ethade, staring into the upper atmosphere. A hand holding a sword appeared out of nowhere. It was similar to the blade Maximus carried, except this one had white flames of fire radiating from it. The sword sliced a rift in the darkness, and a hole formed, unleashing silvery light beams. They looked like little glowing worms. The whole area sparkled. Then a voice said, 'Fly past the second moon, towards the new dawn. A portal to save your friends lies there.' At predawn, I awoke rested and refreshed."

"I dreamt the same thing," confirmed Cndrek.

"About riding a quawner with kids?"

"Not the quawner part, I saw the flaming sword, a hole, and heard the voice. "Have you discerned the meaning?" pressed Cndrek.

"No, not exactly. On the other hand, what if a portal to Eskaonus does lie past Moon Ethade."

"A wormhole? Cndrek chuckled to himself. "No flyer crew has ever encountered one."

"True, and yet we both had the same dream regarding the same phenomenon on the same dusk. I say we seek out this portal, and if it's real, try to enter it. We can use my vessel, the *Old Bella*."

"Hmm . . . if what you suggest is correct, perhaps we should take two flyers in case we run into problems."

"Do you still remember how to pilot an airship, Cndrek?"

"Are you kidding? I was sailing the skies when you were barely learning how to crawl."

"Alright, two floaters it is. We have *The Seeker* harbored at the Dock for upgrades. It's getting new solar sails and a refit on the navdata terminal. Maintenance crews are also upgrading the Triverphol engines and reinforcing the air canopy. It should be ready to sail by earlydawn."

"Works for me." Cndrek grinned, glad that he'd gotten his way.

"My rowmate and midmate are outside on the *Old Bella*. They're always up for an adventure. But you'll need to locate a navigator and engineer. On short notice, I'm not certain who you can find."

"Leave it to me. I've got a couple people in mind."

"Whoever you pick must be discrete. We best keep this endeavor confidential until we're underway. The Council might consider it a foolish effort."

"I wanna go," implored Rauteira.

"I'm sorry, kid, it's too dangerous. If your parents discovered that Cndrek and I took you on a trip into the outer atmosphere, they would probably throw our heinies into a Triverphol flame pit and abandon us."

"Your dataframes might require adjustments, and I still retain Papa Lun's programming binder."

"Let's be honest, Rauteira. You just want to see Seth, right?"

"Well, yes, but I could—"

"I think you should remain here." Runess glanced at Cndrek who nodded in agreement. "Besides being aware of our plans, you're the only contact between Eskaonus and Camayah. However, you can do one thing for us."

"What?" A subdued voice revealed Rauteira's disappointment.

"Configure our communication arrays so we're able to contact them, assuming our ships survive wormhole travel and arrive in Eskaonus in one piece."

Still feeling dejected, she answered, "I guess I can incorporate their frequency into your datacomms. As I recall, Jesse's talkie is set to channel five. I'll also install channel three, although I'm not positive who uses it. Unfortunately, you won't have the enhanced range of Papa Lun's transmitter parts in your comms as I do in my datatop, so you'll need to be near a home planet or system to be heard."

"Thank you, even limited communications would be helpful."

"Are you sure I can't go with you guys."

"Sorry, Rauteira. It's—"

"I know, I know, too dangerous."

Trying to placate her displeasure, Runess added, "If we see Seth, do you have a message for him?"

Her face perked up, her eyes widened. "Tell him I . . . Oh, never mind."

"Enough talk, you two." Cndrek frowned, growing impatient with the conversation. "If we're doing this mission, we better leave before we realize how foolish it is and change our minds."

"Agreed. Let's head over to the docks and refuel while Rauteira upgrades our comms." In single file, the three exited the Science Center and boarded *Old Bella*.

CHAPTER 34

FLIGHT OF THE AIRSHIPS

At the Airship Dock, Runess and Cndrek oversaw the loading of Triverphol fuel for *Old Bella* and *The Seeker* while Rauteira began work on communications. She added the requested databands and set bypasses for channels three and five. With the refueling completed, the men agreed it was best to split up the gathering of supplies. "Come on, Rauteira, you're with me. Let's see if Uewba can teach you how to steer my airship, and after we run a few errands, I'll drop you off at your home." Eyeing Cndrek, he added, "When you finish with your share of the preflight tasks, we'll rendezvous at the old ruins. I'd like to make orbit by halfdawn. Remember, you'll need an experienced navigator and engineer." Runess offered one more admonishment concerning discretion, then he and Rauteira boarded *Old Bella* and lifted off.

Runess approached the Temple Compound first. He landed briefly inside the grounds and talked with the provost and pravost, explaining the situation. Before departing, he asked Malmach and Trikernae to pray for success in their endeavor. His next stop was the Health Center to pick up nutrition and hydration tablets. Since Rauteira had done well with minimum oversight from Uew, Runess let her guide the ship to her housing unit. Upon seeing a floater approach, her parents rushed outside, surprised to see their daughter in the navigator's post.

Once *Old Bella* had settled on the ground, Runess and

Rauteira disembarked. He explained their plan to Rekis and Leetqu, the dangers involved, and why Rauteira shouldn't travel with them. Runess asked them to pray for a successful journey and to keep the matter to themselves. As the adults exchanged farewells, Rauteira tromped off to her quarters to sulk. Leetqu promised she'd talk with her daughter later and try to smooth things over. Hoping that would lessen Rauteira's disappointment, Runess reboarded his vessel and flew to the ruins to wait for Cndrek.

After Runess departed to begin his errands, Cndrek noticed a cluster of sailors sitting idle at the mess table. "Excuse me, gentlemen. I need a couple airmen for a shakedown flight of *The Seeker*. It just finished a refit. Any volunteers?"

No one responded.

"Perhaps I should mention I'll double your pay for the dawn. How does fifty gelts sound?" Fifteen hands rose into the air. "Looking for a navigator and engineer." Two midshipmen stood to their feet. "Okay, mates, you have the jobs. Follow me. We're gonna run *The Seeker* through basic maneuvers, check her upgrades, and then retrieve some gear."

Cndrek and his crew conducted several flight tests, floated the craft to RIFT I, descended for a soft landing, and then entered the facility. "Great job, guys. It seems she handles as advertised. If you two wish to earn a twenty-gelt bonus apiece, I can use a hand loading equipment." The sailors glanced at each other, smiling. "Great. Go down one level to the storage units, and I'll join you once I check in with the S1 at our front desk." The men scurried down the stairwell as Cndrek strode to the counter.

The S1 snapped to attention upon Cndrek's approach. "Fair dawn to you, SSL. I'm surprised to see you here already. The council meeting must have ended early."

"It did. All favorable reports from the councilmembers. I'm sure their official recording will be available on the datacomm terminals by dusk."

"Glad to hear that. How may I be of service, sir?"

"Two things," replied Cndrek. "Can you tell me if Tawehna is in?"

"Yes, she lives in our temporary housing across the hall.

Tawehna walked past me one bout ago." The S1 checked his screen. "Try room H14." He stared at Cndrek, curious why he desired to see the woman, yet realizing it was unwise to question the SSL. "And the other thing, sir?"

"Passcode for our storage lockers. I'm transporting cargo to a secure location."

"The code for this dawn is 53778."

"Got it. Thanks, S1, carry on." And Cndrek rushed downstairs to meet with his helpers. "Alright, guys, let's move to the locker at the end. It has the items we seek." Cndrek punched the numbers into the keypad for unit 12 and motioned for the men to follow him through the sliding door. "We want the cubicles on the left."

Inside the first one were shelves of stunners. "Grab six quispikes and six trispikes while I check the adjacent compartment." Cndrek spotted ten sealed crates stacked along the rear wall. He pried one open and found an unassembled duespike. *I wondered if these deck guns still existed.* He replaced the cover, snatched another crate, and placed both by the exit. *If we can get these weapons to work, they might come in handy.* "Okay, men, the third cubical has an assortment of TPC power modules. I need small and medium cores, four of each; better add two large cores as well. As soon as you're finished, take all this gear up to the floater and load it in the nether deck hold."

"Why are we taking these items, sir?" asked one of the crewmen.

"We're moving them to a different location."

"What location?"

"That's classified, sailor. Just carry the supplies aboard, and hurry, I'm on a time schedule." When the men left the locker, Cndrek entered the fourth cubical and discovered boxes filled with Criunite. He gathered twenty green crystals and stuffed them into his carrier. Feeling he had secured the necessary items for their trip, he walked out of the storage unit and pushed a button on the keypad to close the door. He raced upstairs, located room H14, and knocked on the panel.

Tawehna came to the entry. "Blessings to Yah." She crossed her heart with both arms in the gesture shared among believers. "This is a surprise, sir. Tell me—"

"Sorry for the intrusion, Tawehna. The *sent ones* are in trouble." He went on to explain the situation and asked her to join the effort. "I require an experienced gunner and someone who can navigate an airship."

"Firing stunners I can do. Unfortunately, I know nothing about steering an airship. In fact, I've never been on one."

"Not a problem. I can educate you in navigation. You'll be as good as any rowmate by the time we reach orbit. I'll not kid you, Tawehna, it's a dangerous undertaking."

"Does it have something to do with flying through the outer atmosphere?"

"It does."

"Hmm . . . sounds like a confirmation. During prayer last dusk, I had a vision of a flaming sword slashing a rift in the darkness."

"It appears I knocked on the correct room then. We think this gap might be a wormhole. If so, we hope it'll deliver us to Eskaonus." Cndrek took a deep breath and exhaled slowly. "Well, can you join the expedition?"

"A wormhole, huh? Most people don't believe they're real. Still, my heart tells me to say yes. Give me an interval to pack my satchel, and I'll be ready." She quickly gathered several changes of clothes and her personal items. "I've not forgotten how the *sent ones* saved our planet. If they're in trouble, it's our turn to return the favor."

"I feel the same way." Then the two exited the RIFT and boarded *The Seeker*.

Next, the airship headed to the Science Center. Cndrek left Tawehna on board to review navigation manuals on his datatop while he and the two midshipmen entered the center. "Sorry, guys, I gotta leave you here. I'm sure you'll have no problem catching a flight back to the docks." He thanked them for their assistance and told them to expect double the gelt credits in next event's stipend, including their promised bonuses. "Remember, our efforts this dawn are classified." The men gave their bond to keep it secret.

Cndrek climbed the stairway to Level Two where he found the person he sought. Hiehew held the rank of Program Leader, the senior-most programmer at the Science Center. "You got an interval, PL?"

"For the SSL, I sure do."

"Can we talk privately?"

"Of course, let's use my workstation." The two stepped across the hallway to Hiehew's office and closed the door. "Does it involve Council of Twelve business?"

"Not exactly, although it's of critical importance." Cndrek explained the dire situation and asked for his assistance.

"How can I help?"

"Be my engineer for this mission."

"You mean fly into uncharted atmospheres, search for a speculative wormhole, and travel to a strange land in an unknown dimension."

"Yeah, I guess it sounds a bit crazy."

"Normally, I would agree. I'd probably recommend a reset on your former memory wipe, except last night I had a dream where a flaming sword cut an aperture in the outer atmosphere."

"Then perhaps I was right in approaching you. Are you familiar with airship engines?"

"More than most. I served on the team of programmers who designed the new Triverphol models. In fact, I have the schematics on my datatop. Ya wanna see?"

"No, I believe you." He leaned over the workstation and stared into his eyes. "So, PL, do you want to come with Runess and me? Operating an airship ain't easy by any means. However, with your programming experience, not to mention your knowledge of design, I can teach you to operate a Triverphol engine in no time. Whether yea or nay—you'll have to decide soon. We must depart within the bout."

"If there's a chance to save Jesse and the others who are facing peril, how can I decline? Isn't this what their group did for our planet? Don't we owe them our bond?" Hiehew shuffled around his cubicle, pondering his own questions. Suddenly, he stopped and gazed at Cndrek. "It's decided. I'm in. Should we notify the Council?"

"At this point, the fewer who know, the better. Grab your datatop, extra clothing, any gear you require, and let's shove off."

Cndrek explained the rails to his recruits as they slowly

made their way toward the southern ruins. As they approached the rendezvous site, Cndrek opened ship-to-ship communications on his datacomm. "Runess, this is *The Seeker*. Do you read me?"

"What took so long, Cndrek? You should have been here one bout ago?"

"Complications."

"Stealthy errands are that way sometimes. Who did you get for a rowmate and midmate?"

"Tawehna is my navigator, and Hiehew, the PL from the Science Center, will be my engineer."

"They're not trained flyers."

"Not yet, but they'll acclimate soon enough. Besides, we may need a gunner more than a navigator, and Tawehna is highly experienced with stunner weapons. Remember how well she performed for the raid at Programming and on the moon rescue. She's invaluable. Not only is Tawehna a Yah believer, she received a vision about the flaming sword and wormhole."

"Interesting to say the least. I'll concur with your choice for rowmate. Explain your decision for the midmate."

"Hiehew is as loyal as they come. Besides having strong faith like Tawehna, he's got extensive programming experience."

"That's nice. Being a programmer, though, doesn't make one an engineer."

"Perhaps I should have mentioned that Hiehew designed upgrades for our recent Triverphol engines and wrote most of the dataware for it. Moreover, he had the same dream as you and me. I think it's a good omen. Regarding training, my shipmates reviewed our procedural manuals on the way here, and I believe they're flight ready."

"Alright, if your crew is squared away, set your heading for the upper atmosphere and follow me up. I hope your trainees have learned enough; if not—"

"They did. We'll meet you in orbit. In fact, with our engine upgrades, I'll probably arrive before you." Cndrek chuckled to himself as he hurried to the flight deck.

The ships slowly drifted upward and then engaged their engines.

MOON OF ETHADE

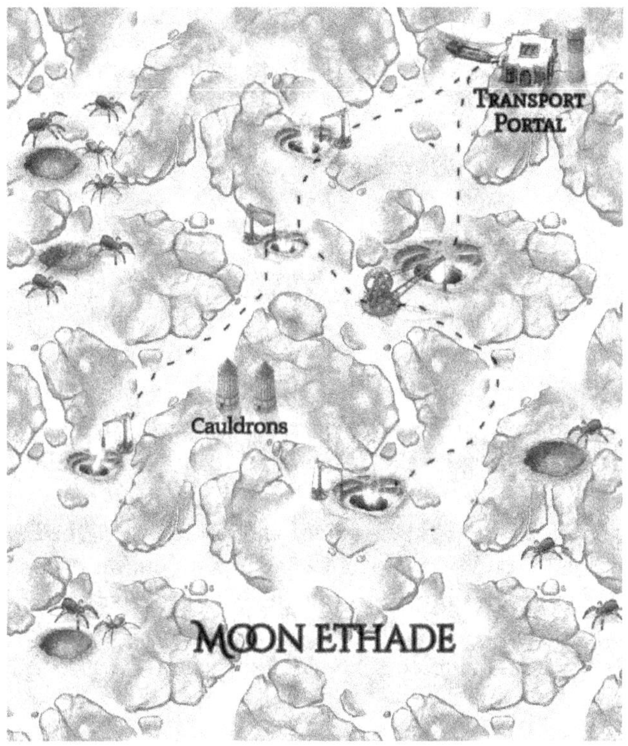

Ethade is the second moon of the Camayah system. The other two satellites are Easteapia, the largest, and Vilmieah, the smallest. Ethade mines and processes Triverphol for fuel. Spiderlike creatures called Quawners have overrun the entire moonscape.

CHAPTER 35

MOON ETHADE

The airship crews achieved orbit by halfdawn. *Old Bella* appeared first, followed by *The Seeker*. Runess opened a secure channel. "Ship-to-ship: I thought you planned to attain orbit before us. You said something about your upgraded engines being better than ours." He laughed into the comm. "So, what happened, Cndrek?"

"We encountered a few challenges on the assent. Nothing we couldn't handle."

"Well, my congratulations to you and your aircrew. Not many people can fly an airship, let alone accomplish an orbital maneuver. Most captains have never tried."

"I'll pass your compliments on to my crewmates. Now that we're circling the planet," asked Cndrek, "shouldn't we lower our booms, install solar sails, and set course for the second moon?"

"Hold off on the sails."

"Why?"

"We have a couple decisions to make."

"I'm listening."

"First, we need to decide on flight methods. If solar sails are deployed, it will take nearly thirty-five bouts to arrive at Ethade. Because of time constraints, I recommend pushing our engines at flank speed. Instead of another dawn or two, we can get there in six bouts."

"Won't this affect our fuel reserves?"

"Majorly," replied Runess. "At an increased rate of consumption, our flyers will barely have enough to reach the moon. We'll hafta refuel upon arrival."

"Based on what Rauteira told us, we better locate this mysterious wormhole as quickly as possible. No time to waste on a pleasure cruise. Let's fly under power," suggested Cndrek. "What's your second concern?"

"Deciding who's in charge of this mission. You have seniority as the SSL."

"True, but your deckhands have more flight experience. We will defer to you."

"Alright then, let's see if we can make Ethade by nightfall, Camayah time."

As the airships approached their destination, Runess hailed the Transport Portal. "Ship-to-shore: This is SL Runess in the *Old Bella*. We have two vessels that require immediate refueling."

The reply crackled over the captain's datacomm. "Welcome to Moon Base Operations. Please descend to sixty marks and stand by while I verify your permission code to load Triverphol fuel."

"Did I mention we're running on fumes?"

"You did, sir. However, we must confirm your authorization" An interval of silence passed. "Not finding anything on my terminal, sir."

"Let me speak to your S3 supervisor!" implored Runess.

"You're talking with him. Floaters don't normally refuel on this moon. In fact, I haven't seen one stop here in stages. Nevertheless, all inbound vessels must log a flight plan prior to arrival. And your crafts have not registered for lunar activities."

"My ship and *The Seeker* are conducting reconnaissance."

"Please elaborate."

"I can't. The operation is classified."

"I'm sorry, Captain Runess. You'll need clearance from the SSL to refuel or dock here."

Cndrek, who was monitoring the call on his datacomm, retorted, "This is Cndrek, the SSL! I'm commanding the aforementioned ship. Consider clearance granted."

"My apologies, SSL. I didn't know you were aboard the

second ship. Please proceed to the caldrons for fueling. One barrow costs 200 gelts. How many will you require?"

"I estimate five barrows per floater."

"Very well, sir. That will be 2000 gelts. You can pay onsite or charge the Airship Dock."

"I would prefer you transfer the bill to me at RIFT I."

"Consider it done, SSL. After fueling, please dock your vessels on the portal's west side. We don't have housing for visitors; therefore, you will have to stay onboard during the dusk. And one more thing."

"Yes."

"Due to quawner issues, I suggest you hover above twenty marks for safety."

Runess rejoined the conversation. "Perhaps you should feed them. You might find the creatures less aggressive if you provided an alternative food source and stopped infringing on their territorial hydrew supply. Planting soreseeds near hollows is working on Camayah."

"Thank you, SL. We received the memo from the Council of Twelve. Because our workers are behind schedule with Triverphol mining and processing, I neglected to implement those protocols. I'll get the situation resolved this phase. Our portal staff wishes you and your crews a joyous dusk. Again, sorry for any inconveniences."

With the fueling completed, *Old Bella* and *The Seeker* returned to the Transport Portal and settled at the thirty-mark elevation. They tied nest abeam and dropped ramps between the vessels, so the captains could exchange provisions and materials. Runess divvied up the nourishment tablets. Cndrek divided the stunners, TPCs, and Criunite crystals he had collected at the RIFT. He left the crates with duespikes in his weapons locker, intending to assemble and test them later. Once everything had been stowed away, Runess brought out Guet and set up the game on his deck. "Who wants to play?"

"We do, Uewba answered." Jawhawtu and Uew sat down and gathered two sets of colored pieces. Uew chose blue and Jaw picked orange.

"I haven't played it in ages, but I'll give it a go." Cndrek grabbed the black.

Runess glanced at Tawehna and Hiehew. "What about you two?" Although Hiehew seemed hesitant, he finally nodded yes and selected the red colors.

"I've never heard of the game." Tawehna studied the odd metal shapes. There were thin rods of different lengths, round objects, squares, triangular and oval shapes, and an eight-sided dice. "Can you explain the rules?"

"Sure thing, Tawehna. Guet is a strategy game played by shipmates to pass the bouts. Each person takes a color and starts with ten pieces. We play it on a table or floor with three to seven players. I'll give you novices helpful suggestions as we go along. However, just so you know . . ." Runess had a glint in his eyes. "That advice will also benefit me."

"Since there is not much else to do this dusk, I guess I'll play." Tawehna picked the white markers. Runess chose yellow and the game began. When the light faded, Cndrek set out green luminous crystals for lighting. Three bouts later, the game ended in a draw between Jaw and Uew.

Runess thanked everyone for playing and returned the pieces to his box. "If circumstances allow, we'll play Guet again next dust. Right now, though, I suggest we hit the hammocks in our quarters. We have an early start on the morrow."

At predawn, the sailors arose, swallowed Tyhydru and Dapferon supplements, and prepped their airships for flight. After notifying the Transport Portal, *Old Bella* and *The Seeker* floated upwards until attaining orbit around Ethade. Not knowing a precise heading, the captains set an easterly course into the outer atmosphere to search for their mysterious wormhole, hoping it would lead them to a land called Eskaonus.

CHAPTER 36

WORMHOLE

Once the airships left Moon Ethade's orbit, they lowered their port and starboard booms and deployed two solar sails to each. The reflective sheets captured light from the sun and pushed the craft forward, increasing its speed as the photons bounced off the sails. Whenever a course correction was needed, the navigators performed a tacking maneuver, similar to a sailboat using the wind to change directions.

Leaving the Camayah system behind, the flyers ventured deeper into unexplored space. *Old Bella* led the way followed by *The Seeker*. The navdata terminals kept track of the passage of time on Camayah since dawn and dusk no longer applied in the outer atmosphere. Other than the red dwarf sun in the background, their surroundings became increasingly dark. Although the vessels had lighting on all decks, the captains tried to conserve TPC powered systems by using Criunite whenever possible. The green luminous crystals also made perfect flashlights.

Other than the occasional ship-to-ship communications between captains, the voyage seemed uneventful, even boring. After nearly twenty bouts of travel, Cndrek asked Hiehew and Tawehna to bring the two crates from the weapons locker, topside. "Alright, let's see if we can assemble what's inside."

Tawehna lifted one of the lids. "Strange device. What is it?"

"A duespike. They existed prior to the Burning. I discovered ten of them in a secret storage area below RIFT I and brought two with us, thinking the weapons might be helpful."

"Is it a stunner?"

"No, not a stunner, per se, but a device with a disruptor beam, capable of shattering objects or burning lenn-sized holes into metal, wood, rock, or other material. I believe airships had the units mounted on their bows as deck guns. Usage was discontinued ages ago due to the damage they could cause."

Hiehew pursed his lips. "What kind of damage?"

"As the rumor goes, the weapon tended to explode, killing the person firing it. The designers never resolved the issue. Therefore, they packed the duespikes away in storage and forgot about them. I wasn't sure any remained until I opened one of the crates."

"Anything else should we know?" Hiehew asked warily.

"I understand they had an extremely long range, double the lenns of a trispike, and came equipped with targeting sights and range finders. I think the disrupters had three settings: single shot, burst, and continuous fire."

"Can these guns be repaired so they don't explode?"

"That's what you're gonna determine, Hiehew. Use your programming skills to locate and fix the flaws, then put one together. When ready, I plan on asking Tawehna, our gunner expert, to test fire it."

"You said the weapon wasn't reliable. What if it blows up?" asked Tawehna as her eyes grew wider.

"Then it will be a fairly short expedition." Cndrek held his stomach and chuckled at his witty remark. "Don't worry; I have faith in your abilities. It's why I chose you two as my shipmates." Hiehew detached an access panel, laid the parts on the afterdeck, and began examining the components. "I'm sure you'll figure out the flaws before we test them, and if we get one unit to work properly, I want the second one repaired and assembled as well. Give me a shout once you're done so I can notify Runess." The captain entered his cabin, smiling to himself.

Several bouts passed by the time Hiehew finished reprogramming the dataware for both disrupters. Tawehna helped him assemble them. She installed a TPC to power the first duespike and mounted it on her navigator post. Cndrek kept peeking from his cabin to check on their progress. When he noticed the mounted deck gun, Cndrek walked over. "It appears we're ready for a test. I'll notify Runess." He hurried back to his quarters and touched the screen on the datacomm. "Ship-to-ship: Runess, are you—"

"Of course, I am. Where else would I be? Did you sight the wormhole?"

"No, just calling with a status report. We are planning to test a duespike." Cndrek explained how he found two at the RIFT and brought them along for protection.

"I thought those things were decommissioned because they were dangerous."

"They were, except Hiehew repaired them. He said most of the defects have been resolved."

"Most?" A long pause ensued. "Give the percentage of success."

"Ninety-five percent."

"Wonderful. You're telling me there's a five percent chance you'll destroy your craft along with mine. Perhaps I should tack *Old Bella* to port for this demonstration."

"Have a little faith. Hiehew is the best programmer on Camayah."

"I hope so. Fine, proceed with your test."

Tawehna aimed the targeting mechanism and set the range at two hundred lenns. She pulled the trigger for a single release. A red light beam shot out and disappeared into the darkness. Next, she engaged the burst. Three red rays blasted forth, causing a slight rattle on the rails.

"Do you think I should try the continuous fire option?"

"No. Let's not push our luck, Tawehna. If we use the third setting, it might shake the quarterdeck apart." He saluted his rowmate to show his gratitude. "I'd say our test was successful. Okay, navigator, bring *The Seeker* alongside *Old Bella* so we can off load the second device. I'll notify Runess."

A half bout later, the airships rendezvoused and tied nest abeam. In this configuration, ships position near one another with one vessel slightly in front of the other. The captains secured their rails and lowered the connecting ramps, which allowed Hiehew to transfer the second deck gun to *Old Bella*. Jaw installed a TPC to power it and mounted the duespike on the bow of their foredeck. Uew tested it, firing red beams into the darkness that reached three hundred lenns. Afterwards, Runess set up Guet and both crews played a game as they discussed their current situation and pondered what lay ahead.

At latedusk, *The Seeker* crew boarded their flyer, detached, and retired to their sleepers. The routine was much the same for the following dawns: moor the flyers together, speculate about the mission, play Guet, and return to their bunks for the dusk. Every third dawn, the sailors consumed nutrition and hydration tablets.

After two events, they observed a faint light in the distance. Assuming it was a sun, the crafts altered course and steered toward it. The captains wondered if the light might be the new dawn in their dreams. During the next several dusks, the outer atmosphere turned darker and colder. On the sixteenth dawn, the air became thin, making it hard to breathe. Runess recalled what Jesse had said concerning interstellar space being airless and requiring special suits to survive the harsh conditions. The captains decided if they didn't sight the fabled wormhole by the morrow, the environment would force them to turn back before everyone suffocated.

Early on the seventeenth dawn, Runess departed his cabin during rounds and stared across the starboard bow. Less than a tick away, an oval-shaped tear in the darkness appeared. Silver beams of light radiated from its perimeter, resembling tiny glowing worms.

He raced to his cabin and opened a channel. "Ship-to-ship: Cndrek, do you see what I'm seeing."

"I do. This silvery vortex matches the one from my dream. I believe it's the singularity we've been searching for."

"Then, this is it; you know the plan."

"Copy."

"Now hear this!" shouted Runess over the intercom. "All hands report to the flight deck! This is not a drill! I repeat; this is not a drill!" Jaw and Uew scrambled from their sleeping chambers on the nether deck. "Snap to it! Remove the solar sails, raise the booms, and secure all hatches. Lock everything down!"

On *The Seeker*, Cndrek roused Tawehna and Hiehew and gave similar orders. Once they finished their assignments, he pressed the icon on his comm terminal. "Ship-to-ship: We're ready, Runess."

"Me too. I'll take *Old Bella* into this rift first. If something goes wrong and my floater implodes, turn around and return to Camayah. Tell our families what happened."

Cndrek and his flight crew hung back and watched. As *Old Bella* entered the event horizon, glistening sparks similar to fireworks encircled it, and the airship disappeared, leaving a broken rail and other debris in its wake. "Oh, no!" screamed Cndrek. "I don't think she survived. We have our orders. Navigator, hard to port. Get us out of here."

"I can't, sir," answered Tawehna in a stressful voice. "A force is pulling us inside."

"Engineer, tie in the Triverphol engines."

"They are offline," replied Hiehew.

"Get them online."

"Unable to comply, Captain. They are not responding to a restart."

"Arrgh! I guess we're following *Old Bella* inside this thing. Well, mates, it's been a hon . . ." He never finished his statement. *The Seeker* vanished, swallowed by the wormhole.

The ships traveled through space and time inside a glowing tunnel that twisted and turned in every direction. After what felt like an eternity, their vessels exited the mysterious vortex into total darkness. There were no suns, no stars, and no point of reference.

CHAPTER 37

THE DEFENDERS

Lady Saephira had arranged for a break-the-fast assembly in the town square for the entire city. As servers set out platters of yarm berry tarts from Ellee's Place, an alarm bell tolled, followed by another. The leaders and residents of Beayama were expecting an enemy attack, yet unsure if it would be an aerial strike from catapults launching skyfire projectiles or a direct incursion. Moments later, a sentry on the main tower yelled, "Breaching poles approaching." He raised the orange rally banner and shouted, "Bar the gates!"

As the alarms continued to sound, safeguards and militia moved to their designated positions encircling the city. Captain Gelr split his twenty guards between the eastern and western positions. Captain Maximus assigned thirty militiamen on the forward entrance and ten on the rearward. The defenders also deployed on building rooftops and in outfacing windows. Some carried slings; others held longbows.

Although walled in certain spots, Beayama wasn't a citadel or fortress city. Most of the secured sections were around the city gates. They contained parapets, which were low retaining walls offering protection to those on the wallwalks. The rest of the perimeters had connected buildings. Beayama featured two gates: a primary on the east and a secondary on the west. The front ingress included two fortified lookout towers on each side of the entry. The rear ingress only supported one tower.

Captain Gelr and Captain Maximus assumed positions at the two eastern towers, armed with longbows. Jesse joined Max and offered what support he could. He bore no weapon, just one of the four communicators. Anna stood near Gelr in the second tower, ready to use her nyeflute if required. She held her sling at the ready. Militia Lead Chepho, who had recovered his health after drinking Ottaar's healing-left tea, commanded the western defenses, assisted by Seth who brought a longbow, sling, and his radio transceiver.

Lady Saephira and Lady Narleen staffed the command center at the Great Hall. AliRoot wandered the hallways, taking in all the activity and excitement, but unlike everyone else, seemed unworried. Narleen used Max's talkie device to monitor communications and relay battle status information to Jesse, Seth, and Militia Chief Phauch. Phauch patrolled the perimeters on a kack, staying in contact with the fourth radio as he searched for weaknesses in their defenses. Holley assisted Ottaar in establishing a mender aid station in the town square. Volunteers rushed back and forth, lugging arrows and stones to restock the defender's weaponry and supply them with food and water.

The first offensive unfolded at forecycle. At the main gate, attackers marched forward, carting a thick pole. "Looks like a battering ram," noted Max. "I assume they cut it from one of our local cottlepines."

At the same moment, Jesse received a call from Seth at the western gate. "Hey, JW, the bad dudes have showed. There are ten guys, five to a side, and they're hauling a log about fifty hands long and nine hands thick with a blunted iron plate attached to the front. I think they plan to crash the entrance."

"Same situation at our end, Seth. Max said those things are battering rams. He's ordering Chepho to fire at will. Perhaps several volleys of arrows and stones will dissuade them. That's our strategy at the main gate, and it seems to be working. The sheer volume of missiles has caused our adversaries to retreat without getting close. We even dropped a few of their log carriers to the ground as well."

"Copy." Seth glanced at Chepho on the wallwalk and

simulated an archery draw with his hands as if he were holding a bow. The lead acknowledged the signal and relayed it to his archers who fired off a salvo. "My outfit and me are wondering why their catapults aren't being used? Not that we want them to."

"I assume they prefer to capture the city, not destroy it. Let's hope they don't change their minds. Max said we have no defense against catapults launching fire-laden weapons."

The second assault occurred one span later. This time, the combatants deployed their battering rams with a company of twenty-five armored soldiers who used their shields to form a covering similar to the Roman turtle shell formation. Their shields created a barrier over the breachers to protect them from arrows and slung rocks.

Archers and slingers launched numerous volleys at the press, wounding just a handful of assailants. The Gahn's defensive shell deflected most of their propelled objects, allowing the ramming units to advance within fifteen paces of the gate.

As the battle raged, Lady Saephira snuck away from the Great Hall and joined the western defense with her longbow. As soon as Chepho noticed Saephira on the wallwalk, he confronted her. "My Lady, it's too dangerous up here. I fear for your safety. I'll escort you back to—"

"Sorry, Lead Chepho, I'm staying. This is my city, and I'll not sit idly by while it's being stormed. I'm experienced as any with the bow. Besides, I've asked the reverend to meet me here with a new weapon." Moments later, Lundy climbed the west tower, carrying a small box and clutching a hollowed-out stick.

"What's the tube thing?" probed Chepho.

"Aye, me glad you asked. It's called a blowgun. I described the concept to Membarb, our woodsmith, and he produced a prototype, along with a full box of carved, wooden darts." He withdrew one from the container, being careful not to touch the point. "This dart fits into the end of me blowgun barrel. Tiny vanes stabilize its flight in much the same way as fletchings do for arrows."

"What can a flying toothpick do? Cause a little scratch? We're in real danger here, Lundy. No time for games."

"Me thinks you should watch." Lundy loaded a dart, inhaled

a deep breath, and blew on the end. A little projectile flew out and struck one of the breachers in the arm. A moment later, the man stumbled backwards and plummeted to the ground. "The dart tips are dipped in a special solution. It's a paralytic mixture developed by Holley on Camayah for use in quawner bombs. It can put a wee elephant to sleep in moments."

"An elephant? Ah, never mind." He watched as Lundy launched another dart. A second soldier staggered and fell. "Alright, squad," Chepho shouted. "Change of orders! Instead of endless volleys that bounce off these shields, pick an open target. Aim for unarmored areas such as hands, arms, or legs. Since we're not having success penetrating their armaments, let's force them to drop their shields and battering rams to deal with injuries to their extremities." Chepho drew his bowstring and launched another arrow toward an open target. "In the meantime, Lundy, keep using your blowgun. The rest of you guys follow his lead. Working together, we may be able to wound enough insurgents with arrows, rocks, and darts so they retreat again."

Seth reported their alternate strategy to JW at eastern gate. Then he notched an arrow, aimed for a shin unprotected by leather greaves, and released. *Whish.* Direct hit. The man let go of the pole and grabbed for his bleeding leg.

At the main gate, they had already realized the difficulty in penetrating their shield covering and switched to a more targeted method, aiming only for exposed extremities. Although it helped, the Gahns were still advancing. Max gave the preassigned signal to put aside their weapons and plug their ears. He yelled to Anabelle in the second tower, "Okay, Miss Anna, show them what a nyeflute can do."

Anna played the confusion tune. As she piped the notes, soldiers took their shields and banged them on the heads of their comrades. Others removed their armor and spun in circles. A few had blank expressions on their faces. The carriers tossed their battering rams aside and danced odd jigs on top of them. Once they came to their senses, the men gathered their armor, picked up their rams, and fled, probably wondering what had happened.

The third onslaught came at midcycle. The enemy used two

breaching poles per gate, plus two companies of fifty men who employed the turtle-shield maneuver. This time, their forces reached the gates. The rear entrance had success turning the tide with support from Lundy's blowgun. He continued to fire his weapon until depleting his paralytic darts. After suffering numerous injuries, the attackers retreated, leaving their poles behind them.

The efforts at the front were not faring as well. Even with targeting unarmored extremities, the breachers had punched holes into the main gate. Before they broke through completely, Max requested Annabelle's assistance again. He signaled his troops to put down their weapons and plug their ears, so they wouldn't be affected by nyeflute music. When the defenders were ready, Anna piped a new melody from her tablature guide, labeled temporary blindness. The song had immediate results. The adversaries began to shuffle around aimlessly, rubbing their eyes, screaming, "I can't see; I can't see!"

Unable to determine their whereabouts or see their comrades, the soldiers providing the defensive shell discarded their shields. Those bearing ramming poles, abandoned them, and raced off in all directions, stumbling over one another. By the time their sight returned, the units were scattered and in disarray. Not wishing to tarry in case something else untoward occurred, the assailants withdrew, defeated for the third time in less than a cycle.

Those individuals with radios reported to Lady Narleen at the command center, detailing their successes in protecting the gates. Soon, cheers rose throughout the city as residents celebrated the brave efforts of the Militia and Safeguards.

CHAPTER 38

ULTIMATUM

By postcycle, the enemy's southern battlegroup, numbering over 250 armored combatants, had redeployed east of Beayama. Near the city entrance, their troops erected a canopy tent, keeping it out of longbow range, and hung a purple pennant to signify the presence of royalty. A delegation of three soldiers approached on foot. One wore a red-plumed helmet, the second a yellow. The third donned a white plume and carried a pike with a truce banner tied to the end. Once the men were within hailing distance of the main tower, they stopped and waved their blue streamer in the air.

"Ho there in the tower!" yelled the person with the red-plumed helmet. "I am LyeDuek, High Commander of the Southern Gahn Battalion. I wish to speak with the militia officer in charge of this city."

"I'm listening," replied Max.

"Who do I have the honor of addressing?"

"I am Maximus Gallius, Captain of the Militia. State your purpose."

"Before I do, I wish to recognize your recent accomplishments. Three times this cycle, your forces repelled our attacks. Although your weapons are unusual, your tactics worked well. You are to be congratulated, Captain."

"We did what we needed to defend our city." Max turned to

Gelr and whispered, "I'm not buying this. What do you think?"

"It's probably a trap. I say we ready our bows and dispatch them."

"Since they're showing a truce banner, let's see where this query goes."

"Okay, Max, but I'm gonna order my safeguards to notch a few arrows just in case."

"Again, I say to you, state your purpose or withdraw," insisted Max. "Our longbows are aimed at you."

"We have been sent by Ruler EdNook. He requests a parley with the witch named Saephira."

"I take issue with your characterization, Commander. Lady Saephira is the honored magistrate of Beayama and devoted leader of the Lower Realm."

"So you say." LyeDuek turned to the soldier in the yellow plume to confer. A discussion ensued for a couple moments, after which LyeDuek said, "My officer and I apologize for the offence. Nevertheless, EdNook, the Ruler of Fate, waits under the purple pennant. If you accept his gracious offer, bring your Lady to the meeting. She can ask two armed escorts to accompany her, except they must keep their swords sheathed. Carry a blue flag with you to indicate your intent. You have one span to respond, or the parley is cancelled." The Gahns then turned around and jogged back to the canopy.

A quarter span later, Saephira, Gelr, and Max rode through the front entrance. Saephira held the blue parley banner at her side. Her group approached the canopy, dismounted, and walked the rest of the way. Eddnok sat at a table underneath the shelter. Commander LyeDuek and the officer in the yellow-plumed helmet stood behind him. The soldier helmeted in a white plume had relocated to the battlegroup's rear position.

When Saephira and her captains were five paces away, Eddnok raised his hand. "That's far enough. Well, well, I see you brought Commander Gelr with you." EdNook pointed him out to his officers. "This man is a traitor like Bolgog. He switched loyalties and joined up with the witch."

Livid at the inference, Gelr reached for his saber. Max leaned over and stopped him. "This is a parley, Gelr. Let's see what Eddnok has to say."

Eddnok studied Maximus. "You must be one of those travelers Lundy mentioned who hails from a mysterious high realm, right?" Max said nothing. "Not talking, huh? Perhaps it's best to keep your mouth shut and listen." Max's eyes widened, his chiseled jaw tightened, yet he held his peace.

Lord Eddnok stood and grinned. "And now for the little witch." Angry at the derogatory slight about Beayama's leader, Maximus moved a hand atop his sword handle, preparing to draw it. LyeDuek and his officer responded by pulling their swords and moving alongside to protect Ruler EdNook. "Put your weapons away, gentlemen, I'll handle this. There's no reason to kill anyone, not yet anyway."

Saephira stepped forward, briefly curtsied, and placed their truce banner on Eddnok's table. "What does this parley entail?"

Eddnok circled around behind Saephira, glaring at her from head to toe, and then returned to his spot. "Yes, yes, I'm glad you asked. Before I get into the details, I noticed you're still using enchantments like floating rocks and magical flying sticks, not to mention shooting toothpicks that cause my warriors to lose consciousness."

"Those things are not sorcery tricks; they're projectiles launched from creative weapons."

"And I suppose playing music, which turns my troops into blind, bumbling idiots, isn't witchcraft either?"

"Some might consider it divine intervention or a miracle."

"I don't believe in such things, my naive lady. At any rate, enough talk. Here are the conditions for your surrender."

"What surrender? I thought you summoned us here in good faith to negotiate," replied Max. "Your delegation waved the blue banner to indicate—"

"Your mistake, sir, and a foolish one." Eddnok laughed so hard he had to place his hands on the tabletop to steady himself. "Truce flags mean nothing to me." He took ahold of their banner and tossed it to the ground.

LyeDuek and his officer glanced at each other and frowned. "Excuse me, my Sovereign," responded LyeDuek, "parley flags are a revered tradition among—"

"Silence! I'm the Ruler of Fate, not you." EdNook sat at the table and unfolded a document. "Here are the conditions, Saephira: You have until midcycle on the morrow to personally surrender to me, or I will destroy the entire Lower Realm, starting with Beayama. This time I will not use soldiers; we'll launch firebombs. Our catapults are already in range of your cities and villages. Your precious settlements will burn to the ground. No one will survive. Moreover, if you don't yield by the designated time, I will proceed with the execution of Commander Bolgog and his two fickle officers, Rennard and Brappt. I've scheduled them to hang on the gallows for treason at midcycle. Your capitulation may buy them a few more spans."

"You are evil, Lord Eddnok or EdNook, regardless of whatever name you use."

"And you, my dear, should have never spurned my sincere marriage proposal."

"You merely wanted another concubine to—"

"Enough! On the morrow, you are to leave Beayama, unarmed, and alone. The choice is yours. I'll await your answer on my flagship. You and your subordinates are dismissed."

Gleeful at the prospect of finally ruling all of Eskaonus, EdNook gathered his entourage and left. The negotiations, or lack thereof, had lasted one span. Saephira, Gelr, and Max, mounted their kacks and returned to the main gate, arriving at latecycle.

"None of this parley is to be discussed. Understood?"

"Yes, my Lady; howbeit, Gelr and I believe you should—"

"Sorry to cut you off, captains. I wish to retire to my quarters and be alone for a while. Please ask Narleen to arrange for an early nightrise banquet in the town square. The seating should accommodate as many families as possible." Saephira realized her residents needed a diversion, as did she. Depending on how she responded to Eddnok's demands, this dinner could be their final one—or hers. Thus far, only Maximus and Gelr knew about the ultimatum. Until she made her decision, she preferred to keep it that way. "Let's make it a celebration feast. I will meet you there later." Then she hurried off to Residential Hall, entered her private room, and closed the door. Saephira threw herself onto the bed and wept uncontrollably.

As twilight approached, locals crowded the square. The

overflow filled the adjacent streets. The banquet included everyone's favorite meats: smoked tarkk, stuffed river eel, and sliced antaloop. Servers set out bowls of roasted maize and platters with freshly baked kin. Dessert entrees featured candied dallups, fresh yarm berries, and a variety of puddings and cakes. For drinks, the guests consumed Azollie tea, slightly fermented yarm, and kunakk, which hosts normally reserved for special functions.

According to the attendees, it was the best banquet in yarns. Afterwards, Saephira thanked the Militia and Safeguards for defending their city. She took a moment to gather her composure, then shared the ultimatum given to her by Eddnok at the parley. As the crowd listened to their leader's options, they were mortified: some moaned, others wept, but most remained silent, simply shaking their heads. As soon as the sighs and murmuring died down, Saephira asked Annabelle to come forward and sing a song. Under the circumstances, Anna could hardly refuse. The crowd grew quiet as she began picking a tune on her glifstring. Soft, harmonious music filled the square. A misty cloud hovered overhead.

"For this solemn occasion, I have chosen one of my favorite hymns called *Higher Ground*. In light of the tragic news we just learned, I pray these words bring hope and encouragement."

I'm pressing on the upward way,
New heights I'm gaining every day;
Still praying as I'm onward bound,
Lord, plant my feet on higher ground.

Lord, lift me up, and let me stand
By faith, on heaven's tableland;
A higher plane than I have found,
Lord, plant my feet on higher ground.

My heart has no desire to stay
Where doubts arise and fears dismay;
Though some may dwell where these abound,
My prayer, my aim, is higher ground.

I want to scale the utmost height,

And catch a gleam of glory bright;
But still I'll pray till heaven I've found,
Lord, lead me on to higher ground.

When the song ended, Saephira stood. "Thank you, Annabelle. Your hymn was indeed timely, and I will cherish it always." After a long pause, she continued. "The time has come for me to bid you farewell. I cannot allow Beayama to be destroyed. Therefore, I have chosen to surrender to Eddnok on the morrow."

Cries of dismay echoed throughout the square.

"Hush now. Don't feel sorry for me. All of you would have made the same decision to save your family and friends." She gazed at Narleen's tear-soaked face. "Vice-leader, would you and your spouse escort me to my . . ." Unexpectedly, Saephira collapsed to the ground. With the mender still attending the injured at her home, Max and Narleen raced over to offer what aid they could. He checked her pulse and breathing while Narleen helped Saephira sit upright. Assuming she had merely fainted, Max lifted her into his strong arms and carried her to Residential Hall with Narleen tagging along beside him. No one said a word.

At firstlight, Saephira walked to the front gate with Max and Jesse holding on to each of her arms. Narleen followed behind her spouse, eyes on Saephira, weeping loudly. Gelr stood at the foot of the east tower, right hand on his sheathed sword. Saephira glanced at him and smiled. It was a sad smile. "Have your safeguards unbar the gates, Captain Gelr."

"Are you sure, my Lady?"

"It's an order, Captain."

"You have until midcycle. Maybe you should wait?"

"No, I must do this while I still have the courage. There's no other way to save our city from being burned and our people killed."

Gelr wiped moisture from his eyes. Reluctantly, he signaled for the tower sentry to crack open the egress. "I fear Eddnok will probably incarcerate you."

"More likely he'll hang me on the gallows along with Bolgog and his commanders."

Overhearing the comment, AliRoot started to cry, calling out, "SaeFear, SaeFear." Lundy drew her close to his side, trying to comfort her. It did little to calm the little girl's anguish. Overwhelmed, Holley and Ottaar stood side by side with tear-soaked cheeks. Seth and Anna simply watched in silence, their hearts broken and numb. Hearing the commotion, several residents left their homes and gathered on the street. Their sorrowful faces told the story.

Suddenly, Jesse's communicator squawked, followed by static, then a voice: "Ship-to-shore." Pause, more static. "Ship-to-shore: This is Runess. Anybody down there named Jesse? We're requesting landing coordinates."

Jesse hurriedly withdrew the radio from his satchel. "Can it really be you, SL? How did you get here?"

"Tell you the how, later. Presently, we need to dock two airships."

"Two?"

Next, Narleen's communicator broke squelch. "Correct! We're answering Seth's distress call. It would appear we are the *sent ones* now."

She quickly handed her radio to Max who asked, "Is that you, Cndrek? Where are you?"

"Hello, big guy. Good to talk with you again. Runess and I are descending from the upper atmosphere. Our crews spent the dusk in darkness after exiting a wormhole tunnel. I figured we had entered an endless void and were doomed, but then yellowish-banded rays appeared out of nowhere without the presence of a sun. As the light dawned, a planet came into view. When we entered the lower atmosphere, our rowmates spotted settlements and a large city surrounded by a horde of hostile forces. Runess and I wondered if we had arrived at the desired location, so we used the datacomm channels Rauteira installed to initiate contact."

"Rauteira knows about our situation on Eskaonus? Please explain."

"She figured a way to access your transceiver frequency; she and Seth have been communicating for half a stage." Max glanced at Seth who sheepishly nodded his head. "You should have taken me up on the SA job offer on Camayah. It would have saved me a long trip just to see your gnarled face." Cndrek chuckled at his jest.

"Yes, sir; however, I'm glad you made the effort. Do you see the large field on the edge of town?" replied Max.

"I have it in my imager now. Starting landing procedures. Runess and I will meet you there in a quarter bout."

"Change of plans, my Lady. You're not surrendering this cycle." Max looked at the sentry in the tower and yelled, "Close and bar the gates! The Lady is not leaving."

CHAPTER 39

BATTLE FOR THE HEART

By the time their two airships landed at the Militia's practice field, a crowd had gathered. After greeting old friends, Maximus and Jesse explained their current situation and introduced Runess, Cndrek, and their aircrews to Lady Saephira, her leadership council, and a growing number of onlookers. As they intermingled, both groups wondered how they were able to understand the other person's language.

Although Narleen wasn't surprised, having portaled with Maxie to a different world, Saephira was first to pose the question: "How are people from Camayah able to speak Eskaonese?"

Runess replied, "We're wondering the same thing regarding your inhabitants. When did you learn the Camayahnite language?"

Before the topic created more confusion, Lundy jumped in with the answer. "Aye, it be a marvel indeed. A similar thing occurred on the Day of Pentecost. Acts 2:6, a revered document from my homeworld, recorded the event. The Holy Spirit made it possible for clans of different dialects to understand one another. We have experienced this wonder previously, and me thinks it's happening again. Let's not get peely-wally over it. Just be thankful an unseen hand is helping us."

"Dudes, I don't mean to drop a heavy, but if we don't devise a plan by midcycle, we'll all be turned into toast."

"The kid's right," said Max. "With two airships to support

our efforts, let's put our minds together and develop a strategy to save the realm. This is nothing less than a battle for the heart and survival of our people; we must not fail." The collective huddled together for several spans to discuss priorities, options, and tactics.

Since the continued defense of Beayama remained a priority, they felt Narleen should stay at the command center to monitor communications. To keep AliRoot from wandering the hallways unescorted, Narleen asked the young child to sit by her and record the mission progress on a central map. As for the others, Militia Chief Phauch, who still carried Anna's radio, led the Militia and Safeguards at the main gate. Squad Leader Bonarb commanded the forces at the rear one. Without a communicator, he used runners on kacks to stay in touch with everyone.

The airship pilots set their datacomms to forward all their communications to Narleen on channel three. Feeling confident with their preparations, the floaters lifted off from the practice field prior to Eddnok's midcycle deadline. *Old Bella* flew south to the Gemous River, and *The Seeker* headed north toward Briacap.

Cndrek piloted *The Seeker*. His mariners included Tawehna, his navigator and gunner, and Hiehew, his engineer. Realizing part of the plan involved storming Briacap to secure the release of Bolgog and his commanders, Cndrek recruited Gelr, Maximus, Seth, and Chepho. More importantly, the four had previously participated in a raid at Briacap and knew the layout. Each brought a longbow and quiver full of arrows.

Once underway, Cndrek distributed stunners. Because Max and Seth had used stun weapons on Camayah, Cndrek armed them with long-range trispikes. He gave Gelr and Chepho the shorter-ranged quispikes and demonstrated how to operate them.

Using their Triverphol-powered engines, *The Seeker* soon passed Tabahir in the Neutral Lands and approached Briacap. "Navigator, I want to get a bird's eye view of this location. Take me up another three thousand marks." From the higher elevation, Cndrek could see the citadel and a fleet of enemy ships docked along the western coastline of the Hallet Sea. "Maximus, you're in charge of this bunch. I'm going to drift down and hover near the battlement on the left and drop lines. We'll provide cover fire while you positon yourself."

"Appreciated," replied Max. "Okay, recruits, to the ropes and prepare to deploy. After we secure the tower, let's establish a defensive line on the wallwalk. Use your stunners to disable the resistance, then we'll advance to the stockade and free our prisoners."

"Sounds as if you have this operation in hand," remarked Cndrek. When his airship reached the desired location, he smiled at Max and pointed to the rails. "Over the edge with your raiders. We're off to the Hallet Sea to scuttle a few boats. Whenever we finish, let's rendezvous back at the tower. Good luck!" The rescue party set their stunners on burst, slung longbows and quivers across their shoulders, and followed Max down the ropes.

Runess piloted the *Old Bella*. His mariners included Uewba, his rowmate, and Jawhawtu, his midmate. Jaw and Uew had cross-trained in navigation and engineering and were both experienced gunners. He added four additional hands: Jesse, Lundy, Annabelle, and Lady Saephira who had insisted on going. Even though Runess specifically requested Jesse and Lundy because of their experience with stun weapons, he also chose Anna in case her nyeflute was required.

Their first priority was to locate and disable a land-based catapult south of the city. Five moments later, *Old Bella* approached the Gemous River and spotted the launcher on the riverbank with a supply transport anchored nearby in the river. Seeing a strange flying craft, the missile team launched a burning projectile at them.

"Hard to port!" yelled Runess. "We're under attack. All hands on deck." He rushed to the navigator's post. "Uew, evasive maneuvers. Keep us away from that fireball. If it hits our air canopy filled with Triverphol gas, we'll explode." Uewba increased speed, dipped left, then right. The firebomb soared past the bow, barely missing them. Seeing Jawhawtu ascending from the lower berth, he shouted, "Jaw, man the duespike! See if you can get a shot off before they reload their launcher." Jesse and Lundy followed Jawhawtu to the foredeck, bewildered, unsure what to do. "Quick, you two go to the weapons locker on the nether deck and grab a couple quispikes. See if you can stun the missile team. We're gonna bring *Old Bella* around for another pass."

As the airship circled, Jaw fired the deck gun. A red beam of light hit the catapult, splintering it into dozens of pieces. When Jesse and Lundy returned, they aimed their quispikes at the soldiers who were standing around, viewing their destroyed equipment. Bursts of yellow rays knocked them to the ground. "Well, that should keep them quiet for a bout or two," chortled the captain. "Alright, Jaw, let's scuttle their ship and get out of here." Jawhawtu aimed the duespike at the stern and pulled the trigger. A red disrupter beam blasted a two-lenn hole into the hull. In mere moments, the craft began to sink, listing to the starboard side. Some of the bevy jumped overboard and swam ashore. He fired a second shot, trying to drop one of the sail masts. Unfortunately, the beam went low, hitting below the quarterdeck, causing a fire to erupt. Soon, it burned out of control. More sailors abandoned ship. "You must have hit the hold containing their accelerants," speculated Runess.

"Did all their shipmates make it to safety?" Saephira asked.

"Not sure, ma'am."

"I thought our plan only involved scuttling vessels and disabling catapults. I realize these Gahns are the enemy. Nevertheless, they're still distant relatives. I hate to see more individuals injured or killed."

"Nor do I, ma'am; however, you're in a war, a battle for survival, facing uncertainties. Loss of life is inevitable. I will try to take every precaution, but not at the expense of losing my mariners or putting our flyer in jeopardy."

"I understand, Runess. I'm merely concerned."

"We all are, Lady Saephira," reassured Jesse.

"Navigator, get me a little altitude. Let's try to find the other two catapult-equipped transports while avoiding their aerial assaults. We almost perished in this last one."

Old Bella rose two hundred lenns in elevation and flew west, following the Cali River. They located the second ship anchored near a ford at the entrance of Onnie Passage.

"Annabelle, can you pipe a nyeflute tune to make our flyer invisible?" inquired Runess.

"I've never tried to hide an entire structure, just small gatherings of people. Let me check my tablature." She dug into her satchel and withdrew the fingering guide. "Hmm, there seems to be two invisibility tunes. I figured the second one was simply a chorus. It has the same notes, except in a lower octave. Maybe it could—"

"Start playing it, and let's see what happens as we approach their position. If they don't see us, great! It'll make our job easier."

The floater dropped in elevation and pulled alongside the enemy vessel. The sailors seemed unware of its presence. Jawhawtu set the range and fired two shots from the deck gun: The first one punched a hole into the stern, causing it to take on water and list to port. His second shot destroyed the catapult and afterdeck. Surprised and bewildered by the red beams of light, a few deckhands immediately abandoned ship. Because the hold also contained firebomb accelerants, it erupted into flames. Fortunately, the remaining bevy escaped into the river before the blaze engulfed the craft.

The comrades continued north and located the third launcher anchored at the mouth of the Upper Fork by Mista Lake. Runess employed the same tactics. Soon, the third vessel was sinking in flames. Having eliminated the three catapults by aftercycle, *Old Bella* turned south toward the coast of Bayegulf.

As soon as Max and his rescue squad landed on the wallwalk, they opened fire with their stunners. Lookouts guarding the battlement, dropped to the ground before they could respond. Their half-plated armor offered little protection against the strange light beams.

Seth raced to the tower, switched his trispike setting to continuous fire, and aimed at those in the plaza below. When the green rays hit the soldiers, they toppled like hewn cottlepines. Chepho took a position on the parapet and released burst after burst of yellow rays from his quispike. Dozens more fell. While Seth and Chepho provided cover, Max and Gelr hurried down the tower steps to the plaza, finding nearly thirty Gahns lying motionless.

Reinforcements scrambled into the courtyard, holding swords and pikes. As they left the barracks, zapping sounds of stunner fire echoed behind them. Green and yellow lights flashed everywhere. Another ten fell to the ground, paralyzed.

Gelr assumed point and led the way to the stockade, followed by Max, who kept glancing over his shoulder, watching for an ambush. He only needed to fire his trispike twice to stun a band of pursuers. For whatever reason, no alarm bells rang. Eventually, the two reached the stockade, and Gelr crashed through the door, startling guards sitting at a table. They drew their swords and charged forward. Four yellow bursts from Gelr's quispike stopped them in their tracks. The duo ran through the hallway, turned right at the first cellblock, finding the chamber locked. Max leaned his trispike against the wall, withdrew his Gladius, and sliced through the lock as if it were butter. Gelr pushed the cell door aside. Inside, three men huddled together wearing tattered clothing. Bruises and cuts covered their bodies.

Once his eyes adjusted to the light coming from the passageway, Bolgog asked, "Is that you Gelr?"

"It is, and Captain Maximus is with me."

"We feared you were the executioners. They planned to hang Brappt, Rennard, and me on the gallows at midcycle, citing the phony charge of treason as their justification. So, how did you get in here? The Gahn army occupies Briacap."

"This is being remedied as we speak. I can answer all your questions later." Max scanned the area. "Where are your guardsmen?"

"Most were killed in the skyfire attacks. Those who survived are locked away in the other cellblock."

"How many?"

"Maybe seventy. Some of those have severe burn injuries."

"I'll go break them out," offered Max. He marched down the left cellblock, cutting off locks from each chamber with his sword and flinging the doors open as he passed. He led the captives to the entrance of the stockade where Gelr, Bolgog, and his two commanders waited. They exited the jail together and beheld the carnage. Bodies of warriors lay across the plaza grounds.

"Are they dead?"

"No, Commander, just stunned." Max and Gelr showed Bolgog the weapons they had used.

"Where did you get those?"

"From travelers who arrived from Camayah," confirmed

Max. "I'll explain the circumstances another time. Right now, you should remove the plated armor from those soldiers before they wake. Gather their weapons and armaments and stow them in a secure location. Then rearm your guardsmen with swords and spears from the armory. Whenever the invaders regain consciousness, drag them to the main barracks and assign ten warders to guard them. Place the remainder of your men along the gates and battlements."

"Those stun devices would sure come in handy for our defense."

"No doubt, howbeit, they're not ours to give. We must return them to the travelers. On the plus side, Gelr and Chepho have offered to stay and help defend the citadel. They carry longbows. With archers and your sixty guardsmen on the ramparts, you should be able to hold the citadel against any outside assaults."

"What about the skyfire attacks? They almost devastated our city."

"Their firebomb launchers are currently being destroyed, and our airships are scuttling their invasion fleets in the Hallet and Nether Seas."

"Airships? Never heard of that kind of sailboat. Can you expound?"

"As I understand it, Commander, the crafts sail the skies by floating through the air. I'm not privy to the specifics, but these flyers are allowing us to defeat the enemy." Bolgog asked several more questions regarding the newcomers, where they hail from, and about their special weaponry. Feeling somewhat satisfied with Max's answers, he ended his queries, entered the nearest tower, removed the white banner from the flagpole, and raised the orange one to rally his forces.

Within a span, the Guards had retaken their city and secured the Gahn prisoners. Soon thereafter, Max and Seth gathered the stunners, leaving their extra arrows with Chepho and Gelr before returning to the battlement tower. While they waited for the rendezvous with Cndrek in *The Seeker*, Seth used his radio to report to Narleen about their success at Briacap.

Old Bella sped south to Bayegulf and spotted seventeen

ships along the coast of the Nether Sea. Most of them had docked near the shoreline. One displayed two flags: a gold-striped banner, indicating it was the flotilla leader, and a solid purple one. Because of the purple pennant, Saephira presumed Eddnok was aboard.

With no catapults to deal with, Uewba relieved Jawhawtu on the deck gun and started punching holes into the brigantine hulls. Since they were close to shore, the scuttled crafts sank halfway, bringing their keels to rest on the seafloor. It required three runs to disable the first sixteen vessels. During the sorties, sailors franticly abandoned their ships and rowed to shore in lifeboats. As *Old Bella* finished her last pass, the flagship raised two sails and departed, setting a northerly course up the eastern coast.

Realizing the frigate planned to escape, Runess turned to Saephira and inquired, "Do you desire it sunk?"

"If it were just Eddnok on the boat, I would say yes, but there are also innocent shipmates on board. Perhaps at some point the residents of Gahneeha will understand the whole truth and enact their own judgment against Eddnok. Let him go."

"Yes, ma'am." Mindful of Saephira's wishes, Runess ordered Uew and Jaw to stand down. He thanked Jesse, Lundy, and Annabelle for a job well done, then entered his cabin to contact Narleen with an update. Next, he placed a ship-to-ship call to *The Seeker,* advising Cndrek to use a higher elevation to avoid firebombs until they eliminated the launchers. With their operation concluded, *Old Bella* changed course and flew to Beayama, arriving during latecycle.

Following the ship-to-ship conversation, Cndrek heeded the advice from Runess. *The Seeker* climbed to an altitude of two hundred lenns, which he hoped was beyond the range of their skyfire launchers. Tawehna had successfully tested the duespike at that distance.

"I'll handle navigation, Tawehna. Get on the deck gun and target those three catapult transports. Aim for the stern and scuttle them. Wait for the crews to safely abandon ship and then fire a couple more rounds to completely destroy the launchers."

As the third one went down in flames, a frigate with a gold-striped banner, raised sails, turned east, and departed. "Cap, she's making a run for it."

"Keep an eye on her, Tawehna. In the meantime, let's maneuver *The Seeker* lower to conduct scrapping runs and scuttle the other sixteen ships before they also leave. I want them half-submerged, their keels sitting on the shoreline floor." Three passes later, the rowmate had disabled all the vessels, burning massive holes into their sterns with red beams from the duespike. As the crafts took on water and listed, the sailors dropped lifeboats and rowed to shore.

"The frigate has caught the wind and is picking up speed," reported Tawehna, confirming the flagship's change of status. "She's steering eastward across the sea. Do you desire to sink her?"

"Hold off. Let me check with Jesse. He and Lady Saephira are on the *Old Bella*." Five intervals later, Cndrek returned to the navigator's post. "Jesse and Saephira believe the ship is sailing to Gahneeha, and they feel it's prudent to let it go, especially if the skipper brings news of their losses."

"Okay, Cap, I'll power off the duespike. And one more thing, sir . . . while you were on the datacomm, a nawmie was released."

"Probably a messenger bird. Did you notice the direction?"

"Southeast."

"Even better. Gahneeha will receive the news faster."

Having accomplished their operation on the Hallet Sea, *The Seeker* turned around and soared to Briacap. Cndrek retrieved Maximus and Seth who were waiting on the wallwalk near the tower. After hearing about the freed captives, subdued occupiers, and the retaking of the citadel by Commander Bolgog, Cndrek called Narleen to report their dual mission had succeeded. Prior to leaving, the floater circled the area to search for signs of regrouping by the Gahn army. All they spotted were scattered units in disarray, so they flew to Beayama, arriving at twilight.

Because Narleen had been monitoring communications, she knew the aircrews would be hungry, so she asked the kitchen staff to set out a small banquet. Although the meal only included a few entrees, the Camayahnite visitors who normally consumed supplements for nourishment, enjoyed eating real food for the first time in ages. During dinner, volunteers delivered food rations to the defenders who remained on watch duty.

Finally, the banquet ended, and people departed to their homes other than Maximus who returned to the main gate. With Captain Gelr helping at Briacap, he assumed command of the Safeguards. Max made the rounds and checked on the men, arranging alternating shifts that allowed the tired detachment to get a little shuteye during darkout. He decided to stay and keep them company until firstlight.

The travelers headed to their airships for the night. Saephira and Narleen hurried to Residential Hall. Jesse and his colleagues trudged over to Ottaar's home. Most of Beayama wondered what dayrise would bring. Would the assailants regroup, counter attack, or lay siege to the city?

Unable to sleep, Saephira arose during darkout. Taking care not to wake AliRoot asleep on the settee, she lit a candle and opened the chest holding the ancient map, four black stones, original scroll, and Taula's *Archive Analyst Report*. She set the items on her table and reread the curator's statement describing the Beays, Brias, and Gahns.

The last section in the report ended with a prophecy concerning a ruler of fate who would emerge, gather the four *TREOW* stones, and join them together. Afterwards, all the clans of *Eskaon* would be reunited in unity and truth.

Separated, the stones remained black, yet each time she placed them adjacent to one another, they turned white. *How does one join these objects together?* Saephira tried many arrangements: First, she stacked them atop each other like gaming cards. Next, she tried a square pattern, then a rectangle, triangle, and diamond configuration. She even positioned them in a straight line, except none of the shapes stayed connected. *If this prophecy was true, they had to link in some way.* Frustrated, Saephira tossed all the items back into the chest and knelt by her bed.

I've never hailed a deity before. I'm not even sure if I know your real name. The gospel scroll Lundy gave me says you are the Word. Annabelle once wrote a song titled the Unseen One. Three cycles ago, she sang a hymn about you being our Vision. I've heard the Camayahnites call you YAH. Others refer to you as Lord or Father. Perhaps who you are is more important than your name or title. That's my assessment.

Regarding the reason for this conversation, I don't care to be a ruler of fate. I've never sought such a title. Still, if I need to connect these four stones in a certain way as a prerequisite to bring unity to our divided land, how do I accomplish it? I've tried numerous times without success. Can you help me discern the correct pattern?

Well, since this is my first prayer and I don't know how to conclude it, I'll simply end by saying Good Nightrise.

Oh, I forgot to mention my name is Saephira.

Feeling exhausted, she climbed into bed and drifted off into a deep sleep. A dream sequence began. Several images were familiar, others strangely beautiful:

Two individuals picking dallups, sunken sailboats floating

A celestial city with golden streets

Blue banner, soldier kneeling

Four white stones in the shape of a cross

CHAPTER 40

THE BIG REVEAL

Although Max planned to leave at firstlight, the missions, raids, and battles, not to mention staying awake during nightrise, had taken their toll. Exhausted, he finally fell asleep in the watchtower with his head leaning against the parapet.

Suddenly, Chief Phauch tapped him on the shoulder. "Sorry to wake you, sir, but you should see this." Max jumped up as if his pants were on fire. "Here, take a look through my magnifier. Two soldiers are approaching at a run."

Max peered through the looking glass. "They appear to be officers. The one in the red-plumed helmet is LyeDuek, a commander in the Gahn army. Other than someone holding a pole with a blue banner, I don't recognize the man wearing the yellow plume."

"Should I have our safeguards notch arrows in case it's a ploy?"

"No, let's wait and see what they want."

When the two men were within paces of the gate, the one with the banner planted his pole into the ground and stepped backwards. The other strode forward. "Ho there in the tower."

"Is that you Commander LyeDuek?" asked Max.

"It is, sir. I assume I'm addressing Captain Maximus."

"You are." Max leaned against the protective wall, resting his right arm on the edge. "State your intentions."

"We request a parley with your leader."

"It's early. I assume Lady Saephira is still asleep." His next comment was a test. "Come back after she breaks her fast."

"Sorry for the inconvenience, Captain. However, this meeting is of utmost importance. We'll wait for your leader at the canopy tent under the purple banner. She may bring a delegation."

"It may be a while."

"Like I said, sir, we will wait." The two messengers turned around and dashed off, leaving the banner pole stuck in the ground."

"Well, Phauch, what do you make of that?"

"Could be a trick?"

"Maybe. Still, they requested a parley, so a parley they shall have. Go wake Lady Saephira and pray she doesn't skin you alive for the early intrusion."

"I hope you're kidding, sir."

Max chuckled at his tease. "I am." Still smiling, he added, "Be sure to tell our Lady that she needs a delegation. I suggest at least a dozen as a show of support. In the meantime, I'll pick a handful of militia and safeguards to serve as her escorts."

Phauch knocked on Saephira's chamber door at Residential Hall and was surprised to see her already dressed in her finest court clothing; her brunette hair lay across her shoulder, braided into a long ponytail. AliRoot, who had been staying with her, wore her usual pink dress and held a small metal chest containing the ancient artifacts. Once Phauch explained the situation, Saephira gave him the names she preferred for emissaries. A span later, she and her entourage galloped out of the city gate, led by Max and four security escorts, all armed with swords and longbows.

Lady Saephira's delegation included fifteen colleagues: Captain Maximus, Militia Chief Phauch, Lundy, Annabelle, Jesse, Seth, Vice-leader Narleen, Mender Ottaar, AliRoot, Cndrek, Runess, a pair of militiamen, and two safeguards. Unfamiliar with kacks or steering them, Runess and Cndrek rode double behind the militiamen. The group dismounted and moved toward the canopy, leaving their animals unhobbled. Standing underneath the covered shelter were the same two officers who had asked for the meeting.

Max marched up to the rectangular table and placed the blue banner on top of it. "We are returning your pennant in good faith."

Following Max, Saephira stepped forward and curtsied. "Good dayrise, Commander."

"It is not a good dayrise at all." LyeDuek sighed. He stared at his comrade and motioned for him to proceed. The officer in the yellow-plumed helmet approached Saephira and handed her a white flag. LyeDuek unstrapped his scabbard and laid it on the end of the table. "As Gahn High Commander, my battalions have no choice other than to capitulate."

Saephira passed the flag to a nearby safeguard, leaving LyeDuek's sheathed sword alone. "I thought you wanted to parley, Commander."

"We do, ma'am."

"Go on. I'm listening."

"The truth of the matter is . . . we cannot battle forces employing flying sticks, floating rocks, and airborne toothpicks as weapons. Nor can we defend against strange crafts that soar through the air, shoot colored lights, sink our ships, and paralyze our soldiers. Our armada numbering forty vessels has been decimated. These tactics must surely be witchcraft."

"They are not sorcery, nor am I the witch that Eddnok led you to believe I am. Several of these weapons we have developed ourselves. Travelers from a distant realm, who came here to help stop this unjustified invasion, provided the others." She pointed at Runess and Cndrek who offered open palms, the customary greeting in their homeworld of Camayah. "Anticipating your concerns, I've asked my colleagues to demonstrate our devices so you can see they're normal weapons of warfare, not divination."

Maximus withdrew an arrow from his quiver, notched it in his longbow, drew the bowstring, and fired. *Whish*. The projectile flew toward a cottlepine a hundred paces away and pierced the trunk with a loud twang. "These so-called flying sticks are arrows," said Max. "They are effective and deadly."

Annabelle shuffled sideways a pace, loaded a rock in her sling, twirled it over her head to build momentum, and released it. The stone flew high into the sky and disappeared in the distance. "This is a sling." Anna handed it to LyeDuek. "It launches stones, not magical flying rocks." The commander carefully inspected the sling and returned it.

Lundy moved forward a couple paces, holding his blowgun in one hand and a dart in the other. "When you place this tiny shaft in me wooden tube, blow into the end, it'll shoot out a toothpick-sized object. Mender Holley coated the tip with a medication she developed. It's a fast-acting formula able to put a person to sleep in mere moments. Would one of you care to volunteer for a wee demonstration?" Both Gahns declined. Lundy just grinned and returned to his place.

"We could talk all cycle regarding unusual weapons," continued Saephira, "including the skyfire devices your troops employed to burn our settlements and destroy our fishing fleet. No doubt, you have more questions, as do I. Let's table those queries for now. We are here for parley negotiations." Saephira pointed at the small band of soldiers who were standing thirty paces away. "If those in white plumes are junior officers, please invite them to join us."

LyeDuek signaled for the group of two women and ten men to advance. Once everyone had gathered under the canopy, the commander asked, "What are the conditions for our surrender?"

"Before we discuss those, I must show you a few artifacts." Saephira asked AliRoot to bring the chest and set it on the table. "I see by the look on your faces that several of you recognize her hairstyle and clothing. Yes, AliRoot is from Gahneeha. I met her there on an eastern sojourn to your city. She traveled here to Beayama, surviving the Nae Wilderness, to bring me these." Saephira opened the chest, removed two black stones, and set them on the table.

"Those belong to us!" exclaimed LyeDuek.

"Actually, only one does, and it will be returned at the proper time. The other one was stolen from the Archives in Briacap by your deceptive ruler, EdNook, who is none other than the infamous Eddnok, a disgraced lord." She withdrew two more stones and spaced them apart on the table. "We discovered this third one buried at the ruins on Onnie Passage—and the fourth from a cave inside the Blighte—along with this chest, a map of *Eskaon*, and an ancient document."

She unfolded the map and spread it on the table. "This map shows three settlements named Beay, Bria, and Gahn," With her finger, she pointed to each location. "They later became known as Beayama, Briacap, and Gahneeha." Next, she held up a document. "This manuscript was written in a unique text, using codes and ciphers to keep the information hidden. Our archivists unraveled the scroll's codex and translated it." She placed the original document next to the map and beckoned Narleen to move closer. "Vice-leader, please pass out copies of Taula's *Archive Analyst Report*."

While Narleen handed the sheets to their curious officers, Saephira said, "I encourage you to take a moment and read our senior curator's statement." As the Gahns studied the information, murmurs arose. Some shook their heads in disbelief; others nodded to one another, seeming to agree with the findings.

"As you can see, Commander LyeDuek, we are distant relatives, descendants from *Eskaon*, a land we currently call Eskaonus. Let me draw your attention to the prophecy in the last section about the black stones. It states a ruler of fate would emerge, collect the four *TREOWs*, join them together in a certain way, and afterwards, all the clans of *Eskaon* would be reunited in unity and truth—never to be separated again."

She slid the *TREOW* objects closer to each other, and they turned white. As the Gahns watched the transformation, their eyes grew wide, prompting more murmuring. Then remembering her dream, Saephira assembled the rectangular stones in the shape of a cross. As soon as she did, they snapped together like magnets and glowed. She raised the cross high for every soul to see.

LyeDuek dropped to his knees "We have been deceived by EdNook. You are the promised ruler, your Majesty."

"I am not royalty, nor a queen, only a simple leader who desires what's best for our people, wherever they reside. Whether or not I'm this fated person isn't important right now."

"But the translated material says whoever can join the sacred tokens together is the true Ruler of Fate, the foretold one." More junior officers dropped to their knees. "My Lady, we are your slaves."

"You are not slaves; rather, displaced relatives who were deceived by the false ruler, Eddnok. Even so, there must be consequences for your unprovoked attacks."

"Name them. We will comply with all, including the

executions of my senior officers and myself. However, please don't punish our warriors; they were simply obeying orders."

Saephira returned all the items to the chest, paused for moment before replying, "Here are my conditions for full surrender: First, you will inform your forces to stand down immediately. Do you have a way to contact them?"

"Yes, ma'am. We use homing flyers. In fact, messages have been arriving since last nightrise, reporting sunken ships, destroyed catapults, and units in disarray. Fleeing sailors confirmed our two flagships somehow escaped the carnage. I assume Skippers JaeLuet and TaeVook are returning to port."

"They did not escape; we allowed their crews to leave in hopes the news of your ill-fated invasion is reported to the leadership in Gahneeha."

"May I ask one question?"

"If it's pertinent to these proceedings."

"I haven't heard from NiaLuck, my subordinate commander from the northern battalion, which currently occupies Briacap."

"No Longer. She and her assailants were captured during a raid. Leader Bolgog has retaken control of the citadel. His prisoners are safely detained, pending the outcome of this parley."

"Thank you. As her senior commander, I worried for her welfare and for those under her command."

"Understandable. Second, your forces must disarm, remove their plated-armor, and relinquish shields and weaponry to my militia. There will be no exceptions."

"We will comply."

"Third, whenever that's done, our residents will help your sailors repair their scuttled ships, allowing your troops to return to Gahneeha. Anyone who wishes to stay and settle here may do so without fear of retribution. In the meantime, we will provide food and housing. Gahn volunteers are encouraged to assist us in rebuilding our destroyed settlements. Howbeit, the latter is not a condition of this surrender."

"You have our pledge. Until your settlements are restored, we will remain under your charge."

"Fine, then a truce has been declared. There's been enough fighting and dying, most of it on our end. Sadly, these losses cannot be undone. Nevertheless, as the appointed leader of our combined Lower and Upper Realms, I hereby grant amnesty to each soldier, sailor, and any Gahn who participated in this assault. On the morrow, I will take a delegation to Gahneeha by airship, meet with Magistrate QuiQuot, and offer a peace agreement between our peoples. This parley has ended."

"Ma'am?"

"You and your comrades are dismissed to carry out the obligations of your surrender. And as the prophecy promised, I pray there'll finally be unity between all the clans of *Eskaon* and their descendants. We are, after all, brothers and sisters."

CHAPTER 41

DIPLOMATIC MISSION

At forecycle, Lady Saephira and AliRoot rode to the Militia's practice field where the flyers remained docked during nightrise. She had promised the little girl three things: a ride in an airship, ownership of her white-striped kack, and safe passage home. Because Jesse had met Magistrate QuiQuot on their earlier sojourn to East Eskaonus, she asked him to join her on the diplomatic mission. Runess' aircrew had prepped *Old Bella* and stood ready to depart as soon as their passengers and an animal named Salie boarded the flight deck.

The plan entailed flying to Tabahir and conducting aerial surveillance over the city to determine how it fared since the invasion. If the situation appeared secure, they would continue to Briacap and land in the plaza to consult with Senior Commander Bolgog. Saephira wanted to talk with him in person about the Gahn surrender, detail the conditions of the truce, and explain her rationale for amnesty. Following the meeting with Bolgog, she'd instruct Runess to fly past the Lost Forest, across the Nae Wilderness, and land in the port city of Gahneeha. Unsure how the Gahns would view their intrusion, the latter destination troubled her the most.

"The big guy said I would find you two here." Cndrek smiled as he entered the mender's home. Ottaar had just pulled two loaves from her stove. The smell of baked kin filled the air. Lundy, Annabelle, Seth, and Holley sat around the kitchen table, waiting to break their fast.

"Which two?" Holley asked.

"Annabelle and Seth. I need a navigator and engineer for a short excursion."

"What happened to your rowmate and midmate?" Seth wondered.

"Oh yeah, I gave Tawehna and Hiehew the dawn off. They wanted to hike the Cali River trail to Mista Lake and view your vast supply of hydrew. We don't have lakes and rivers in Camayah. We hardly have any surface liquids at all. They also plan to visit a few shops and eateries in the town square."

With his interest piqued, Seth leaned forward in his chair. "Where's the excursion?"

"To this blighted area. I have theories regarding its formation, and Max says you have the coordinates."

"I do. I've been there on my hoverboard. The Blighte is hot and desolate."

"So, when does a little hot weather bother you? You lived on Camayah for a while. Besides, we'll be flying in the lower atmosphere. The temps should be much cooler."

Seth glanced at Annabelle who nodded her agreement. "Sure, Anna and I are down for it."

"Aye, me care to see the Blighte as well. Got room for old Lundy?"

"Plenty of space for sightseers," replied Cndrek.

"How about it, Hol? You've never flown on an airship before. It's totality awesome, like soaring on the wind. Much cooler than a hoverboard ride."

"I guess. I'm not doing much else this cycle."

"I'd enjoy flying the wind," added Ottaar. "How long are you going to be gone?"

"A couple bouts, no more than four or five."

"Wonderful. I'll bring a haversack of kin and sliced antaloop roast in case we get hungry."

"Hold on, dudes, let me grab several waterskins. The Blighte's heat can suck the moisture right out of your mouth." Wondering if Seth's comment was true or a witticism, the now wary group of explorers plugged along behind Cndrek to the practice field and boarded *The Seeker*.

The floater sailed across the western skies, entered the Blighte, and in less than a bout, arrived at the dry lake. "Let's hover here for an interval," ordered Cndrek. Annabelle brought the craft to a stop, and Seth put the engines on standby. Lundy, Holley, and Ottaar leaned over the rails to see the ancient settlement of *Eskaon*. Cndrek pulled a magnifier out of his pocket and scanned the area. "This place reminds me of Camayah after the Burning. I think it may have suffered a similar catastrophe."

Eventually, the others lost interest and gathered into subsets to visit. Holley and Ottaar walked to the bow and sat by the starboard rails. Lundy and Anna wandered to the stern. Seth, however, stayed on the navigator's post with Cndrek.

"Hey, Seth, come take a peek through my magnifier. Do you see the steam rising from that dry lakebed and the encrusted yellow material surrounding it? I think this entire basin contains underground accelerants."

Seth adjusted the focus on the looking glass. "You mean Triverphol?"

"No, but something similar, and the awful odor comes from light air being released."

"On earth we call it hydrogen sulfide, which is a highly flammable compound that smells like rotten eggs."

"Whatever the gas is, it can probably be mined and used for canopy lift and airship fuel."

"Why? You're not running low. I checked. The hold has at least four barrows left."

"I don't need more fuel; although, you might."

"What does that mean?"

"It means I'm leaving *The Seeker* here on Eskaonus. I don't have a crew to fly her home to Camayah, unless you and Anna offer to sail with me."

"What happened to Tawehna and Hiehew?"

"They've decided to stay on Eskaonus. Both lost their bonds in the Purge. They are middle-aged, single, and neither has living family on Camayah. I think they plan to rebond, or as the Eskaonites term it, get betrothed."

"Ya think?"

"I do. Noticed them snuggling the other dusk when they thought no one was watching." Cndrek stepped closer and stared into Seth's bluish-green eyes. "Well, are you interested in going? I'm sure Rauteira would love to see you. She said you're the only blond-haired boy on the whole planet, and all the young girls want to bond with you, she most of all. With your engineer training and other talents, I can see you becoming an airship captain in five stages."

"I'm sorry. Your offer sounds cool, even tempting, except Jesse says we're dipping out soon."

"To the high realm?"

"Actually, it's called heaven." Seth gazed skyward as he pondered the situation. "So, if you leave the floater, how are you getting home?"

"I'll hitch a ride on *Old Bella* with Runess." He sighed in obvious disappointment. "If you change your mind, or Annabelle does, let me know. We are leaving at dawn on the morrow.

"I will mention it to Anna, but I'm fairly sure her answer will be no."

"Well, I had to inquire." Cndrek flipped on the ship's intercom. "Navigator to post. Set course for Beayama. Time to head home." And *The Seeker* flew to the city, arriving at midcycle.

After stopping at Briacap so Saephira and Bolgog could meet, *Old Bella* lifted off and continued east to Gahneeha. While Uewba kept AliRoot occupied at the navigator's post, showing her how to steer a flyer, Saephira and Jesse met in the captain's cabin with Runess. He asked, "May I examine those black stones?"

"Sure, they're in the metal chest I brought aboard. Give me a moment." Saephira hurried to the first sleeper on the nether deck, grabbed her little box, and returned. She opened the lid and handed Runess one of the rectangular objects.

"Interesting." He turned it around in his hand, feeling the smoothness. "These things are similar to datastones used prior to the Burning. Sadly, they were lost during the Event, along with most of our records and technology." He rubbed his finger over the *TREOW* symbol. "Hmm, do you mind if I try an experiment on my terminal." Saephira nodded her approval.

Runess placed it on top of his comm reader and touched *Examine* on the monitor. Immediately, the screen flashed and multiple lines of data appeared, revealing images, illustrations, and vast sections of text.

"What does this mean?" Saephira shuffled nearer to study the images.

"I believe it means your ancestors were more advanced than you thought." He removed the stone and tried a second one. It displayed the exact same data, as did the third and fourth ones. "All of these are duplicates."

"Can you explain? I'm not sure I comprehend. Is it tekknowledgie?"

"The data could include technology. However, I think it's a type of archive." He pointed to the *TREOW* symbol engraved on the front. "According to Lundy, an expert in linguistics, *treow* is an archaic word meaning tree."

"A family tree?" questioned Jesse.

"Perhaps. With a portion of those images being faces of individuals, I would say this record is a registry of the Gahn, Beay, and Bria families of *Eskaon*."

"Wow! If so, Saephira, this is an incredible find. You may have discovered the long-lost history of your ancestors."

"I concur with you, Jesse." Runess gave the stones back to Saephira who placed them into her tin holder. "Okay, this is what I can do. I have a spare datatop in my cabin. I'll give the device to your archivists so they can research and translate the data."

"Datatop device? We don't understand how to use your tekknowledgie."

"It's easy. The *sent ones* can show you."

Saephira scrunched her face. "*Sent ones?*"

"It's what the Camayahnites call us," advised Jesse.

"I see. Then I'll ask Lundy and Annabelle to assist our archivists in—"

Suddenly, the ship's intercom sounded in the cabin. "Rowmate to captain. We are approaching a large city. What are your orders?"

Runess raced to the navigator's post. "Set her down in the empty space by those docks."

Old Bella descended to a soft landing. Within a quarter

span, a mass of people surrounded the oddly built craft. In front of the crowd stood armored soldiers, some with pikes, others with swords—and behind them, diverse groups of men, women, and children.

Runess paced from port to starboard, scratching his chin. "I don't like the look of this, ma'am. Jaw, you better man the duespike. Uew, go to the weapons locker and break out three trispikes. And hurry. We may get rushed."

"Runess, please raise the parley flag and give the hail I told you." Saephira peered over the rail to see if is she could spot a familiar face. "Let's hope we can avoid any more fighting."

As soon as the blue flag rose to the top of the mast, a large man ambled forth from among the throng. "My name is QuiQuot, the acting magistrate of Gahneeha. Who requests this parley?"

Runess leaned on the rail and replied, "As captain of the airship, *Old Bella,* I've been instructed to tell you that SaeFear, JayEsse, and AliRoot have requested it."

"AliRoot is with you?"

"I am." AliRoot peeked through the railings. "Stop being naughty, QuiQuot. We aren't here to harm anybody. SaeFear has come to make peace. Come aboard and see the kack she gave me."

The magistrate turned around and motioned for the city militia to lay down their weapons. "I will go see this strange vessel and conduct a parley." Runess dropped the ramp, and QuiQuot boarded the ship, holding the hand of MiaRoot. When the two reached the flight deck, AliRoot saw her mother and ran to embrace her.

"Momma, I told you I'd come back. You would be so proud of me."

"I am, dear. We all worried about you. Where did you go?"

"Across the Nae to find JayEsse and SaeFear. He's a good man, and she's the true Ruler of Fate. I brought the sacred stones to her so she could save us from the bad, bad EdNook. SaeFear is the one who gave us silver and bronze tokens to move out of that horrible Camp Gahn."

"I did leave the camp, brave daughter, and relocated to the city. In fact, QuiQuot and I are attached."

"I'm happy for you, Momma. I knew it would happen. Is QuiQuot my papa now?"

"He is." AliRoot dashed over to him, jumped up, and hung on to his neck.

"I missed you, little one." QuiQuot gave her a quick kiss on her cheek. As he put her down, a frown formed on his face. "At some point, AliRoot, I need to inquire concerning the missing black talismans."

"Yep, I took them, and I'm glad I did. SaeFear will tell you why." She skipped across to the foredeck and removed the hobbles on her kack. "Momma, this is Salie. Do you wanna go for a ride?"

MiaRoot eyed QuiQuot and mouthed the words, "Is it alright?"

"Sure. Don't be gone too long." AliRoot hopped on Salie, helped her mother climb on behind, and together they trotted away. Once on the street, AliRoot steered her ride past the onlookers, traveling toward the city square. QuiQuot waited until the two had rounded the corner. "Before we begin this parley, SaeFear, I wish to know everyone's real names."

"I am Lady Saephira. My comrade is Jesse Walt. Our captain is Runess."

"After considering the recent homing flyer messages describing our defeat, I cannot say it's good to meet you three. Aside from the few cargo ships and harpooning trawlers in the harbor, our entire military fleet, numbering forty vessels, is reported sunk. I assume the Gahn army has been slaughtered as well."

"No, they have not!" retorted Saephira. "Other than a handful of soldiers lost in this unprovoked invasion, your people were spared. Not the case with mine." Anger flared on Saephira's face, her posture stiffened, her voice rose, and tears began to flow. She could no longer hold back her feelings. "Your losses involved military personnel, soldiers whose job it is to fight and die. On the other hand, we lost hundreds of families to your skyfire weapons, including innocent women and children. Your settlements remain intact. Several of ours are decimated, homes and buildings burned to the ground. Discounting the six catapult boats that caught fire and sank, the rest of your armada has only been scuttled. The damage can be repaired, the crafts refloated. As for us, our small fleet of fishing vessels sits on the bottom of the sea, their crews dead."

"It appears your anger is justified. Then I assume this is not really a parley; rather, it's a demand for our capitulation."

"That's not why we journeyed here. I simply desire for this foolish war to end and for there to be peace between the eastern and western realms. We are not seeking surrender but a truce, not occupation of Gahneeha but an alliance. And if you will permit me, I will show why we should be allies, not enemies."

For the next span, Saephira presented the same information she shared with Commander LyeDuek about finding a chest with the map of *Eskaon* and other artifacts. She gave QuiQuot a copy of the archiver's report, connected the four *TREOW* stones, and confirmed the prophecy relating to fate and unity. She explained her offer of amnesty, assisting the Gahns in repairing their ships, and the safe return of all sailors and soldiers to their homeland.

"I understand why AliRoot believes you are this ruler of fate. And I'm inclined to agree with her. It appears we've been greatly deceived by EdNook, I mean Eddnok. What do you want us to do with him?"

"My thoughts are conflicted on this matter. Part of me feels he ought to pay dearly, even with his life. Whatever you decide, don't let him see another dayrise as a free man."

"Perhaps you can devise a novel punishment to fit his many crimes," suggested Jesse.

"Okay, I will arrest him when or if he shows his face in Gahneeha. We will hold a trial and let the elders decide his fate."

As the conversation wound down, AliRoot returned with MiaRoot. "Did you and your mother have a nice ride on Salie?"

"We did, SaeFear, we did. Salie is wonderful, and Momma agrees. Salie seems to recognize everything I say." She skipped over to hug Saephira, stopped, and closed her eyelids for a moment. When she reopened them, she said, "You and JayEsse are leaving, aren't you? Can't you stay and play with me? I'll even let JayEsse win at flinging rocks in the river."

"I'm sorry, dear one. We must depart for Beayama."

AliRoot grabbed Saephira's neck and whispered in her ear. "Tell JayEsse you love him."

"If he will listen to me, I'll try."

She blinked her eyes again. "Maximus and Narleen will birth a baby girl named Cassia." Saephira released the embrace and stepped backwards with an odd look on her face. "Don't be mad at me," implored AliRoot.

"I'm not. Your insights still amaze me."

Next, she hugged Jesse around the waist. "You have a good heart, JayEsse. Practice your throwing, and next yarn, I'll challenge you to another contest of skipping rocks." Jesse smiled, yet didn't have the heart to tell AliRoot he'd never see her again.

Before *The Seeker* departed, Saephira handed QuiQuot the *TREOW* that had originally belonged to the Gahns and promised to visit in one yarn to finalize their alliance.

CHAPTER 42

RETURNING HOME

Instead of flying across the Nae to return to Beayama, Saephira asked Runess to follow the coastline, hoping to spot Eddnok in his fleeing flagship. After a league of travel, Uewba shouted, "Ship off the starboard bow. It's sailing northeast and flying a gold-striped banner on the main mast." Runess, Saephira, and Jesse rushed to the foredeck and peered over the rails.

Runess focused his magnifier. "I see a purple pennant on the second mast. It must be Eddnok's vessel. You may not get another chance, ma'am; shall we sink her?"

"I'd like nothing more. I'm sorry I still feel this way. Eddnok deserves to die for the many crimes and murders he's committed these past yarns, but not along with the crew who are just followers of his deceptive orders. Let the ship pass. QuiQuot promised me that Eddnok would face judgment when he arrives in port."

Old Bella continued southwest for three more leagues until a whistle sounded in the captain's cabin. "Small craft adrift off the port bow, Cap. Do we investigate?"

"Yes, Uew, drop us down for a closer look." Runess switched on his intercom. "This is the Captain. All hands on deck for rescue operations."

By the time everyone arrived, *Old Bella* hovered above a

tiny boat with five listless bodies. "I think this could be the lifeboat Master Haleema released before her flagship perished," reasoned Saephira. "Can you land this airship in the water?"

"We're still a ship, ma'am. Of course we can." He turned to his navigator. "Uew, splash her down next to the boat and prepare to lower our ramp." As the floater descended, Runess called to Jaw and Jesse. "Grab the gaff lines in my cabin and stand by to recover bodies."

The little skiff was half-full of water and barely afloat. Jesse and Jawhawtu tossed their lines, pulled the craft nearer, and jumped into it. "Are any of them alive?" asked Saephira.

"We'll know in a moment," Jesse replied. They quickly checked the five men for life signs. "The sailors are unconscious with shallow breathing. All are severely dehydrated."

One by one, Jesse and Jaw hauled them aboard and laid them by the stern. "These guys better receive medical assistance soon, or they may not make it. I wish we had Ottaar with us." Jesse hailed Runess on the quarterdeck. "Do you have a first aid kit?"

"No, however, I have an idea. In my cabin is a chest with hydration and nutrition tabs. Grab a handful of Tyhydru and Dapferon. The pills may help revive them." Jesse raced to the cabin, withdrew ten oval tablets: five reddish, five greenish, and backtracked to the afterdeck. Runess managed to force the tabs into the sailor's mouths without choking them. "We need to give those supplements a chance to work, so I want three hands to move this crew to the sleepers. Right now, rest is what they need most." Jawhawtu, Uewba, and Jesse acknowledged the command, lugged the men below, settled them into bunks, and returned to the flight deck for more orders.

"Jaw, engage the engines and give me full power. I would like to reach Beayama as soon as possible. In the meantime, I'll contact Narleen and Cndrek on my datacomm to advise them of our current situation, and then I'm going below to keep an eye on the condition of our survivors. Uew, you have the helm. And Jesse, you're dismissed to swab the deck." Runess laughed, hoping Jesse realized he was kidding.

A bout later, Runess passed by Saephira and Jesse as he made his rounds. "The castaways are doing better. They're sleeping soundly. All in all, a good dawn, I'd say. The negotiations went well, and we recovered five marooned shipmates. It appears our work here on Eskaonus has concluded. Cndrek and I feel it's time for us to fly back to Camayah. Therefore, we've decided to leave at predawn."

"Are you sure you can't stay a little longer?" pressed Saephira, hoping for a yes. "I was planning a celebration banquet for next cycle."

"I'll hafta pass, ma'am. We best ride the wormhole to our world before it closes. Those phenomena are tricky things. I felt you and Jesse deserved a heads-up about our plans."

"How do we ever thank you? You helped save Eskaonus."

"No thanks needed, ma'am. It's what *sent ones* are supposed to do, right Jesse?" Jesse merely nodded with a blank stare, as if his thoughts wandered elsewhere. "*Old Bella* should be arriving in Beayama in a couple bouts. Until then, enjoy the view over the rails. I have lots of preflight prep to accomplish prior to dawn. Joyous dusk to you." Runess entered his cabin and shut the door.

Saephira and Jesse stood at the rails and watched the coastline go by. A long period of silent reflection transpired between them until Jesse spoke. "Saephira, I've been waiting for the proper time to tell you . . ."

"What? Is there something wrong?"

"We are leaving, too."

"To the high realm?" Saephira exhaled a deep sigh. "Already?"

"Our collective only planned to stay here for a few cycles, but then your fishing vessels were lost at sea, Eddnok reappeared, and the invasion occurred. Now that everything seems resolved, it's time for us to depart as well."

"Please wait another cycle, at least until the celebration banquet?"

"I'm sorry, Saephira."

"So am I." She sighed again and slowly stepped away from the rail.

"Where are you going?"

"To check on the welfare of my sailors." And Saephira descended the rungs to the nether deck. Jesse didn't notice the tears in her eyes.

Old Bella landed in Beayama during twilight. After checking once again on the conditions of her seamen, Saephira took the chest of artifacts and walked to the ramp. Jesse followed her. "Would you like me to escort you to Residential Hall?"

"No, that's okay. Uewba has offered to accompany me to my quarters. However, I'd appreciate it if you asked a mender to check on our castaways."

"Ma'am, the mariners can spend the night on my flyer. I'm sure they'll feel fit in the dawn. Those supplement tabs can do wonders."

"Thank you, Captain Runess. Your nourishment pills, aerial transportation, and general assistance have been invaluable. Without it, we might have all perished." Saephira moved closer and kissed him on the cheek. Surprised at the unexpected show of affection, Runess' face turned slightly red. Next, she curtsied to Jesse and said, "Good nightrise." With Uewba holding Saephira's arm, the two departed *Old Bella*. Jesse felt slighted, even though he probably deserved it. As the women strolled down the street, he heard muffled weeping.

For a moment, Jesse considered trying to catch up to them and offer Saephira an apology for disappointing her. Instead, he entered the engineering bay to visit with Jawhawtu and say goodbye. Later, he returned to the quarterdeck and offered a farewell to Runess. With one last glance at *Old Bella*, Jesse exited the ship and hurried to the mender's house. He entered Ottaar's front door to find his group sitting around the kitchen table. Lundy, Anna, Seth, and Holley were eager to hear what happened in Gahneeha. Following a brief summary, he asked, "Where's Ottaar?"

"She went to bed a span ago," confirmed Holley. "Why do you ask? Is someone in need of mendering?"

"Yeah. During our flight home, we rescued five stranded deckhands from Master Haleema's flagship. The men are spending nightrise on Runess' airship. Saephira wondered if a mender could check on them."

Holley stood and grabbed her medical bag. "Since I'm a mender now, I'd be happy to." She darted for the door, then stopped suddenly. "Jesse, will you still be up when I finish my treatments? I've been meaning to talk with you."

"It's nearing darkout. Can the conversation save until the morrow? I'm exhausted. It's been a long dayrise."

"Sure, I simply—"

"Hold up, Hol. I'll go with you." On the way out, Seth grabbed a torch on the landing, and the two rushed away, heading toward the practice field where Camayah's floaters were docked.

After they left, Jesse addressed Annabelle and the reverend. "I'll meet everybody at firstlight to break our fast. Since our mission is done here, we'll be departing for heaven in the morning. Pack your satchels ahead of time and make sure Seth and Holley know the itinerary."

Ignoring their questioning faces, Jesse climbed the stairwell and entered his bedroom. He placed his candle lamp on the dresser and flipped the lid to ignite the flame. A warming glow and the smell of frankincense filled the room. Jesse pulled out his journal, wanting to add the next entry, but changed his mind and started reading his previous logs, remembering their earlier adventures and experiences. By the time he finished, several spans had elapsed. Being past darkout, he could hardly keep his eyelids open. Jesse extinguished his candle lamp and crawled into bed, planning to write a diary log in the morning before breaking fast with his team members. Within moments, he was sound asleep.

CHAPTER 43

THE AFTERMATH

Glancing out the window, Jesse could tell it was past forecycle. He had overslept. Realizing his colleagues were waiting for him, he dressed quickly, packed his satchel, and bolted down the stairs. His team members were sitting around the table, sipping tea and talking. "Sorry I'm late, guys. I assume you've already broken your fast?"

"Ottaar served a meal over a span ago," advised Holley. "She left kin rolls on the counter for you before she departed for shopping."

"Naw, I'm not really hungry." He scanned the room. "Where's Seth? We're supposed to be leaving for heaven this morning."

Everyone had odd expressions on their faces as if they were hiding something. Finally, Anna answered, "Seth took off at firstlight. He left this letter for you." She slid it across the table to him.

Hey JW. I dropped by your bedroom at firstlight to talk, except you were sound asleep, snoring the hinges off. By the time you read this, I'll be on my way to Camayah. I told Max everything, so he can fill you in on the details. Since Cndrek no longer has an aircrew, he left his airship behind at the Militia practice field. He felt The Seeker might come in handy while the Lower Realm replaces their fishing fleet.

If I work hard, Cndrek thinks I can become a flight captain in five years; I mean yarns or is it stages? All these calendar timeframes still scramble my brain. Anywho, Tawehna and Hiehew are staying in Eskaonus. They can handle the navigation and engineering duties on the ship. In fact, the programmer dude understands floater crafts better than most. Hiehew even designed their Triverphol engines.

Cndrek believes the Blighte may have an adaptable fuel source underneath the dry lake. Max has the information on how to access it. Well, I gotta dip. Us dudes have a wormhole to catch. Oh yeah, I'm taking my hoverboard and radio with me. Hope this doesn't break some heavenly rule. Besides, you may need to contact me one day; I mean cycle, dawn, or whatever. In case you're wondering about Rauteira and me, all I can say is that dayrise will bring what it brings.

I will miss Max the most; don't tell him I said so. Thanks for the adventure, JW. You're the coolest boss ever. Remember Rule Number One.

Seth

"Did you guys know about this?"

"Aye, we read the letter. Me thinks the kid will do fine," replied Lundy. "Perhaps God has called him there for an important task." Jesse plopped down in a settee by the table and began chewing on his lower lip. He leaned forward, closed his eyelids for a few moments, and seemed to zone out.

Holley cleared her throat to draw his attention. "I wanted to visit with you last night, Jesse. However, you were already in bed by the time I returned from mendering the sailors. I'm not sure how to say this . . ." Her voice softened to almost a whisper. "I've decided to stay in Eskaonus."

"What?" Jesse sprang to his feet. "You're kidding, right?"

"No. Ritwell Village needs a mender. My heart is here with these people. I made this decision a while ago. Ottaar already knows—as does Lady Narleen. I can accomplish more in Eskaonus than I ever could walking the golden streets in heaven."

"Wow, I never realized . . . are you sure?"

"Yes, I believe it's my calling. I'm an official mender now." She slung her medical bag over her shoulder and adjusted her purple sash with the five tassels. "Bonarb has offered to escort me to the village to establish an aid station." She smiled as she spoke. "I think he likes me, too. We're almost the same age and have interests in common. Sorry to rush off; Bonarb is waiting for me at Ellee's eatery." She hurried to the front door, stopped suddenly, turned around, and curtsied. "Thank you, Jesse, for making my dream of being a doctor come true." She opened the door and scurried outside, closing it behind her.

"I hate to be another bearer of unexpected news, Jess, but I'm also staying." Anna's voice cracked, followed by a flood of tears. "Reverend, can you explain. I just can't . . ."

"Aye, expounding things is me specialty. You best take your seat again, Brother Walt. You see, Annabel and me have been talking ever since we visited the ruins at High Springs. We think the place was a temple complex long ago, maybe even a monastery, and I wish to help the Eskaonites rebuild it. Always felt I should be pastoring churches again. This is me chance to make a difference."

"On the morrow, we travel up Onnie Passage to begin the restoration process. Chepho offered to lead the expedition. He's organizing a group of smiths and rock masons to assist with the rebuilding. Even Mender Ottaar is participating. She looks forward to harvesting more fruit and healing leaves from the life tree. Gelr arrived from Briacap yestercycle and has already asked for safeguard volunteers to ferry supplies to the site."

"As soon as the sanctuary is completed, I'll start teaching on spiritual matters. I'm convinced the Unseen One of *Eskaon*, Yah from Camayah, Yahweh from earth, and the Word from John's gospel are the same deity. Annabel plans to use her glifstring and nyeflute to lead praise and worship, teach songs, and if congregants are interested, start a choir. Tawehna and Hiehew, who are already Yah believers, want to be involved as well. Me thinks it's the main reason they're staying here in Eskaonus. We have a grand project on our hands."

Stunned, Jesse stared glassy-eyed at Lundy.

"Me and Annabel have scheduled an organizational meeting with Chepho, Tawehna, and Hiehew regarding the trip. We're on a time schedule and need to finish our deliberations by midcycle, so she and Gelr can go mushroom picking."

"Reverend, you weren't supposed to say that. It's a secret."

"Accept my wee apology, Annabel. Us preachers can't help but share good news. In me defense, though, Luke 8:17 says nothing is hidden that shall not be known."

"I figured you'd come up with a justifiable verse. I'm not mad. I am glad folks know. Concerning Gelr, our friendship goes back to the cycle I found him bemoaning his evil deeds with Eddnok and encouraged him to change his destiny by doing good."

Finally, Jesse's befuddled mind cleared. "So, you and Gelr are courting. How long?"

"With time being relative in different places, I'm not exactly sure. Perhaps a month."

"Apparently, I'm the last to find out these things."

"Maybe your thoughts have been focused elsewhere."

Jesse bolted from the settee. "And where would that be?" His face reddened and posture stiffened.

"On your relationship with Saephira."

"We don't have one!"

"Sorry, Jess, perhaps I've misread things. Either way, Lundy and I must leave now." She hurried over and gave Jesse a hug on the neck. "Thank you for saving me during the rockslide on Onnie Passage and for your caring leadership thereafter. Seth was correct; you are the best boss ever." Her tears began flowing again. "Say hello to Chesedel for us when you get back to heaven." Then she and Lundy departed, leaving Jesse standing all alone.

He could hardly believe what just happened. Jesse moved to a stool by the table, opened his satchel, removed his journal, and primed his pen. "This will make for an interesting log." Instead of writing entry twenty-two, he scribbled:

Final Entry

I am not sure how to put this . . .

Startled by Saephira entering, he shut the journal cover and stood.

"Lady Saephira, I didn't expect to see you again. I figured I'd offended you one too many times."

"Not at all. Last nightrise, I was disappointed to learn you were leaving so soon. I had hoped you could stay a little longer. I later realized we all have obligations to keep, including me." She approached closer, noticing Jesse's journal on the table. "I came by to wish you and your colleagues a safe journey to the high realm."

"Apparently, they aren't traveling with me."

"What happened?"

"Pull up a chair, and I'll tell you." Jesse perched on the stool. In a dejected tone, he proceeded to give her the somber details. Once Jesse finished, he asked, "Were you aware of these decisions?"

"No. This is the first I've heard regarding your team staying on Eskaonus, and I knew nothing about Seth leaving, either. Narleen did mention Max and her were picking dallups this cycle. I had no idea Annabelle had invited Gelr to do the same. It's customary for couples to court those they're interested in betrothing. If you recall, gathering mushrooms is the preferred method for women to attract eligible suiters in Eskaonus."

"Yeah, I remember."

"You should be happy for them."

"I guess . . ." His voice dropped off like a bucket in a well.

"Really, you don't sound very pleased."

"Sorry, I don't care to discuss it. Nothing personal, Saephira."

"Understandable, considering . . ." She leaned against the backrest, pondering how to finish her thought. "Because this is the last time I'll see you, I'm gonna take AliRoot's advise and say it."

"Say what?"

"That I love you, yet for some reason you've ignored my repeated hints, and several of those were not so subtle. Therefore, I'm officially inviting you to pick dallups with me. I will tarry at the stables until midcycle." Without waiting for a reply, she arose, pushed her chair aside, and slipped out the front entrance.

Jesse sat motionless for the longest time, his thoughts skewed, his eyes closed. When he opened them, he noticed his journal, picked up his pen, and continued where he left off.

Final Entry

I am not sure how to put this, but my team isn't returning to heaven. Seth departed for Camayah in an airship this morning. Lundy wants to stay here and build a church, and Annie has agreed to serve as his worship leader. As for Holley, she recently accepted a village mender positon in Ritwell. Can redeemed saints do such things? Are they able to dwell or serve God outside of heaven as mortals? And with respect to falling in love with someone in an outer realm world, is it kosher or even allowed?

I'm torn, confused, maybe I should . . .

Before he finished the sentence, Ottaar walked in with two armloads of supplies. She set the bags on her counter and stared at Jesse. "What are you doing here by yourself?"

"Writing an entry in my journal." He closed the cover and set his ink pen aside. "Can I ask you a question?"

"Sure, what's on your mind?"

"Do you know what's going on with my associates?"

"I'm the city mender. I know everything. And I'll tell you this, Jesse Walt, if you don't rise from your seat this very moment—go over to the stables and apologize to Lady Saephira for being an idiot—then I'll use my cane to drive you there." She reached for a shortened, wooden staff that leaned against the wall by her counter and raised it high in the air. "Well, what's it gonna be?"

Jesse rose warily to his feet, left his journal and pen on the table, and raced through the open door.

"Don't worry, I'll close it." Ottaar slowly shook her head and chuckled, which developed into a fit of laughter. Afterwards, she unpacked her bags and poured herself a cup of Anatora tea.

CHAPTER 44

THE FULLNESS OF TIMES

Uzziel and Chesedel strolled along Straight Street discussing recent events. Much had occurred following the wars in heaven and on earth. There were seven bowl judgments, the destruction of Babylon the Great, and news that Satan had finally been defeated and locked in a deep pit:

"And I saw an angel come down from heaven, having the key of the bottomless pit and a great chain in his hand. And he laid hold on the dragon, that old serpent, which is the Devil, and Satan, and bound him a thousand years, And cast him into the bottomless pit, and shut him up, and set a seal upon him, that he should deceive the nations no more, till the thousand years should be fulfilled: and after that he must be loosed a little season" (Revelation 20:1–3).

"The world has endured ages of deceit, and Satan has only been bound temporarily?"

"Sadly, elChesed, this is true. Prophecy says the devil will be freed from his prison cell when a thousand earth years have concluded. God has his reasons. Perhaps the Almighty hopes Satan will repent, or his release will serve a higher purpose. We are not privy to God's wisdom. What we do know is that these final events will usher in *The Greatest Moment*. In the meantime, the inhabitants of the earth will have a millennium to rejoice."

Chesedel smiled. "The residents of heaven will celebrate as

well."

"They already are. Soon their praises will fill eternity." The two angels stopped at the Walled Terrance to sit down. "Since we have a short thousand-year break," Uzziel laughed at his quip, "tell me about Eskaonus and Eddnok's invasion of the western realms. I'm concerned."

"As was I. Jesse's journal logs stopped at *Entry Twenty-One*, or so I thought. Therefore, I dispatched a winged sentinel to Eskaonus to observe. He just returned."

"What did the winged one discover?"

"Their resident evil had finally been defeated, the invasion halted, and the three realms of Eskaonus reunited, yet not before the southern province and their people suffered much loss. Fortunately, a handful of Camayahnites in airships traveled through a wormhole to save them from further destruction."

"My sources tell me you made this portal jump possible."

"I simply provided the means and pointed the way. At no time did I waver from our rules concerning angelic encounters."

"Good, it appears your promotion to the rank of cherubim was warranted. Aside from the sentinel's observations, have we received any additional updates from Jesse? You indicated there may be another log."

"There is. Although I believed twenty-one to be his last, a subsequent log recently arrived at the Hall of Records, and it's perplexing."

"Please clarify."

"Jesse called it his *Final Entry*. He wrote that his team isn't returning. Holley wants to remain in Eskaonus as a village mender to provide medical care. Lundy and Annabelle desire to rebuild a destroyed temple and continue its ministry. As for Seth, he returned to Camayah. None of them are coming back to heaven."

"What about Jesse?"

"His log is unclear regarding his intentions. Thus far, our gate watchers have not reported his presence anywhere in the heavenly realm."

"And this bothers you?"

"Greatly. Weren't our envoys supposed to return once they completed their mission?"

"Hmm." Uzziel stood and wandered over to the Tree of

Life. "Maybe God has a higher purpose for the Redeemed. And I don't think it involves staying in heaven for eternity, and to quote a cliché, to float around on clouds and play harps forever and ever."

Chesedel followed closely behind him. "Why do most saints think reaching heaven is the ultimate goal?"

"Tradition perhaps." Uzziel picked two life fruits and handed one to Chesedel. "Apparently, outreach to lost and needy worlds in God's vast kingdom has been His purpose from the beginning—and one of the reasons for redemption."

"Will we ever see Jesse and his colleagues again?"

"Most assuredly." Uzziel devoured his purple fruit and placed the pit on top of the Walled Terrace. "Prophecy states 'that in the dispensation of the fullness of the times He might gather together in one all things in Christ, both which are in heaven and which are on earth—in Him.'"

"Isn't this passage from Ephesians 1:10 in the New King James Version?"

"Correct. The words are likewise found in other Bible translations, always reflecting the same promise." Uzziel walked to the River of Life and stared at the waters flowing crystal clear.

As he pondered the prophecy, Chesedel joined Uzziel at the riverbank. "After eons of endless turmoil, can such oneness truly occur?"

"So it would seem, my friend. One day there will be unity, not only on the earth, but throughout the heavens."

"Does this include the people of Eskaonus, Camayah, and inhabitants beyond the outer realms?"

"The prophecy indicates all things in all places," confirmed Uzziel.

"Even us angels in heaven?"

"I would assume the 'gather together in one' also includes immortal beings since they likewise dwell in our heavenly domains. Well, elChesed, it seems as if we have our work cut out for us. Finish eating your life fruit and then let's go."

"Where?"

"To the Fountain of Living Water. There's another group of *Abrahams* waiting for an assignment to minister in a world facing peril. In fact, we have many willing parties, all because of Jesse and his envoys who responded to the first call. Their selfless examples have stirred a revival of sorts in heaven."

"Who is giving the appeal to this group at the fountain?"

"You are."

"Me! Are you sure I'm ready?"

"Yes, you're one of the cherubim now. Don't worry; I'll stand by your side in case you need me. Remember to show the saints your flaming sword so they know you're a ranked cherub."

"I will. What's the mission this time?"

"I'll tell you on the way." The two angels entered the unseen realm and instantly arrived at the fountain. And a new outreach began on *the day after always.*

CAST OF CHARACTERS

This directory contains major and minor characters from all three books in *The Day After Always* series. Not every character is a player in each novel. The names are provided for reference, review, and their connection to the various storylines.

Abdiel (AB-dye'l): High-ranking angel. His name means servant of God. He manages Outreach & Supply in Central Heaven.

Ahboen (ah-BOW'n): Former Program Assistant (PA) on Camayah, missing.

AliRoot (AL-ee-root): A gifted young girl from East Eskaonus.

Bio: AliRoot lives in Camp Gahn with her mother, MiaRoot, who is a strict yet loving parent. The child is highly curious, often impetuous, and loves to play games. She is friendly, helpful to her friends, mischievous at times, and very perceptive for a nine-year-old.

Annabelle Altshuler: Also called Anna, Annie, and Annabel. Messianic believer, anointed songwriter, musician, raptured saint. Envoy to Eskaonus.

Bio: Annabelle was born in Ghana. When her parents died, a Jewish family in England adopted her. She attended their synagogue, and later, a messianic fellowship where she had a charismatic experience. God began giving her prophetic dreams and spiritual songs, which certain folks in her congregation didn't appreciate. They asked Anna to keep those revelations and songs to herself or leave. After praying for wisdom, she decided to move on. Soon thereafter, the Rapture occurred.

Bolgog (BOWL-gog): Senior Commander in the Guards. He later became the de facto leader of the Upper Realm when Lord Eddnok disappeared. Lives in Briacap.

Bonarb (BOW-narb): Younger brother of Chepho, squad leader in the Militia, resides on Eskaonus.

Bovi (BO-vee): Former concubine in Eddnok's household. Her fraternal twin sister is Seirlai. Bovi currently lives with relatives in Briacap.

Brappt (BRAP't): Sub-Commander in the Upper Realm.

Calrin (cal-RIN): Teenager from Beayama, harpoon angler, friend of Seth.

Chepho (CHE-foe): Militia Lead in the Lower Realm.

Chesedel (CHESS-a-del): Official name is *elChesed*. Faithful messenger, Jesse's guardian angel. His name means mercy of God.

Cndrek (KUHN-drek): Senior Security Leader (SSL). He oversees all Sectors and RIFTs on Camayah, serves on the Council of Twelve.

Eddnok (ED-nock): Lord Eddnok, deposed ruler of the Upper Realm, former magistrate in Briacap. He later adopted the name of EdNook.

Bio: Eddnok is self-centered, cunning, helps those who are faithful to him, and turns on those who are not. He consumed fruit from the cloned knowledge tree and embraced evil. He was last seen entering the Lost Forest. He later resurfaced in East

Eskaonus as EdNook.

EdNook (ED-nook): Ruler EdNook, same person as Lord Eddnok.

Ellee: Owner of Ellee's Place, an eatery in Beayama.

Flissae (FLISS-ay): A prostitute who worked for Eddnok. Recently moved to Tabahir and opened a tavern.

Fruit Vendor: Angel who operates the mobile produce stand in heaven.

Gelr (GEL'er): Former Upper Realm commander who defected to the Lower Realm. Promoted to Captain of the Safeguards by Lady Saephira.

Haleema (ha-LEE-mah): Master Skipper, senior flagship captain from Bayegulf.

Hiehew (HI-hue): Program Leader (PL) at the Science Center on Camayah, serves on the Council of Twelve, Yah believer.

HieHoot (hi-HOOT): Sailor, first mate on QuiQuot's cargo ship. Lives in Gahneeha.

Holley Rossie: Also called Hol, Doc, and healer. Former nurse practitioner, recent resident of heaven. Now a mender on Eskaonus.

Bio: Holley worked in an emergency care facility on earth before she arrived in heaven. She regretted not going to Eskaonus with Jesse and the team. Later, Holley realized her healthcare knowledge was why the angels chose her for the first outreach. A medic would have been advantageous, considering the dire conflicts the team encountered. When presented with another opportunity, she joined the second outreach to Camayah.

Hyneil (HIE-neal): Magistrate of Bayegulf.

JaeLuet (jay-LOOT): Gahn flagship skipper, northern armada, Hallet Sea.

Jawhawtu (jaw-HAH-too): Also called Jaw, airship midmate, engineer.

Jesse Walt: Also called Jess, JW, Sir, Brother Walt, and JayEsse (jay-ESS-ee). Served in the Navy, former police officer, raptured saint, chosen as team leader for the Eskaonus outreach.

Bio: After high school, Jesse enlisted in the Navy and became an MP. When he got out of the service, he took a position as a small-town police chief. Due to an unfortunate DUI accident, the department forced him to resign. He had trouble finding work until a convenience store hired him as a clerk. Jesse is inquisitive, caring, and sometimes conflicted. He enjoys journaling. After the Rapture, he was asked to lead a group of emissaries to Eskaonus, and then later to Camayah.

Layshura (lay-SURE-ah): Operational Leader (OL) at the Health Center on Camayah, serves on the Council of Twelve.

Leeda (LEE-duh): Senior elder from Nakk Village.

Leetqu (LEET-kue): Inhabitant of Camayah, serves on the Council of Twelve, Yah believer, married to Rekis, her daughter is Rauteira.

Lucifer: Also known as Satan, the devil, the great dragon, and that old serpent.

Lundy MacBain: Also called Reverend, Rev, Preach, Master Lundy, and Papa Lun. Scottish minister, Bible scholar, language translator, missionary, martyred saint, resident of heaven. Envoy to Eskaonus.

Bio: Reverend Lundy ministered for many years as a pastor. He lived in Scotland 400 years ago. One day, he encountered a mob of agnostics who didn't care for his preaching. They pulled knives and killed him. His soul emerged in heaven. He spends his time in prayer and meditating on Scripture.

Lurah (LOO-rah): Postal Overseer for the central mail tower in Beayama. Her teenage brother is Raydoo.

LyeDuek (LIE-dook): High Commander of the Southern Gahn Battalion.

Malmach (maul-MOK): Spiritual leader, called the provost, Yah believer, serves on the Council of Twelve on Camayah, married to Trikernae. Along with his spouse, he oversees the ministry at the Temple Compound.

Maximus Gallius: Known as Max, Maximum, Maxie, and the big guy. Roman soldier who found faith in Christ during the first century, longtime resident of heaven. Currently staying on Eskaonus, married to Narleen. Promoted to Captain of the Militia by Lady Saephira.

Bio: Maximus was a Roman soldier, a centurion, in charge of ninety men. He worshiped the false god of war, Mars. While away on an eastern campaign, barbarians raided his hometown. They killed everyone in the village and raped his beloved, Cassia, before murdering her. His plans for marriage and children ended. He grew distraught, bitter, and angrier by the season. Then one day, Max met a fisherman who told him about the one true God. He and several of his legionnaires accepted His Son as Savior and were baptized. Later, Caesar discovered their new allegiance to the Christ and put the group to the sword. Max awoke in heaven.

Melmandus (mel-MAN-dus): Former Captain of the Militia. Perished in a rockslide.

Membarb (MEM-barb): Woodsmith in Beayama, friend of Ottaar.

Menarbat (MEN-ar-bat): Called *the Tracker*, former Overseer of Provisions in Beayama, traitor. Last seen entering the Lost Forest with Eddnok.

MiaRoot (MY-uh-root): Mother of AliRoot from the Root family. Lives in Camp Gahn with her daughter.

Nanlon (nan-LAWN): Owner of the Copper Rail Tavern in Tabahir. He is the barkeep, cook, and housekeeper. His son, Natt, works in the stables.

Narleen (NAR-lean): Lady Narleen, my lady, Vice-leader of the Lower Realm, assistant magistrate in Beayama, married to Maximus.

Bio: Narleen served as Saephira's lady-in-waiting in Beayama before being promoted to Vice-leader of the Upper Realm. She is trustworthy, compassionate, supportive of others, and sometimes impetuous.

Natt: Stable boy at the Copper Rail in Tabahir, son of Nanlon.

NiaLuck (nye-LUHK): Under Commander of the Northern Gahn Battalion.

Operational Leader: (OL) at the Termination Facility on Camayah. Replaced by Layshura.

Ottaar (OH-tarr): Mender in Beayama, medic and physician. Promoted to Mender of the Realm by Lady Saephira. Also called the lead mender.

QuiQuot (kwie-KWAHT): Cargo shipmaster, appointed temporary magistrate of Gahneeha.

Phauch (PAW'sh): Militia Chief in the Lower Realm.

Preaverca (pray-VER-ca): Former Postal Overseer in Beayama, traitor. Last seen entering the Lost Forest with Eddnok.

Program Master: (PM), AI ruler on Camayah, program deleted.

Raetila (ray-TILL-ah): Security Assistant (SA) from RIFT II on Camayah, mixed loyalties.

Rauteira (rah-TEER-uh): Tech-savvy teenager, daughter of Rekis and Leetqu, resides on Camayah.

Raydoo (RAE-do): Teenager from Beayama, harpoon angler, friend of Seth.

Rekis (REE-kis): Inhabitant of Camayah, serves on the Council of Twelve, Yah believer, married to Leetqu, his daughter is Rauteira.

Rennard (REN-nard): Commander in the Upper Realm.

Runess (ROO-ness): Security Leader (SL) over the Airship Dock for Sector One on Camayah, serves on the Council of Twelve.

RyeYook (RIE-yook): Magistrate of Gahneeha, murdered.

Saephira (sa-FEAR-uh): Lady Saephira, my Lady, Leader of the Lower Realm, senior magistrate in Beayama. Also called SaeFear (SAY-fear).

Bio: Saephira is the magistrate of Beayama and leader of the Lower Realm. When her parents died, she inherited their leadership roles. She was betrothed to Eddnok of the Upper Realm with the hope of creating an alliance between the two warring provinces. Before the wedding, Saephira discovered

Eddnok only desired her as one of his concubines, so she declined the arrangement. She is wise, discerning, and honest.

Seirlai (ser-LAY): Former concubine in Eddnok's household. Her fraternal twin sister is Bovi. Seirlai currently lives with relatives in Briacap.

Seth Cahir: Also known as recruit or the kid. A teenager, athletic, marathon runner, rock climber, loves all outdoor sports except surfing. Accepted Christ as his Savior during the Jesus People Movement in the 1970s, resident of heaven. Envoy to Eskaonus.

Bio: One day in Malibu, Seth was floating past the breakwater, waiting for a ten-foot wave, when a great white attacked him, biting his surfboard in two. He made it to shore, swimming, but the shark chased him all the way in. Afterwards, he swore he'd never enter the water again. Then one day during a bike ride, Seth was run over by a drunk driver, which paralyzed him from the waist down. Later, the doctors discovered a cancerous brain tumor. When they tried to remove it, he started hemorrhaging. Seth died in surgery and awoke in heaven.

SiaVoot (SIGH-voot): Manager of Camp Gahn in East Eskaonus.

TaeVook (tay-VOAK): Gahn flagship skipper of the southern armada, Nether Sea.

Tawehna (tah-WAY-nah): Experienced with stunner weapons, Yah believer from Camayah.

Trikernae (TRY-ker-nay): Spiritual leader, called the pravost, Yah believer, serves on the Council of Twelve on Camayah, married to Malmach. Along with her spouse, she oversees the ministry at the Temple Compound.

Uewba (YEW-baw): Also called Uew, airship rowmate,

navigator, resides on Camayah.

Uzziel (use-ZI-el): Called *the Cherubim*, high-ranking cherub angel, carries a flaming sword. His name means strength of God.

VieRook (veye-ROOK): Sailor, second mate on QuiQuot's cargo ship. Lives in Gahneeha.

Waubush (WAH-bush): Former Captain of the Safeguards. Perished in battle.

Winged Ones: Sentinel angels.

Yhmim (yah-MIM): Deposed Vice-leader of the Lower Realm, traitor, serving a lengthy prison sentence.

Yosah (YOH-sah): Official from the city of Midvill on Eskaonus.

GLOSSARY: ESKAONUS

OVERVIEW OF ESKAONUS

Eskaonus (Es-KAY-nohs) is an offworld planet or place with two provinces: Upper Realm in the north and Lower Realm in the south. It has two seas, one landlocked. The Nae Wilderness lies to the east and the Blighte to the west. Both are extremely arid and largely unexplored. There are rumors about an eastern realm or settlement past the Nae.

The world has no sun or moons. During the day, a glowing light similar to an aurora borealis shines forth until fading into a gloomy twilight. Afterwards, nighttime takes over, followed by total darkness. Residents use torches during these darkouts.

Humid southlands have rivers, farmlands, and abundant plant life. Arid northlands are mostly barren with limited resources. Tall exotic trees called cottlepines cover the forests. Most animals are larger than those living on earth. Some have similar sounding names. Predator fish known as tarkks inhabit the seas, lakes, and lower tributaries. Slimy eels swim the rivers. Inhabitants use four-footed creatures with long hairy manes, called kacks, for riding and as pack animals.

Eskaonites harvest yarm berries, maize, root vegetables, squashes, and mushrooms. Their main diet is fish from harpoon angling, but they also hunt for bush varmints and antaloops. Foods are heavily spiced to preserve them. Families generally eat two meals a day: one in the morning and a hearty dinner banquet after twilight. Drinks include various flavors of tea, yarm beverages, and kunakk.

<u>KEY PLAYERS</u>

Annabelle Altshuler: Musician, emissary sent from heaven.

Bolgog (BOWL-gog): Senior Commander of the Guards. De facto leader of the Upper Realm.

Brappt (BRAP't): Sub-Commander in the Upper Realm.

Calrin (cal-RIN): Teenager from Beayama, harpoon angler, friend of Seth.

Chepho (CHE-foe): Militia Lead in the Lower Realm.

Eddnok (ED-nock): Deposed ruler of the Upper Realm. Whereabouts unknown.

Ellee: Owner of Ellee's Place, an eatery in Beayama.

Flissae (FLISS-ay): Owner of Flissy's Place, a brothel in Tabahir.

Gelr (GEL-er): Captain of the Safeguards in the Lower Realm.

Haleema (ha-LEE-mah): Master Skipper, senior flagship captain from Bayegulf.

Holley Rossie: Experienced medic, emissary sent from heaven.

Hyneil (HIE-neal): Magistrate of Bayegulf.

Jesse Walt: Former police officer, emissary sent from heaven, team leader.

Lurah (LOO-rah): Postal Overseer for the central mail tower in Beayama. Her teenage brother is Raydoo.

Maximus Gallius: Captain of the Militia, married to Narleen.

Menarbat (MEN-ar-bat): Called *the Tracker*. Whereabouts unknown.

Lundy MacBain: Minister, language expert, emissary from heaven.

Nanlon (nan-LAWN): Owner of the Copper Rail Tavern in Tabahir.

Natt: Stable boy at the Copper Rail in Tabahir, son of Nanlon.

Narleen (NAR-lean): Vice-leader of the Lower Realm, married to Maximus.

Ottaar (OH-tarr): Mender of the Realm, medic, physician.

Phauch (PAW'sh): Militia Chief in the Lower Realm.

Preaverca (pray-VER-ca): Former Postal Overseer. Whereabouts unknown.

Raydoo (RAE-do): Teenager from Beayama, harpoon angler, friend of Seth.

Rennard (REN-nard): Commander in the Upper Realm.

Saephira (sa-FEAR-uh): Leader of the Lower Realm, senior magistrate in Beayama.

Seth Cahir: Athletic teenager, emissary sent from heaven.

Yosah (YOH-sah): Official from the city of Midvill.

Although the Eskaonites have forenames and surnames, the latter indicating their family heritage, they prefer using first names only.

LOCAL GREETINGS

Good dayrise: Good morning
Good nightrise: Good evening

TIMES AND SEASONS

Firstlight: Predawn, also called morning twilight
Twilight: Time before nightrise
Morrow: Tomorrow, as in on the morrow
Dayrise: Daytime or morning time
Nightrise: Evening or nighttime
Darkout: Midnight or later, darkest part of the night
Darkness: Middle of the night
Dark, the: Short form for darkout
Day: Short form for dayrise
Night: Short form for nightrise

Yestercycle: Yesterday
Forecycle: Later morning
Midcycle: Noon or around noon
Aftercycle: Afternoon
Postcycle: Late afternoon
Latecycle: Later afternoon, nearing twilight

Moments: Minutes, sometimes as seconds
Span/Spans: Hour/hours
Cycles: Days
Periods: Months, sometimes as undetermined
Yarns: Years, as in a few or many yarns
Ages: Long time, many years, long ago
Eons: Centuries, extensive periods of time, past eras

DISTANCES AND MEASUREMENTS

Leagues: Distance, approximately 10 miles, sometimes as undetermined

Paces: One pace = 3 feet (for height, width, stride, and distance)

Stones: Weight

Hands: One hand = 4 inches, 18 hands = 6 feet (mainly for height)

Comparisons: Tall as a cottlepine. Strong, big, or wide as a kack.

<u>MILITARY AND ARMIES</u>

(SOUTHERN PROVINCE)

Militia, the: Lower Realm soldiers

Safeguards, the: Lower Realm tower guards, sentries, and gatekeepers

Captains: Senior officers in the Militia or Safeguards, similar to Colonels

Militia Lead: Junior officer, similar to a Lieutenant

Militia Chief: Commissioned officer with authority like a Sergeant Major

Squad Leader: Enlisted soldier, similar to a Sergeant

Gatemen: Keep or entryway sentries

Militiamen: All soldiers, ranked or unranked

(NORTHERN PROVINCE)

Guards, the: Upper Realm soldiers

Commanders: Common designations for any officer in the Guards

Senior Commander: Command rank officer, similar to a Colonel

Commander: Middle rank officer, similar to a Major

Sub-Commander: Junior officer, similar to a Lieutenant

Squad Leader: Non-commissioned rank with authority

like a Sergeant

Guardsmen: All guards, including officers, sentries, warders, and sentinels

<u>PLANTS AND ROOTS</u>

(IN TEAS AND MENDER REMEDIES)

Anatora: Flowering plant, mild tranquilizer
Azollie: Spiny root, stimulant, similar to caffeine
Helixzon: Oily plant, utilized in making healing salves
Netherute: Root, pain reliever, promotes sleep
Soaproot: White porous root, antiseptic qualities
Utondra: Antidote for yarm berry poisoning

<u>VINEYARDS</u>

Kunakk Vineyards (kue-NACK): Trellised vineyards near Nakk Village. Local vinedressers cultivate the grain pods to produce a beverage called kunakk.

Yarm Vineyards (Yah'rm): A farm collective raising yarm berries. Vinedressers from nearby Ritwell Village tend the crop and ship the berries throughout Eskaonus to create juices and fermented drinks as well as fresh desserts.

<u>CITIES AND VILLAGES</u>

Bayegulf (BAY-gulf): Port city, sailors, fishing, shipping center, allegiance to Lower Realm, city mender.

Beayama (bee-YAH-ma): Capital of the Lower Realm, non-fortress, militia headquarters, trading center, commercial shops, woodshop, metalworking, forges, city mender.

Briacap (BRY-uh-cap): Capital of the Upper Realm, fortress, large battalion, nearby mining operations, metalworking, woodshops, forges, alchemist, city menders.

Cali Village (CAL-lee): Lower Realm settlement, fishing at Mista Lake and along the Cali River, village mender.

Falein Village (FAY-leen): Lower Realm settlement, fishing at Falein Lake, farming, bush varmint hunting in the Neutral Lands, village mender.

Midvill (MID-vill): Neutral city, allegiance to Lower Realm, trading center, small militia garrison, city mender. The city straddles the middle of the boundary lines.

Nakk Village (NACK): Upper Realm settlement, vinedressers for Kunakk Vineyards, small garrison, no local mender.

Ritwell Village (RIT-well): Lower Realm settlement, vinedressers for Yarm Vineyards, fishing along the Gemous River, bush varmint and antaloop hunting in the Heill Void, no local mender.

Tabahir (TAB-uh-her): Nonaligned city in the Neutral Lands influenced by Briacap. Commerce comes from taverns, lodging, and brothels. Known for trading, smuggling, and bush varmint hunting. Lawless vicinity, no local mender.

WILDERNESS AND DESERTS

Blighte, the: Western badlands, barren, deadly hot, dry, no plants, no animals, inhospitable.

Heill Void (he-EL): Also called ***the Void***. Arid desert, sand dunes, windy, sparse vegetation, large spiny cactus, herds of antaloop, dens of bush varmints. Located southeast of the Nae Wilderness.

Nae Wilderness (NAY): Also called ***the Nae*** and ***the Wilderness***. Mostly unexplored, dangerous, borders the Lost Forest. Settlements are rumored to exist in the east. Explorers and trackers seldom travel more than a league into the region.

Those who do, rarely return. The Nae is lifeless and desolate. It has no flowing water except in the southern part where the Gemous River intersects with the Heill Void.

Northern Expanse: Parched wastelands, scorching temperatures, unexplored.

Southern Expanse: Uninhabited region south of the Gemous River, chilly climate.

<u>MOUNTAINS AND SUMMITS</u>

Birgo Summit (BUR-go): Second highest elevation in Eskaonus.

Colrath Mountains (COAL-rath): Highest mountain range, red rocky shale, three abandoned mines, borders the Blighte on the west and Narmoot Forest in the south. Notable mounts are Gaulmore Peak and Birgo Summit. No minerals.

Gaulmore Peak (GAUL-more): Highest elevation in Eskaonus, south of the Northern Expanse.

Mnnie Mountains (MIN'nee): Southern mountain range, steep cliffs, deep dry canyons, ancient ruins, fresh water spring. Closest rivers are the Cali and Gemous. Veins of tin and copper are scattered among the ridges.

Narnj Mountains (NARN-jay): Second highest mountain range, located north of the Lost Forest, borders the Hallet Sea. It has two working mines with major deposits of tin and copper ore.

Onnie Passage (ON'nee): A pass through the Mnnie Mountains with steep cliffs and deep canyons.

Outlook Point: An overlook area by the Gemous River that lies east of Yarm Vineyards and south of the Lost Forest. Last familiar landmark before entering the Nae Wilderness and

Heill Void.

MINING OPERATIONS

Dig, the: Copper mine in the Narnj Mountains.

Pit, the: Tin mine in the Narnj Mountains. Laborers take the ore from both mines to Briacap to smelt and forge into bronze.

Red Drop: An abandoned mine in the Colrath Mountains. The dig collapsed and buried the miners inside. Later became a graveyard memorial.

Surface Mining: The Mnnie Mountains have small veins of tin and copper on the exposed ridges. Smiths transport the ores to Beayama for processing.

FORESTS

Lost Forest: A large forest of cottlepines bordering the Nae Wilderness. It earned its reputation because people who entered the dense interior never returned.

Narmoot Forest (NAR-moot): A sparse forest below the Colrath Mountains. Half the trees are dead or dying. Most of the ones growing in these woods are strangely deformed.

SEAS AND OCEANS

Hallet Sea (HAL-let): Northern landlocked ocean, surrounded by steep mountains and the Northern Expanse wastelands, unexplored.

Nether Sea (NETH-er): Southern ocean, port access, harpoon fishing, coastal sailing.

LAKES

Falein Lake (FAY-leen): Shallow waters, docks, boats, harpoon angling, net fishing for eels, water supply for Falein Village.

Mista Lake (MISS-tah): Deep waters, docks, boats, harpoon angling, net fishing for eels, water supply for Cali Village.

<u>RIVERS, SPRINGS, AND WELLS</u>

Cali River (CAL-lee): A tributary of the Gemous River with an upper fork. Supplies water to Mista and Falein lakes. The river is teaming with river eels.

Dry Well: An abandoned well near Briacap, one of many that dried up after the Event.

Gemous, the (GEM-oh-us): Main river system of lower Eskaonus. It runs through the Heill Void and into the Nae Wilderness with a lower fork branching from the Nether Sea. The waters contain endless schools of slimy eel and migrating tarkks.

Hidden Springs: Mineral spring near the Narmoot Forest.

High Springs: Artesian spring located in the Mnnie Mountains along Onnie Passage, non-alkaline, sparkling clean water.

Trobell Springs (TRO-bell): The main water source for Nakk Village and Briacap.

Yarm Springs (Yah'rm): A deep well near the Gemous River. Yarm Springs is the main water source for irrigating the nearby vineyards.

Waterways: Rivers and streams follow the contour of the land, generally flowing upstream instead of downstream. All are silty.

<u>OTHER LOCATIONS</u>

Boundary Lines: Northern and southern borderlines separating the provinces.

East Eskaonus: A land rumored to exist, exact location unknown.

Farmlands: Found entirely in the Lower Realm. They grow maize, varieties of gourds, starchy roots similar to yams, and vegetables.

Neutral Lands: Formerly called the Disputed Lands. An area between the Upper and Lower Realms. Barren, lawless, and overrun by bush varmints.

Ruins, the: An ancient settlement in the Mnnie mountain range, origin unknown.

<u>ITEMS AND INFORMATION</u>

Alchemy: The forerunner of chemistry.

Antaloop: Deer-like animal with four horns. Numerous herds inhabit the Heill Void along the Gemous River. Locals hunt them for their tender, sweet-tasting meat.

Brand: Old name for a sword or brandished weapon.

Breaking Fast: First meal after fasting through the night, more commonly known as breakfast.

Bush Varmint: A three-legged, hopping creature with one front leg and two hind ones. Similar in size to a large jackrabbit, except the bush varmint has short ears and a long bushy tail. They live in burrows in the Neutral Lands and Heill Void. Cooked or stewed varmints are a popular entree in the northlands.

Communicators: Five radios given to Jesse by an angel from Outreach & Supply in heaven. They are capable of receiving signals over great distances. They're fully powered, pocket sized, voice activated with five separate channels, and transmit on any band or frequency. The units seem to have an unlimited range and feature a homing signal.

Cotta: A yellowish-tan plant with spiny branches. Weavers use the soft, fibrous tips to make clothing, cloth products, ropes, cords, and lines. Similar to cotton.

Cottlepines: Type of evergreen pine tree with oak-shaped leaves on their branches instead of needles. They grow to a towering height.

Dallups: Mushrooms in Eskaonus. They flourish in the southern lands, propagated by seeds instead of spores. The larger ones keep the patch full by spreading their seeds during darkout. Residents only harvest the middle-sized dallups. The caps are shaped like little Christmas trees, pointed at the top with green gills underneath.

Glifstring: An eight-string musical instrument, half guitar, half harp, which never needs tuning. It comes with a shoulder strap.

Homing Flyers: Fast flying predatory birds able to navigate at night and deliver messages. They are the size of a large raven with a smooth underbody and grayish fuzz-covered wings.

Hoverboard: A shuttle given to Seth by an angel from Outreach & Supply in heaven. A portable, two or three-person, all-terrain, solar and battery powered hovercraft. It's extremely fast. The unit folds in quarters and fits into a handy carrying case.

Hunting Mushrooms (or dallups): A courting ritual.

Generally employed by women as a way to meet interested suitors.

Laddie: Scottish slang. Although often associated with men or boys, in the past, laddie was used as a nickname for women or girls. In the plural form, laddies, like guys and dudes, can also refer to a mixed group. Some consider the name gender-neutral.

Medkit: Holley's medical satchel containing antibiotics, various medications, diagnostic equipment, first-aid supplies, and a procedural manual. With it, she could handle most medical situations, even minor surgeries.

Mender: Physician or medic.

Kacks: Four-footed creatures with longhaired manes, which the locals ride as mounts and outfit as pack animals. They are good swimmers, fast runners, hardy, and can travel for long periods of time without drinking water.

Kin: Crispy baked bread made with maize. Considered a main food staple.

Kunakk (kue-NACK): A dark, frothy liquor produced from vine-ripened grain pods cultivated in the Kunakk Vineyards. The distilling process makes the drink highly intoxicating.

Maize: An orangish-brown vegetable, similar to corn, grown on stalks in the farmlands below the southern boundary line. The dried kernels are ground to make kin. Weavers use maize fibers, called sillk, to produce twine and threads. Papersmiths dry the husks and roll them into thin sheets to create scrolls.

Nyeflute: A golden brown flute with carved intricate designs. The heaven-issued instrument fits into a tubular-shaped holding pouch with an attached shoulder strap. It comes with a fingering tablature for different songs or tunes. When played, the songs cause certain effects such as sleepiness, confusion, and invisibility. Others instill confidence, encouragement, and alertness. It's similar to a Celtic Boehm flute but slightly shorter in length.

Sentinels: Upper Realm soldiers who function as lookouts, sentries, or watchmen.

Settee: Two or three-person couch similar to an ancient Roman lectus. Used for reclining and sometimes as a spare bed.

Sillk: Fibers on the maize plant. It is dried and woven together to make durable twine, threads, and fishing leaders.

Slimy Eels: Also called greenbacks, slimies, river eels, and elvers. They are greenish, non-predator fish that spawn in the seas before migrating upriver into the lakes where they can grow to over ten-feet long. Anglers catch them with hook and line or by netting.

Tarkks: Predator fish found in lakes and the lower forks of rivers, similar in size to great white sharks or killer whales. The sea varieties are huge, growing to over a hundred feet.

Tarkkies: Juvenile tarkks, smaller but still large, about the size of a twelve-foot shark.

Tijvah: A Hebrew word for hope, expectation, and possibilities. It also refers to a rope or cord, which comes from a root word meaning to bind together, collect, expect, or wait upon. Common expression: hope is a rope.

Warders: Upper Realm soldiers who function as security guards, jailors, or stockade custodians.

Yarm: A drink made from the yarm berry, a grape-sized, pinkish berry harvested from bushes in the Yarm Vineyards. Yarm is a lightly fermented drink, which is usually diluted with water for children and adolescents. It's the preferred beverage in both realms.

<u>FORTIFICATIONS</u>

Alure: Access pathway in battlements (see wallwalk).

Battlement: A type of parapet on top of a rampart with spaced gaps that allow the launching of projectiles from shielded positions (see crenels and merlons).

Citadel: Fortress or strongly fortified building or structure.

Crenels: Gaps between the raised sections (*merlons*) in parapets, battlements, or fortified towers. Defenders observe and deploy weapons through the crenels.

Fortress: Stronghold with a military presence often included in a town or city.

Garrison Quarters: Where soldiers are housed and fed when on active duty.

Merlons: Raised sections between the gaps (*crenels*) of a parapet, battlement wall, or fortified tower. Defenders could hide behind the merlons for protection.

Parapet: Low retaining wall, often part of battlements, offering protection to defenders on the wallwalk behind it. A rampart is the main wall. The parapet is a lesser wall with a height ranging between chest-level and the top of someone's head.

Rampart: The main defensive wall in a citadel or fortified structure. It usually has a broad top with a wallwalk and parapet.

Stockade: Prison, holding area, or jail.

Wallwalk: Walkway running along the interior part of a

fortified wall or parapet.

<u>WEAPONS</u>

Blowgun: The blowgun was invented long ago, perhaps dating back to the Stone Age. The earliest written references were from Rome in the second century. The maximum range was about hundred yards. Blowgun users often constructed their darts from wood, but they used other materials as well. Basic darts had a whittled wooden tip. Lundy dipped his tips in a mixture that caused paralysis.

Dagger: Handheld knife, shorter than a throwing knife. Effective in combat and for self-defense.

Fighting Staff: Also called a quarterstaff, battlestaff, and according to Max, *the persuader*. Wielded in sparring and combat. Common fighting techniques included lunge, strike (reverse, counter, or spin around), block, parry, sweep, fake, dodge, and deflect.

Gladius, the: A Roman medium length sword, double-edged, with a honed point suitable for cutting, chopping, and thrusting. The iron blade fit into a wooden sheath surrounded by either leather or bronze. Max's heaven-issued sword was patterned after the same basic design but forged with a superior metal of unknown origin. The edge was razor-sharp and the blade practically unbreakable.

Longbow: Although the longbow was commonly associated with the Celts in Wales, various ancient cultures employed them for hunting and warfare. Often made with yew but different woods were also utilized. The bow could shoot arrows over half a mile and were deadly accurate at 200 feet.

Saber: Curved, single-bladed sword produced in the Upper Realm.

Sling: Ancient slings were constructed with a holding

pouch connected to two cords. One cord ended in a loop, which slingers would slide over their fingers so when the other cord was released, the sling stayed attached to their hand. Rounded stone projectiles flung from slings could reach distances beyond 600 feet and had a high degree of accuracy at 150 feet.

Spears: The Guards preferred long-handled spears with bronze points. They measured eight feet in length. Militia spears were shorter at six feet. Soldiers could toss both types like javelins. The accuracy range was between forty and fifty feet. Soldiers often carried two.

Swords: All swords from Western Eskaonus were bronze forged and tempered. Guardsmen favored curved, single-bladed swords (called sabers) while militiamen wielded straight, double-edged ones.

Throwing Knives: Common weapons in both realms and carried in pairs. Depending on a person's expertise, thrown knives had an accuracy range of thirty feet.

MILITIA SWORDSMANSHIP TECHNIQUES

Block: Prevent a weapon from landing
Chop or Strike: A downward hit
Deflect: Ward off an attack
Dodge or Evade: Step out of the way
Fake: Feint one move and use another
Parry: Defend from an assault with a countermove
Slash: A sweeping motion
Stab or Lunge: Thrusting with a pointed weapon

BANNERS, FLAGS, AND PENNANTS

Black: Advance or attack
Black-striped: Disembark
Blue: Truce or parley
Gold-striped: Flagship
Green: Proceed with orders

Green-striped: Launch weapons
Orange: Rally
Purple: Royalty or Sovereign
Red: Cancel orders
Red-striped: Retreat or escape
White: Surrender
Yellow: Use caution
Yellow-striped: In peril

RADIO CHANNELS

One: Seth
Two: Annabelle or Phauch
Three: Maximus or Narleen
Four: Rauteira's datatop
Five: Jesse

RULES

Rule Number One: Always expect the unexpected.
Rule Number Two: Face your fears to overcome them.
Rule Number Three: In due season you will reap if you don't quit or lose heart.
Rule Number Four: If all else fails, RUN!
Rule Number Five: Stand our ground.
Rule Number Six: You're only defeated if you think you are.

BUILDINGS AND HALLS

Archives, the: Both Beayama and Briacap maintain a storage library with ancient documents, detailing their history and cultures, much of it vague and incomplete.

Great Hall, the: A building in Beayama with a large hall for public events such as banquets, exhibitions, and business meetings. It contains conference rooms and two kitchens.

Postal Tower: Also called the mail tower. The structure includes a delivery room, residential quarters, a clerk's sorting desk, and roosts for the homing flyers. Cities staff at least one tower for communications between communities. Villages operate postal huts run by volunteers.

Residential Hall: Living quarters for Saephira and other governmental officials.

GLOSSARY: CENTRAL HEAVEN

<u>CENTRAL HEAVEN</u>

Locations and landmarks in Central Heaven are speculative. Notwithstanding, several are based on Scripture, others inspired by tradition.

"But as it is written, Eye hath not seen, nor ear heard, neither have entered into the heart of man, the things which God hath prepared for them that love him" (1 Corinthians 2:9).

<u>KEY PLAYERS</u>

Chesedel (CHESS-a-del): Official name is *elChesed*. Faithful messenger, Jesse's guardian angel. His name means mercy of God.

Lucifer: Also known as Satan, the devil, the great dragon, and that old serpent.

Uzziel (use-ZI-el): Called *the Cherubim*, high-ranking cherub angel, carries a flaming sword. His name means strength of God.

Winged Ones: Sentinel angels.

<u>CHERUB ANGEL OR CHERUBIM</u>

Cherub or cherubim in the plural form are celestial beings. They serve God and follow His will. The cherubim were first introduced in Genesis: "So he drove out the man; and he placed at the east of the garden of Eden Cherubims, and a flaming sword which turned every way, to keep the way of the tree of life" (Genesis 3:24). Although their biblical descriptions vary, cherubim are thought to have wings and carry fiery swords or *brands*. Before his rebellion and fall from heaven, Satan was a cherub (see Ezekiel 28:11–15).

Brand: An ancient term for sword or brandished weapon. A blade that flashed when swung.

<u>HEAVENLY SALUTATIONS</u>

Peace to You, Shalom, Blessings, Precious One, Beloved, Favored Ones, Dear Ones, Maranatha, and Godspeed.

<u>LOCATIONS AND LANDMARKS</u>

Dwelling Places: Housing for the saints.

"In my Father's house are many mansions: if *it were* not *so*, I would have told you. I go to prepare a place for you. And if I go and prepare a place for you, I will come again, and receive you unto myself; that where I am, *there* ye may be also" (John 14:2, 3).

Fountain of Living Water: A wellspring in Central Heaven that disperses the waters of life. Sometimes called the Fountain of Life.

"And he said unto me, It is done. I am Alpha and Omega, the beginning and the end. I will give unto him that is athirst of the fountain of the water of life freely" (Revelation 21:6).

"And the Spirit and the bride say, Come. And let him that heareth say, Come. And let him that is athirst come. And whosoever will, let him take the water of life freely" (Revelation 22:17).

Fruit Cart: Vendor's mobile produce stand on Straight Street.

Hall of Records: A storage facility where all the records and histories from the beginning of time are kept, including the Scroll of Life, scrolls of works, and all other related documents. The Hall of Records also contains a scroll room where residents can access Scripture, prophecies, hymns, poetry, and other writings to study, read, and enjoy. *Note: In biblical times, books were generally in the form of scrolls.*

"And I saw the dead, small and great, stand before God; and the books were opened: and another book was opened, which is *the book* of life: and the dead were judged out of those things which were written in the books, according to their works" (Revelation 20:12).

Judgment Seat: The place where Christ delivers judgments and hands out rewards.

"For we must all appear before the judgment seat of Christ; that every one may receive the things *done* in *his* body, according to that he hath done, whether *it be* good or bad" (2 Corinthians 5:10).

Orientation: An informational center to help with directions, suggestions, and guidelines for new arrivals. The facility also carries starter kits and offers a wide selection of clothing.

Outreach & Supply: A place to requisition materials, tools, musical instruments, Bibles, Torahs, and other items appropriate for use in heaven.

Patriarch Plaza: The most popular plaza in Central Heaven. It has a lecture podium and unlimited seating.

Paths of the Patriarchs: All interconnecting footpaths in Central Heaven.

Prayer Gardens: Special gathering places set aside for solitude and prayer. Some theologians believe certain biblical references or terms might foreshadow landmarks found in heaven.

GARDEN OF MEDITATION (Philippians 4:8): Located on Straight Street.

GARDEN OF PRAYER (1 Thessalonians 5:17): Junction by Damascus Road.

GARDEN OF SUPPLICATION (Philippians 4:6): Corner of Charity Street and Narrow Way.

Pearl Gates: The pearl gates are traditional names for entries, passageways, or portals into heaven. They are based on descriptions from Revelation 21:12–21, which mention twelve gates made with twelve single pearls. Each gate contains the written name of one of the twelve tribes of Israel. The three gates below are hypothetical.

GOLD PEARL (Matthew 13:45–46): Pearl of great price.

ROSE PEARL (Song of Solomon 2:1): Rose of Sharon.

WHITE PEARL (Isaiah 1:18, Revelation 2:17): White represents purity, newness, and forgiveness.

River of Life: A river with life-giving properties.

"And he shewed me a pure river of water of life, clear as crystal, proceeding out of the throne of God and of the Lamb" (Revelation 22:1).

Everything will live wherever the river goes (see Ezekiel 47:9).

A river went out of Eden and watered the garden (see Genesis 2:10).

Streets and Roads: Thoroughfares to various locations in Central Heaven and elsewhere. Some theologians believe roadways in heaven, like streets, are foreshadowed in Scripture.

DAMASCUS ROAD (Acts 26:12–13).
FAITH AVENUE, HOPE LANE, AND CHARITY STREET (1 Corinthians 13:13).
NARROW WAY (Matthew 7:14).
STRAIGHT STREET (Acts 9:11).

"And the street of the city *was* pure gold, as it were transparent glass" (Revelation 21:21*b*).

Throne Room: The place where the Ancient of Days resides.

"I beheld till the thrones were cast down, and the Ancient of days did sit, whose garment *was* white as snow, and the hair of his head like the pure wool: his throne *was like* the fiery flame, *and* his wheels *as* burning fire" (Daniel 7:9).

"After this I looked, and, behold, a door *was* opened in heaven: and the first voice which I heard *was* as it were of a trumpet talking with me; which said, Come up hither, and I will shew thee things which must be hereafter. And immediately I was in the spirit: and, behold, a throne was set in heaven, and *one* sat on the throne" (Revelation 4:1, 2).

Tree of Life: Ancient tree that grows and flourishes by the River of Life.

"In the midst of the street of it, and on either side of the river, *was there* the tree of life, which bare twelve *manner of* fruits, *and* yielded her fruit every month: and the leaves of the tree *were* for the healing of the nations" (Revelation 22:2).

"And out of the ground made the LORD God to grow every tree that is pleasant to the sight, and good for food; the tree of life also in the midst of the garden, and the tree of knowledge of good and evil" (Genesis 2:9).

The fruit did not fail nor did the leaves wither. Leaves were used for medicine and fruit for food (see Ezekiel 47:12).

Tree of the Knowledge of Good and Evil: Current status and location unknown.

"But of the tree of the knowledge of good and evil, thou shalt not eat of it: for in the day that thou eatest thereof thou shalt surely die" (Genesis 2:17).

"And the serpent said unto the woman, Ye shall not surely die: For God doth know that in the day ye eat thereof, then your eyes shall be opened, and ye shall be as gods, knowing good and evil" (Genesis 3:4, 5).

Waiting Line: An overflow area where people wait to appear before the Judgment Seat.

Walled Terrace: Scenic walkway in Central Heaven adjacent to the River of Life.

GLOSSARY: GAHNEEHA

OVERVIEW OF GAHNEEHA IN EAST ESKAONUS

East Eskaonus not only includes the Nae Wilderness, it's the same place. For ages, the residents in western realms believed only a wasteland lay beyond the Nae. They didn't know that the Realm of East Eskaonus actually existed. There were rumors, of course, but no one had successfully explored the arid eastern lands and lived to tell about it. The truth only came to light after Lady Saephira and Jesse sojourned there.

East Eskaonus has a major port city called ***Gahneeha***, which is home to the Gahn people. Neighboring the city limits is Camp Gahn, a tent settlement where agricultural laborers live. The Gahns built their civilization along the Wyntarie River. It has farms, vineyards, an artesian water well, and storage facilities. The province maintains an army and a large fleet of sailing vessels. They mine and process iron for weapons and tools.

As in all areas of Eskaonus, there are no suns or moons. During the day, a glowing light similar to an aurora borealis shines forth until fading into a gloomy twilight. Afterwards, nighttime takes over followed by total darkness. Residents use torches during these darkouts.

Lands surrounding Gahneeha are mostly barren with limited resources. Tall exotic trees grow in the nearby cottlepine grove. Predator fish known as tarkks inhabit the Nether Sea and Wyntarie River, along with schools of slimy eels. Residents use four-footed creatures, called kacks, for riding and pack animals.

Gahneehanites harvest maize, vegetables, squashes, and dallups. Their main diet is fish, but they also hunt for bush varmints and antaloops. Drinks include various flavors of tea and kunakk.

KEY PLAYERS

AliRoot (AL-ee-root): A gifted young girl from East Eskaonus. Lives in Camp Gahn.

EdNook (ED-nook): Ruler EdNook, same person as Lord Eddnok.

HieHoot (Hi-HOOT): Sailor, first mate on QuiQuot's cargo ship. Lives in Gahneeha.

JaeLuet (jay-LOOT): Gahn flagship skipper, northern armada, Hallet Sea.

LyeDuek (LIE-dook): Gahn military commander in the southern battalion.

MiaRoot (MY-uh-root): Mother of AliRoot from the Root family. Lives in Camp Gahn with her daughter.

NiaLuck (nye-LUHK): Gahn military commander in the northern battalion.

QuiQuot (kwie-KWAHT): Cargo shipmaster, appointed temporary magistrate in Gahneeha.

RyeYook (RIE-yook): Magistrate of Gahneeha, murdered.

SiaVoot (SIGH-voot): Manager of Camp Gahn in East Eskaonus.

TaeVook (tay-VOAK): Gahn flagship skipper of the

southern armada, Nether Sea.

VieRook (veye-ROOK): Sailor, second mate on QuiQuot's cargo ship. Lives in Gahneeha.

The latter half of their names indicates family heritage.

<u>TIMES AND SEASONS</u>

Firstlight: Predawn, also called morning twilight
Twilight: Time before nightrise
Morrow: Tomorrow, as in on the morrow
Dayrise: Daytime or morning time
Nightrise: Evening or nighttime
Darkout: Midnight or later, darkest part of the night
Darkness: Middle of the night
Dark, the: Short form for darkout
Day: Short form for dayrise
Night: Short form for nightrise

Yestercycle: Yesterday
Forecycle: Later morning
Midcycle: Noon or around noon
Aftercycle: Afternoon
Postcycle: Late afternoon
Latecycle: Later afternoon, nearing twilight

Moments: Minutes, sometimes as seconds
Span/Spans: Hour/hours
Cycles: Days
Periods: Months, sometimes as undetermined
Yarns: Years, as in a few or many yarns
Ages: Long time, many years, long ago
Eons: Centuries, extensive periods of time, past eras

<u>MILITARY AND ARMIES</u>

Commanders: Common designations for command officers

Gahns: Common name for all East Eskaonus soldiers
Guards: Entryway sentries and jailers
Skippers: Captains of military vessels
Shipmasters: Captains of cargo ships

High Commander: Command officer, similar to a Major General, red-plumed helmet
Under Commander: Subordinate officer, similar to a Brigadier General, red-plumed helmet
Commander: Middle rank officer, similar to a Major, yellow-plumed helmet
Junior Officer: Lower rank officer, similar to a Lieutenant, white-plumed helmet
Squad Leader: Non-commissioned rank with authority like a Sergeant

Vineyards

Vineyards: Unnamed trellised fields. Vinedressers cultivate the grain pods and produce a beverage called kunakk.

Cities and Settlements

Camp Gahn: Tent settlement for agricultural workers.

Gahneeha (gaw-KNEE-haw): Port city, fishing commerce, trading, shipping center, woodsmiths, metalsmiths, alchemist, foundry, forge, shipbuilders, commercial shops, stores, military complex, sailor's hall, city menders.

Wilderness and Deserts

Eastern Expanse: Parched wastelands, scorching temperatures, unexplored.

Heill Void (he-EL): Also called ***the Void***. Arid desert, sand dunes, windy, sparse vegetation, large spiny cactus, herds of migrating antaloop, dens of bush varmints. Located southeast of the Nae Wilderness.

Nae Wilderness (NAY): Also called ***the Nae*** and ***the Wilderness***. The Nae is a wasteland that extends east from the Lost Forest. It is lifeless and desolate. It has no flowing water except in the southern part where the Gemous River intersects with the Heill Void. Settlements are rumored to exist on the other side of the desert, past the Lost Forest in the west.

MOUNTAINS AND SUMMITS

Narnj Mountains (NARN-jay): Rugged mountain range that surrounds the Hallet Sea, located north of the Lost Forest and Nae Wilderness. It has one working mine with major deposits of iron ore.

MINING OPERATIONS

Mine: Unnamed iron mine in the Narnj Mountains. Cargo ships take the ore to Gahneeha for processing.

Surface Mining: The Narnj hills have veins of tin and copper on the exposed ridges. Cargo ships transport the ore to Gahneeha for processing.

FORESTS

Lost Forest: A large forest of cottlepines bordering the Nae Wilderness. It earned its reputation because people who entered the dense interior never returned.

SEAS AND OCEANS

Hallet Sea (HAL-let): Landlocked ocean surrounded by steep mountains and wastelands of the Northern and Eastern Expanse. Too alkaline for fishing. Sea monster sightings.

Nether Sea (NETH-er): Vast ocean, harpoon fishing, clam digging along the shorelines, and coastal sailing.

RIVERS, SPRINGS, AND WELLS

Gemous, the (GEM-oh-us): Main river system of lower Eskaonus. It runs through the Heill Void and into the Nae Wilderness with a lower fork branching from the Nether Sea. The waters contain endless schools of slimy eel and migrating tarkks. The river disappears into a hollow.

Well: Unnamed fresh water supply for Gahneeha, Camp Gahn, and surrounding areas. Artesian spring, non-alkaline.

Wyntarie River (Win-TARR-ee): Waterway between the Nether Sea and Hallet Sea. The river has migrating tarkks and is teaming with river eels.

Rivers and waterways follow the contour of the land, generally flowing upstream instead of downstream. All are silty.

OTHER LOCATIONS

Cottlepine Grove: A stand of trees north of the city, mainly used for shipbuilding.

Docks: An area for loading and unloading cargo and processing catches of fish.

Farms: Unnamed fields that grow maize, varieties of edible gourds, starchy roots similar to yams, sweet melons, and vegetables. Yarm berry plants are not cultivated in East Eskaonus.

Hollow, the: Mystical hole in the Gemous River.

Ruins, the: Ancient settlements in the Narnj Mountains, abandoned, origin unknown.

Stables: Animal stalls for kacks in Camp Gahn. The camp has two locations.

Storage: A series of huts set aside for storing food, lumber, and other products.

<u>ITEMS AND INFORMATION</u>

Alchemy: The forerunner of chemistry.

Antaloop: Deer-like animal with four horns. Numerous herds inhabit the Heill Void along the Gemous River. Inhabitants hunt them for their tender, sweet-tasting meat.

Attached: Married or betrothed.

Bartering: Gahneehanites do not use credits for payments like those in Upper and Lower Realms. Instead, they trade products for products to pay for rent, food, comfort, and everything else they need or desire.

Brigantines: Two-masted sailing vessels with square or rectangular sails. Also called Brigs.

Bush Varmint: A three-legged, hopping creature with one front leg and two hind ones. Similar in size to a large jackrabbit, except the bush varmint has short ears and a long bushy tail. They live in burrows in the Heill Void. Cooked or stewed varmints are a popular entree.

Cottlepines: Type of evergreen pine tree with oak-shaped leaves on their branches instead of needles. They grow to a towering height.

Detached: Divorced or separated.

Dallups: Mushrooms in East Eskaonus. They flourish near cottlepine groves, propagated by seeds instead of spores. The larger ones keep the patch full by spreading their seeds during darkout. Residents only harvest the middle-sized dallups. The caps are shaped like little Christmas trees, pointed at the top with green gills underneath.

Gahnatine, the: Eddnok's flagship.

Homing Flyers: Fast flying predatory birds able to navigate at night and deliver messages. They are the size of a large raven with a smooth underbody and grayish fuzz-covered wings.

Kacks: Four-footed creatures with longhaired manes, which the locals ride as mounts and outfit as pack animals. They are good swimmers, fast runners, hardy, and can travel for long periods of time without drinking water.

Kin: Crispy baked bread made with maize. Considered a main food staple.

Kunakk (kue-NACK): A dark, frothy liquor produced from vine-ripened grain pods cultivated in the local vineyards. The distilling process makes the drink highly intoxicating.

League: Range or distance, approximately 10 miles, sometimes as undetermined.

Maize: An orangish-brown vegetable, similar to corn, grown on stalks in the farms. The dried kernels are ground to make kin.

Menders: Physicians and medics.

Metal Smithing: The process of working with metals. A foundry melts the metals in furnaces and casts them into molds. A forge or hearth heats them prior to hammering them into shapes.

Slimy Eels: Also called river eels. They are greenish, non-predator fish that spawn in the seas before they migrate upriver into lakes where they can grow to over ten-feet long.

Tarkks: Predator fish found in lakes and the lower forks of rivers, similar in size to great white sharks or killer whales. The sea varieties are huge, growing to over a hundred feet.

Tarkkies: Juvenile tarkks, smaller but still large, about the size of a twelve-foot shark.

TREOWs: Ancient black stones thought to be sacred talismans or tokens, purpose unknown.

<u>WEAPONS AND ARMAMENTS</u>

Armor: Gahn soldiers wore iron half-plate armor, comprised of shaped metal plates that covered the wearer's upper body.

Battle Rams: A battering ram was a breaching device with a metal head, sometimes resembling a male sheep, designed to break down walled fortifications or splinter wooden gates. In its basic form, the weapon was a long, heavy pole carried by a group of people and rammed against an obstacle.

Catapults: General name for weapon launchers causing extreme damage. The ones built by the Gahns were similar to trebuchets, but much larger and capable of slinging firebombs great distances. They had a range of a quarter league or more depending on trajectory and size of the projectile.

Greaves: A piece of armor protecting the shins. Gahns used leather greaves attached by straps.

Helmets: Gahn officers wore three types: red-plumed for high and under commanders, yellow-plumed for commanders, and white-plumed for junior officers. Enlisted soldiers were not outfitted with them.

Phalanx: A rectangular unit of infantry armed with long spears or pikes. The Greeks employed this military formation to great advantage.

Pikes: Twelve-foot spears with iron metal tips.

Shell Shielding: Similar to the Roman Turtle formation. Soldiers covered their heads with shields, one person holding it over the soldier next to him, creating a type of shell.

Shields: Gahn warriors carried medium-sized oval shields, carved from cottlepines, covered by leather and lettered with GN across the front.

Skyfire Projectiles: Wooden barrels filled with liquid fire, a napalm-like formula devised by Eddnok. These firebombs came in two sizes: full and half-barrel loads.

Swords: All swords from East Eskaonus were iron forged and tempered. Although officers carried their swords in scabbards, regular troops preferred unsheathed blades, strapped to their tie belts. Iron swords offered a slight improvement over their bronze counterparts, in that they were somewhat stronger, making them less likely to break or bend during a battle.

BANNERS, FLAGS, AND PENNANTS

Black: Advance or attack
Black-striped: Disembark
Blue: Truce or parley
Gold-striped: Flagship
Green: Proceed with orders
Green-striped: Launch weapons
Orange: Rally
Purple: Royalty or Sovereign
Red: Cancel orders
Red-striped: Retreat or escape
White: Surrender
Yellow: Use caution
Yellow-striped: In peril

BUILDINGS AND HALLS

Annex, the: Guarded facility that displays the black stones.

Archives, the: Storage library with ancient documents, dealing with Gahn history and culture, much of it vague and incomplete.

Forge: Building with a hearth where artisans heat iron and other metals prior to hammering them into shape.

Foundry: Facility that melts metals in furnaces and casts them into molds.

Military Complex: Compound with barracks, practice field, and armory.

Postal Tower: Also called the mail tower. The structure includes a delivery room, residential quarters, a clerk's sorting desk, and roosts for the homing flyers. Camp Gahn operates a postal tent run by volunteers.

Sailor's Hall: Meeting place for sailors to share information, relax, and tell tall tales about their voyages.

Shipbuilder's Facility: Shop where skilled workers build and repair sailing vessels.

GLOSSARY: CAMAYAH

<u>OVERVIEW OF CAMAYAH</u>

Camayah (ka-MAY-ah) is an advanced world employing science and technology. The landmass is divided into five sectors, the majority of those being in the northern hemisphere.

Most of the populace perished in an event called the Burning. A past supernova from a distant sun may have caused this catastrophe, but the facts remain sketchy. After the disaster, Camayah became an arid wasteland. The few who lived, struggled to survive. Over time, the survivors developed into four classes of people: programmers, operators, laborers, and security. The planet is currently undergoing terraforming.

Camayah's local sun is a red dwarf that emits a dim, reddish light. The planet has three orbiting moons.

<u>PLANET AND MOONS</u>

Camayah (ka-MAY-ah): System planet
Vilmieah (vill-MY-ah): First moon
Ethade (ETH-aid): Second moon
Easteapia (eas-tee-PIE-ah): Third and largest moon

<u>KEY PLAYERS</u>

Cndrek (KUHN-drek): Senior Security Leader (SSL) for all Sectors.

Hiehew (HI-hue): Program Leader (PL) at the Science Center, Yah believer.

Jawhawtu (jaw-HAH-too): Also called Jaw, midmate, airship engineer.

Layshura (lay-SURE-ah): Operational Leader (OL) at the Health Center.

Leetqu (LEET-kue): Married to Rekis, daughter is Rauteira.

Malmach (maul-MOK): Married to Trikernae, spiritual leader, called provost. Along with his spouse, he oversees the ministry at the Temple Compound.

Rauteira (rah-TEER-uh): Daughter of Rekis and Leetqu.

Rekis (REE-kis): Married to Leetqu, daughter is Rauteira.

Runess (ROO-ness): Security Leader (SL) for the Airship Dock.

Tawehna (tah-WAY-nah): Experienced gunner, Yah believer.

Trikernae (TRY-ker-nay): Married to Malmach, spiritual leader, called pravost. Along with her spouse, she oversees the ministry at the Temple Compound.

Uewba (YEW-baw): Also called Uew, rowmate, airship navigator.

<u>LOCAL GREETINGS</u>

Fair Dawn to You: Good morning
Joyous Dusk to You: Good night
Blessings to Yah: Religious greeting used by believers

TIMES AND SEASONS

Interval: Minute
Bout: Hour
Dawn: Day
Predawn: Firstlight
Earlydawn: Midmorning
Halfdawn: Middle of the day
Latedawn: Afternoon
Nightfall: Twilight
Dusk: Night
Latedusk: Midnight or later
Event: Week
Phase: Month
Stage: Year, sometimes an event
Era: Undetermined period of time
Age: Century, long ago

Yesterdawn: Yesterday
Morrow: Tomorrow, later
Morn: Sunrise or morning
Eve: Sunset or evening

DISTANCE

Stride: Three feet
Tick: Mile
Leggs: Leagues or longer distance, sometimes undetermined

MEASUREMENTS

Notch: Inch
Mark: Foot
Lenn: Yard

WEIGHT

Masses: Pounds

Load: Ton
Crate: Twelve tons
Cubes: Ounces (fluids)
Beaker: Gallon (fluids)
Barrow: Fifty gallons (fluids)

<u>DATA TERMINOLOGY</u>

Assimilated: Facilities connected to the datastream
Beamed Data Transfers: Communications between portals, facilities, and airships
Data: All codes and information
Databands: Data channels
Datacode: Password or keyword
Datacomm: Communication device or pathway
Dataflows: Same as datastream
Dataframes: Small computers
Datapass: ID wristband or temporary DIN
Datastream: Flow of data
Datatop: Laptop
Data Systems: Computer programs
DIN: Data Identification Number or Data ID Number
Mainframes: Large computers

<u>DINs</u>

Although no longer required, all inhabitants are encouraged to have Data Identification Numbers (DINs).

<u>STUNNERS</u>

Bospike: Contact weapon, carried by S1s.
Quispike: Short range, fifty lenns, three firing settings, yellow light beam, carried by S2s.
Trispike: Long range, ninety lenns, three firing settings, green light beam, carried by S3s.
Duespike: Extremely long range, unknown lenns, airship deck gun with targeting sight, red light beam, rumored to exist before the Burning.

POWER

TPC: Triverphol Power Cores. The modules (or cells) have a viewing window that gives off a yellow flaming glow. The cores come in three sizes: Large for mainframes, airships, portal systems, and cranes. Medium for programming terminals, general data equipment, and communications. Small for stunners, lighting, hand scanners, and minor devices.

SUPPLEMENTS AND COSTS

Nutrition
Tycozide: 3 gelts (daily dose)
Dapferon: 6 gelts (extended release)

Hydration
Hydru: 3 gelts (daily dose)
Tyhydru: 6 gelts (extended release)

Pleasure
Cradphenanill: 1 gelt (rapid release)
The Council has banned the use of pleasure tabs.

PILL DESCRIPTIONS

Tycozide: Round tablet, reddish-brown
Dapferon: Oval tablet, reddish-brown
Hydru: Round tablet, greenish-blue
Tyhydru: Oval tablet, greenish-blue
Cradphenanill: Cube, white

LOCATIONS AND PLACES

Airship Docks: Docking areas for airships that provide travel to locations not connected by transport portals. Airships can also travel to the moons and are equipped with solar sails.

Health Center: Formerly called the Termination Facility, the facility is now involved in medical research. The operators oversee the production of nourishment tabs and vaccines.

Holding Area: Formerly a jail for discontents and fanatics. The Council of Twelve converted the property into a religious center called the Temple Compound.

Housing: Living units for laborers. Most were built from metal scraps and secondhand materials found in the ruins.

Pit Mines: Underground cavities containing Triverphol and other minerals or substances.

Programming Center: Former governmental complex for the planet. Corrupt leaders used part of the facility to reprogram discontents and fanatics. The Council of Twelve changed its purpose and renamed it the Science Center.

RIFTs: Multipurpose facilities with numerical designations. All have the same basic layout. The main level contains an information counter, accounting kiosk, communication terminal, pill dispensary, classrooms for instruction, recreation areas, and temporary housing. RIFTs communicate through beamed data transfers with other facilities, including airships, and with all portal locations.

RIFT is an acronym:

REHO (Recreation)
INDO (Instruction)
FEYO (Feeding)
TAEO (Taxation)

Ruins: Remnants of buildings, former spaceports, and abandoned or destroyed temples. Broken objects and general debris are scattered throughout the area. Laborers scrounge these ruins for reuseable materials, pieces of solar sails, discarded relics, and any salvageable trash to make household items, tools, protective clothing, and other things needed for survival.

Science Center: The center is the computer hub of the planet and the meeting place of the Council of Twelve. It's a large complex that specializes in scientific research, development, and implementation.

Temple Compound: This compound is a religious center for Yah believers but is open to all faiths. It conducts worship services, offers religious teaching, and hosts prayer gatherings. A provost and pravost run the facility and serve as ministers.

Termination Facility: An elimination center that formerly terminated the sick and those considered unprogrammable. It has been decommissioned, and the facility converted into the Health Center.

Transport Portals: Travel hubs between connected locations on Camayah and the planet's three moons.

<u>ITEMS AND INFORMATION</u>

Airships: Floating crafts powered by Triverphol-fueled engines and equipped with solar sails for atmospheric travel. Also called floaters and flyers.

Battle Frenzy: A mental state where combatants feel they have superhuman strength and are impervious to pain. Sometimes called *Battle Heat.*

Battle Trance: A condition of heightened senses where events appear to move slowly. The fighter sees things in slow motion, giving him or her time to react beforehand. Fear disappears. The person is focused. Time, itself, seems to linger. When the trance lifts, the flow of time returns to normal.

Believers: Yah worshipers.

Bonded: Married.

Bondedmoon: Similar to a honeymoon.

Burning, the: Also called the Event. A cataclysm that destroyed most of the planet. It may have been a chemical disaster, fusion explosion, or unknown supernova event. The cause was never determined. All flora and animal life perished. Water evaporated. Only a few individuals survived.

Caldrons: Processing and storage facilities for Triverphol.

Council of Twelve: The newly formed governmental authority on Camayah. It has twelve councilmembers representing the various factions on the planet: the SSL and four SLs from the RIFTs, a ship's captain on behalf of the Airship Docks, the provost and pravost speaking for the Temple Compound, an OL from the Heath Center, the PL for the Science Center, and two senior workers standing in for the Laborers.

Cradphenanill: Also known as pleasure tabs or cubes. Usage discontinued.

Crane: Heavy equipment with a bucket used to remove liquid Triverphol.

Criunite: A green luminous crystal that gives off light. Locals find them in Triverphol pits, exposed ridges in the hills, near hollows, and around ruins. Supplies are limited.

Diggers: Handheld mining and raking tools.

Event, the: Also called the Burning. A past supernova from distant sun may have caused the cataclysmic event.

Foeca (FOE'ca): A sticky, milky substance found in round balls around quawner cave entrances.

Gelts: Digital currency.

Guet: A strategy game that airship personnel play to pass the time.

Hydrew: Liquids or fluids on Camayah, emerald-colored, similar to water.

Jumpsuits: Protective clothing.

Midmate: Airship engineer.

Nawmies: Rare birds.

Nest abeam: In this configuration, ships typically position side by side, with one ship slightly ahead of the other.

Outer Atmosphere: Unexplored space.

Prebonded: Engaged, betrothed.

Provost and Pravost: Pastors.

Quawners: Large spider-like creatures with six legs. They have tough outer skins and spit venom to immobilize their prey. The creatures are most active during the night. They use stealth to track their prey and clicking sounds when attacking. Quawners live in deep, underground burrows.

Recycled Body Chemicals: Processed from terminated individuals and used in various pills and products. The Council ordered the practice discontinued.

Reprogramming: There were two types: limited (mind wipes) and complete (resets). The reset was an extensive brainwashing. It masked memories, replaced names with coded numbers, made people more compliant, which turned them into nameless drones. The Council of Twelve has stopped this practice. All those who received these procedures are being deprogrammed.

Rowmate: Airship navigator.

Solar Sails: A solar sail is a large reflective sheet that captures photons from a sun. These particles bounce off the sail, causing momentum, driving the attached craft forward. Normally, the photons push the vessel away from a sun, but with a tacking maneuver similar to a sailboat using the wind, a pilot can change the direction. Unlike spaceships that usually coast after reaching their maximum speed, crafts equipped with solar sails can continue accelerating.

Soreseeds: Also called soreseed sets, are a variety of plant types. Some germinate into corn-like plants called maza; others grow into shrubberies, edible gourds, and various vine or bush vegetables. The plants need ground liquids to survive, but can also draw moisture from the air during a misty night.

Supernova: Supernovas occur during the last moments of a star's life. The gigantic explosion can devastate nearby planets and solar systems.

Tabs: Tablets, pills, sometimes called cubes.

Terraforming: A process of modifying the landscape of a planet, moon, or other desolate place to make it more habitable.

Triverphol: A highly flammable liquid mined from the flame pits on Camayah and its three moons. The substance is processed and converted into light air, airship fuel, and power cells.

Triverphol Sickness or ***Triverphol Disease:*** Also called the Disease. The symptoms of infection are a yellowish rash, followed by blisters, then decaying skin, weight loss, weakness, muscular degeneration, and finally, death. During later stages, the sickness seems to spread to unaffected people and children. It had no known cure until the Health Center, under the direction of Holley Rossie, developed a healing-leaf formula from the life tree on Eskaonus. There have been no recurrences.

Upper Atmosphere: The area between planetary orbit and a moon.

Venom: A substance that quawners spray to immobilize their prey. It has paralytic and hypnotic effects.

Wormhole: A hypothetical connection between vast regions of space and time.

Yah: Yahweh, YAH, God.

VACCINATIONS

Floksillin: Vaccine to prevent general diseases, seventy percent effective.

Ploksillin: Vaccine to protect against the effects of Triverphol Sickness, fifty perfect effective.

The Health Center has discontinued production of these vaccines in favor of the healing-leaf cure.

STAFFING, POSITIONS, AND RANKS

LABORERS: The common workforce on Camayah.

Laborers: Hired workers who mine for Triverphol and other minerals, rake for Criunite crystals, gather Foeca, dig wells, and cultivate crops.

OPERATORS: Specialists who staff the Health Center. They produce nutrition and hydration pills, vaccines, and health-related products. Operators and their families have residences at the facility.

Operational Leader (OL): Command position, main overseer at the center.
Operational Assistant (OA): Second in command.
Operational Technician (OT): Skilled operator.

Operator: Common name for all Health Center staff.

PROGRAMMERS: People with coding experience who are involved in scientific research, development, and implementation. All programmers and their families live at the Science Center.

Program Leader (PL): Overseer of the center.
P3: Supervisor, highest-ranked programmer, seniority.
P2: Mid-level position, moderate experience.
P1: Trainee.
Programmer: Common name for all programmers.

SECURITY: Guards who oversee security at all facilities, RIFTs, airship docks, and mining sites. Security and their family members have complimentary residences in the local RIFT and enjoy other benefits.

Senior Security Leader (SSL): Manages all security personnel on the planet.
Security Leader (SL): Second command position. Each RIFT has one.
Security Assistant (SA): Third command position. Each RIFT has one or more.
S3: Supervisor, highest-ranked guard.
S2: Mid-level position.
S1: Trainee.

APPENDIX: JESSE'S JOURNALS

Entry One

No changing of days, or nights, or light from the sun. Normal time continues on earth, I think. Here, it's basically one, long, everlasting day. Therefore, I'm calling this eternal era "the day after always," a day that goes on forever and ever.

I have not seen any little children or babies, only teens, who I would estimate to be around thirteen years old. A book I read once said people in heaven would be in their prime, yet I see a ton of older individuals, like Abraham, who looks to be the age described in the Bible. There are all ages here, just no little ones. If all the saints were thirty years old, it might feel like a cult or something. I plan on asking someone in the know about these matters. As for me, I look the same age I was before I arrived, except I don't need eyeglasses anymore or have a sore knee. And I feel strong and energetic.

Entry Two

Hope you enjoy the book. I made you a waterproof satchel to carry it in. Your pen is inside, full of ink, and ready to go. Take the journal with you. It may come in handy. I also recycled the old fruit pit I found on your desktop. Everything has a purpose here.

Godspeed, elChesed

Entry Three

Made it to Eskaonus. Rev. Lundy is missing. He didn't arrive with the rest of us. I'm getting a bit worried. We'll search for him in the morning. Built a shelter and made camp for the night. We are all feeling tired. Annie says she's a little sick to her stomach. Probably nerves. Hope things are better tomorrow. Will try to make contact with the Eskaonites and do some investigating. I don't want to give away our purpose, not until I know who's friend or foe.

Entry Four

Interesting couple days. Everyone poisoned by yarm berries. We had no immunity. Search party from the southern lands found us and took us to local medic for treatment. Almost lost Annie. Attacked by assailants this afternoon. Not sure why. Concerning the evil, I haven't determined much. I think it concerns Eddnok and the northern lands. Big dinner tonight. Hope to find out more.

Entry Five

Dinner went OK. Gathered good intel. Expedition planned for tomorrow to see some old ruins. They may provide clues to what happened here and why there's no knowledge of God or belief system. Saephira thinks it may be an ancient temple. If so, why was it destroyed or abandoned? Need more facts. The leader has discerning dreams and seems open to spiritual matters. Not yet sure what evil lurks here on Eskaonus. Something, however, isn't right. We're all really tried. It's been a day. Praying for a restful sleep.

Entry Six

Really sleepy, so I'll make this entry short. Lots happened today. Discovered a buried scroll, must be old, yet it looks new, like the ones in heaven. The ruins are probably an old temple. How or why destroyed, I don't know. The answers might explain why there's no knowledge of God or religion here. Uncovered two carved symbols. They seem familiar to me. Starting to trust Saephira. Plan to tell her more about our purpose here, just waiting for the right opportunity. Preaverca hiding something. Lundy still missing. The rest of us are doing okay.

Entry Seven

Massive rockslide at ruins, many injuries, Anna paralyzed, townspeople dead, Lundy lost. It's all my fault. Guess I'm still a failure. I'm not gonna . . .

Entry Eight

Second day of red sky. Fewer windstorms. I imagine all of heaven knows about my failures from last night. Everyone in my group does, yet they continue to support me as leader. Not sure I would do the same. If someone is listening, all I can say is I'm sorry. I tried to erase my last entry, except for some reason, the ink is permanent. Couldn't tear out the page either. Max said things made in heaven are eternal. Apparently, this goes for my journal, the ink written thereon, as well as the satchel itself. Chesedel told me heaven is the place of second chances. I pray there's a third one for me. I sure blew my first two.

Annie feels we will receive word on Lundy soon. I hope so. She exhibits an uncanny discernment in these matters. Annie also mentioned Chesedel visited her room last night. If so, that's wonderful. Miracle or otherwise, she's fully recovered. We are planning a rescue mission for Narleen who was abducted by the Upper Realm. Our answers lay there, I think, including the evil we were sent here to confront. Well, time for bed.

Entry Nine

Attempting a rescue mission tomorrow night. Hope to find Lundy and Narleen who are being held as prisoners and break them out of jail. Saephira hasn't pressed me on our purpose in Eskaonus, how we got here, or where we came from. I will probably share what I can tonight. Lord, grant me wisdom in this. Right now, however, everyone is focused on the night raid at Briacap. Praying for success and safety.

Entry Ten

Busy few cycles, I mean days, so I haven't been recording entries. Good news. We found and rescued Lundy, along with eight other prisoners who were being held captive by Lord Eddnok. He's as wicked as they come. I suspect Eddnok is behind the evil influence here.

Lundy translated an ancient manuscript that reveals a hidden cave with a mysterious treasure (attachment below). It might hold the answers we are seeking. He thinks we should focus on finding it. Me too. Except getting there is another matter. We'll decide in the morning.

Attachment

If treasure is what you seek then don't be meek, nor forgo the rift near the highest cliff. Buried deep within lies a secret twin of the richest gift known to gods or men. Take an uphill pace to seek a taste of wisdom sublime and power divine. So follow the trail to the mountains red, through the forest dead, past waters shed, and peaks that grow during daylight glow. Past ancient grave lays hidden cave where treasure awaits for a ruler of fate.

Entry Eleven

We may have discovered why evil has become so widespread. The mysterious treasure appears to be a knowledge tree clone. According to Lundy, it produced forbidden fruit like the tree in Eden and even had a similar appearance. I'm not exactly sure how or why this occurred. Notwithstanding, we think Eddnok consumed the fruit, then ignored the good knowledge and allowed the evil knowledge to spread in his already corrupted heart. If so, many have perished because of his wickedness, including Falein Village, which is now in ruins. In regard to the hidden cave and what became of the knowledge tree, I haven't a clue. Chesedel may have the lowdown since he was present at the end. All we know for sure is the tree miraculously disappeared.

Our group helped rescue Narleen for a second time and restored Saephira to her rightful place as Leader. Most of the conspirators have been rounded up, all except Eddnok. Concerning other news, we were just invited to a planning dinner. I suspect we'll be asked to help participate in an effort to stop Eddnok before more of his wickedness takes root. Countering evil was one reason we came here, right? As for the second part, to bring the truth of God and His ways back to Eskaonus, we're still working on it.

This may be my last entry for a while. It's been a learning experience for all of us, especially me. I wasn't sure I could say this and mean it until recently, but thank you for sending us here. I look forward to finishing our mission, returning to heaven and sipping a cool drink from the Fountain of Life. The water here tastes like mud.

Entry Twelve

We detoured to Eskaonus. Since these entries are duplicated in the Hall of Records, I suppose heaven already knows about our side trip. Located Max and gave him an overview of our assignment to Camayah. I asked him to join our efforts. Although his support would be invaluable, my request created more conflict. Narleen, his wife now, and Max got into a heated discussion. She doesn't want him to go anywhere without her. And here's another concern: If Max does volunteer and Narleen insists on going with him, can she make the portal jump with the rest of us? No doubt I'll find out soon enough. Like Ottaar the mender often says, "Dayrise will bring what it brings." In other news, the alliance is doing fine. I'm glad Holley is with us. Her doctoring skills may be necessary before this mission concludes. Guess that's about it for this entry.

Entry Thirteen

Arrived in Camayah. Max and Narleen came with us. The transport made her sick, but Holley treated her. She seems to be doing fine. First contact was with a local family. They were wary, yet helpful. I plan to press them for more information tonight. We visited one of their RIFT facilities. RIFT is an acronym for Recreation, Instruction, Feeding and Taxation. In regard to Feeding, it's a misnomer. This world has no food or water. The inhabitants use nourishment pills to survive. This place has huge six-legged creatures called quawners. They may be a problem. No other animals. They perished in an event called the Burning. No vegetation either. Hope to learn more about what happened here. Plan to split up and do some investigating this afternoon. Being watched. Gotta go . . .

Entry Fourteen

I haven't posted for several days, I mean dawns. A lot has transpired since my last entry: Two locals, Leetqu and Rekis, never returned home from working in the flame pits. When Narleen, Holley, and I went to check on their whereabouts, we were subdued and confined in Holding, a jail facility. Fortunately, Max and two of our party members stormed Holding and saved us before we were reprogrammed, or worse, terminated. This world is really messed up.

Seth and Holley located the missing Yah believers and their ministers on a moon named Easteapia. We have hatched a plan to remove them from their self-imposed exile. I asked Max to handle the military planning for this and other strategic operations. I don't think we would have been successful without him.

We only have two of the five radios in working condition. One was incorporated into a portable computer called a datatop.

The other two transceivers are in pieces. I hope Rauteira, a tech-savvy teenager, can put them back together.

Since my journal entries are seen in heaven, I have a request. We need angelic intervention. As stated in the above addendum, Anna can protect us with her nyeflute songs, namely, the invisibility tune. However, we have no way to hide these exiled believers once we return them to their planet, which is complicated because Security now considers us as discontents.

There's an old emergency shelter in some nearby ruins. Lundy believes it was part of a destroyed temple complex. It does look similar to the ruins along Onnie Passage in Eskaonus. It would only be a temporary hiding place until we can sort things out. Just wondering if a couple of guardian angels can watch over the refugees? If not, we'll make do.

Busy day tomorrow. I better get a couple hours of sleep beforehand. I'm trying to project confidence to my colleagues, but inside I'm worried.

Entry Fifteen

Our team is resting today. Anna calls it a Sabbath. Not an actual one, since several are working on projects. Holley is analyzing samples and substances, searching a cure for Triverphol Disease. Lundy is coding, and Anna is making slings. Max, of course, is strategizing.

During the moon rescue, we ran into all sorts of problems. Eventually, we retrieved all the exiled believers. When it seemed like certain disaster, a solar eclipse occurred, and we escaped during the darkness of totality. Several locals were hurt by stunner fire, a type of laser beam, but they're recovering.

We all returned safely to the shelter, where I found a heaven-made candle lamp, just like the one I took to Eskaonus. Lundy and Anna believe it's the same one. Whether it is or isn't, the intended message is clear. Heaven heard my appeal for angelic intervention. Although I can't see any angels, I believe they are keeping us safe. I say us, because everyone is staying in the emergency bunker now. The residence we were living in was burned down by security forces. The fire almost killed six partners, but with the help of Annie's nyeflute, the group escaped in the nick of time. With the addition of the seven believers from Easteapia, our collective has grown to eighteen.

We're having a planning meeting later, probably tomorrow, to see what can be done about the Programming and Termination facilities. We want to stop the practice of brainwashing, called reprogramming, and the senseless killing of unhealthy individuals for their body chemicals. Those issues seem overwhelming.

Please thank Chesedel for me. I assume he was the one who left the candle lamp. Besides being an encouraging sign, it will come in handy for light. And it makes this dingy place smell nice.

Entry Sixteen

I'll start this entry with the big reveal. The esteemed leader of this planet, known as the Program Master, is a fraud. He never existed. He, or rather I should say it, was a maintenance program gone awry. This planet was being run by artificial intelligence. After a cataclysm befell Camayah, this so-called PM emerged and instituted changes based on lies. I'm not sure how the devil fits into all this, or if he does, but I am reminded of the Scripture that says Satan is the father of lies.

Our team pulled the plug on this deceptive program, creating an opportunity for a replacement government. Accordingly, we hope to reestablish the Council of Twelve, the ruling body the Program Master program eliminated when it took over. We will offer guidelines to this new council and perhaps, point them in a better direction.

In other news, the moon rescue was a difficult operation yet successful. On a subsequent mission, Max and Seth found water, what the residents call hydrew. It lies deep underground. Since this is an advanced society, I will suggest they pump it to the surface. We also believe the RIFTs have stockpiled seeds. It wouldn't take much to restore vegetation on the planet, at least in certain places. Perhaps this dead, arid place can be terraformed.

Lundy and others are trying to undo the programming forced upon residents to erase their memories and control their minds. Holley developed a cure for an unknown disease using healing leaves. And Runess, a former airship captain, wants to show me something in the lower hemisphere.

We transported everyone from the shelter to guest housing at the Programming Center, so I guess we no longer require angelic intervention. Never saw a single angel, yet I felt their presence. Thank Chesedel or whoever came to support us.

I have a difficult meeting to chair and expect contention from several of the citizenry invited to serve on this board. I'll be sharing practical and spiritual solutions. What happens thereafter is on them. Free choice, right? Besides, it's their planet, not mine. I pray the meeting ends well. If it does, I'm gonna take Runess up on his little airship tour. I plan to ask Seth and Annabelle to join me.

Entry Seventeen

The first meeting of the Council of Twelve went well. I got them started by appointing delegates to represent the various factions on this planet. I outlined the main issues facing them and gave the membership proposals to consider. Afterwards, Anna, Seth, and I departed in an airship to their south pole. This is where the revelations began.

Apparently, native flora and most of the animal species survived the Burning, which had devastated the rest of the planet. We discovered a shielded crater containing its own little biosphere. It wouldn't take much to reestablish life here, if they pump water to the surface and plant soreseed vegetation. Then animals could be reintroduced in the middle and northern sectors. Over time, the inhabitants may be able to terraform their entire planet.

Regarding our mission goals, we accomplished most of them. The believers were freed from their moon exile. The practice of reprogramming an individual's mind to take away their will and identity has been halted, and the process is being reversed. Other changes are underway, too. Most importantly, Yah worshipers are free to practice their religion without the threat of being imprisoned or killed. The deceptions that plagued this world have been exposed, and because of Holley's efforts, a terrible disease now has a cure.

We plan to depart Camayah and return to Eskaonus after we thank the people who supported us. This has been an exhausting assignment for all involved. My colleagues deserve a break, so we're going to spend a couple days in the Lower Realm to recuperate. As for me, I look forward to a moderate climate, lush greenery, and attending a banquet with actual food and drink.

If I have learned anything during these last two outreaches, it is this: Eternity is not about us and what we want. It's about helping others, not only with spiritual concerns, but with practical ones.

NOTE FROM THE AUTHOR

We sometimes assume life is the same for all created beings wherever they might exist—that individuals fit into the same mold, follow the same customs and laws, embrace the same plan of salvation, worship the same way, and end up in the same afterlife—or that spiritual warfare and physical conflicts no longer occur in the hereafter. Eternity may reveal this is not the case.

Concerning conflicts, a quick look through the Bible will detail much death and destruction endured by humanity. Some of those struggles are seen in Sodom and Gomorrah and in the violent clashes between Israel and Judah as they sought or rejected God's will. We should never assume that similar scenarios can't repeat elsewhere in God's infinite kingdom. Nor presume immortality merely involves floating on clouds as we play harps or that the final dispensation (Ephesians 1:10) means the Lord has completed His agenda. Regarding the latter, I believe our Creator has more to accomplish. And so do His redeemed.

God is the same yesterday, today, and forever (Hebrews 13:8), but His many worlds and realms, whether known or unknown, will not remain the same. Even our familiar cosmos will change. His new heaven and new earth (Revelation 21:1) will likely be distinctive, present new challenges, and offer opportunities for continued ministry. Redemption, after all, has an ongoing purpose, and eternity, an everlasting timeframe.

ABOUT THE AUTHOR

Charles Earl Harrel is a Christian writer with more than 650 published works. His articles, inspirational stories, and devotionals have appeared in various periodicals and in forty-one anthologies. Charles is also a nine-time contributor to Chicken Soup for the Soul. He has written four books: *The Ministry of Divine Healing, The Greatest Moment, The Day After Always,* and *The Always Realms.*

He pastored for thirty years, serving churches in California, Nevada, and Oregon, before stepping aside to pursue writing. Charles holds a doctorate in ministry. He and his wife, Laura, live in Portland, Oregon. They enjoy hiking, community outreach, and teaching from God's Word.

THE DAY AFTER ALWAYS (Book One)
The adventure begins. Follow the intriguing story of five associates as they embark on a spiritual journey to discover the possibilities and perils waiting in the time beyond time.

<u>THE ALWAYS REALMS</u> (Book Two)
The saga continues. The advocates travel to Camayah, an advanced civilization facing peril, to help the inhabitants before their culture slides into chaos.

<u>THE ALWAYS REALMS</u> (Book Two)
The saga continues. The advocates travel to Camayah, an advanced civilization facing peril, to help the inhabitants before their culture slides into chaos.